W9-AMP-851

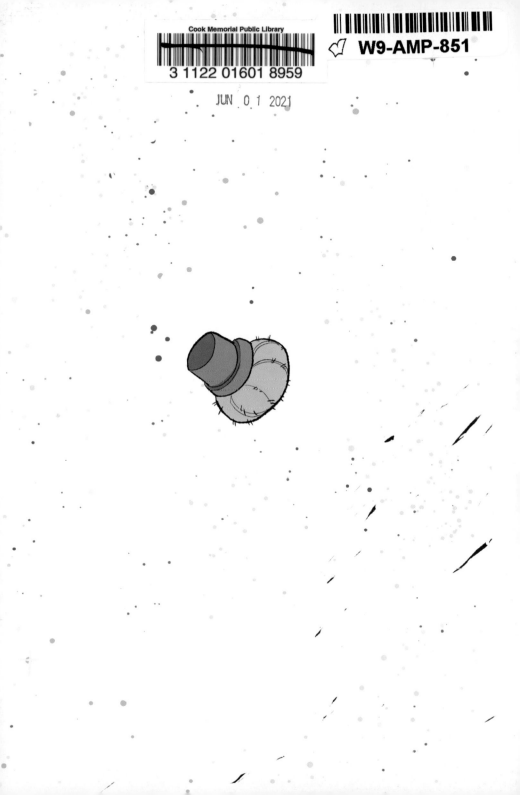

Stephen McCranie's

SPACE BOY

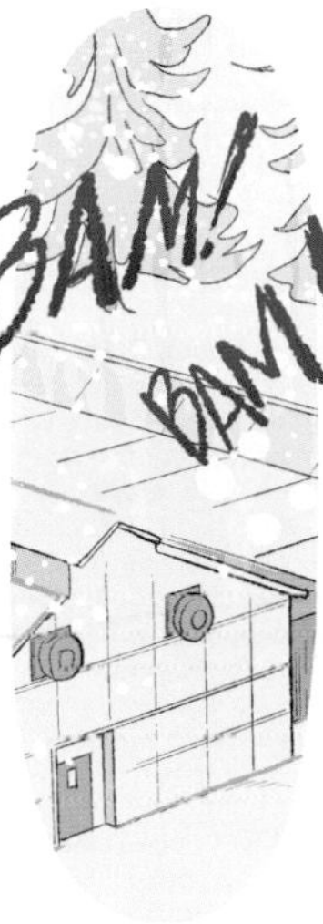
BAM!
BAM!

VOLUME 9

Written and illustrated by
STEPHEN McCRANIE

DARK HORSE BOOKS

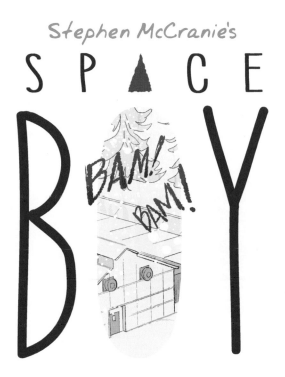

President and Publisher **Mike Richardson**

Editor **Shantel LaRocque**

Associate Editor **Brett Israel**

Designer **Anita Magaña**

Digital Art Technician **Allyson Haller**

STEPHEN McCRANIE'S SPACE BOY VOLUME 9

This book collects *Space Boy* episodes 127–143, previously published online at WebToons.com.

Library of Congress Cataloging-in-Publication Data

Names: McCranie, Stephen, 1987- writer, illustrator.
Title: Space Boy / written and illustrated by Stephen McCranie.
Other titles: At head of title: Stephen McCranie's
Description: First edition. | Milwaukie, OR : Dark Horse Books, 2018- | v. 1:
   "This book collects Space Boy episodes 1-16 previously published online at
   WebToons.com."--Title page verso. | v. 2: "This book collects Space Boy
   episodes 17-32, previously published online at WebToons.com."--Title page
   verso. | v. 3: "This book collects Space Boy episodes 33-48, previously
   published online at WebToons.com."--Title page verso. | v. 4: "This book
   collects Space Boy episodes 49-60, previously published online at
   WebToons.com."--Title page verso. | v. 4: "This book collects Space Boy
   episodes 61-75, previously published online at WebToons.com."--Title page
   verso. | v. 6: "This book collects Space Boy episodes 76-92, previously
   published online at WebToons.com."--Title page verso. | Summary: Amy lives
   on a colony in deep space, but when her father loses his job the family
   moves back to Earth, where she has to adapt to heavier gravity, a new
   school, and a strange boy with no flavor.
Identifiers: LCCN 2017053602| ISBN 9781506706481 (v. 1 ; pbk.) | ISBN
   9781506706801 (v. 2 ; pbk.) | ISBN 9781506708423 (v. 3 ; pbk.) | ISBN
   9781506708430 (v. 4 ; pbk.) | ISBN 9781506713991 (v. 5 ; pbk.) | ISBN
   9781506714004 (v. 6 ; pbk.) | ISBN 9781506714011 (v. 7 ; pbk.)
Subjects: LCSH: Graphic novels. | CYAC: Graphic novels. | Science fiction. |
   Moving, Household--Fiction. | Self-perception--Fiction. |
   Friendship--Fiction.
Classification: LCC PZ7.7.M42 Sp 2018 | DDC 741.5/973--dc23
LC record available at https://lccn.loc.gov/2017053602

Published by Dark Horse Books
A division of Dark Horse Comics LLC
10956 SE Main Street | Milwaukie, OR 97222
StephenMcCranie.com | DarkHorse.com

To find a comics shop in your area, visit comicshoplocator.com

First edition: February 2021
ISBN 978-1-50671-883-5
10 9 8 7 6 5 4 3 2 1
Printed in China

[redacted]

[redacted]

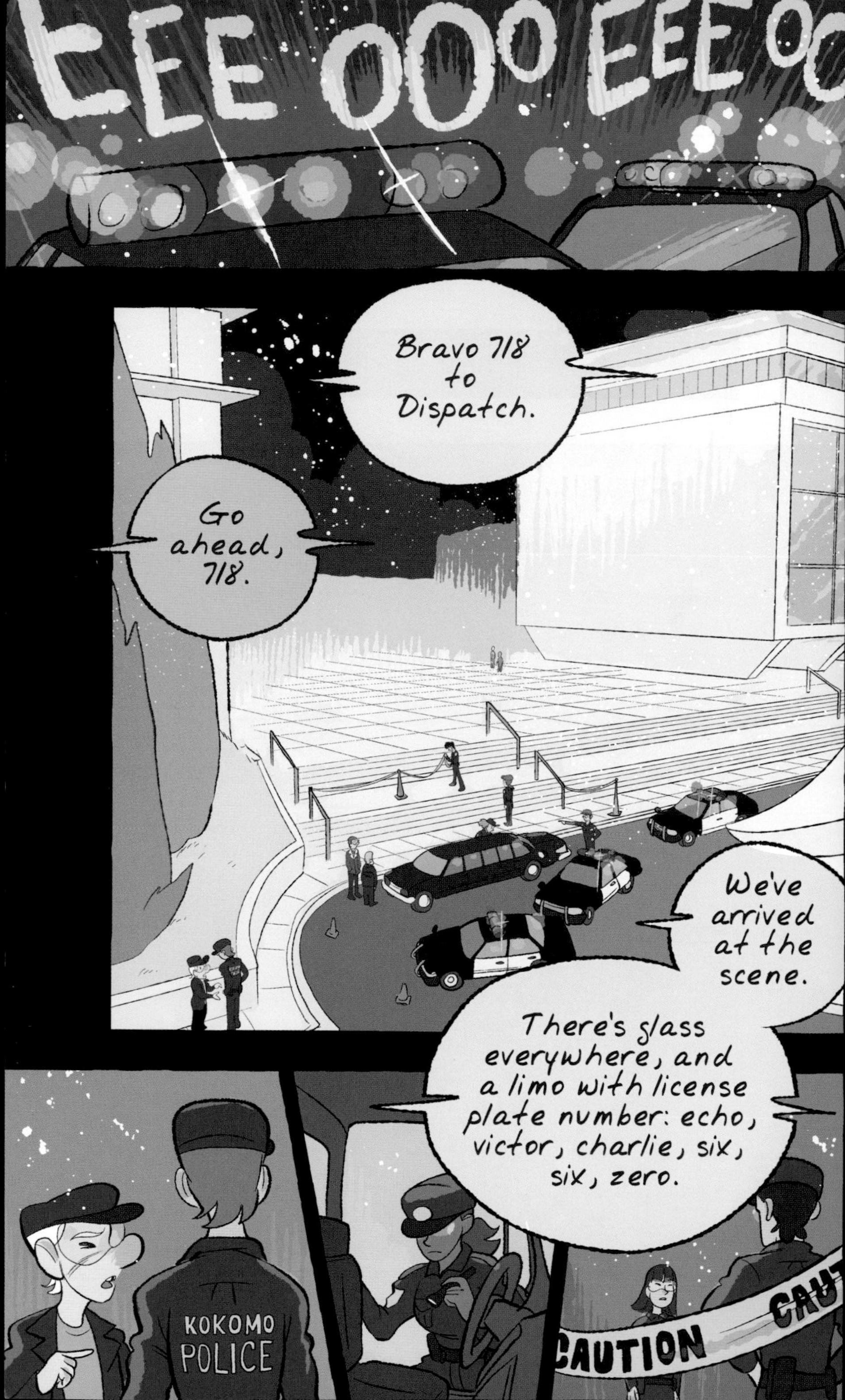
EEE OOO EEE OO
Bravo 718 to Dispatch.
Go ahead, 718.
We've arrived at the scene.
There's glass everywhere, and a limo with license plate number: echo, victor, charlie, six, six, zero.
KOKOMO POLICE
CAUTION
CAUT

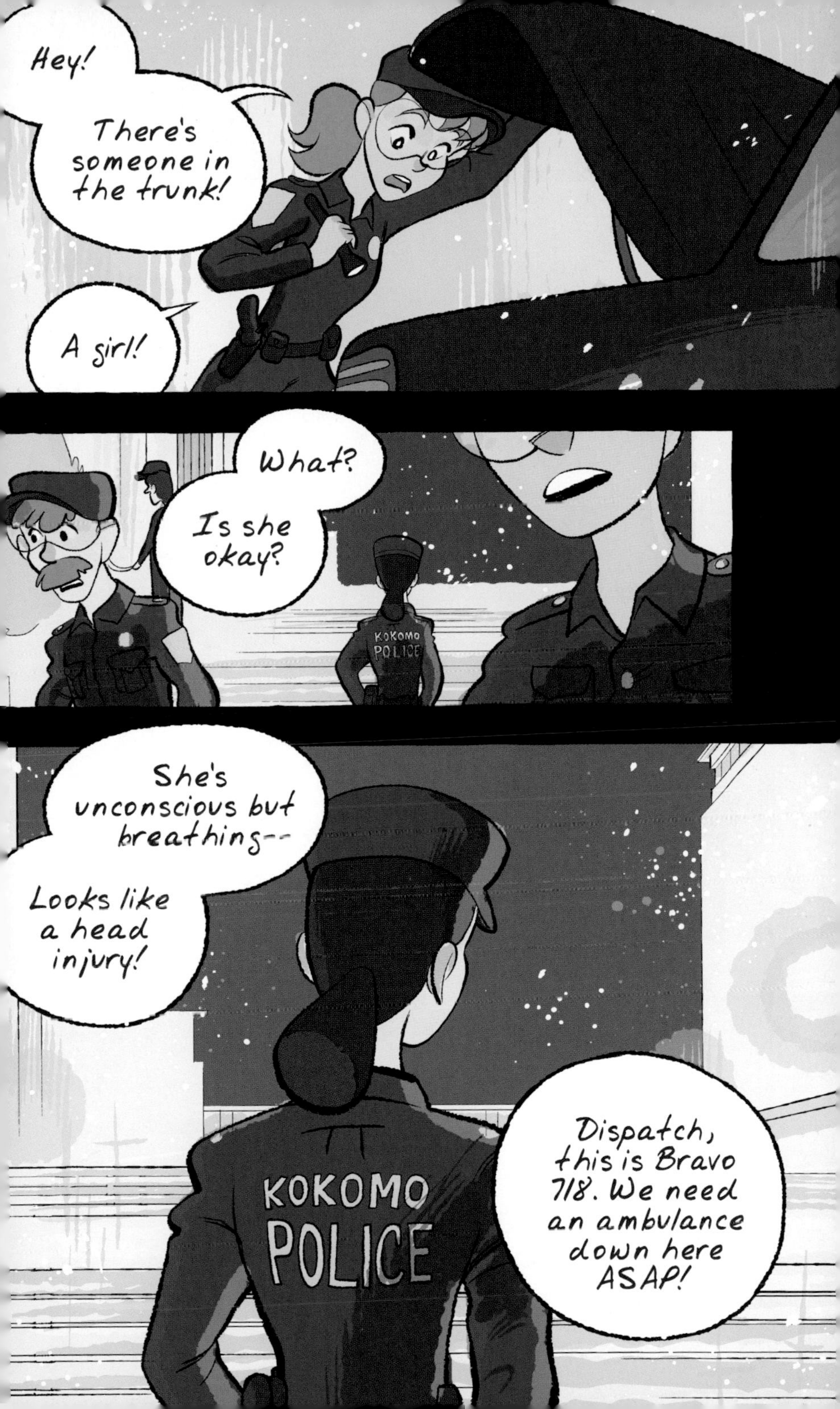
Hey!
There's someone in the trunk!
A girl!
What?
Is she okay?
KOKOMO POLICE
She's unconscious but breathing--
Looks like a head injury!
KOKOMO POLICE
Dispatch, this is Bravo 718. We need an ambulance down here ASAP!

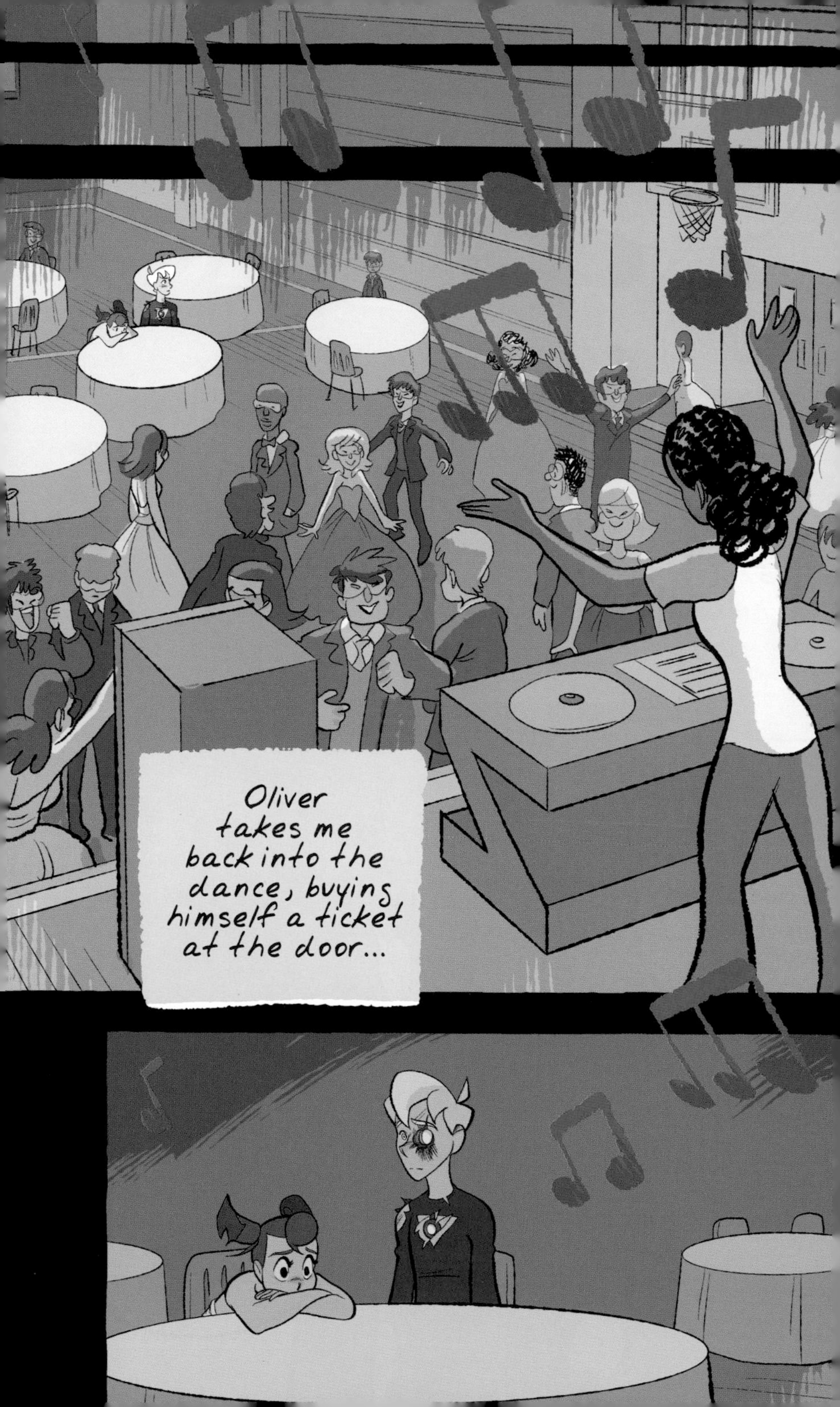
Oliver takes me back into the dance, buying himself a ticket at the door...

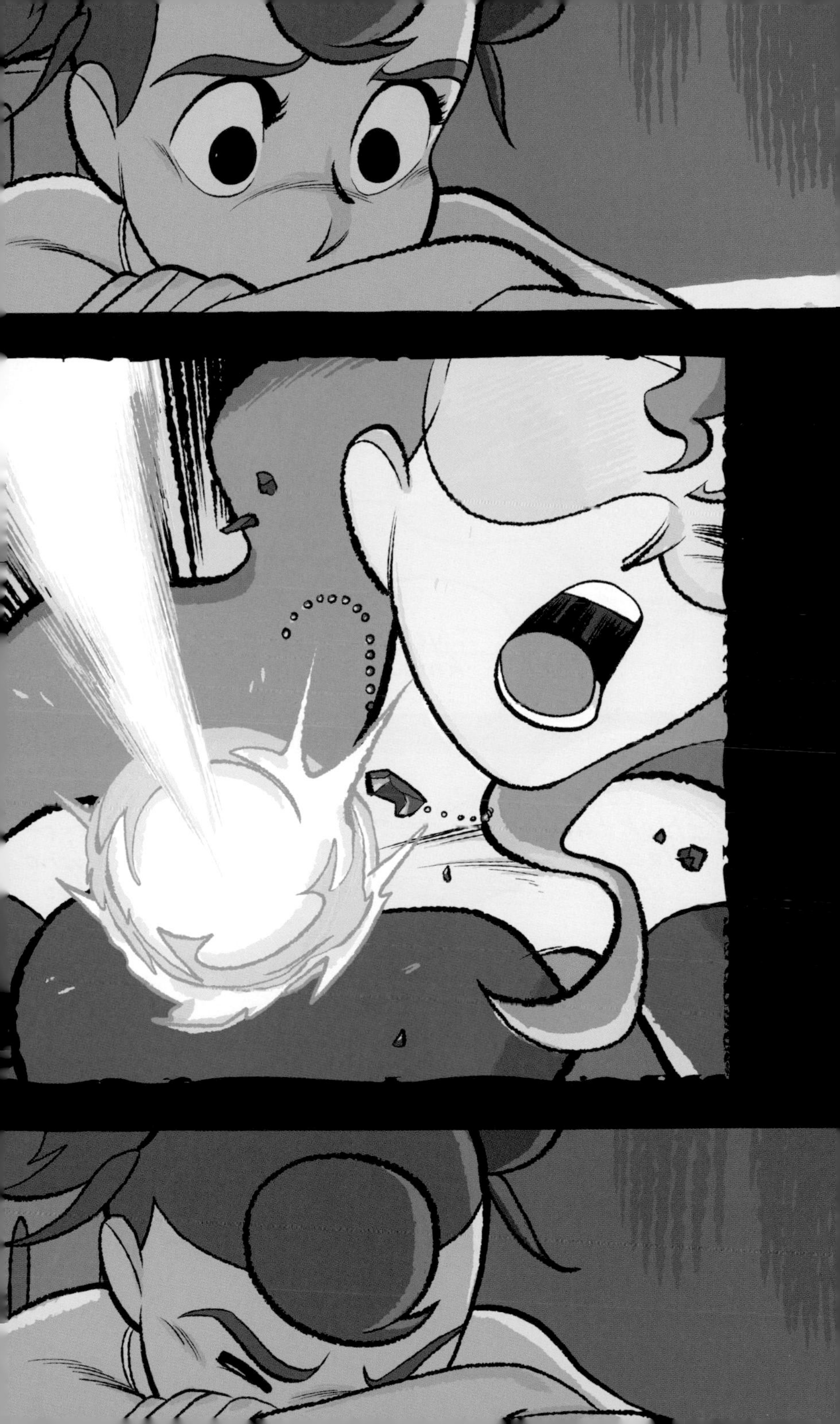

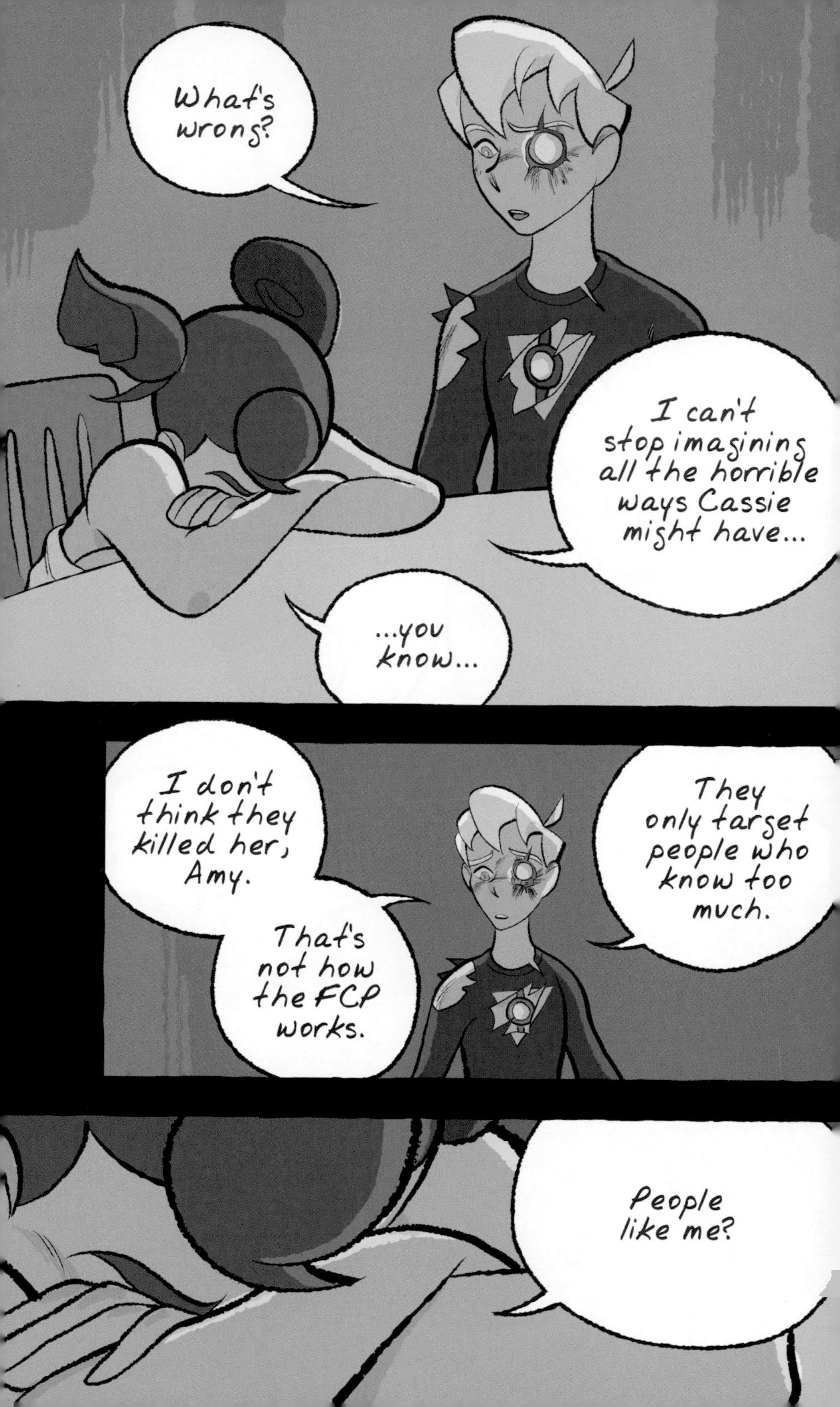
What's wrong?
I can't stop imagining all the horrible ways Cassie might have...
...you know...
I don't think they killed her, Amy.
That's not how the FCP works.
They only target people who know too much.
People like me?

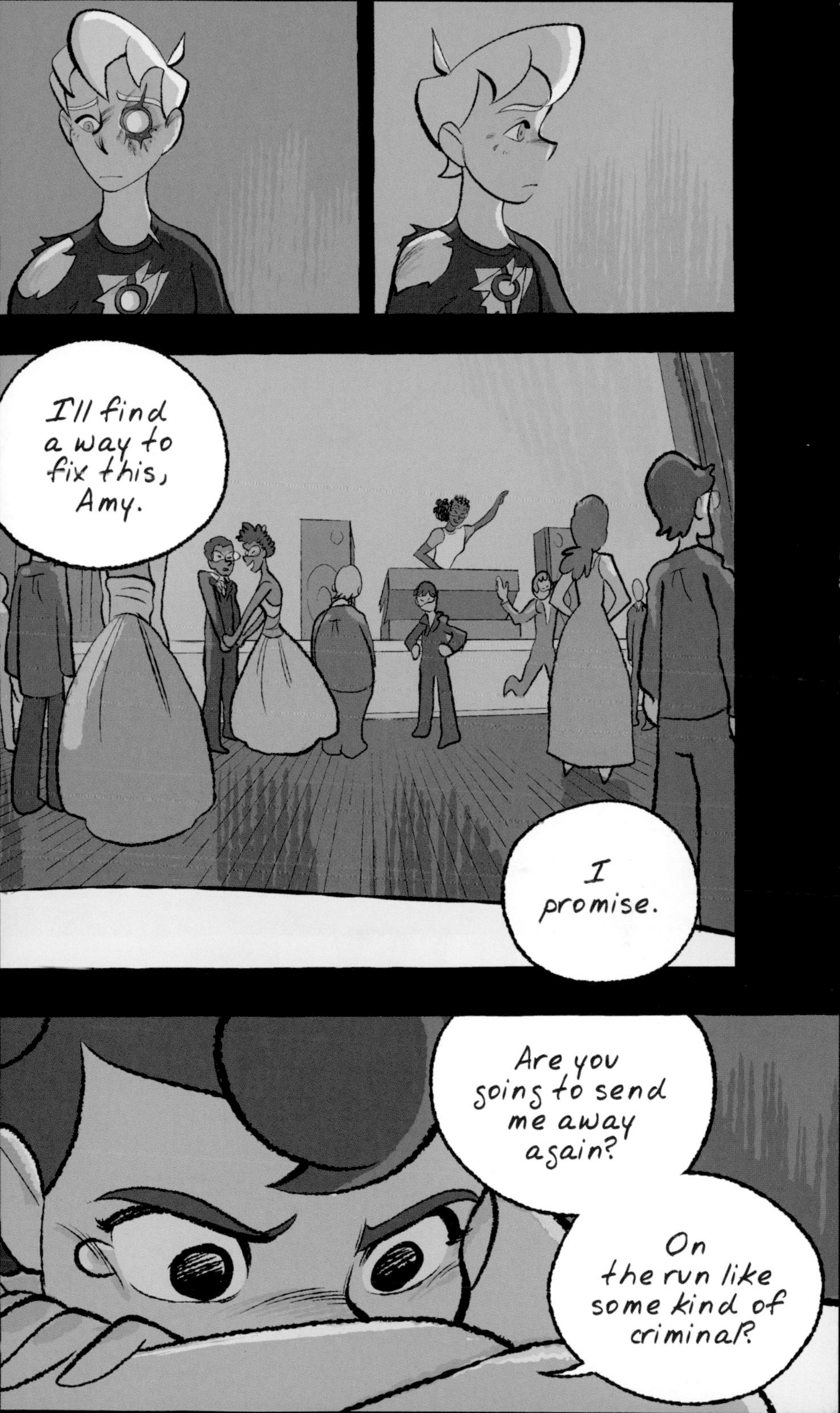
I'll find a way to fix this, Amy.
I promise.
Are you going to send me away again?
On the run like some kind of criminal?

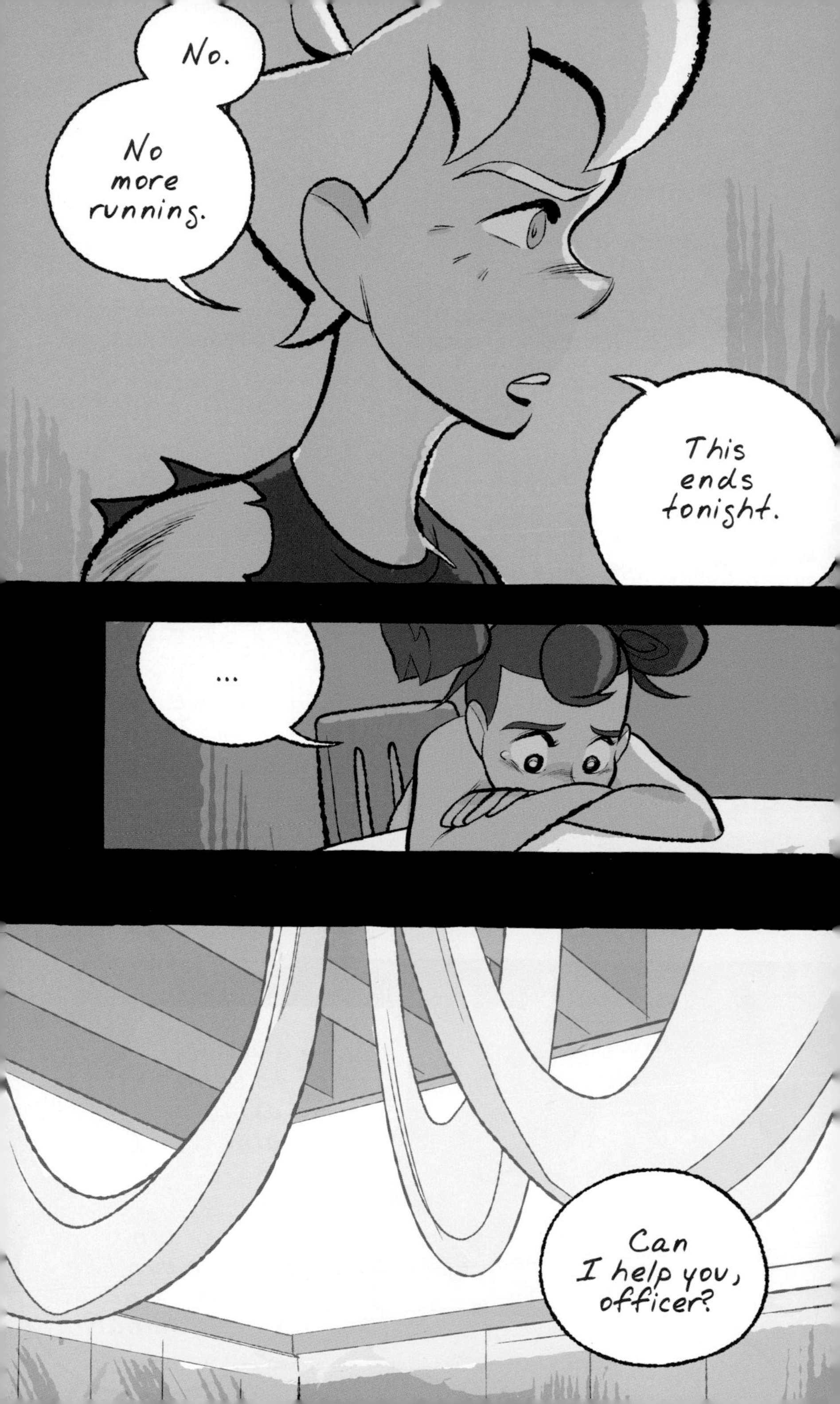
No.
No more running.
This ends tonight.
...
Can I help you, officer?

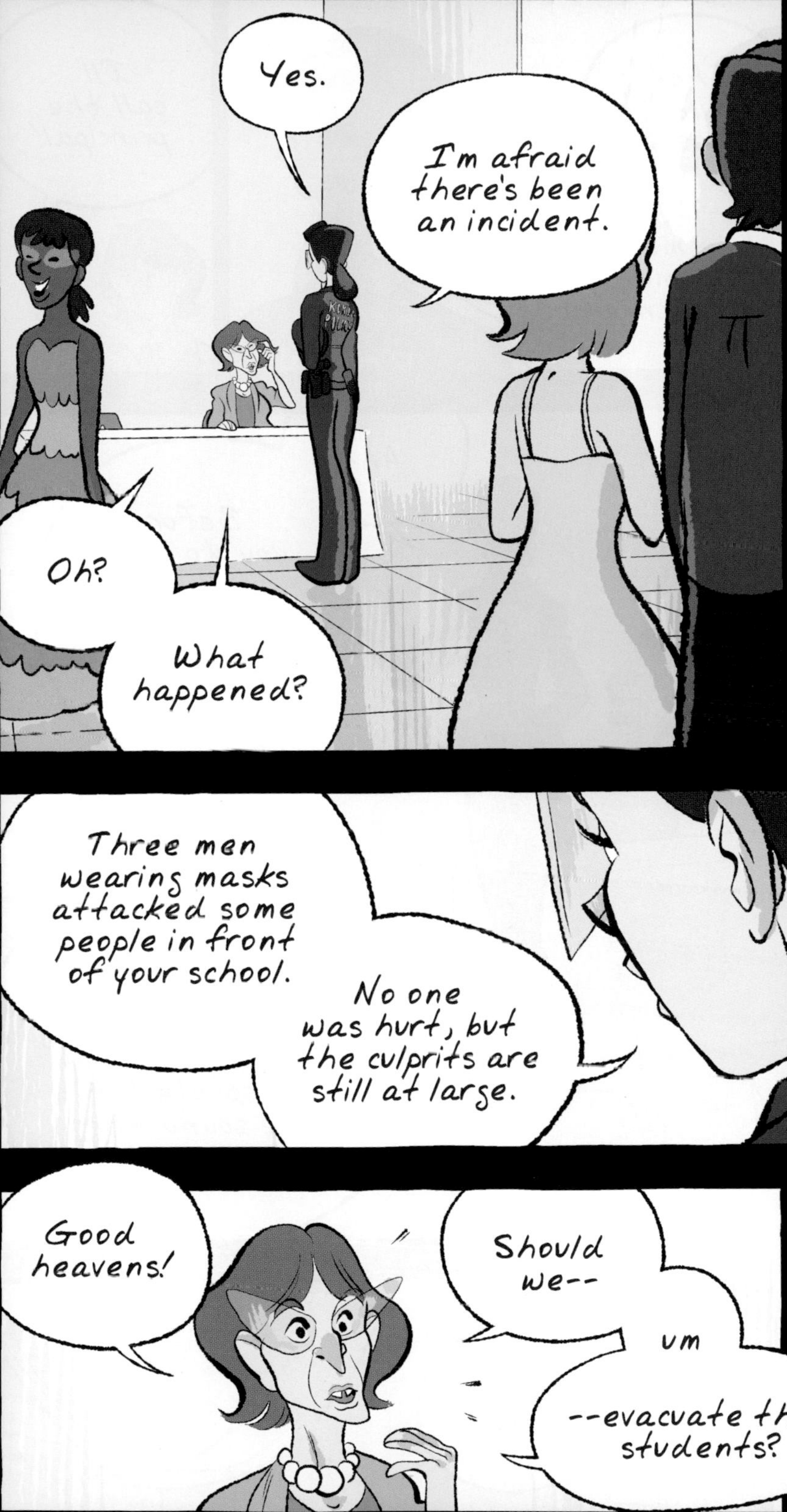
Yes.
I'm afraid there's been an incident.
Oh?
What happened?
Three men wearing masks attacked some people in front of your school.
No one was hurt, but the culprits are still at large.
Good heavens!
Should we--
um
--evacuate the students?

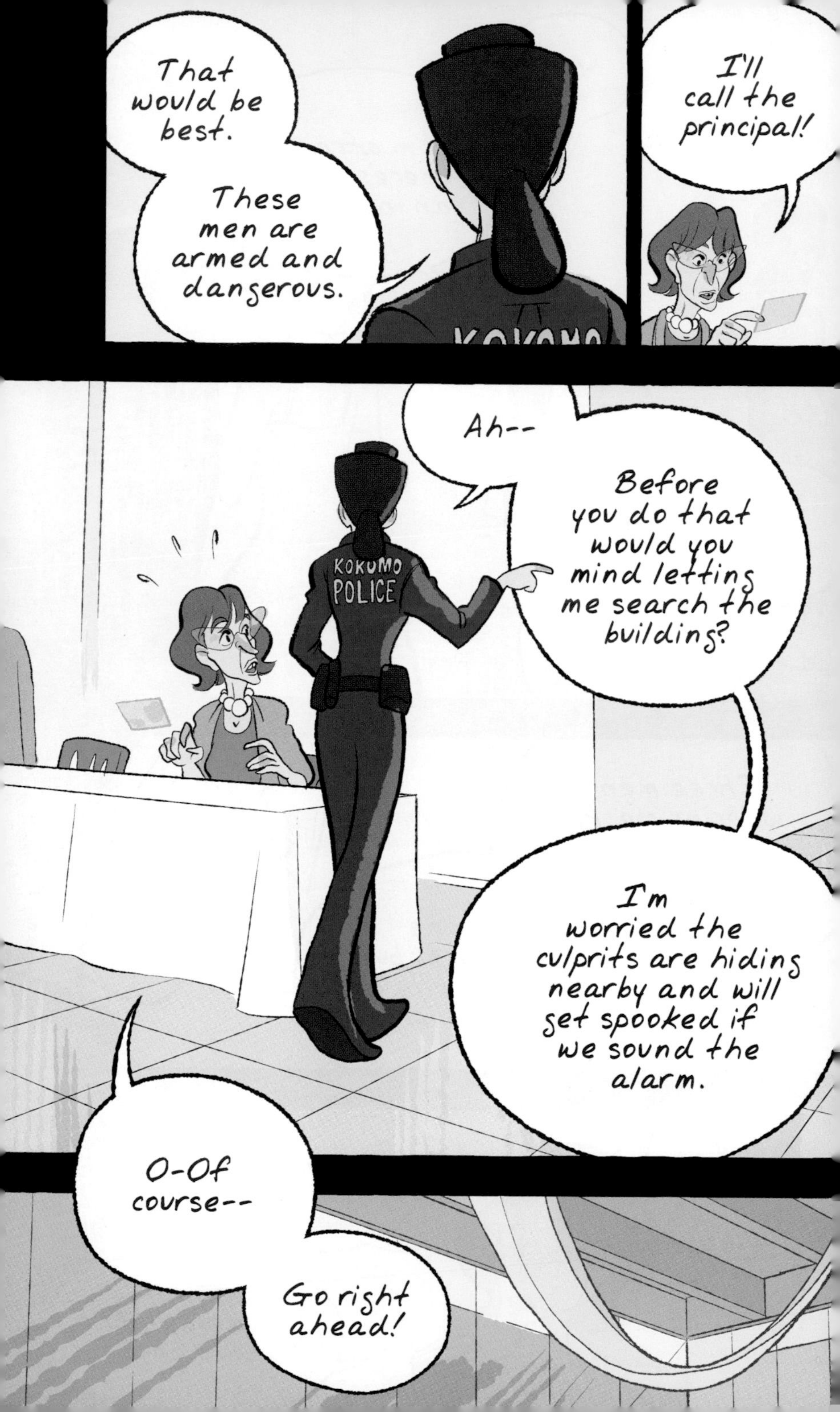
That would be best.
These men are armed and dangerous.
KOKOMO
I'll call the principal!
Ah--
KOKOMO POLICE
Before you do that would you mind letting me search the buildings?
I'm worried the culprits are hiding nearby and will get spooked if we sound the alarm.
O-Of course--
Go right ahead!

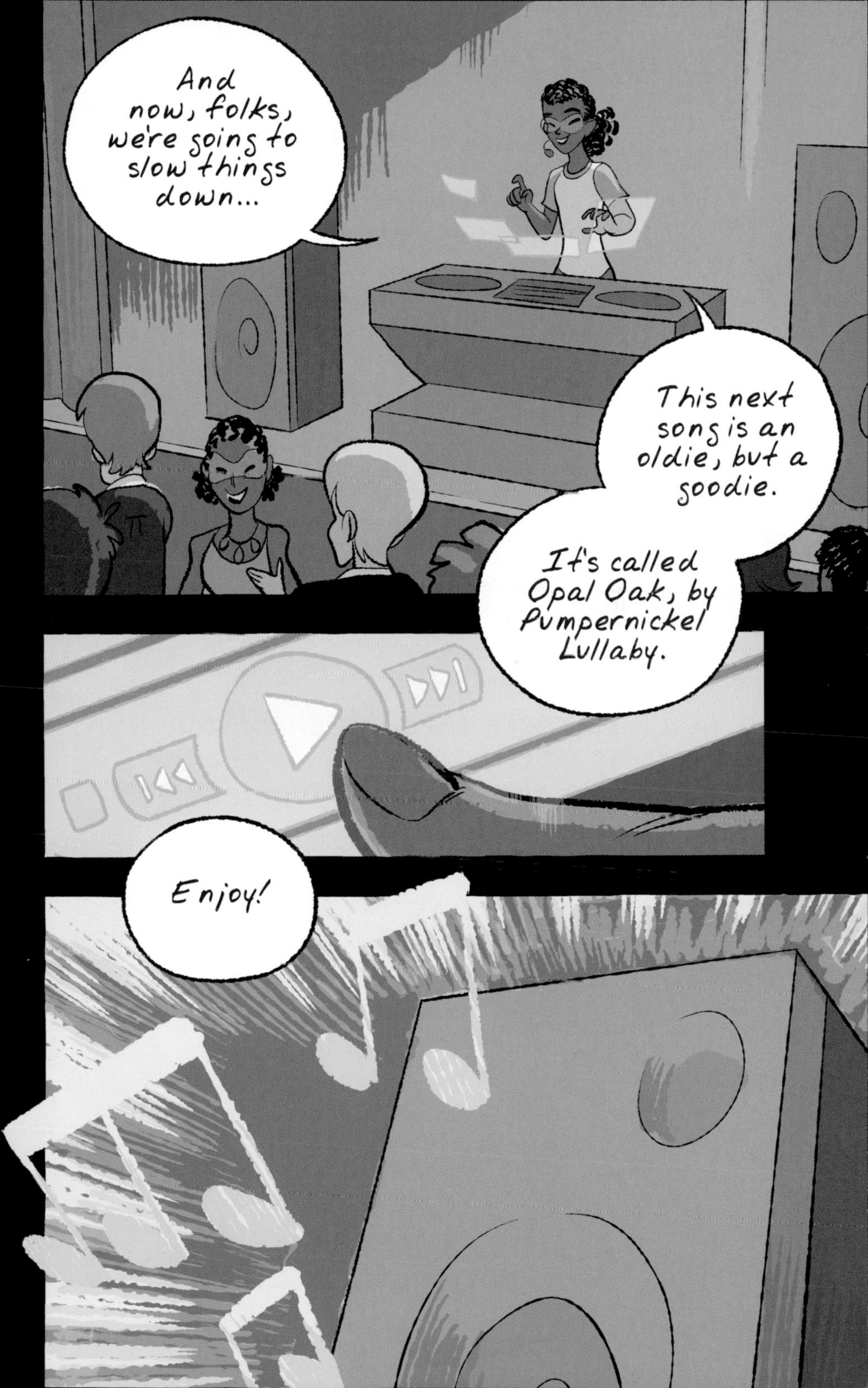
And now, folks, we're going to slow things down...
This next song is an oldie, but a goodie.
It's called Opal Oak, by Pumpernickel Lullaby.
Enjoy!

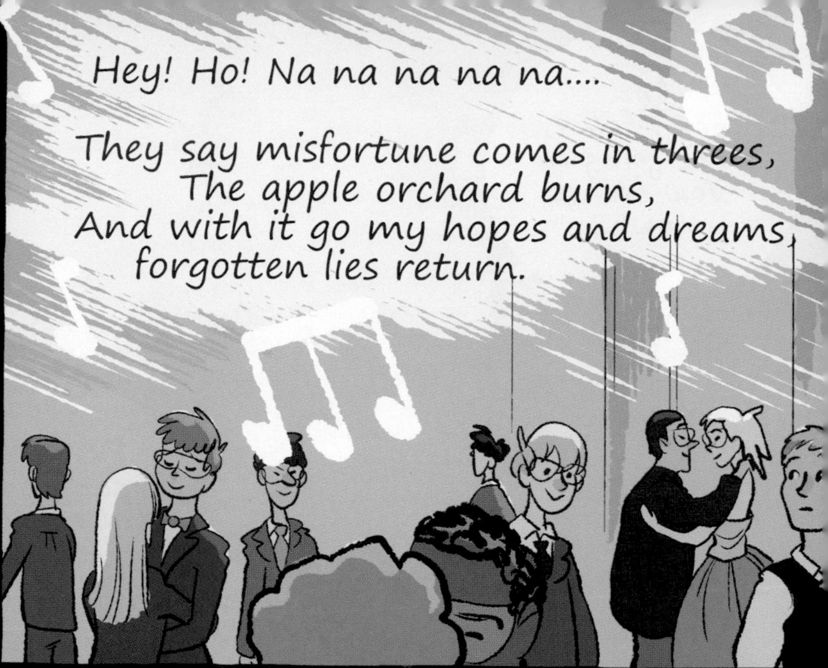
Hey! Ho! Na na na na na....
They say misfortune comes in threes,
The apple orchard burns,
And with it go my hopes and dreams,
forgotten lies return.

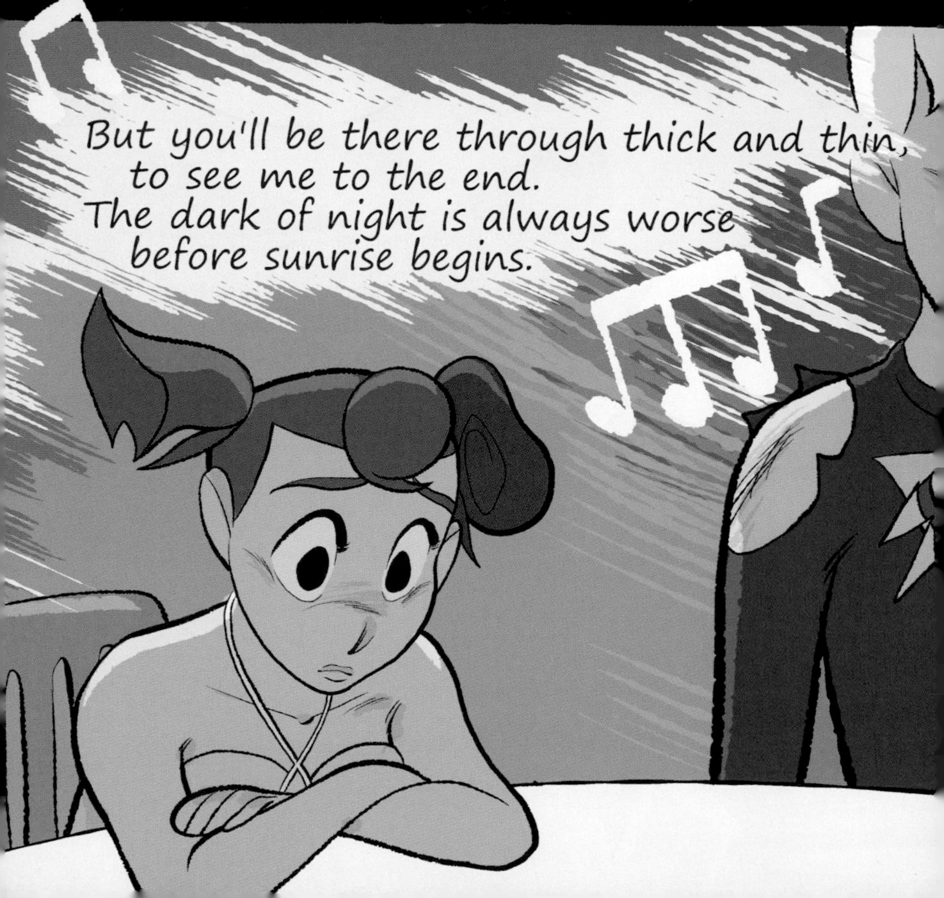
But you'll be there through thick and thin,
to see me to the end.
The dark of night is always worse
before sunrise begins.

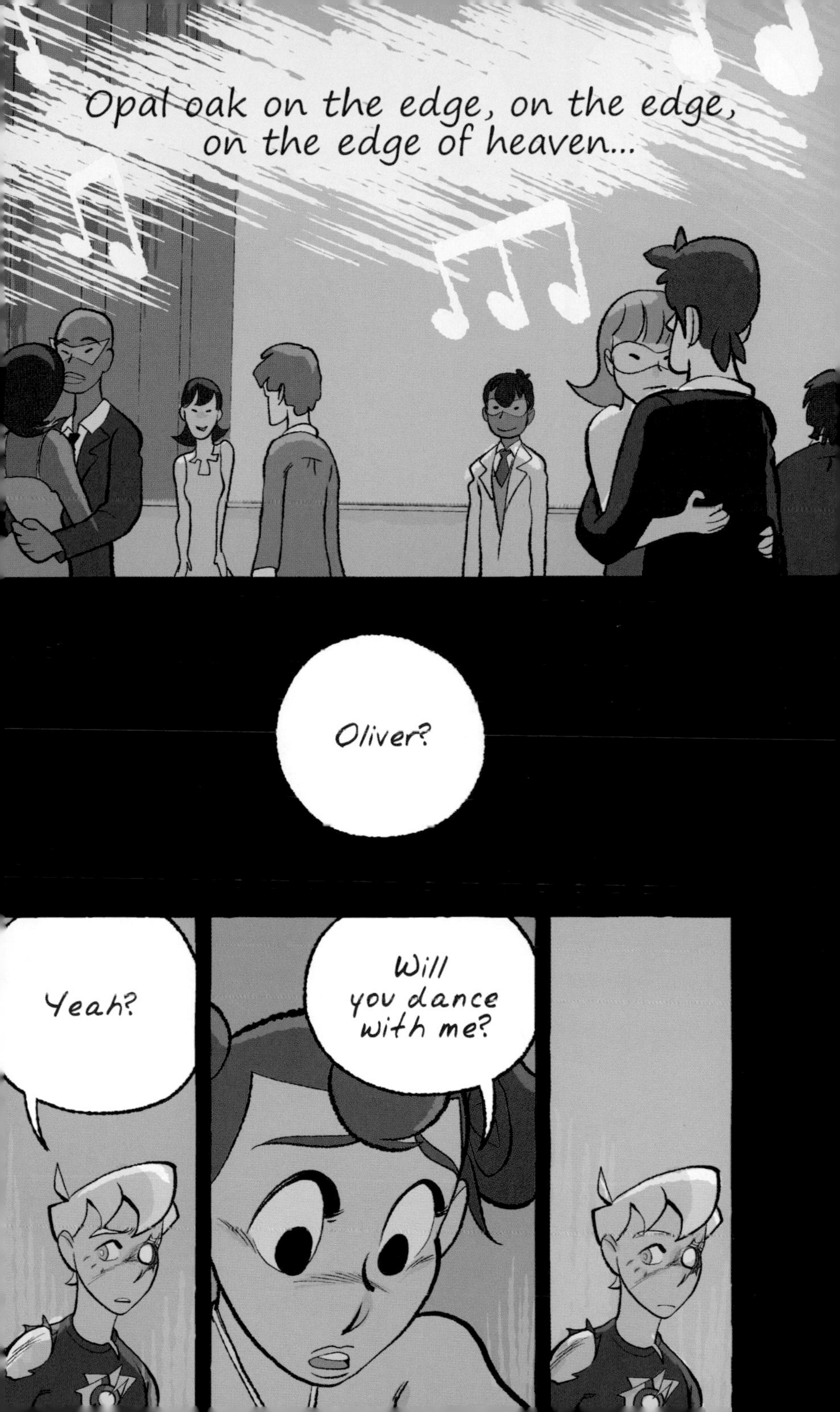
Opal oak on the edge, on the edge, on the edge of heaven...
Oliver?
Yeah?
Will you dance with me?

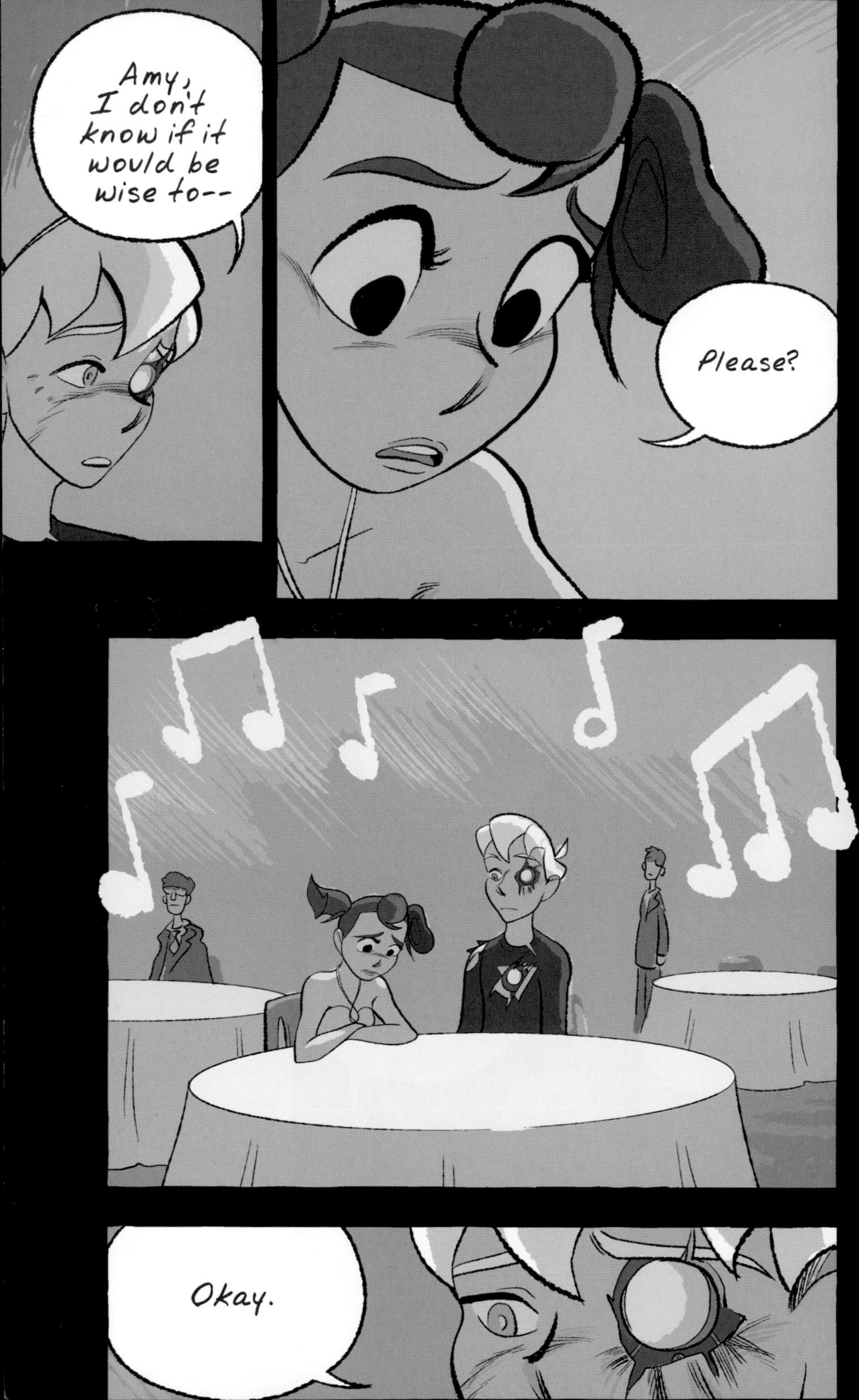
Amy, I don't know if it would be wise to--
Please?
Okay.

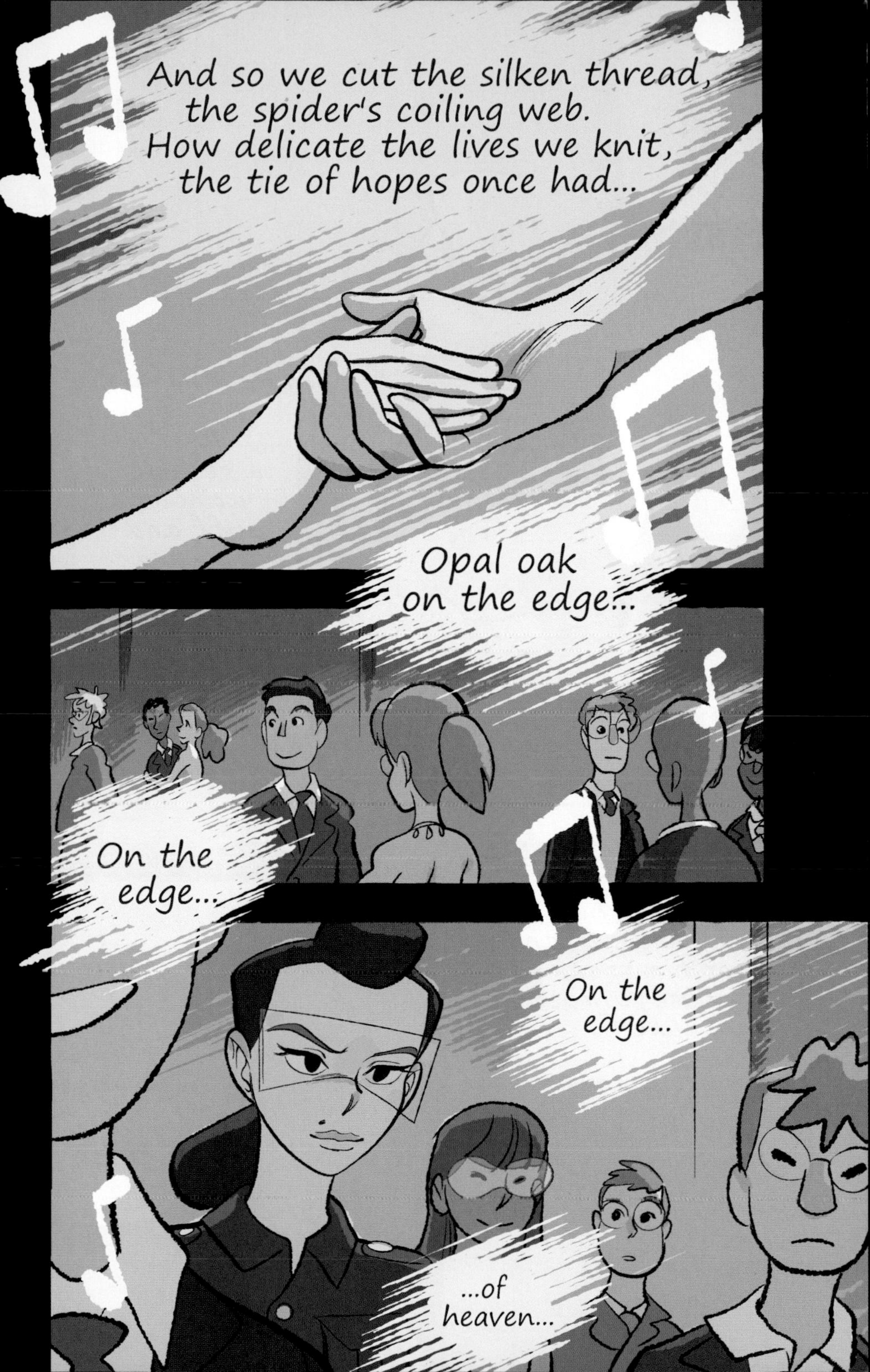
And so we cut the silken thread,
the spider's coiling web.
How delicate the lives we knit,
the tie of hopes once had...
Opal oak
on the edge...
On the
edge...
On the
edge...
...of
heaven...

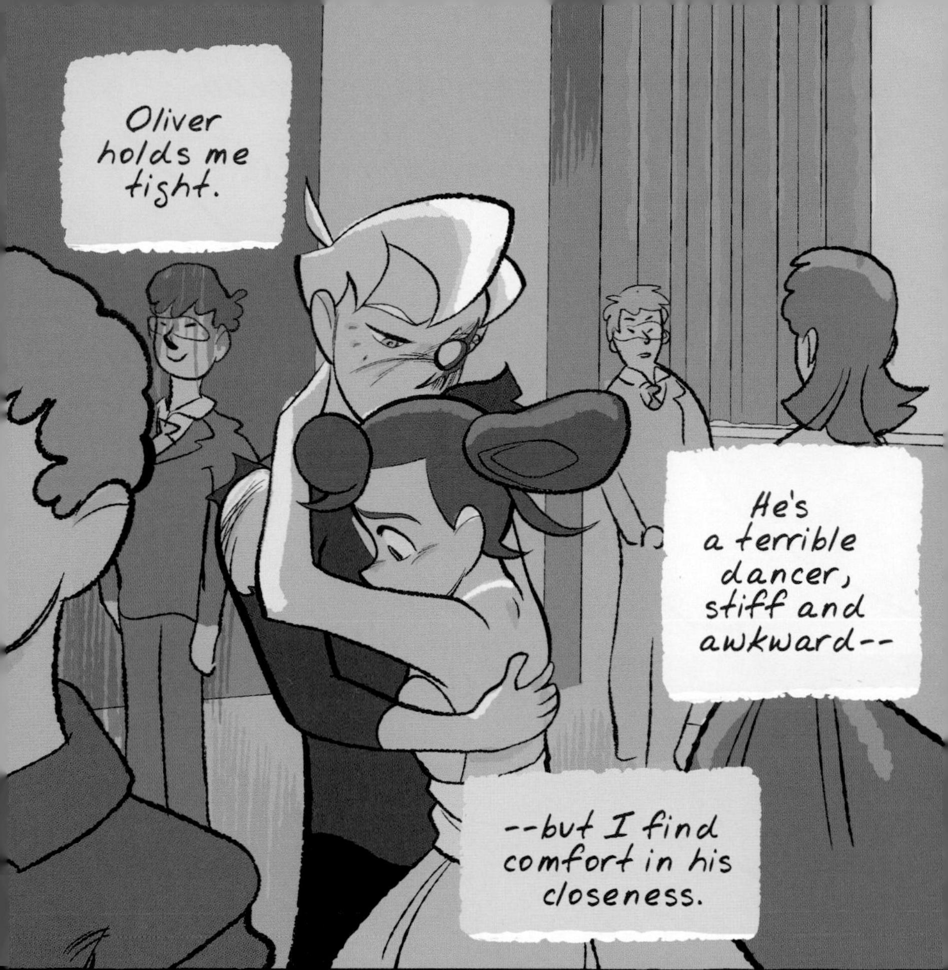
Oliver holds me tight.
He's a terrible dancer, stiff and awkward--
--but I find comfort in his closeness.

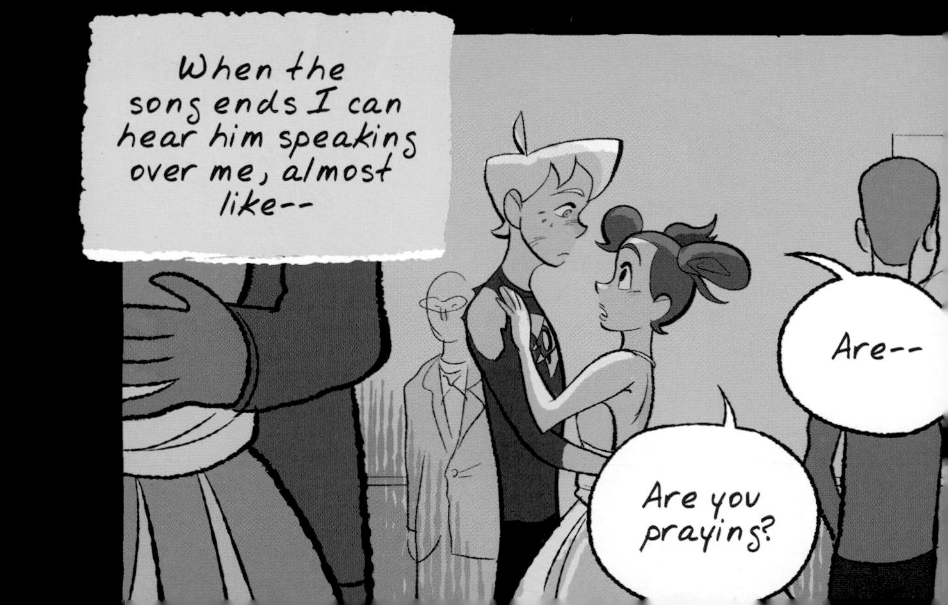
When the song ends I can hear him speaking over me, almost like--
Are--
Are you praying?

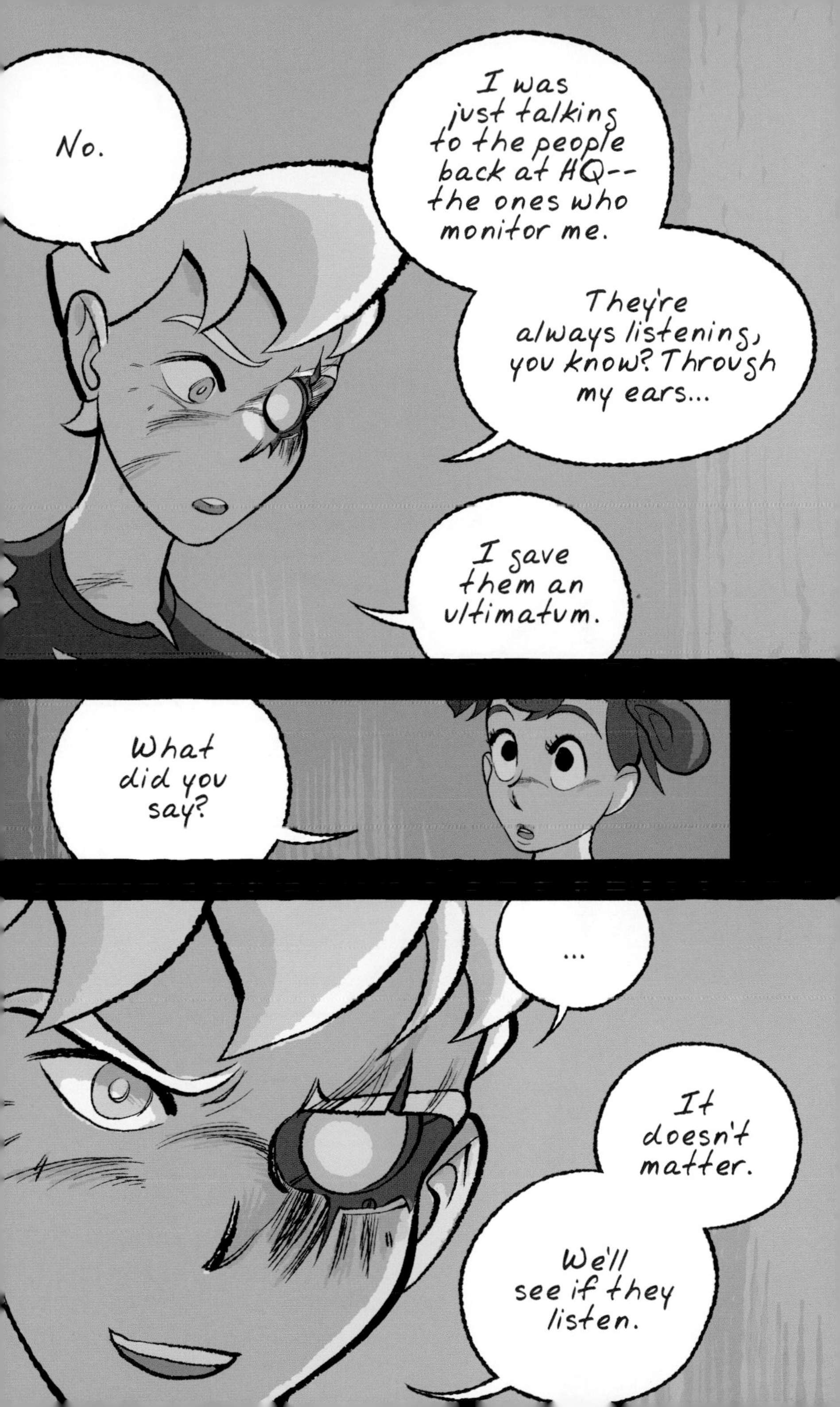
No.
I was just talkins to the people back at HQ-- the ones who monitor me.
They're always listening, you know? Through my ears...
I save them an ultimatum.
What did you say?
...
It doesn't matter.
We'll see if they listen.

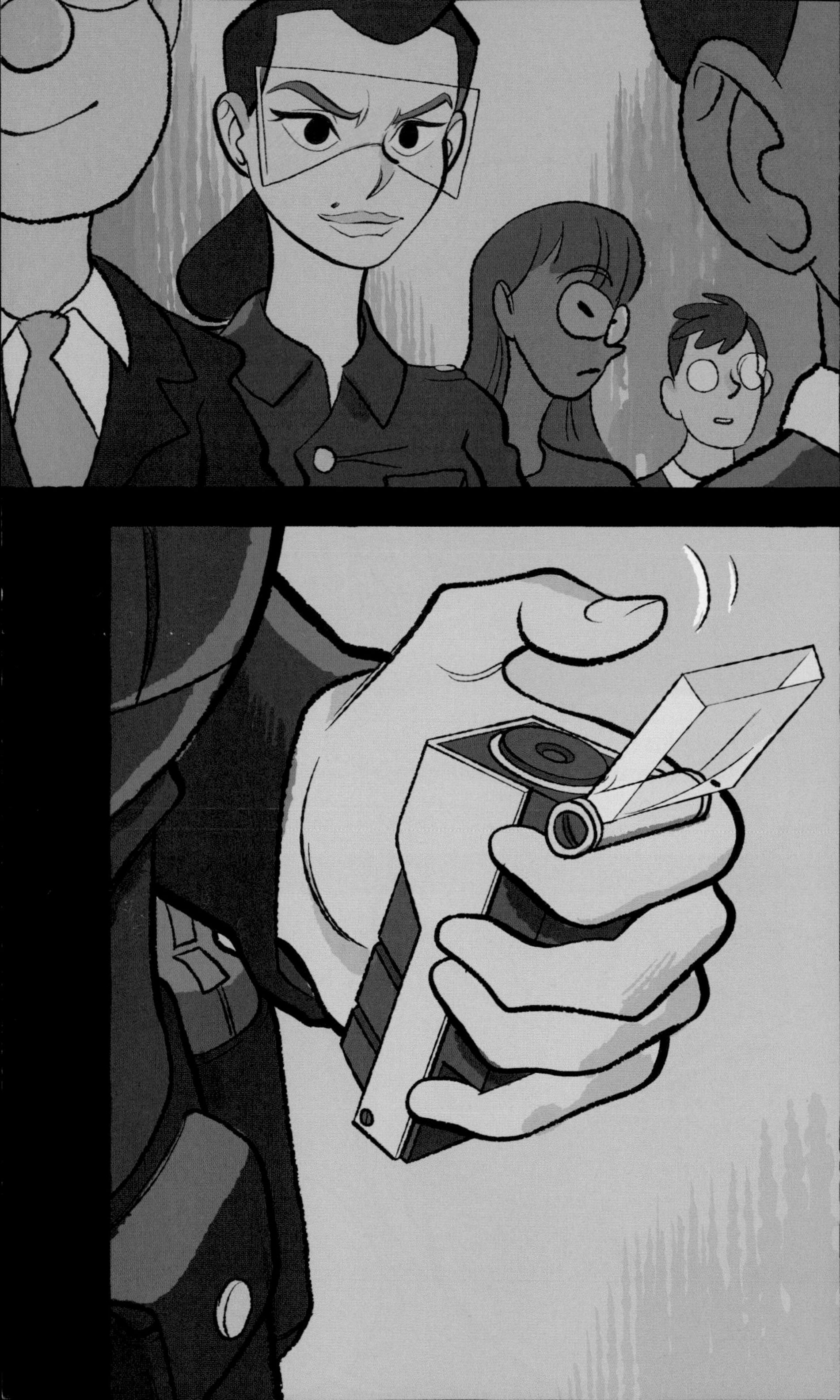

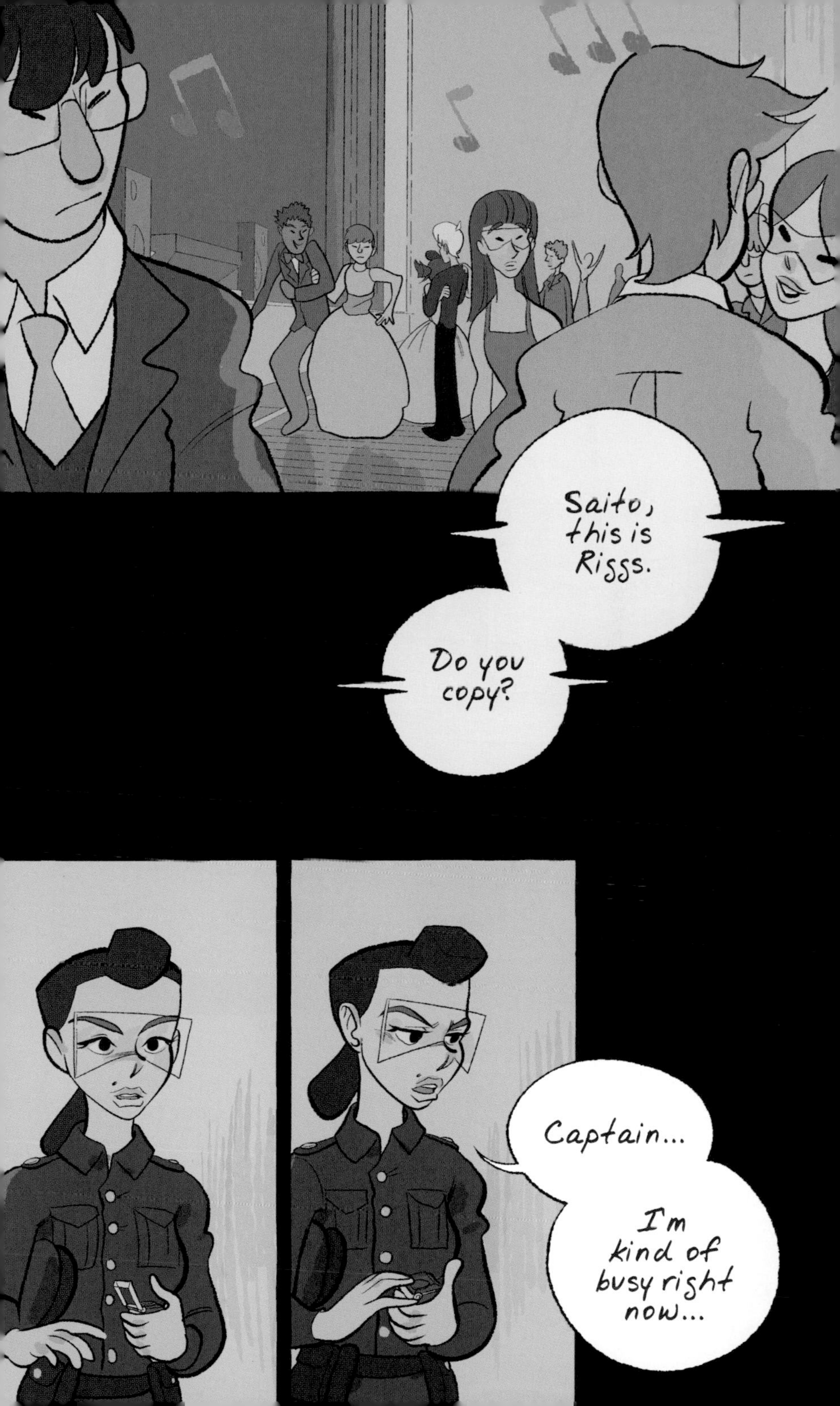
Saito, this is Riggs.
Do you copy?
Captain...
I'm kind of busy right now...

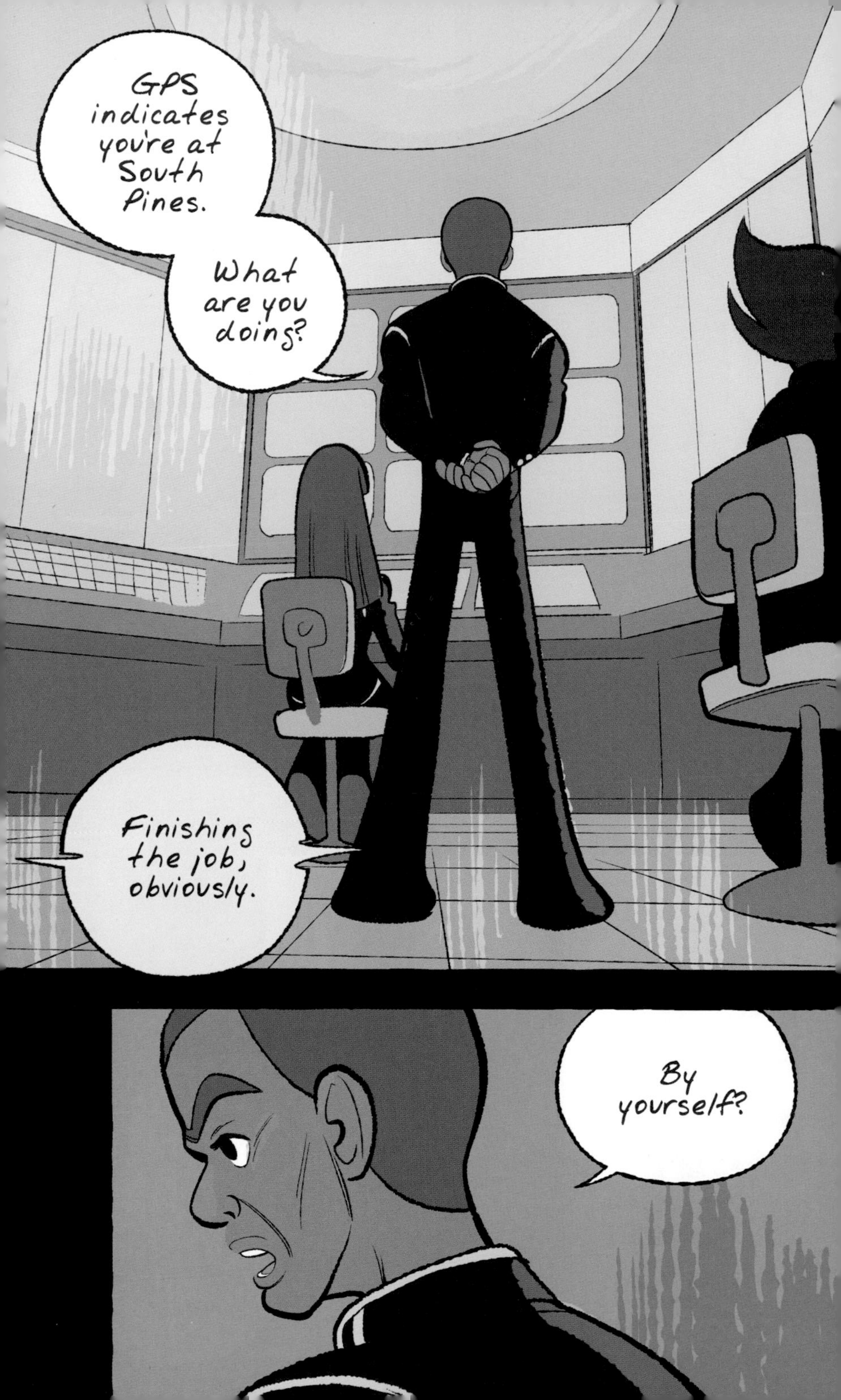
GPS indicates you're at South Pines.
What are you doing?
Finishing the job, obviously.
By yourself?

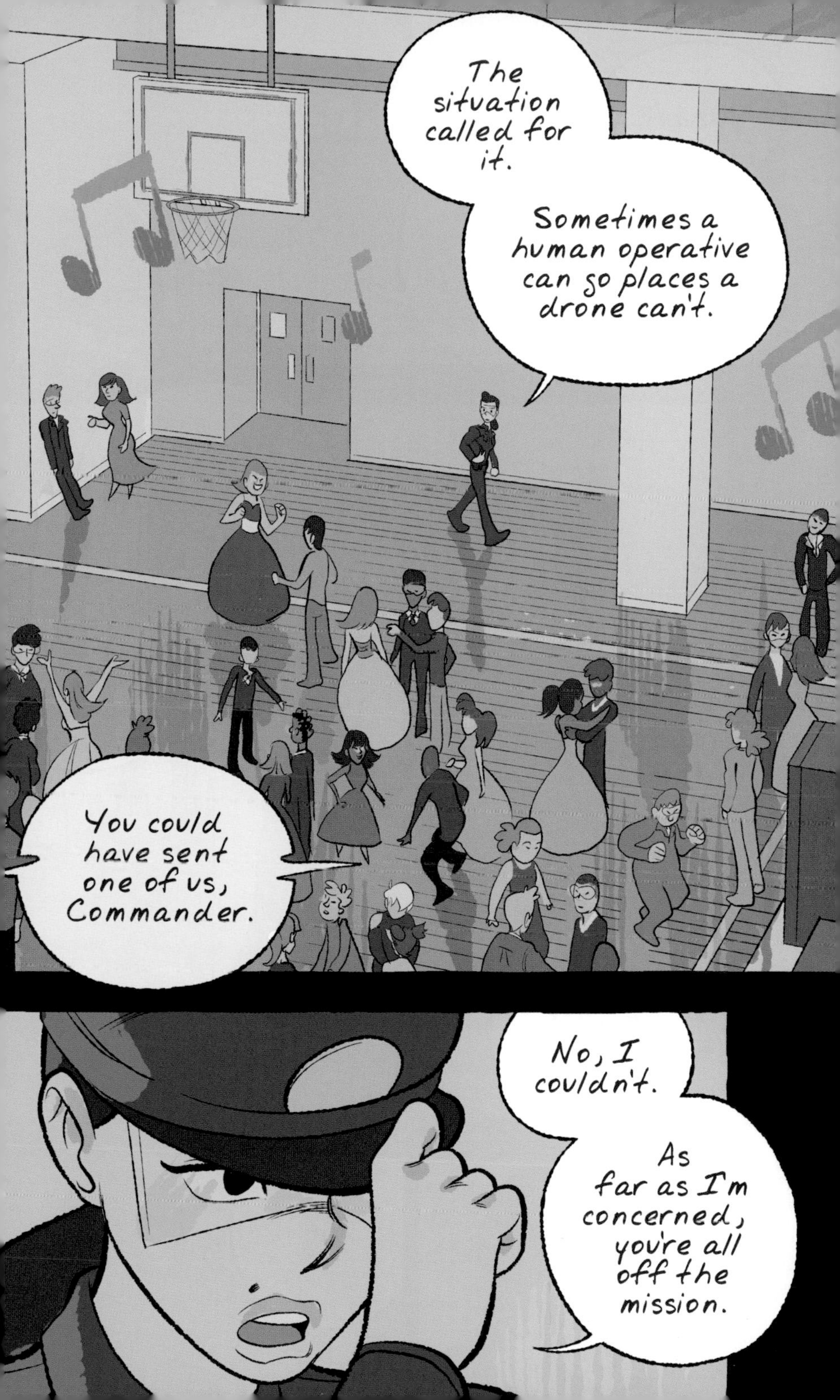
The situation called for it.
Sometimes a human operative can go places a drone can't.
You could have sent one of us, Commander.
No, I couldn't.
As far as I'm concerned, you're all off the mission.

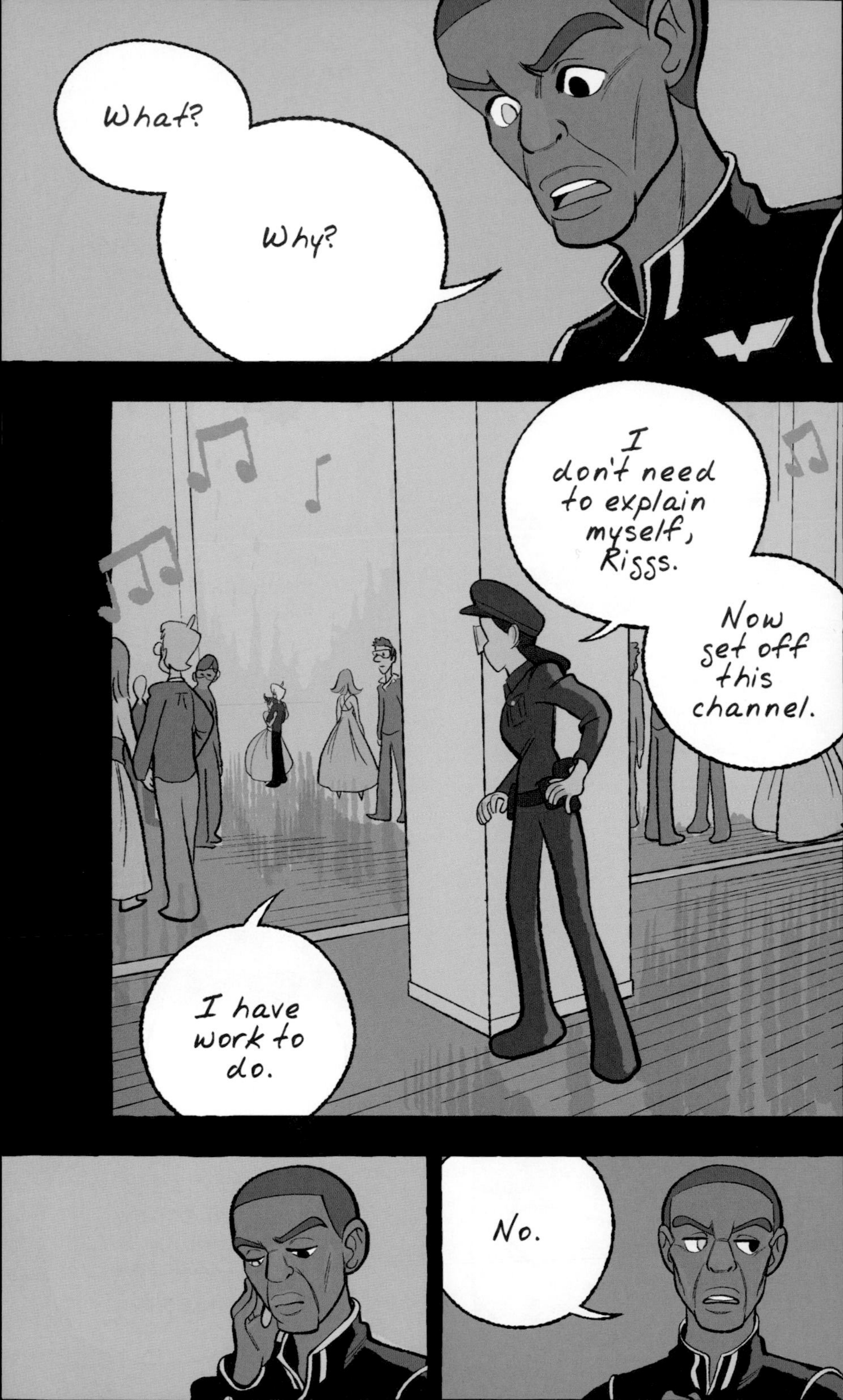
What?
Why?
I don't need to explain myself, Risss.
Now set off this channel.
I have work to do.
No.

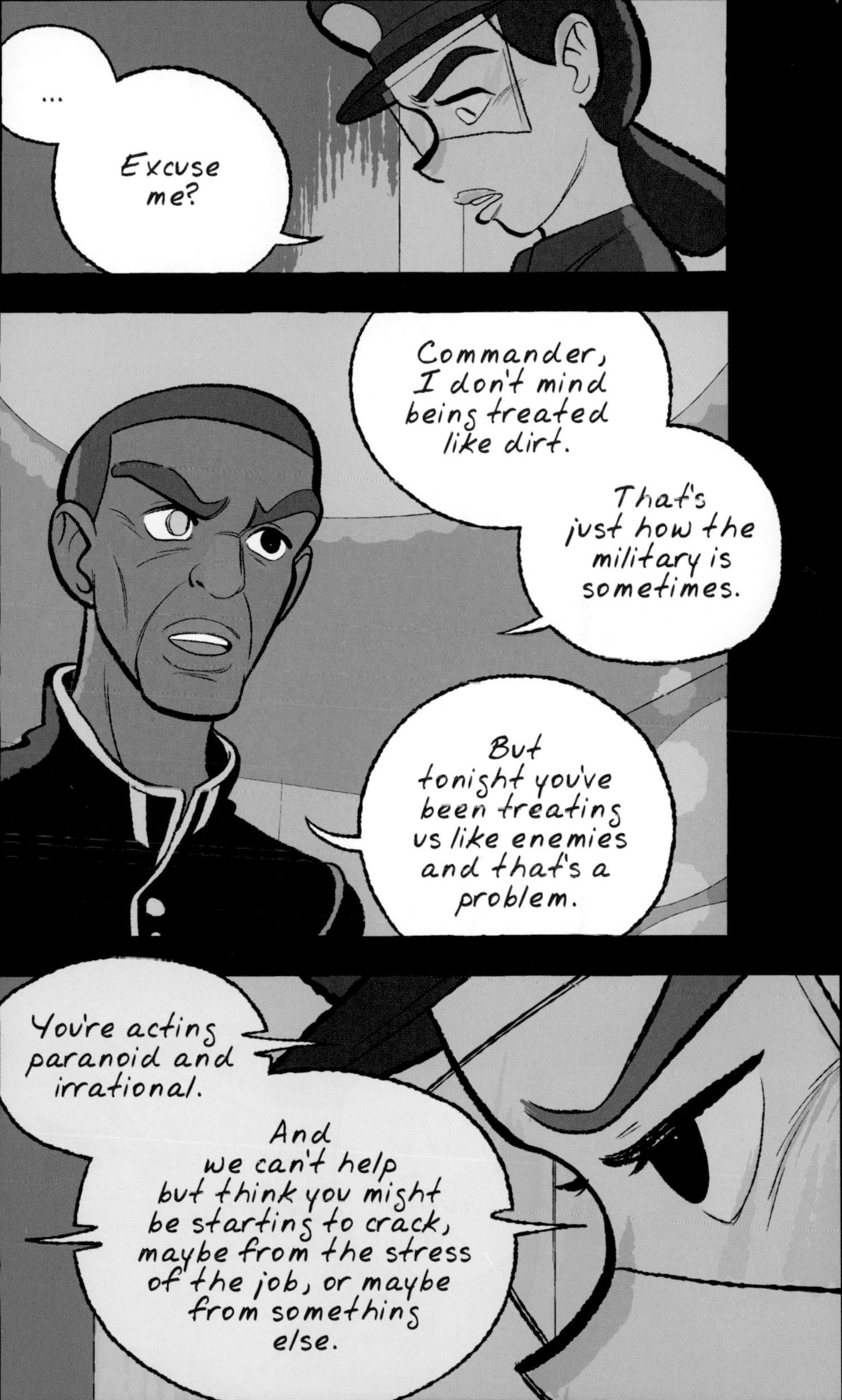

...
Excuse me?
Commander, I don't mind being treated like dirt.
That's just how the military is sometimes.
But tonight you've been treating us like enemies and that's a problem.
You're acting paranoid and irrational.
And we can't help but think you might be starting to crack, maybe from the stress of the job, or maybe from something else.

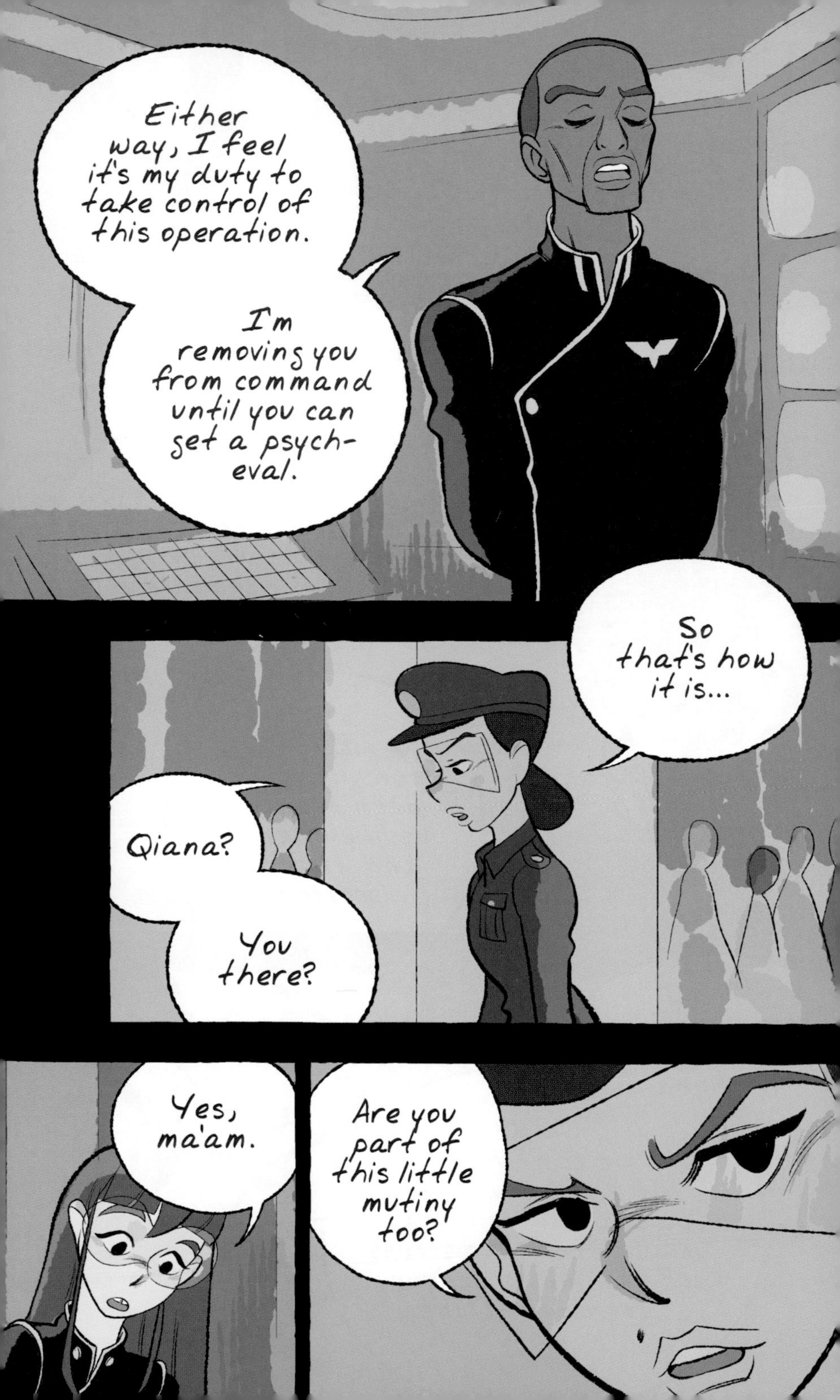

Either way, I feel it's my duty to take control of this operation.
I'm removing you from command until you can get a psych-eval.
So that's how it is...
Qiana?
You there?
Yes, ma'am.
Are you part of this little mutiny too?

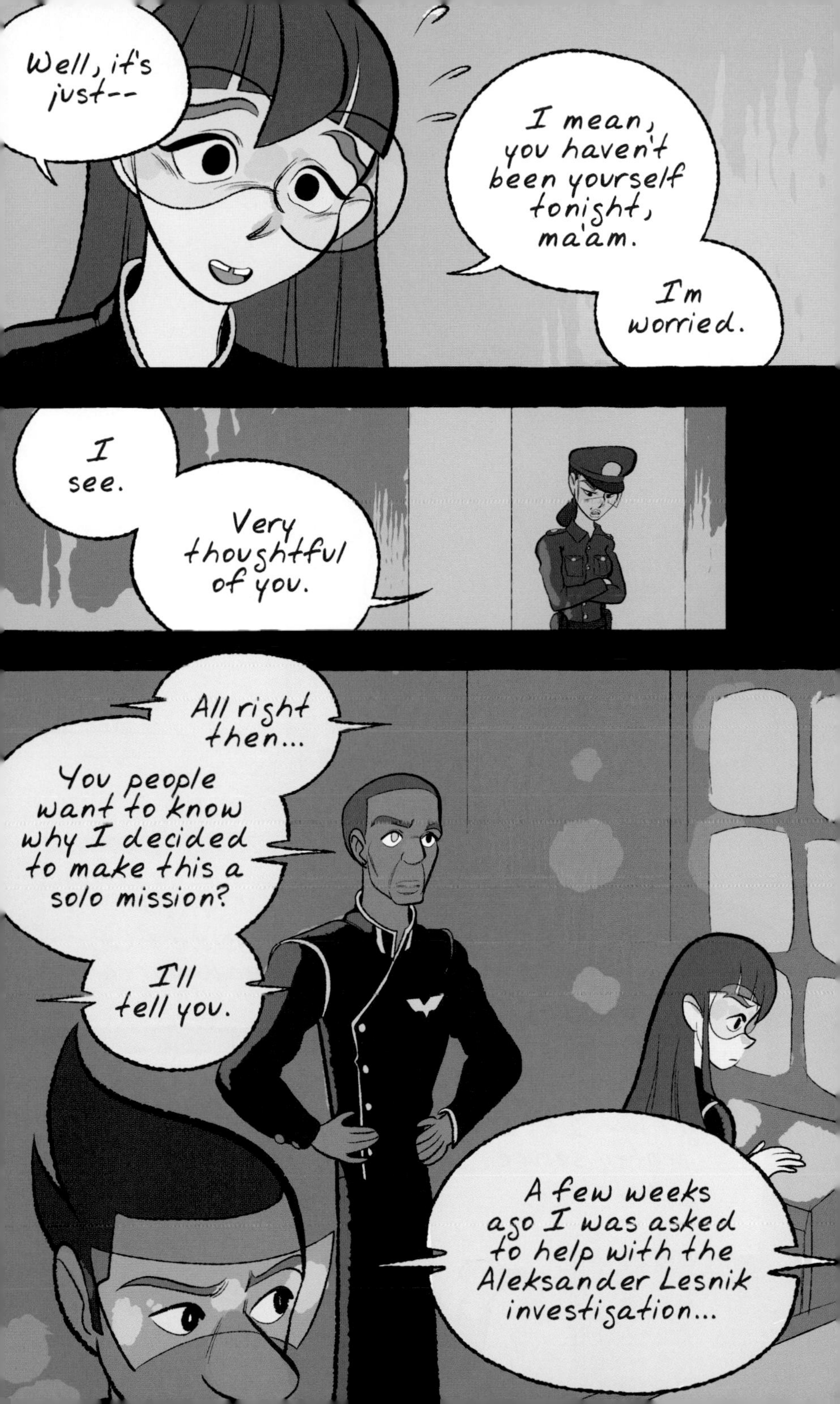
Well, it's just--
I mean, you haven't been yourself tonight, ma'am.
I'm worried.
I see.
Very thoughtful of you.
All right then...
You people want to know why I decided to make this a solo mission?
I'll tell you.
A few weeks ago I was asked to help with the Aleksander Lesnik investigation...

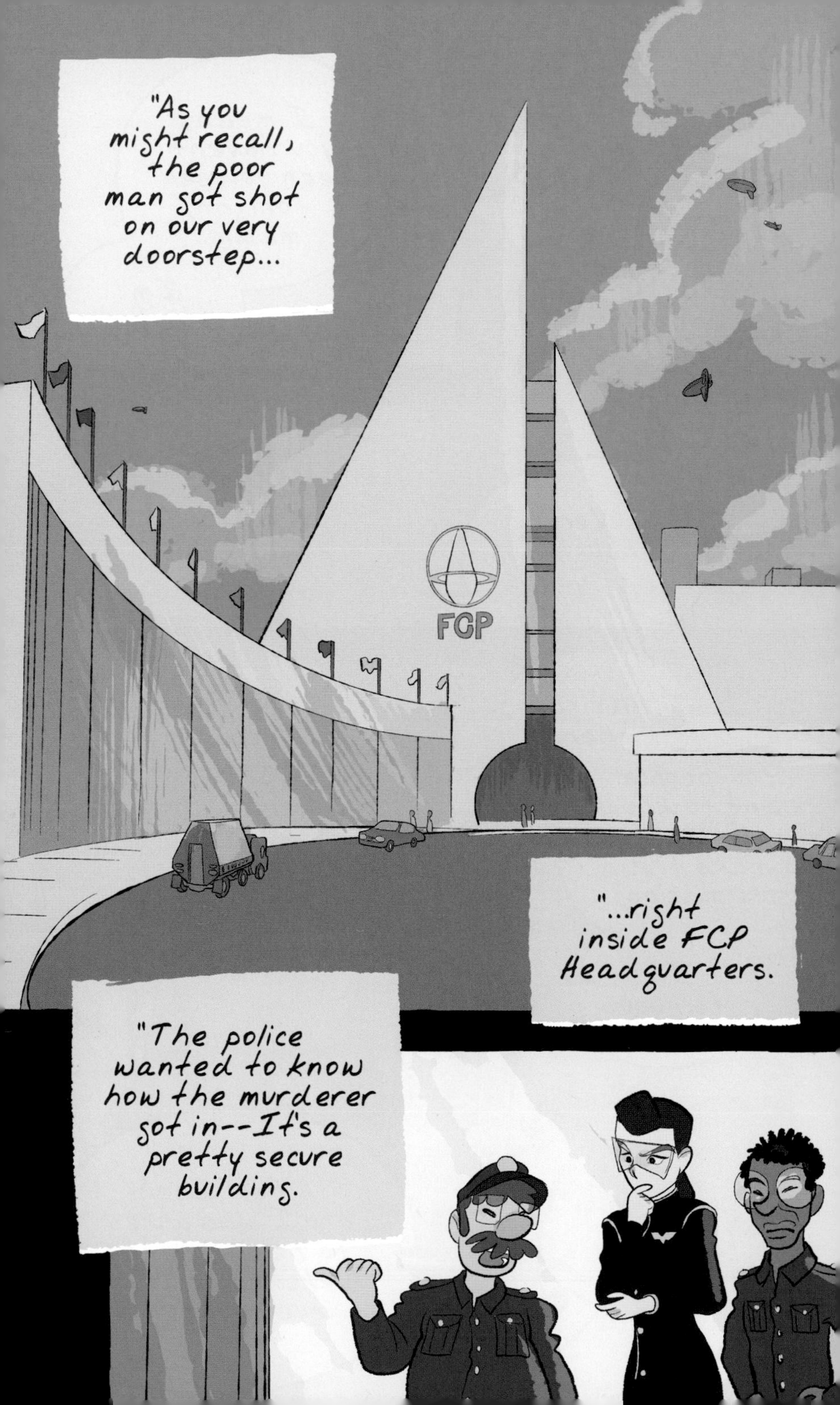
"As you might recall, the poor man got shot on our very doorstep...
FCP
"...right inside FCP Headquarters.
"The police wanted to know how the murderer got in--It's a pretty secure building.

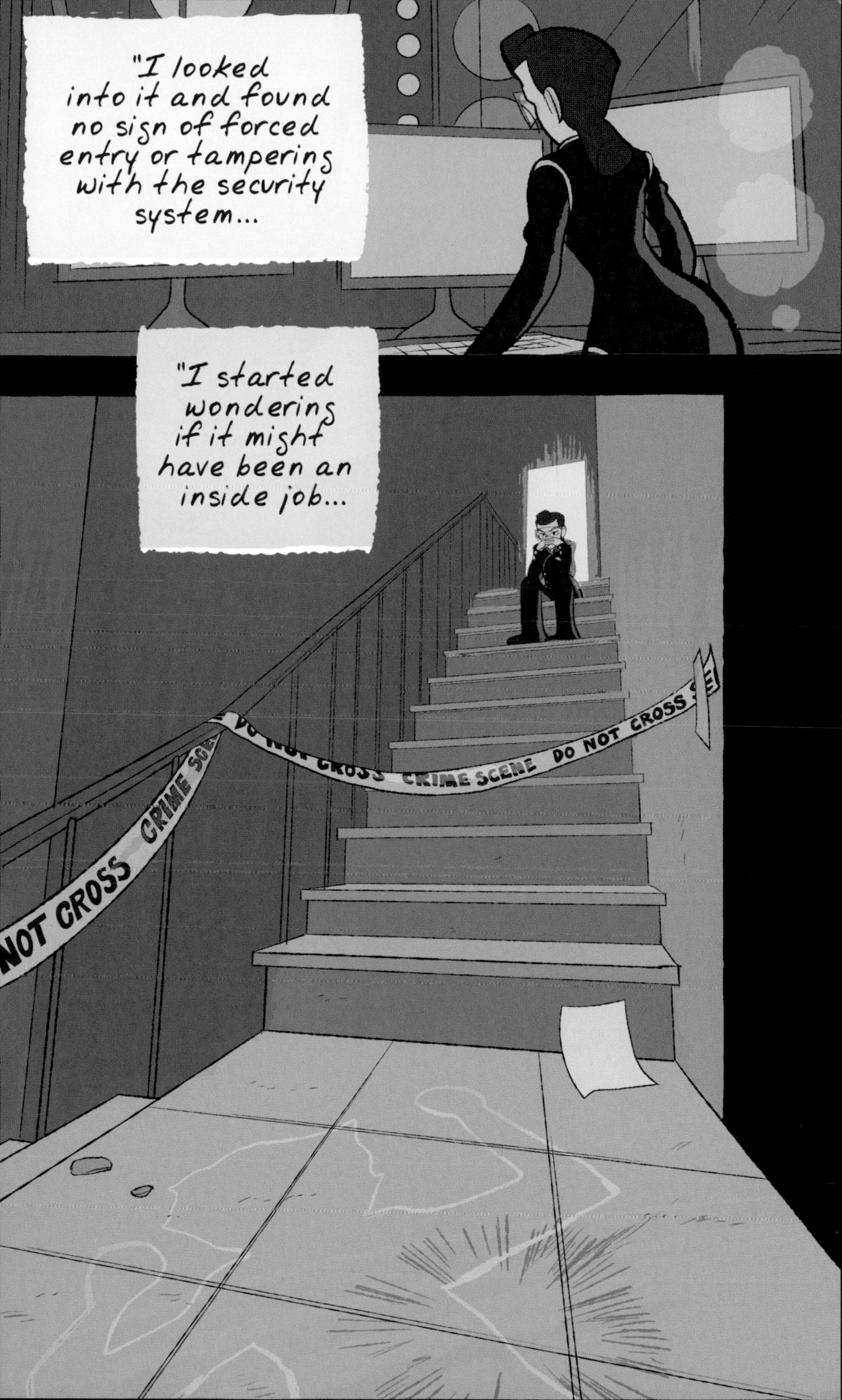
"I looked into it and found no sign of forced entry or tampering with the security system...
"I started wondering if it might have been an inside job...
DO NOT CROSS
CRIME SCENE
DO NOT CROSS
CRIME SCENE
NOT CROSS

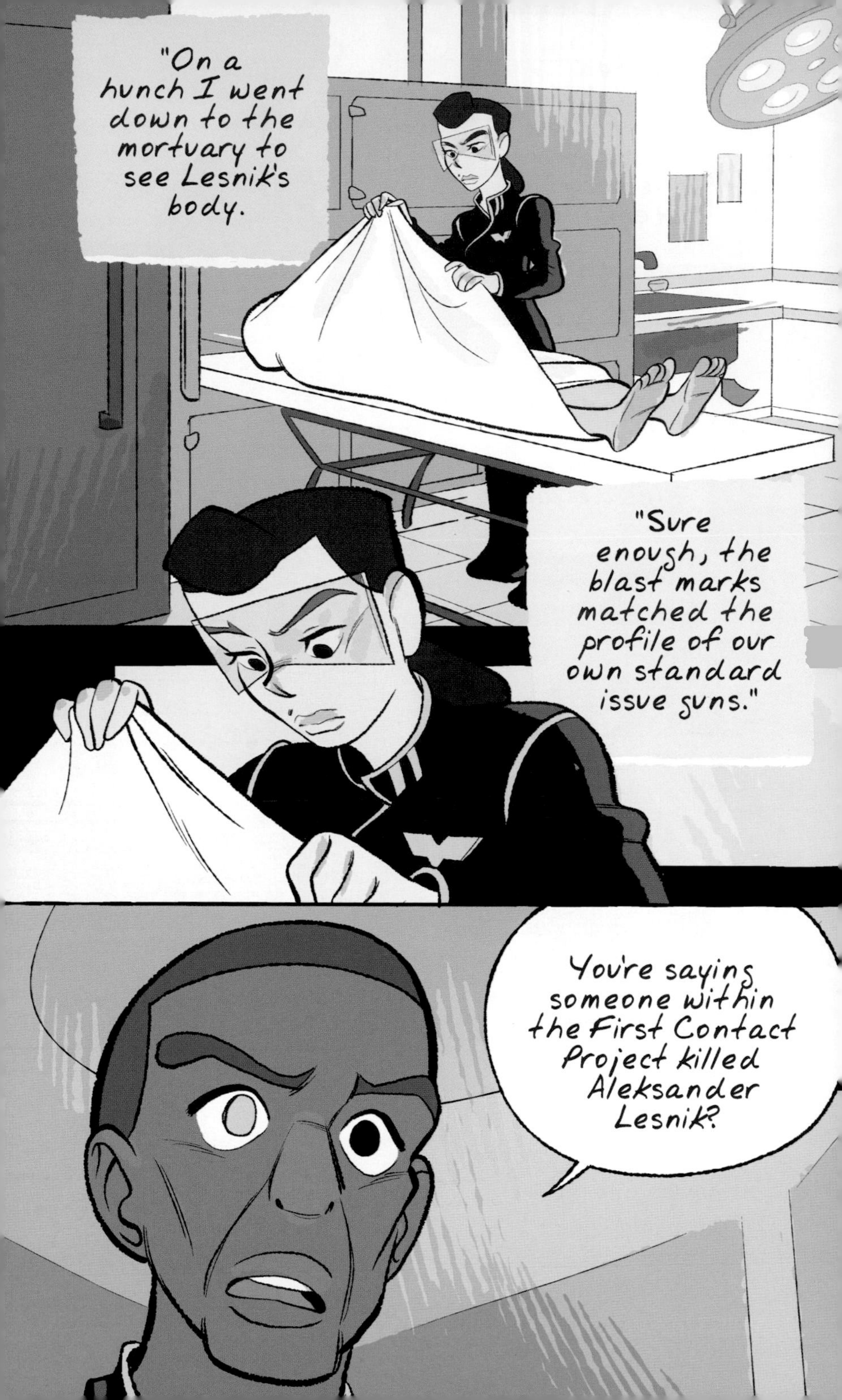
"On a hunch I went down to the mortuary to see Lesnik's body.
"Sure enough, the blast marks matched the profile of our own standard issue guns."
You're saying someone within the First Contact Project killed Aleksander Lesnik?

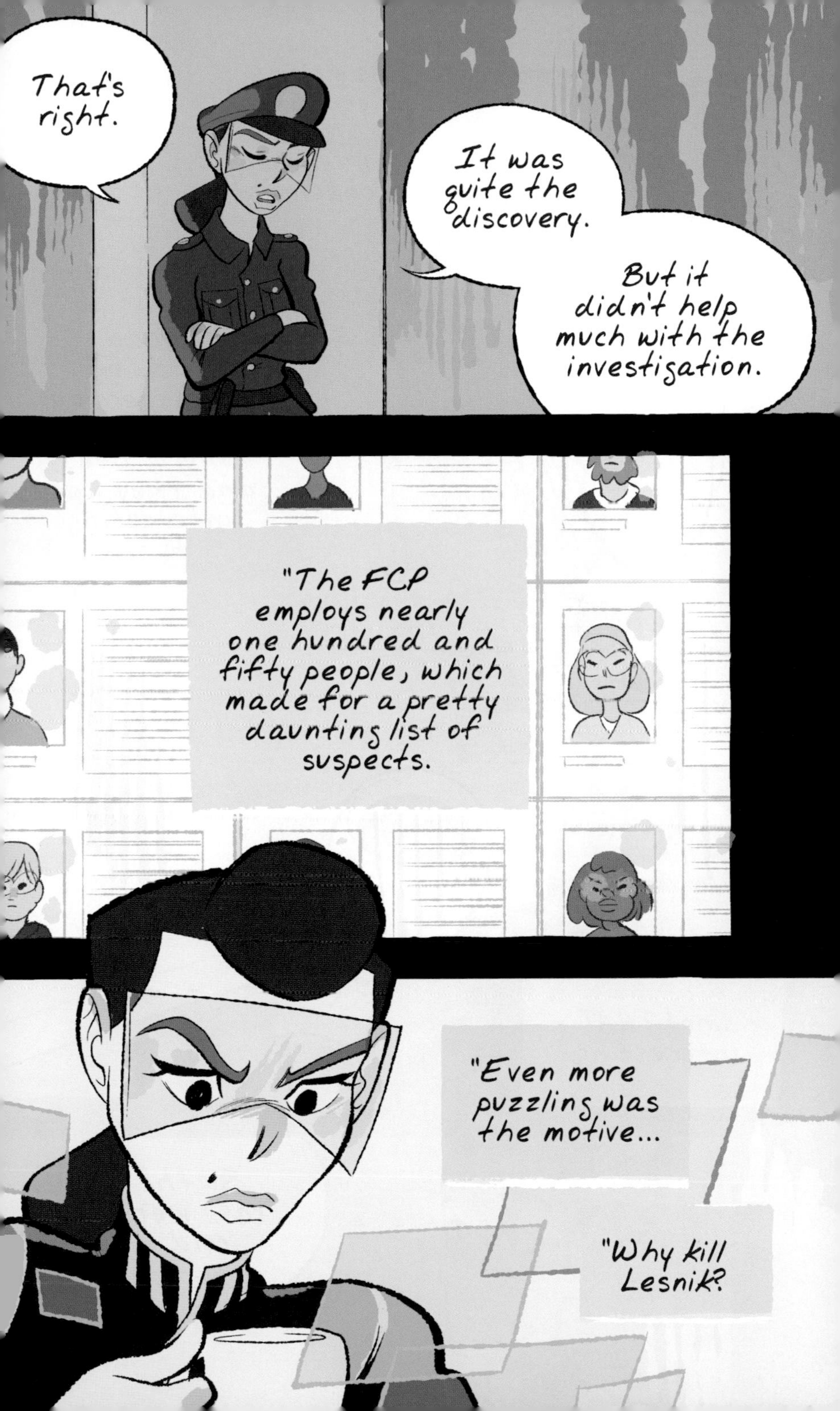
That's right.
It was quite the discovery.
But it didn't help much with the investigation.
"The FCP employs nearly one hundred and fifty people, which made for a pretty daunting list of suspects.
"Even more puzzling was the motive...
"Why kill Lesnik?

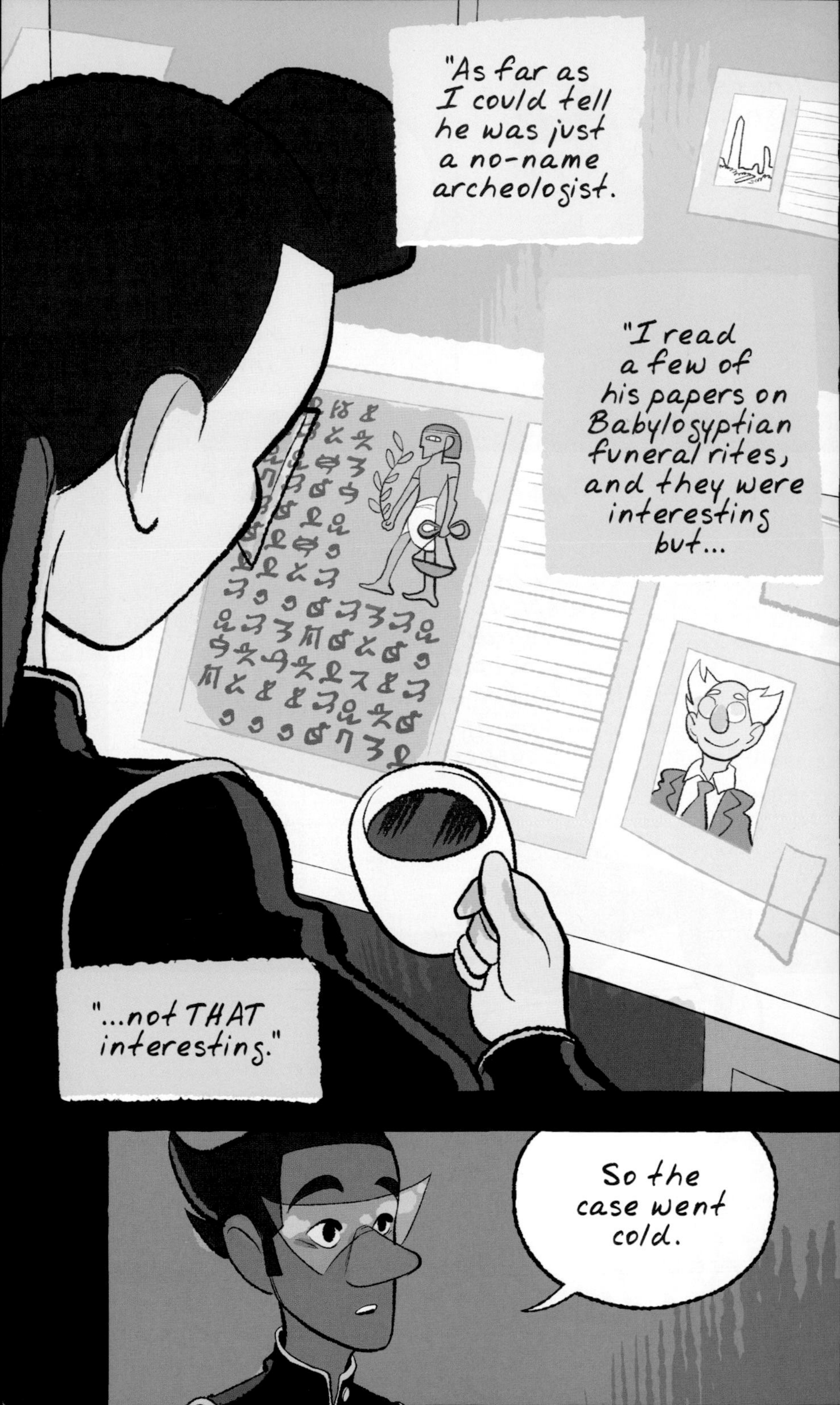
"As far as I could tell he was just a no-name archeologist.
"I read a few of his papers on Babylosyptian funeral rites, and they were interestins but...
"...not THAT interestins."
So the case went cold.

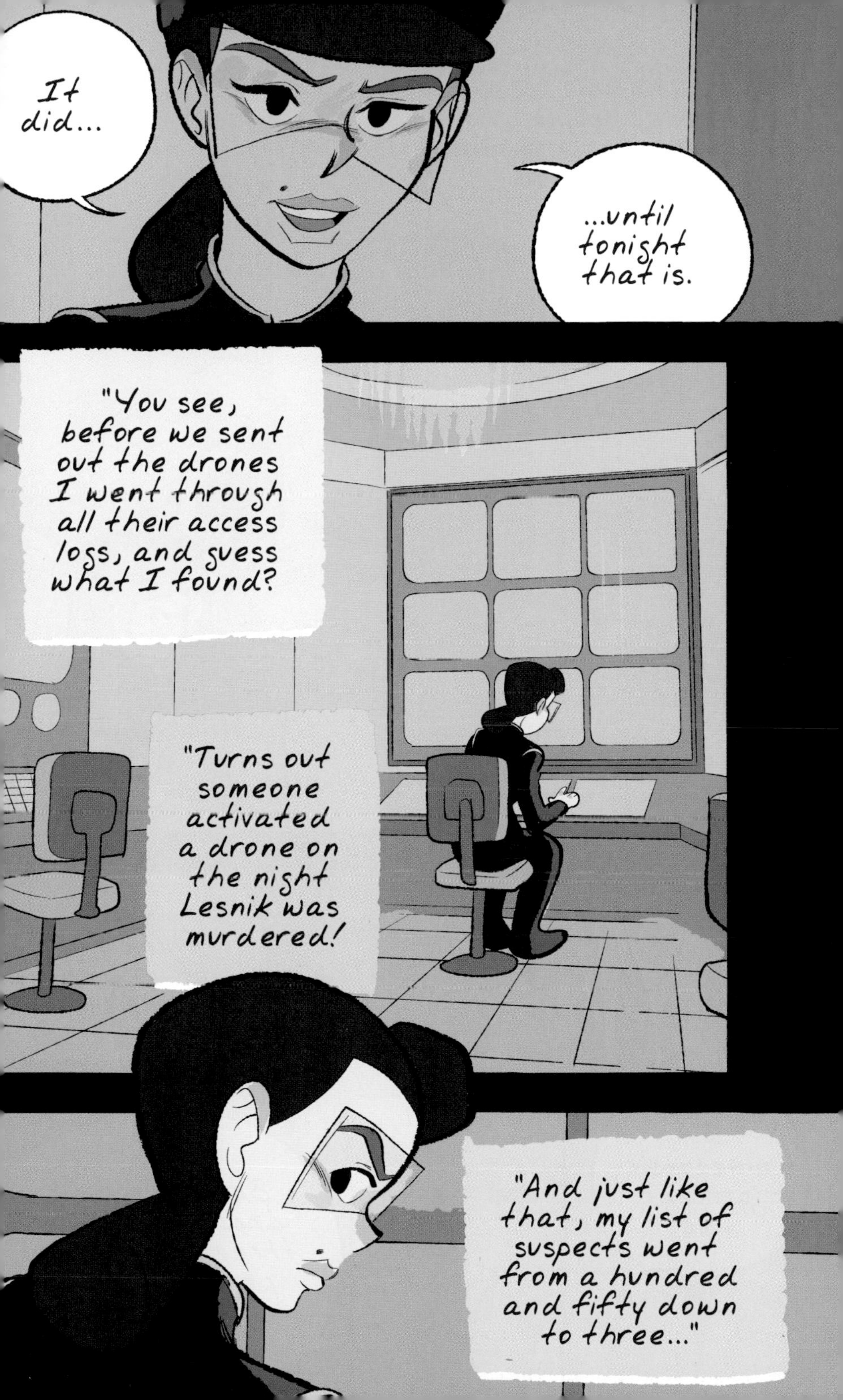
It did...
...until tonight that is.
"You see, before we sent out the drones I went through all their access logs, and guess what I found?
"Turns out someone activated a drone on the night Lesnik was murdered!
"And just like that, my list of suspects went from a hundred and fifty down to three..."

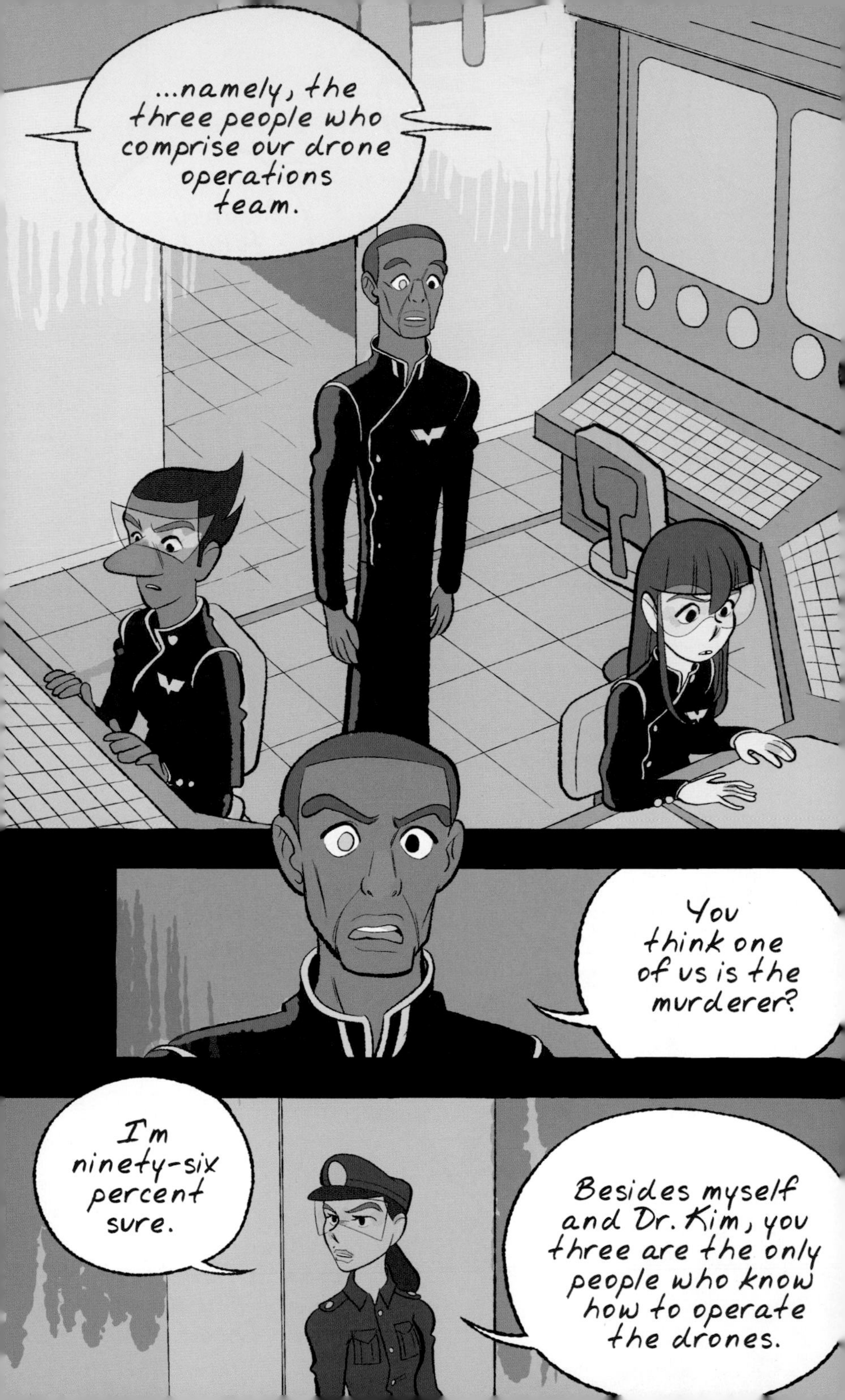
...namely, the three people who comprise our drone operations team.
You think one of us is the murderer?
I'm ninety-six percent sure.
Besides myself and Dr. Kim, you three are the only people who know how to operate the drones.

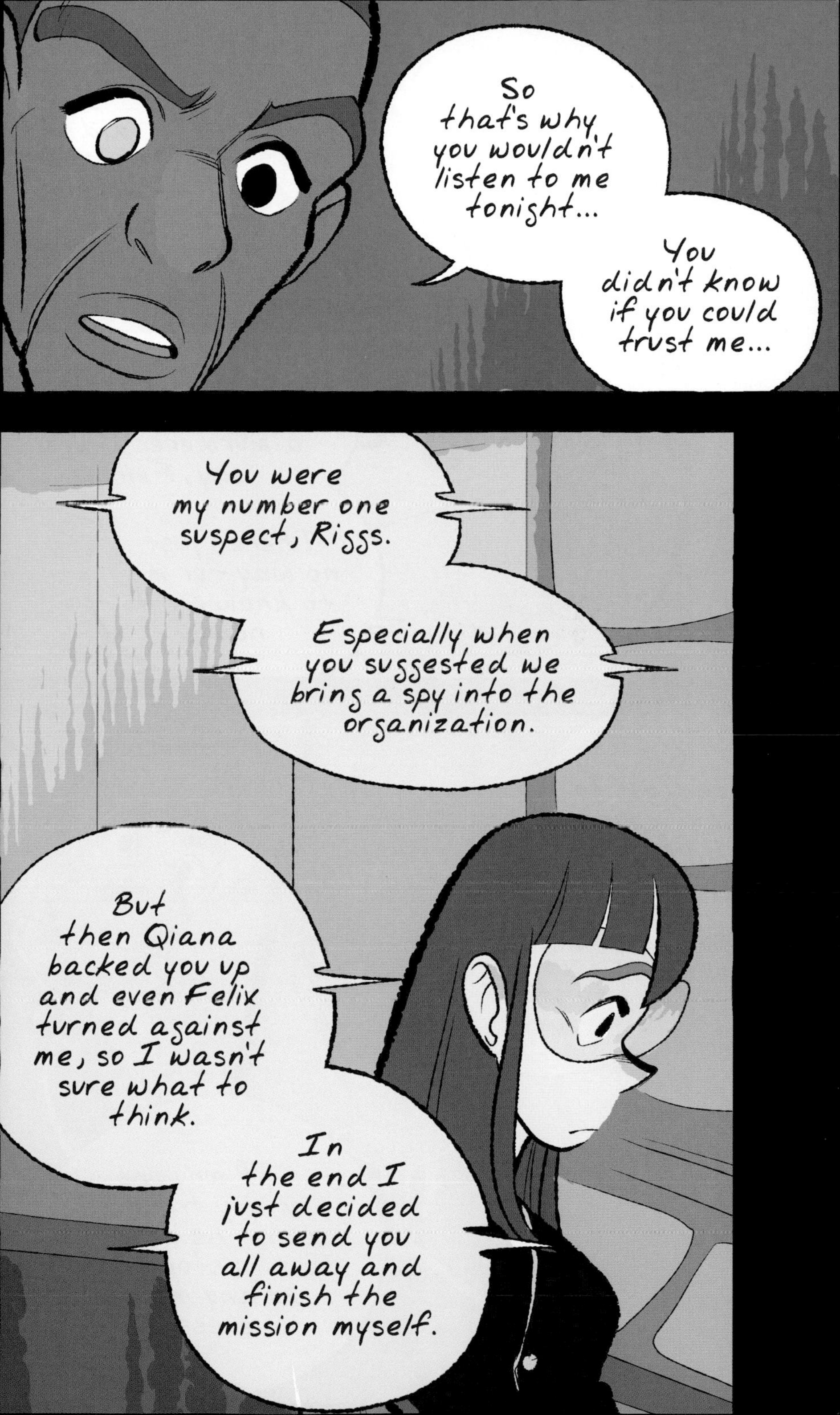
So that's why you wouldn't listen to me tonight...
You didn't know if you could trust me...
You were my number one suspect, Risss.
Especially when you suggested we bring a spy into the organization.
But then Qiana backed you up and even Felix turned against me, so I wasn't sure what to think.
In the end I just decided to send you all away and finish the mission myself.

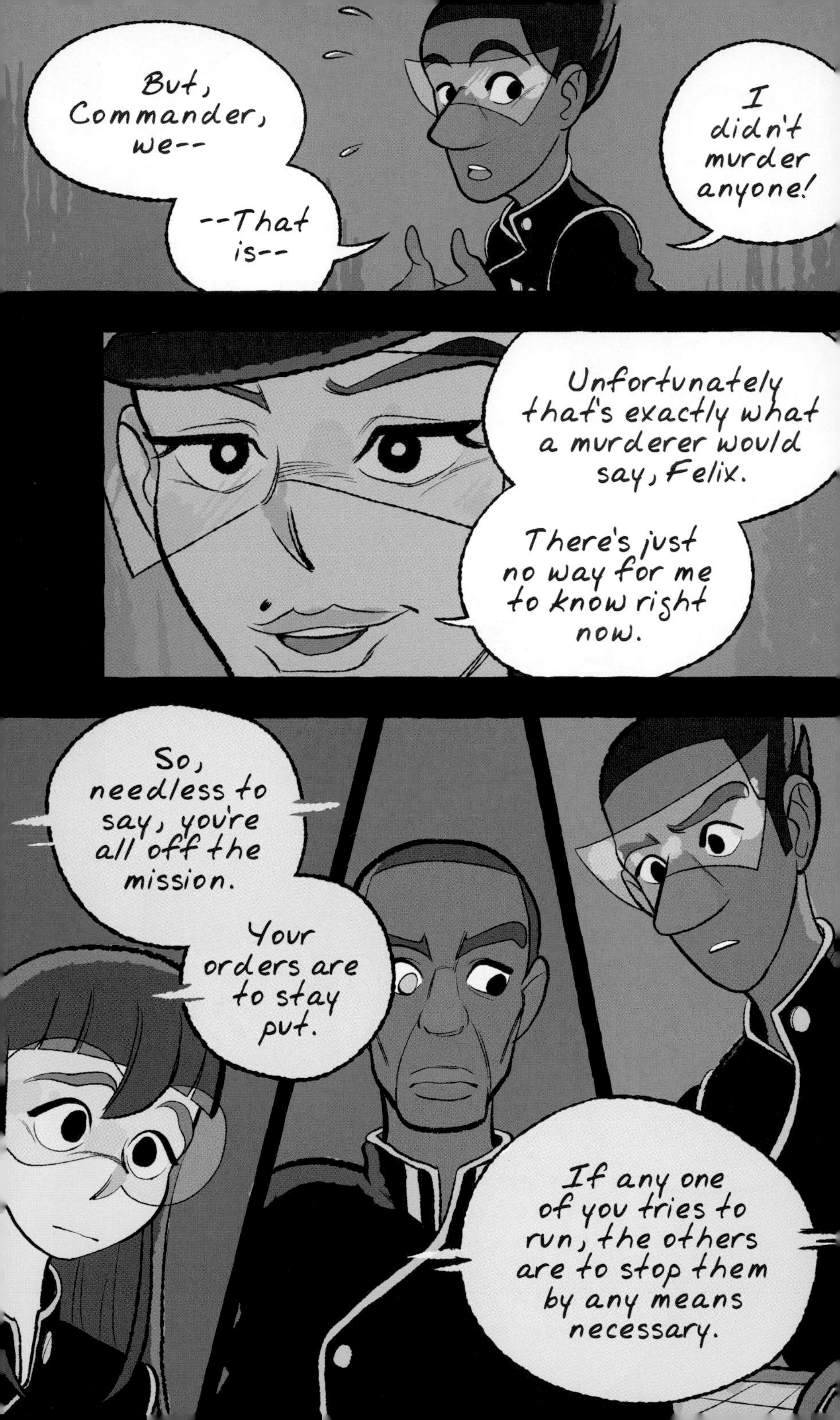
But, Commander, we--
--That is--
I didn't murder anyone!
Unfortunately that's exactly what a murderer would say, Felix.
There's just no way for me to know right now.
So, needless to say, you're all off the mission.
Your orders are to stay put.
If any one of you tries to run, the others are to stop them by any means necessary.

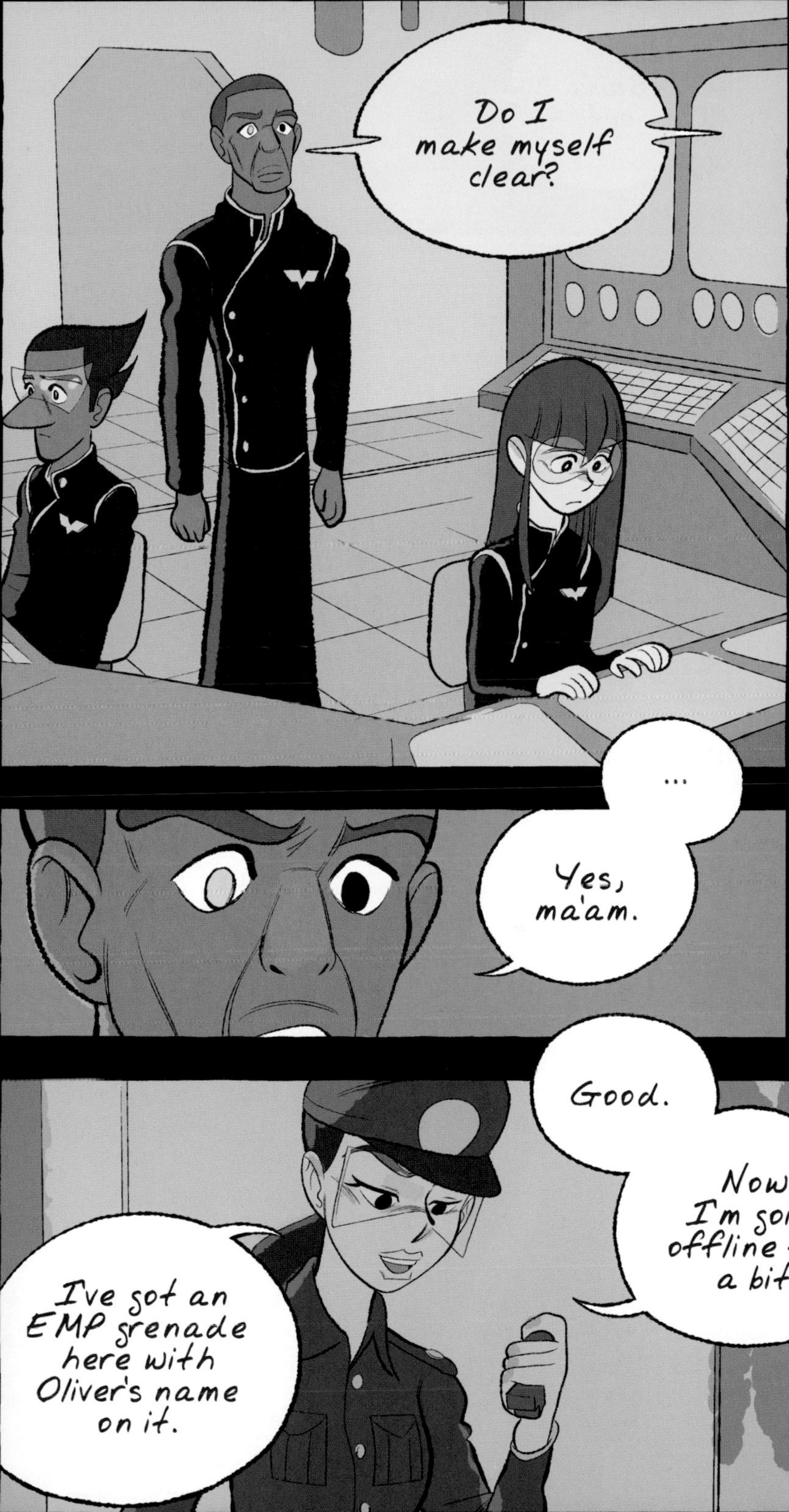
Do I make myself clear?
...
Yes, ma'am.
Good.
Now, I'm going offline for a bit.
I've got an EMP grenade here with Oliver's name on it.

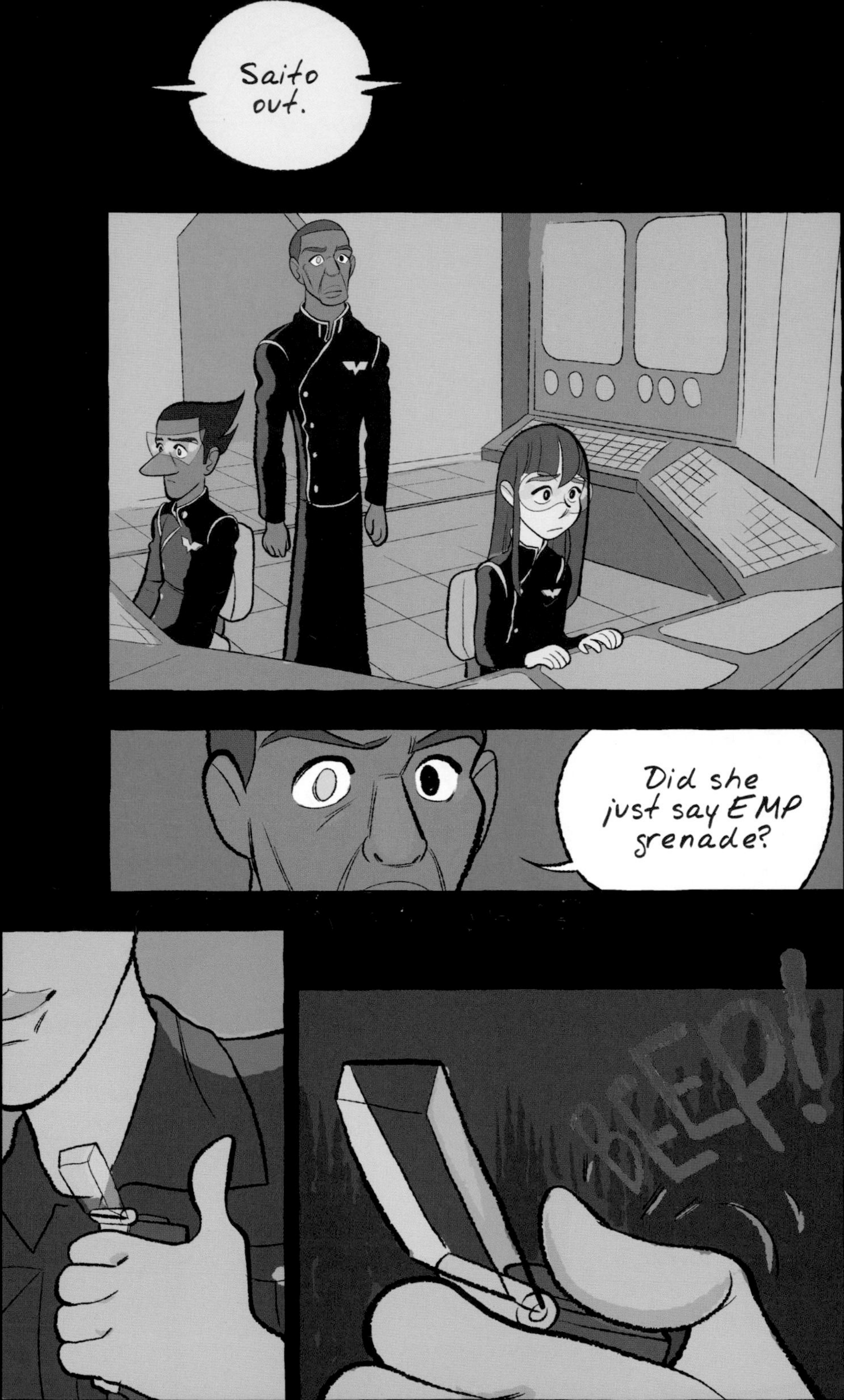
Saito out.
Did she just say EMP grenade?
BEEP!

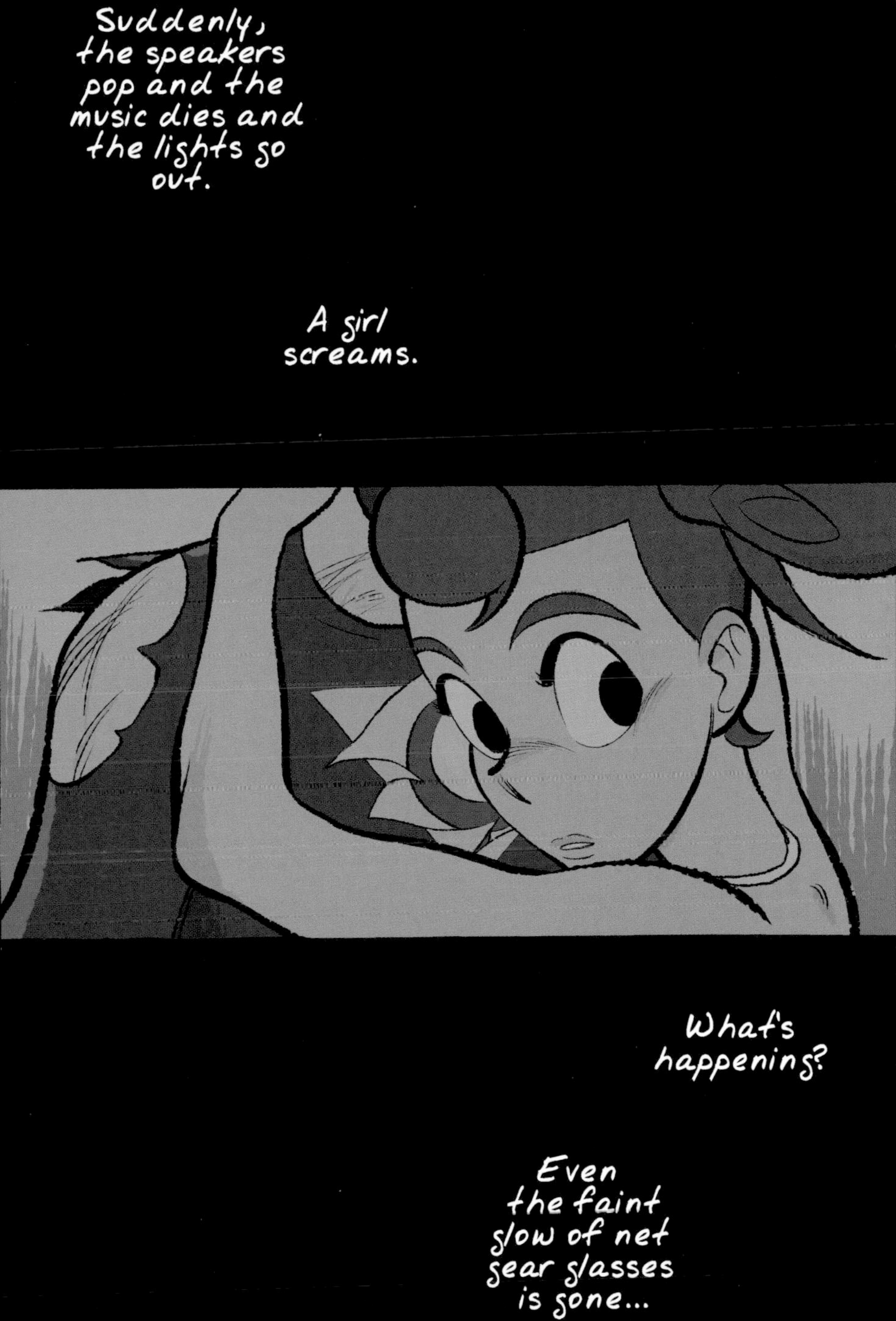
Suddenly, the speakers pop and the music dies and the lights go out.
A girl screams.
What's happening?
Even the faint glow of net gear glasses is gone...

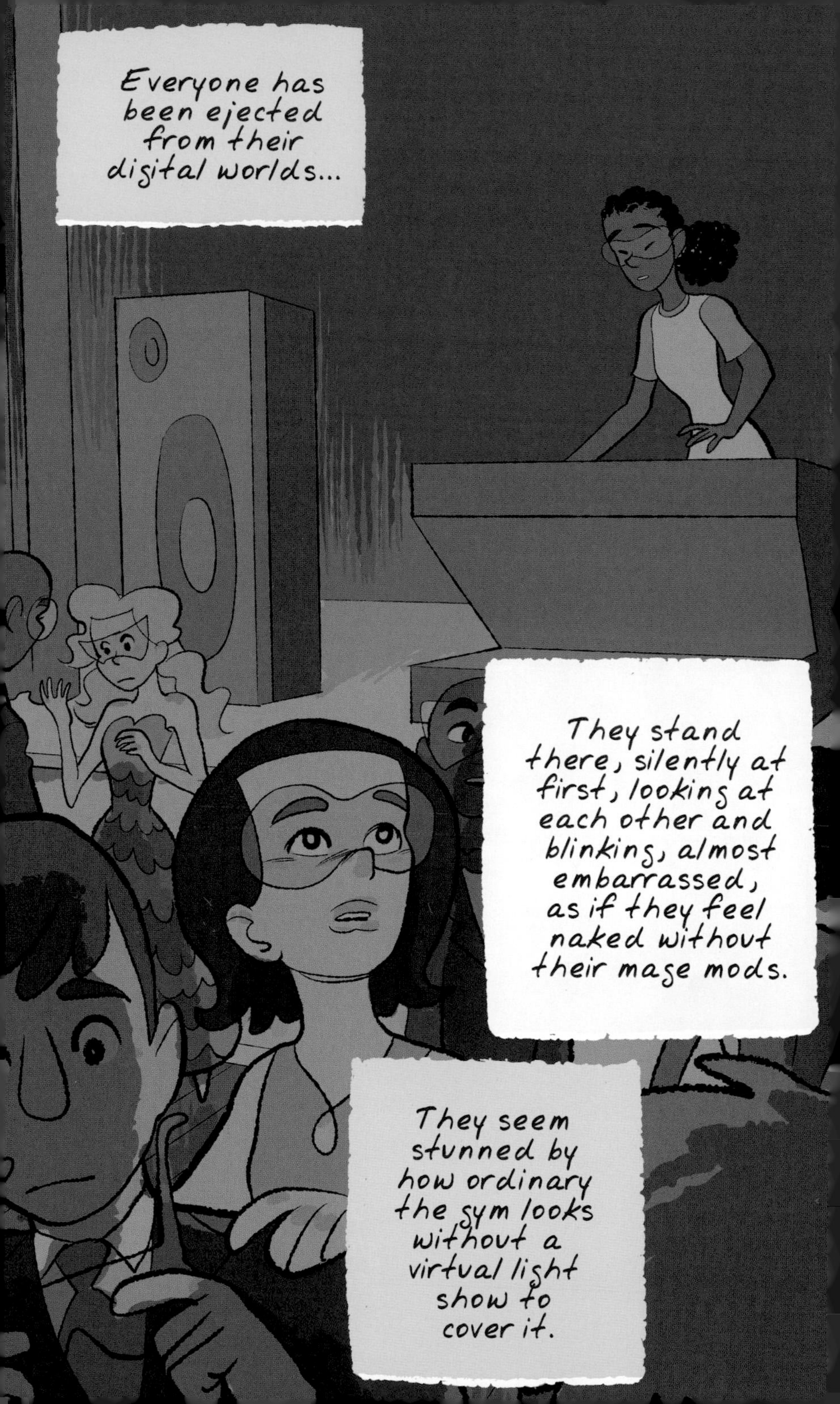
Everyone has been ejected from their digital worlds...
They stand there, silently at first, looking at each other and blinking, almost embarrassed, as if they feel naked without their mage mods.
They seem stunned by how ordinary the gym looks without a virtual light show to cover it.

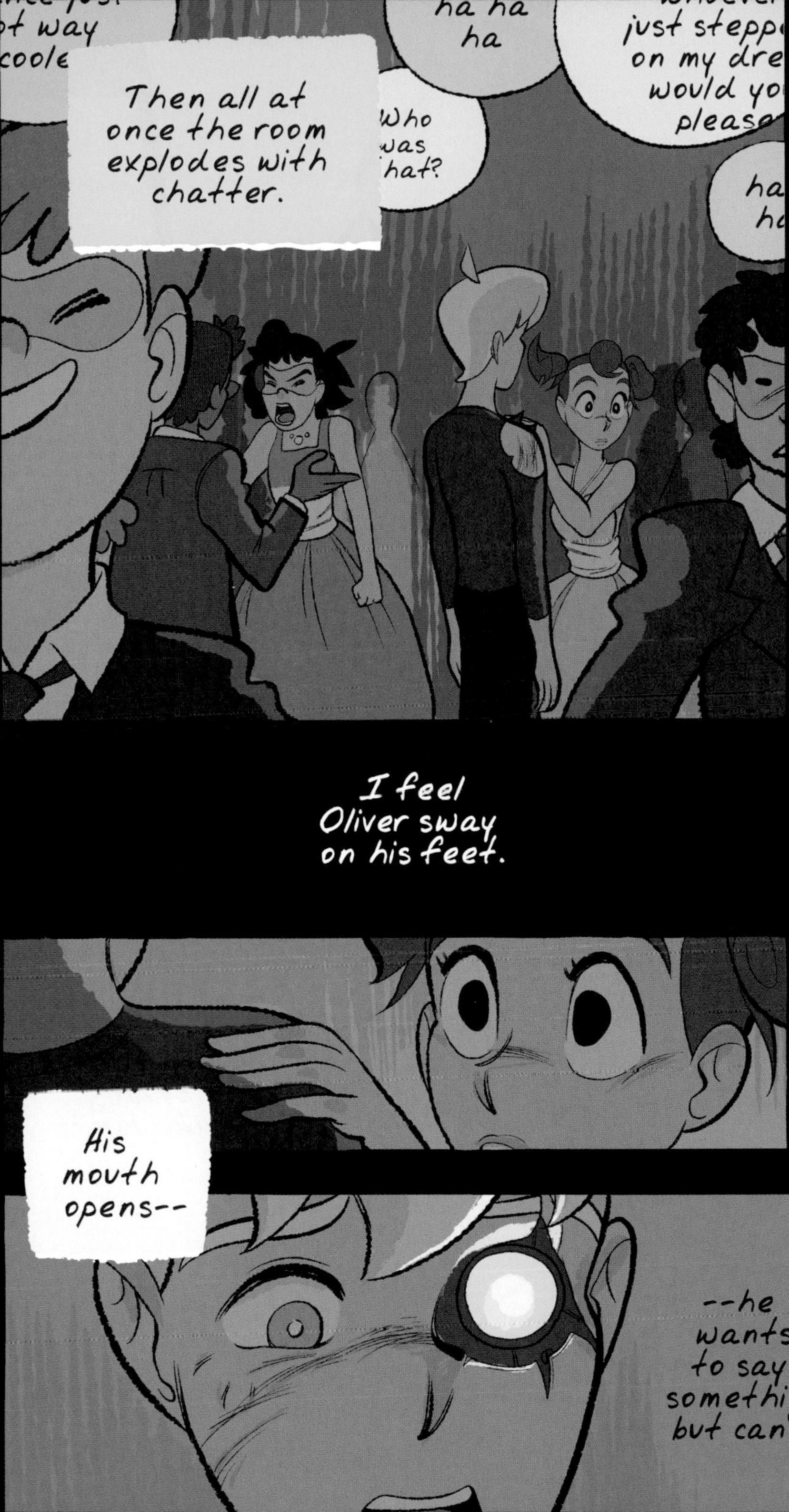
Then all at once the room explodes with chatter.
ha ha ha
Who
just
on my
would
I feel Oliver sway on his feet.
His mouth opens--
--he wants to say something but can't.

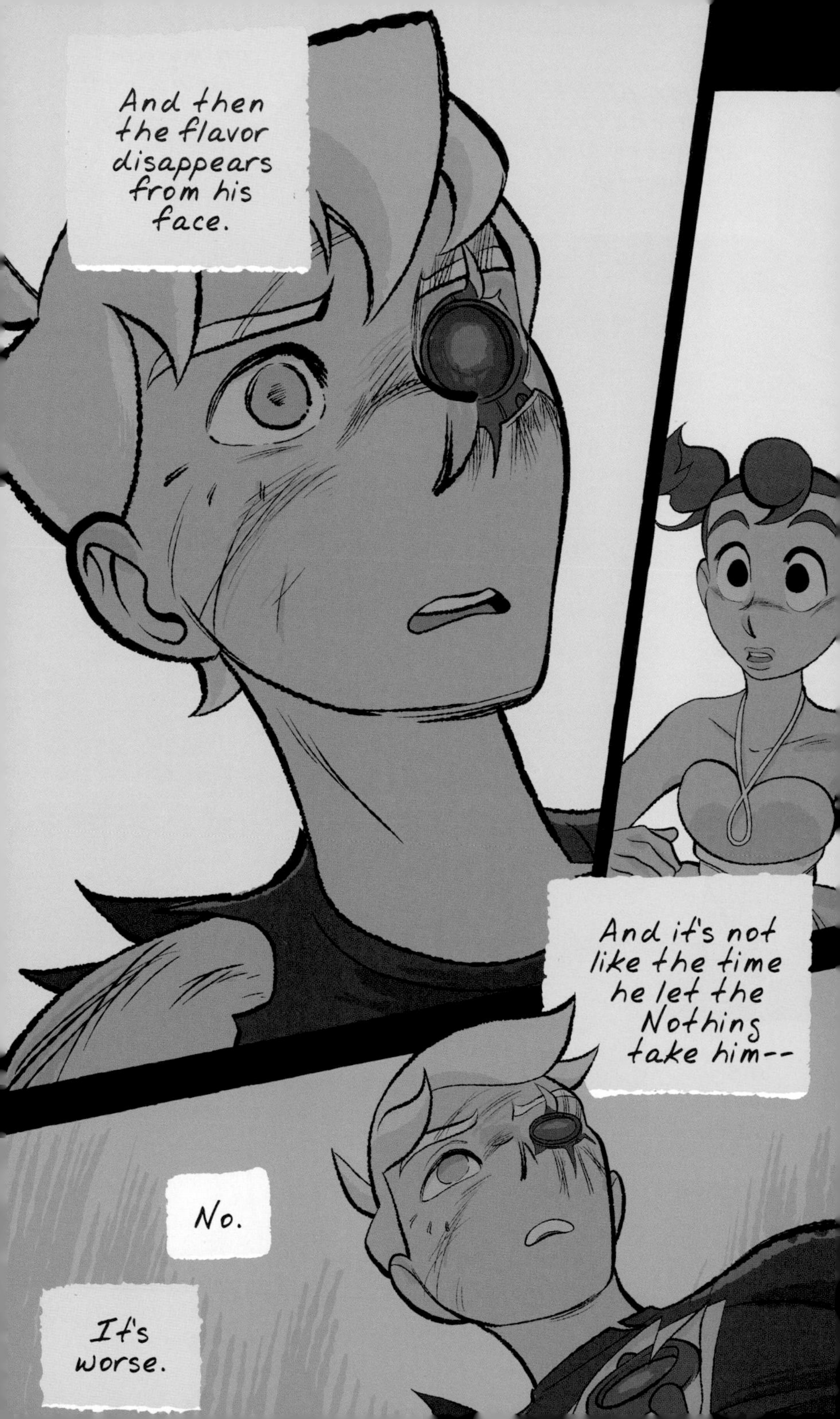
And then the flavor disappears from his face.
And it's not like the time he let the Nothins take him--
No.
It's worse.

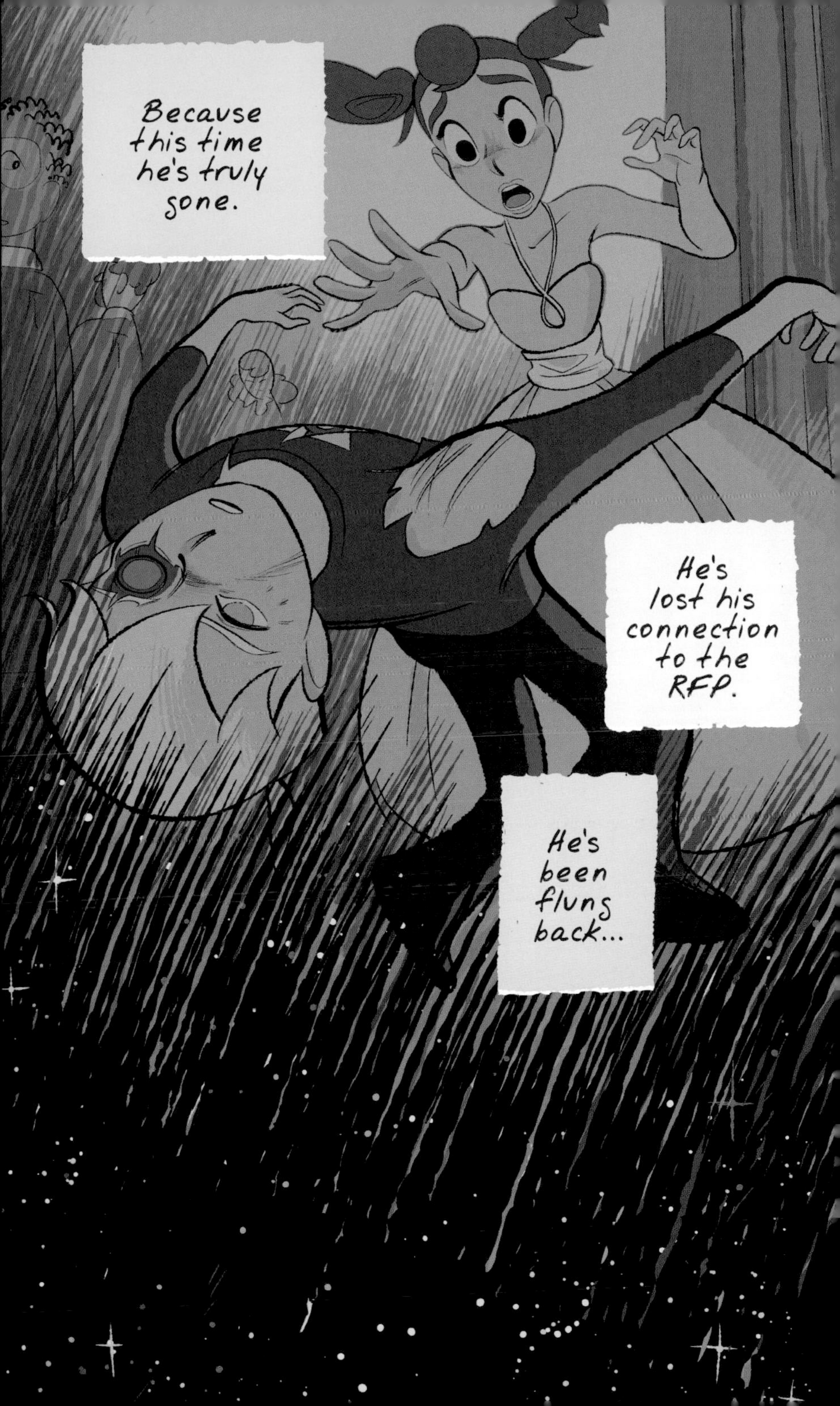
Because this time he's truly gone.
He's lost his connection to the RFP.
He's been flung back...

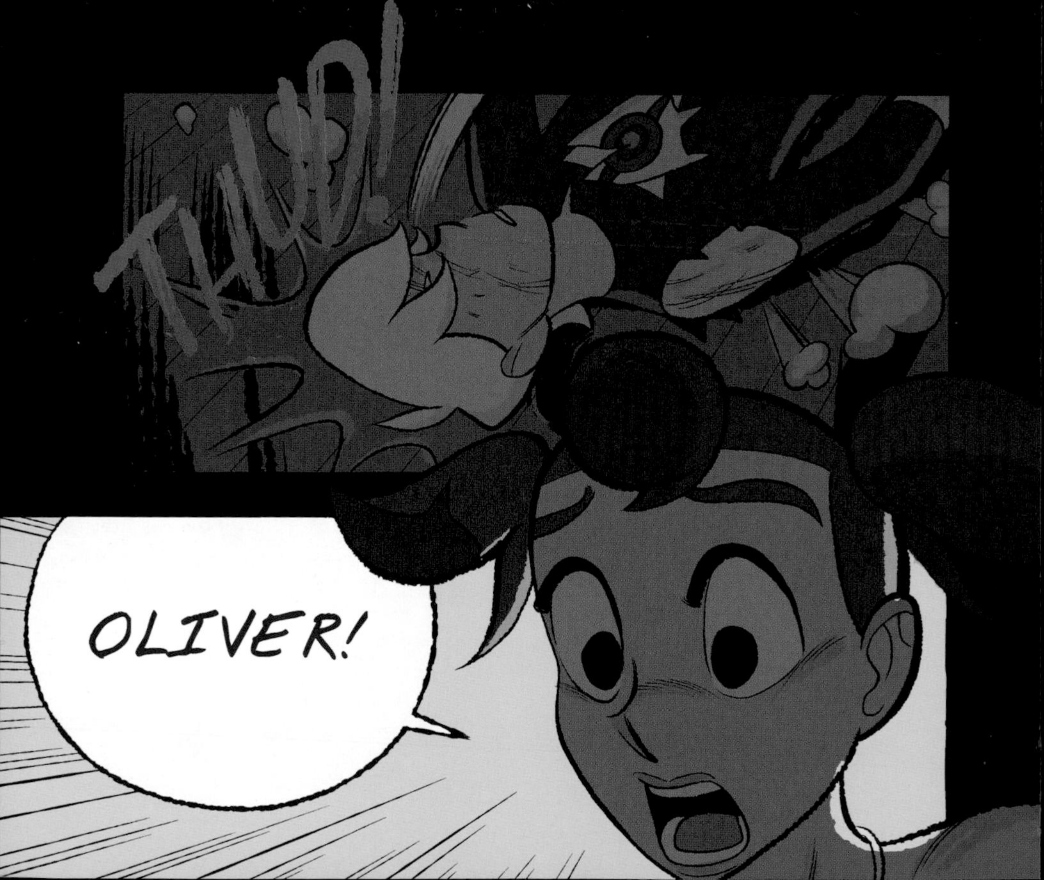
OLIVER!

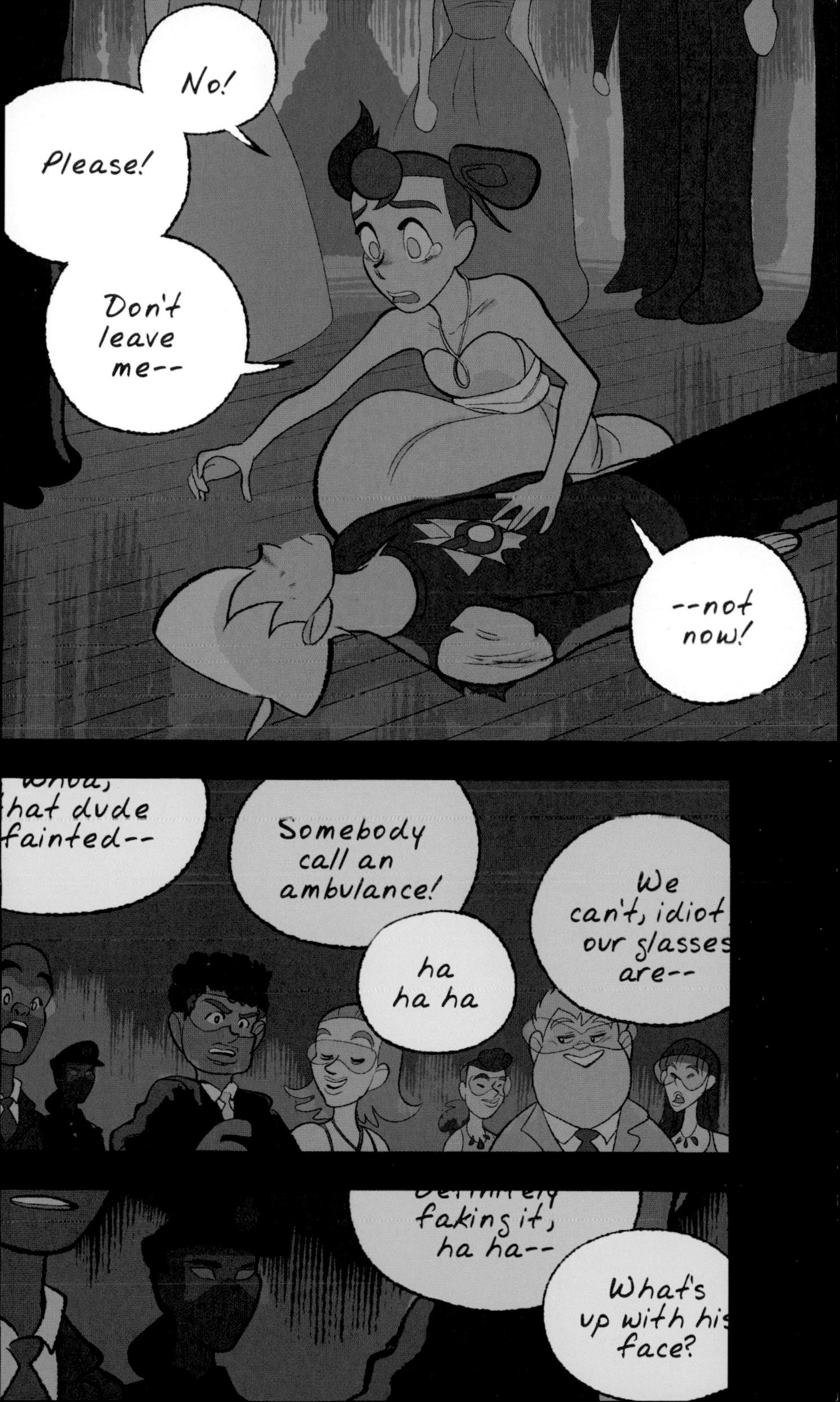

No!
Please!
Don't leave me--
--not now!
hat dude fainted--
Somebody call an ambulance!
We can't, idiot our glasses are--
ha ha ha
faking it, ha ha--
What's up with his face?

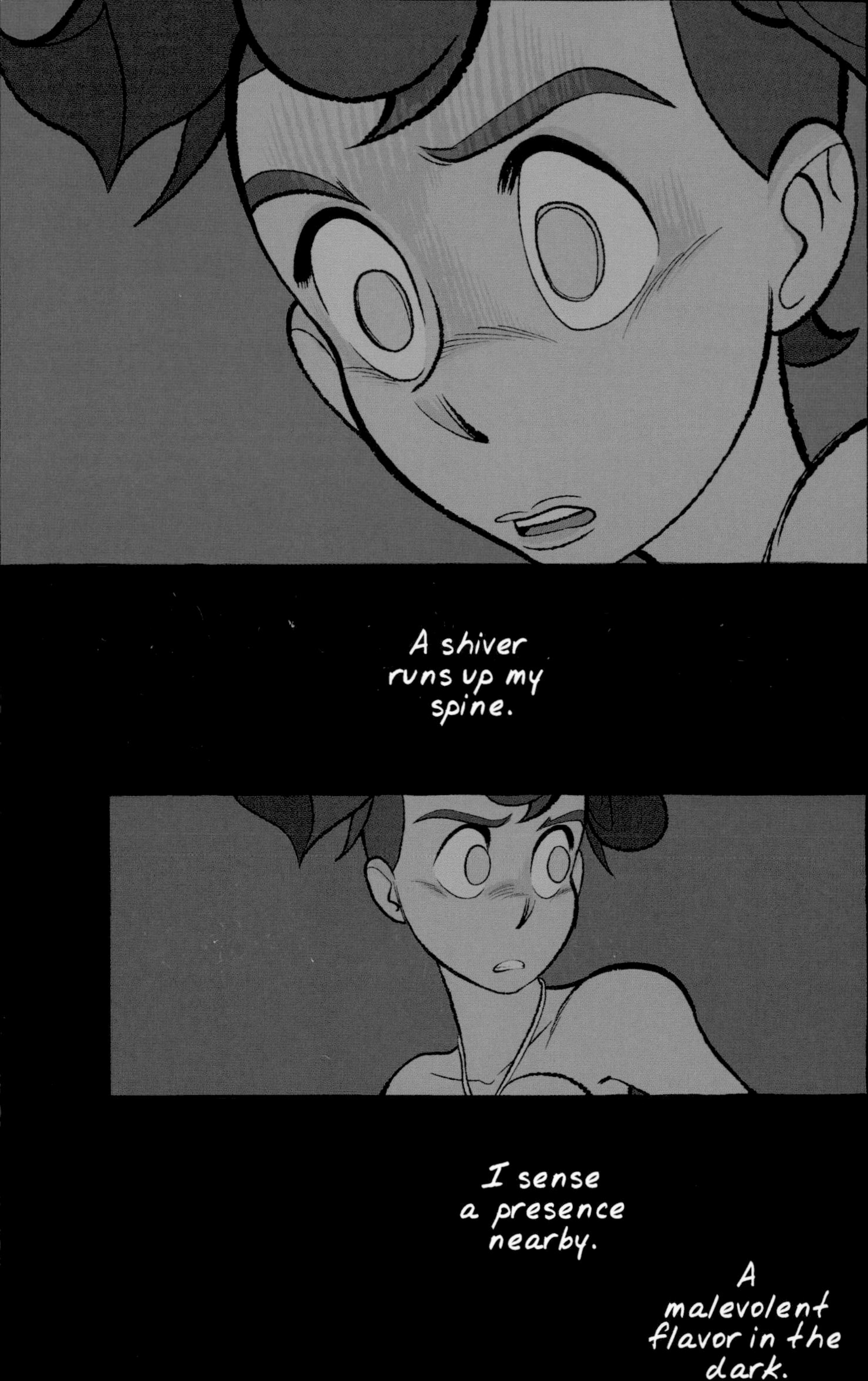
A shiver runs up my spine.
I sense a presence nearby.
A malevolent flavor in the dark.

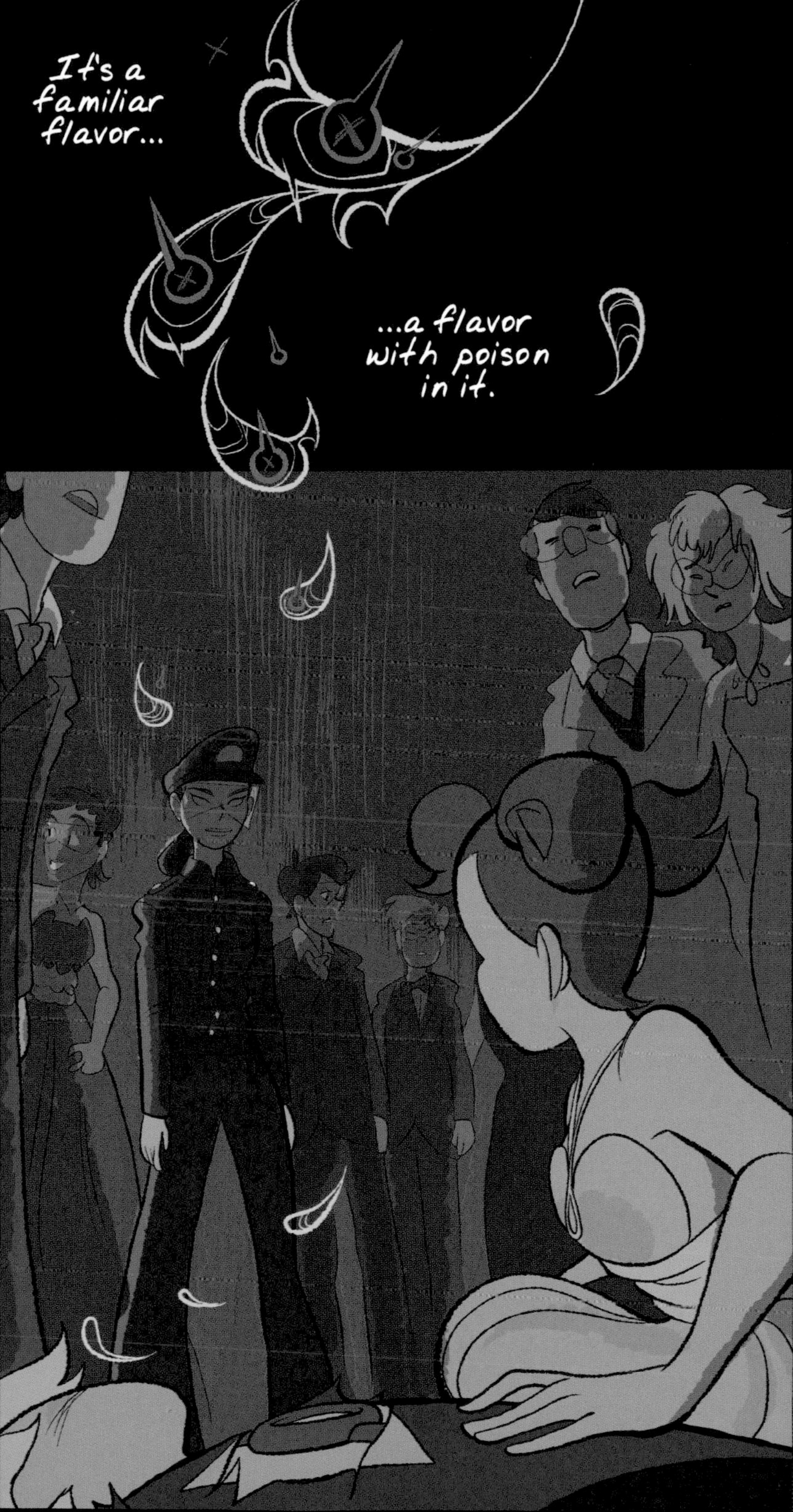
It's a familiar flavor...
...a flavor with poison in it.

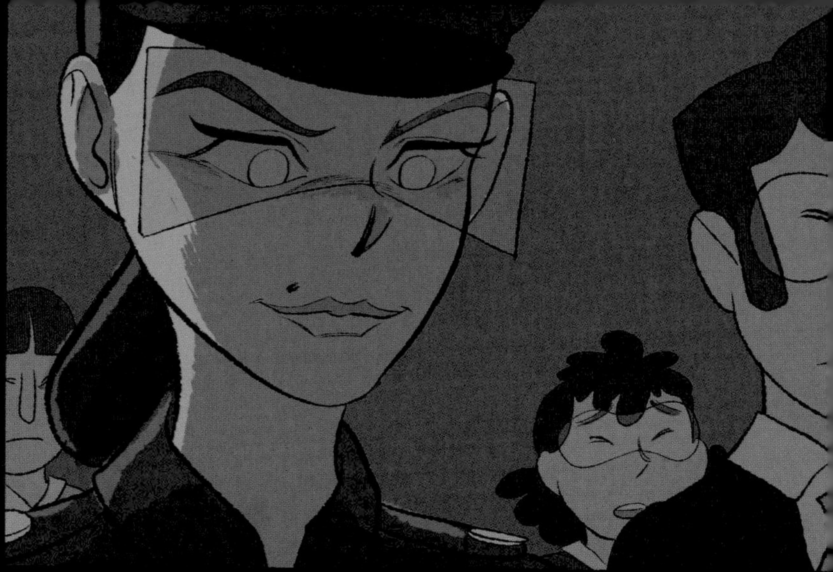

And
I run.

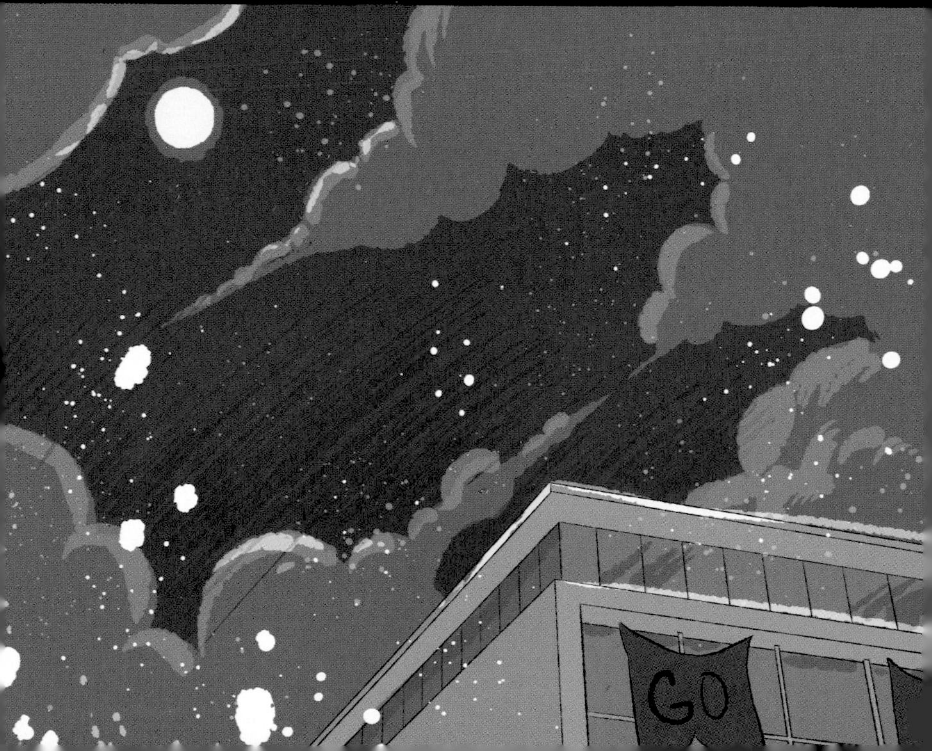
GO

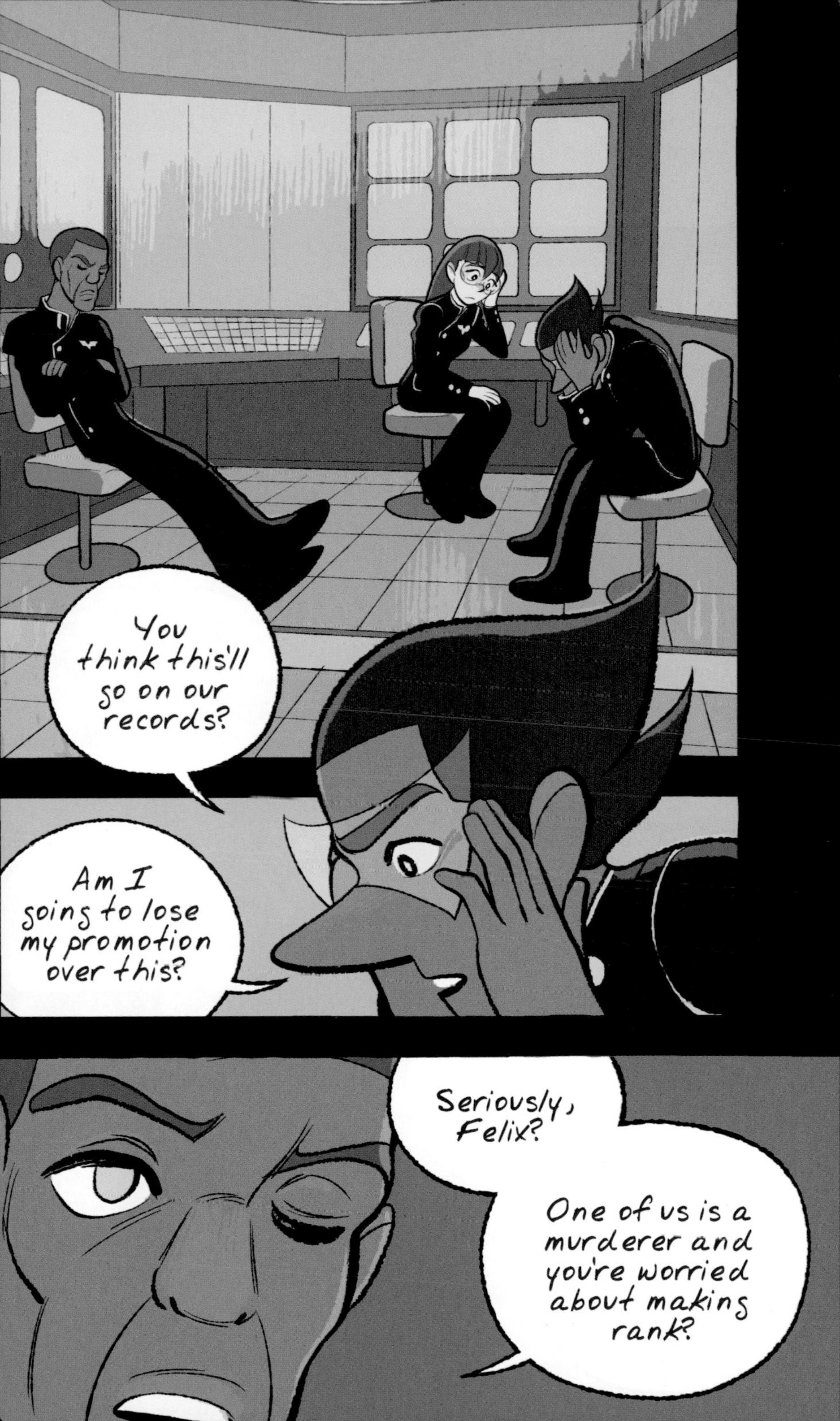
You think this'll go on our records?
Am I going to lose my promotion over this?
Seriously, Felix?
One of us is a murderer and you're worried about making rank?

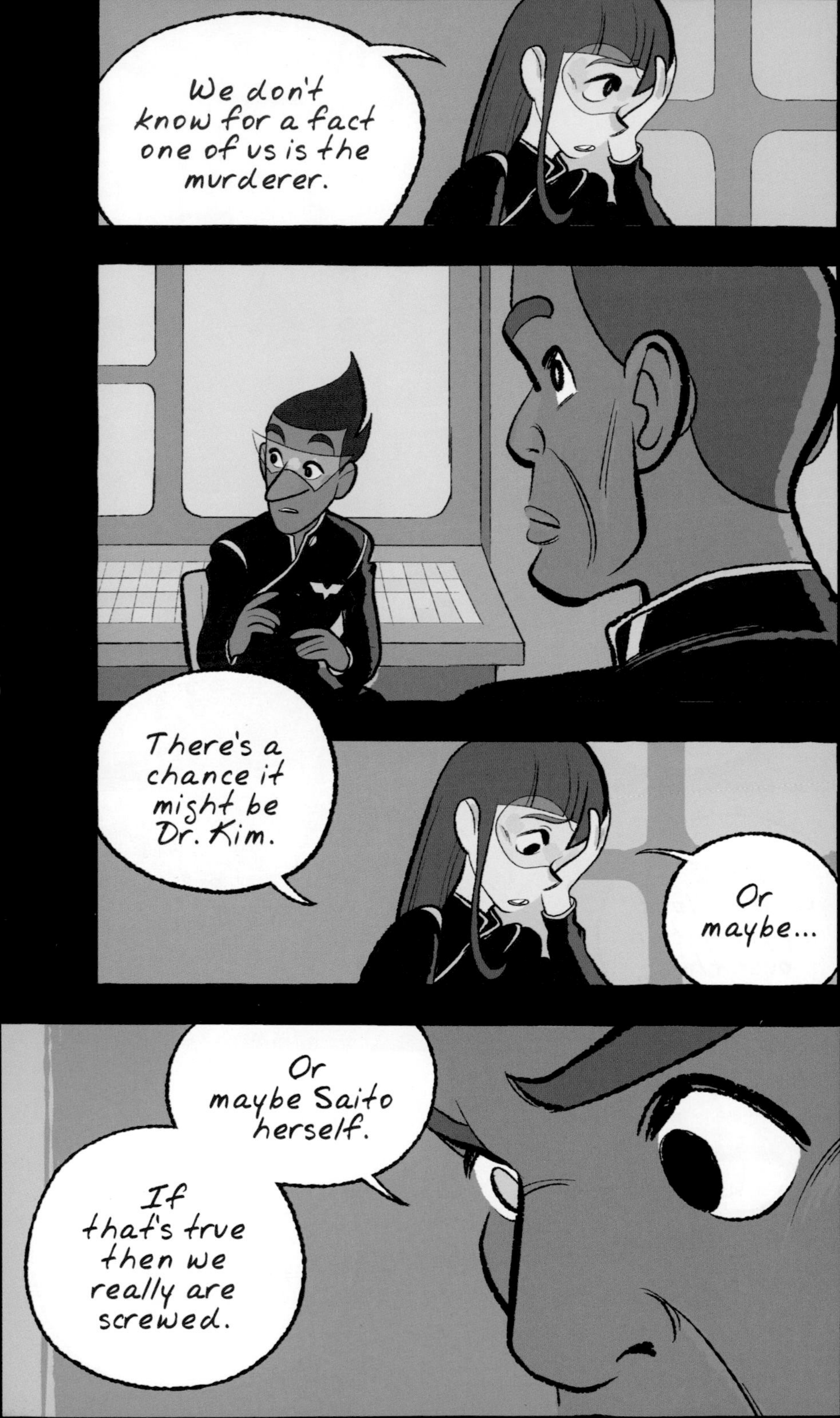
We don't know for a fact one of us is the murderer.
There's a chance it might be Dr. Kim.
Or maybe...
Or maybe Saito herself.
If that's true then we really are screwed.

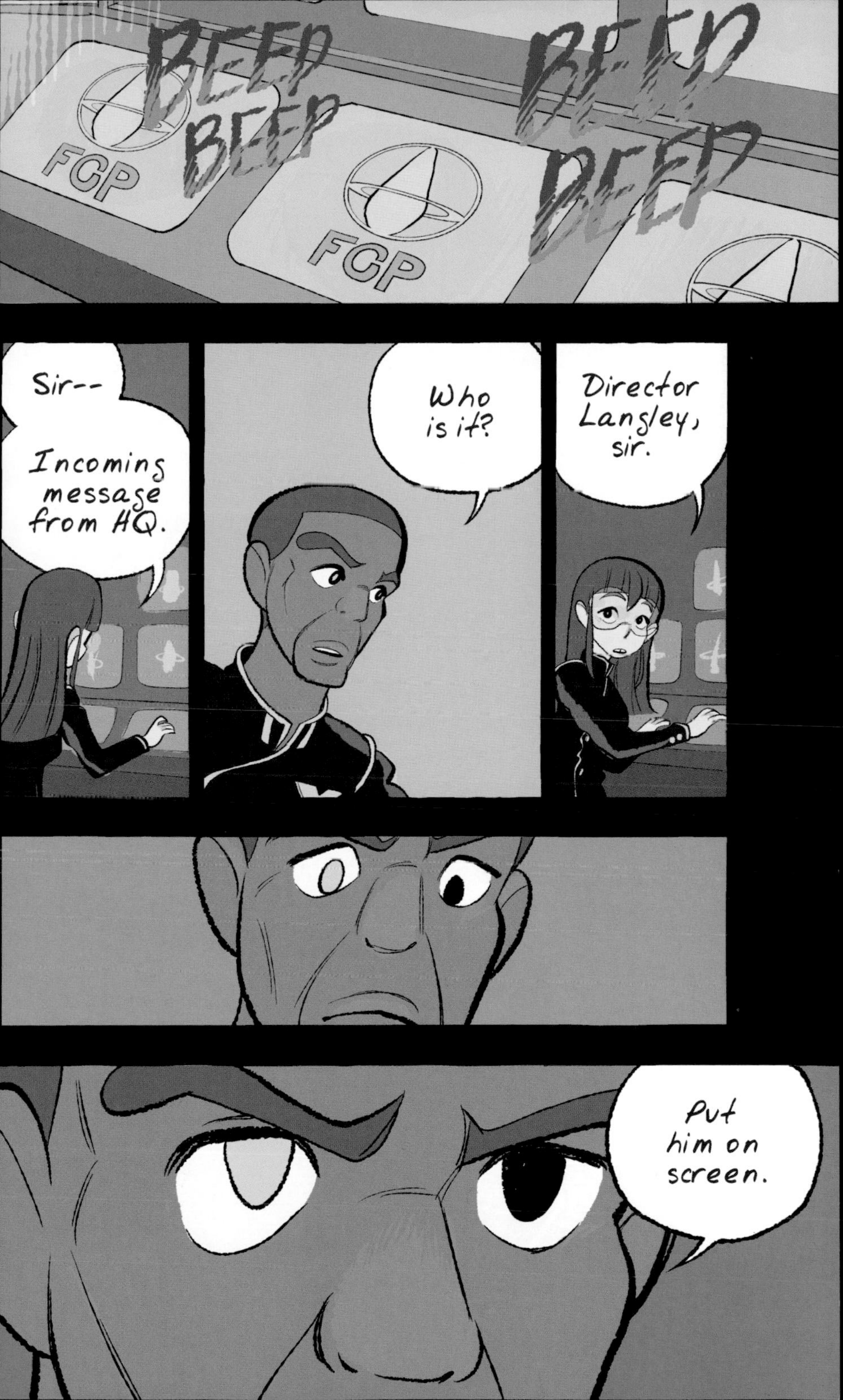
BEEP BEEP
BEEP BEEP
FCP
FCP
Sir--
Incoming message from HQ.
Who is it?
Director Langley, sir.
Put him on screen.

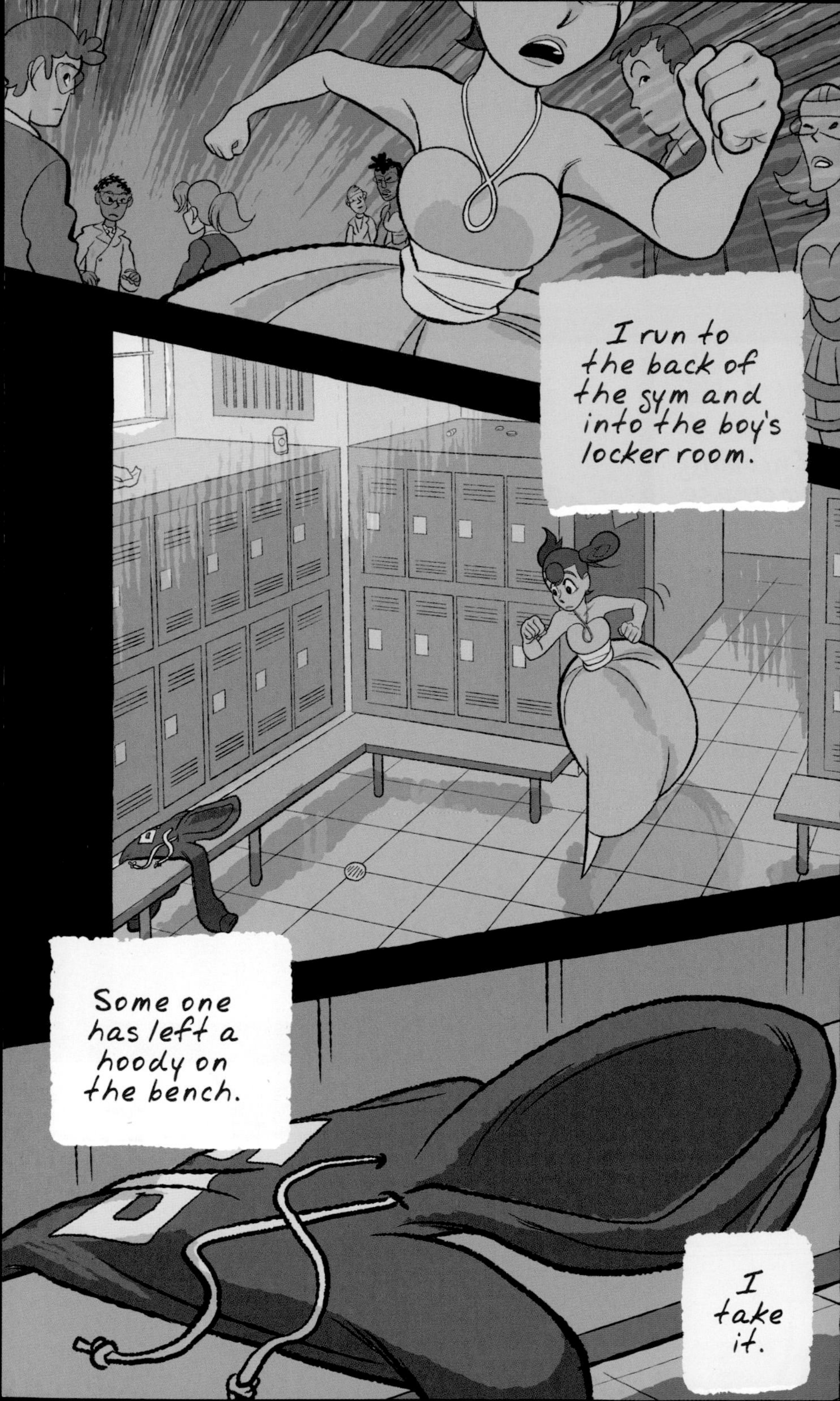
I run to the back of the sym and into the boy's locker room.
Some one has left a hoody on the bench.
I take it.

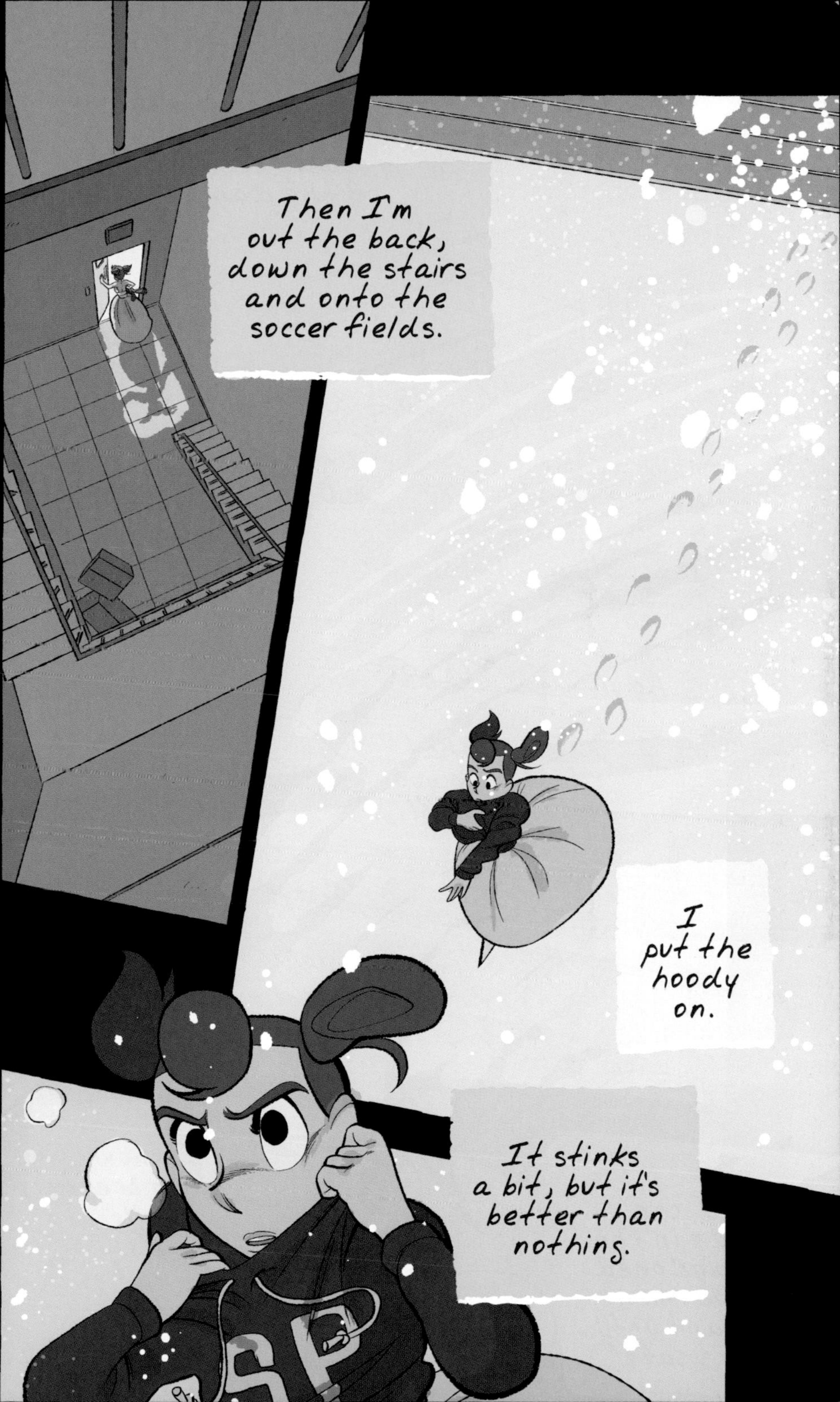
Then I'm out the back, down the stairs and onto the soccer fields.
I put the hoody on.
It stinks a bit, but it's better than nothing.

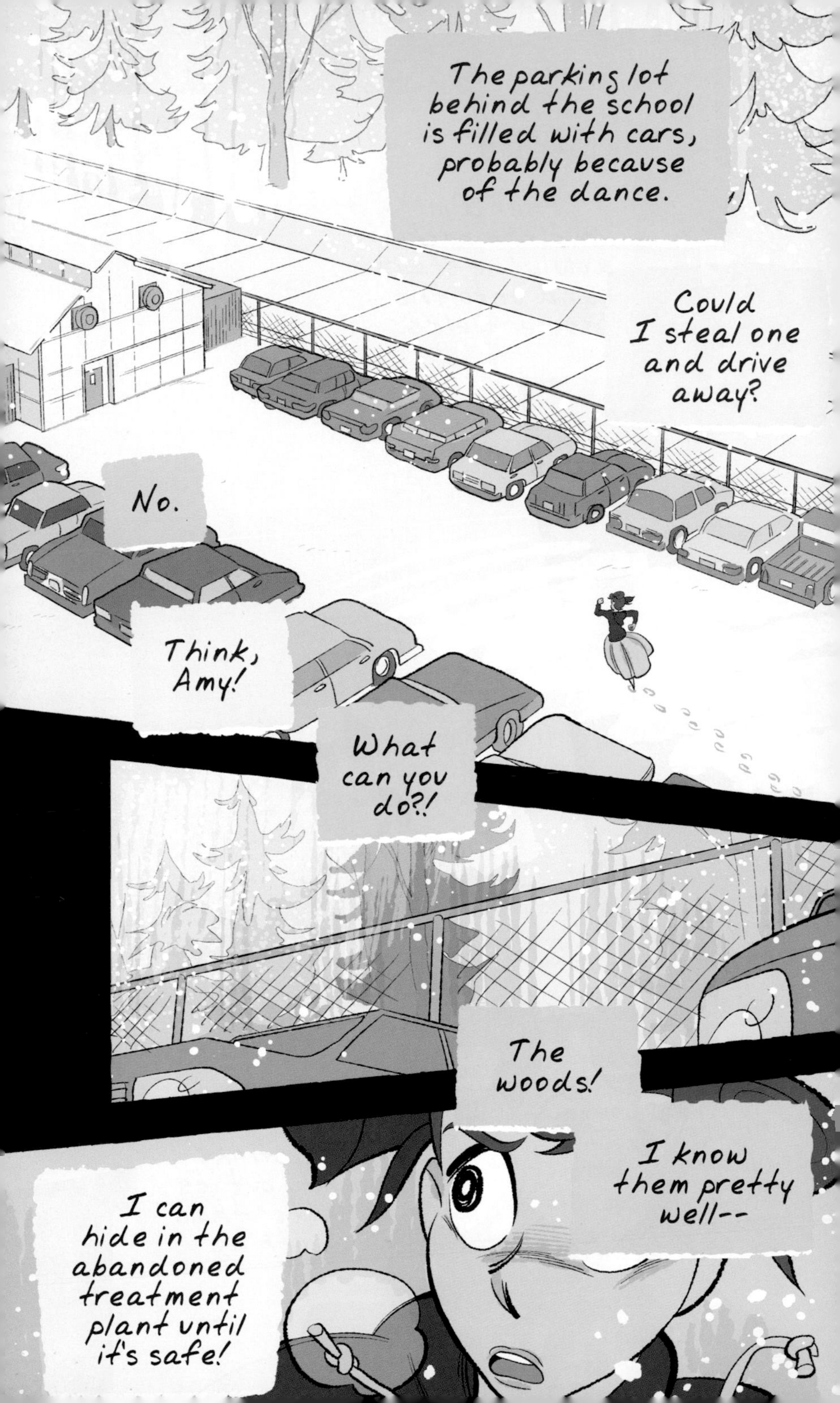
The parking lot behind the school is filled with cars, probably because of the dance.
Could I steal one and drive away?
No.
Think, Amy!
What can you do?!
The woods!
I know them pretty well--
I can hide in the abandoned treatment plant until it's safe!

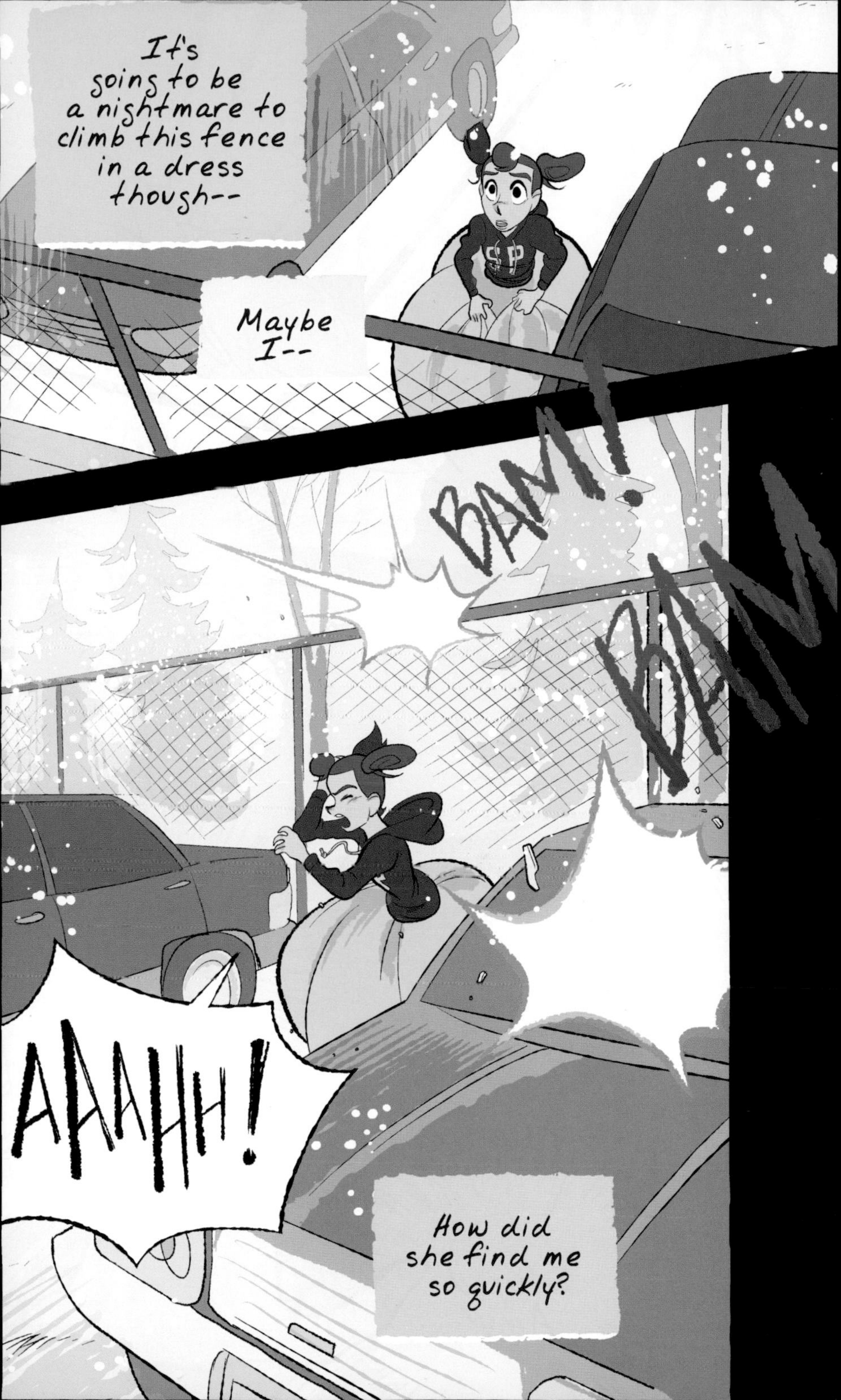
It's going to be a nightmare to climb this fence in a dress though--
Maybe I--
BAM!
BAM
AAAHH!
How did she find me so quickly?

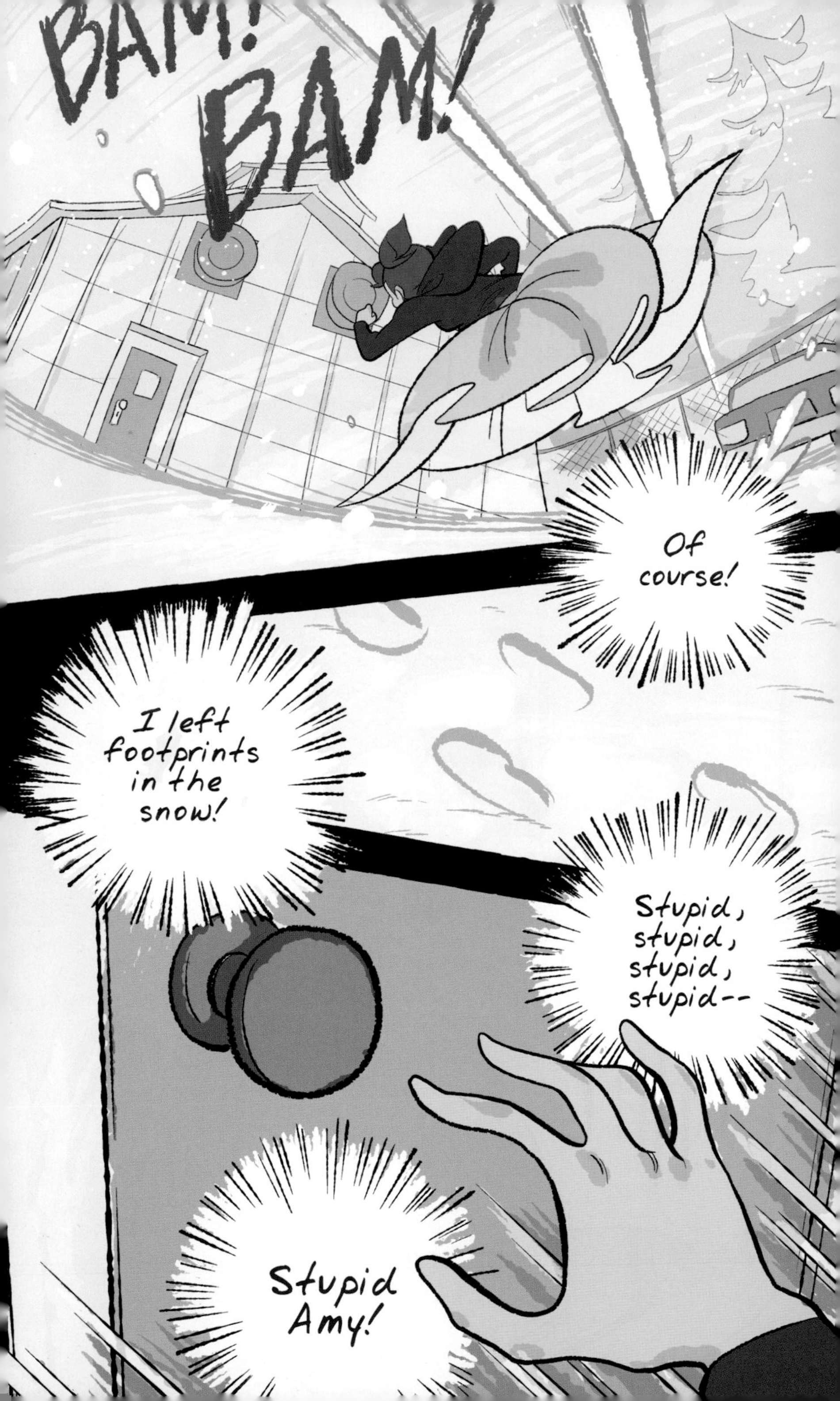
BAM! BAM!
Of course!
I left footprints in the snow!
Stupid, stupid, stupid, stupid--
Stupid Amy!

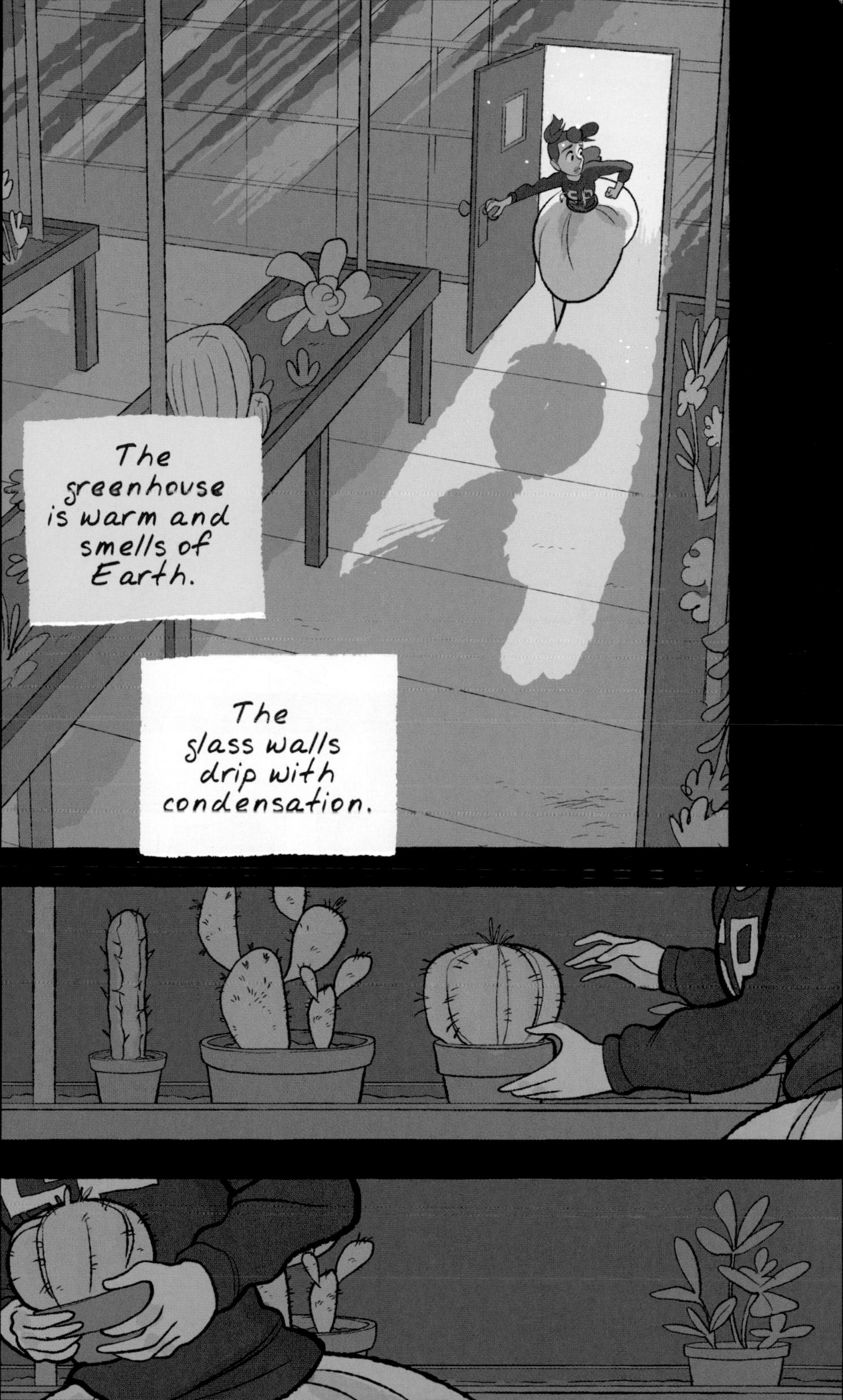
The greenhouse is warm and smells of Earth.
The glass walls drip with condensation.

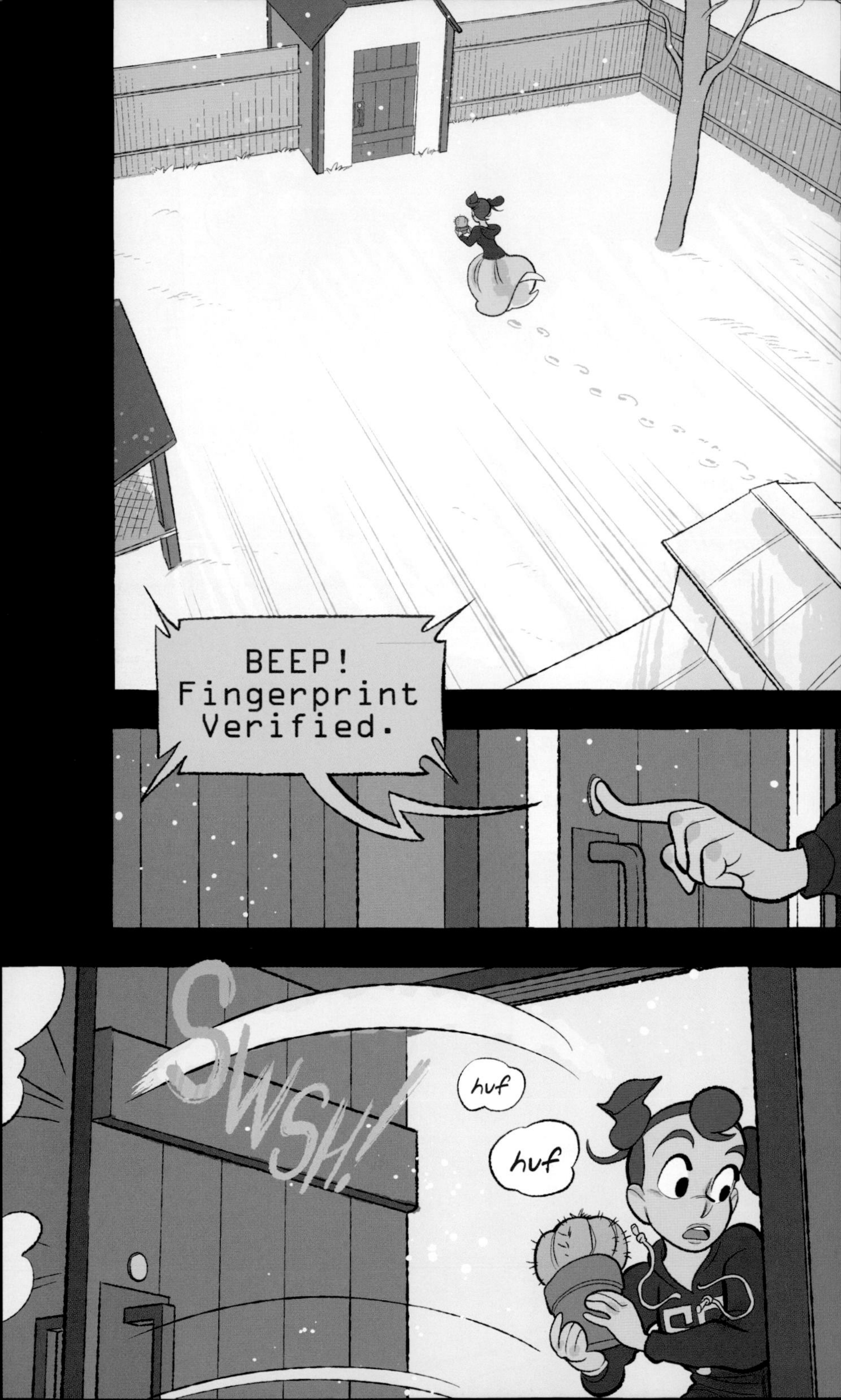
BEEP! Fingerprint Verified.
SWSH!
huf
huf

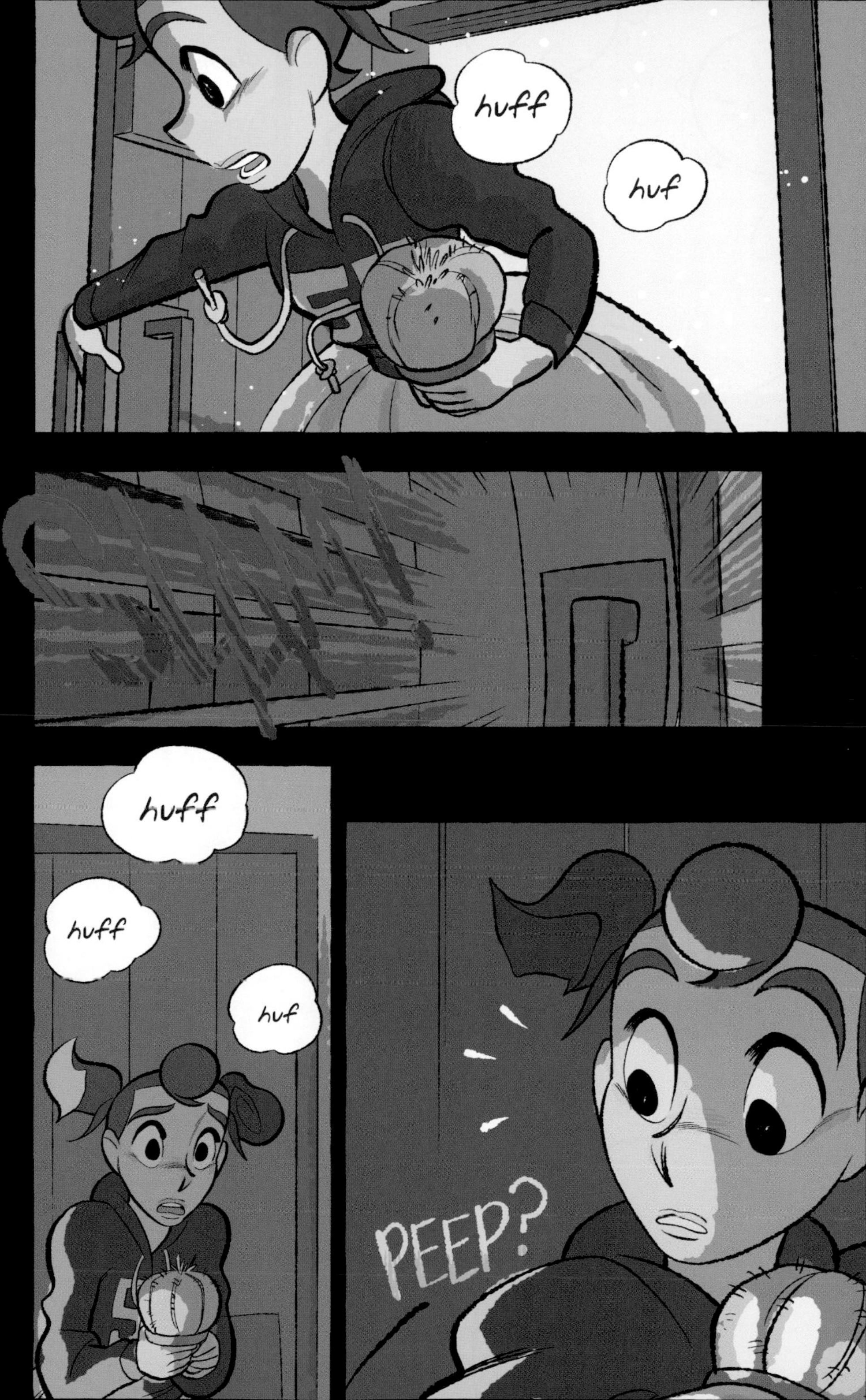
huff
huf
huff
huff
huf
PEEP?

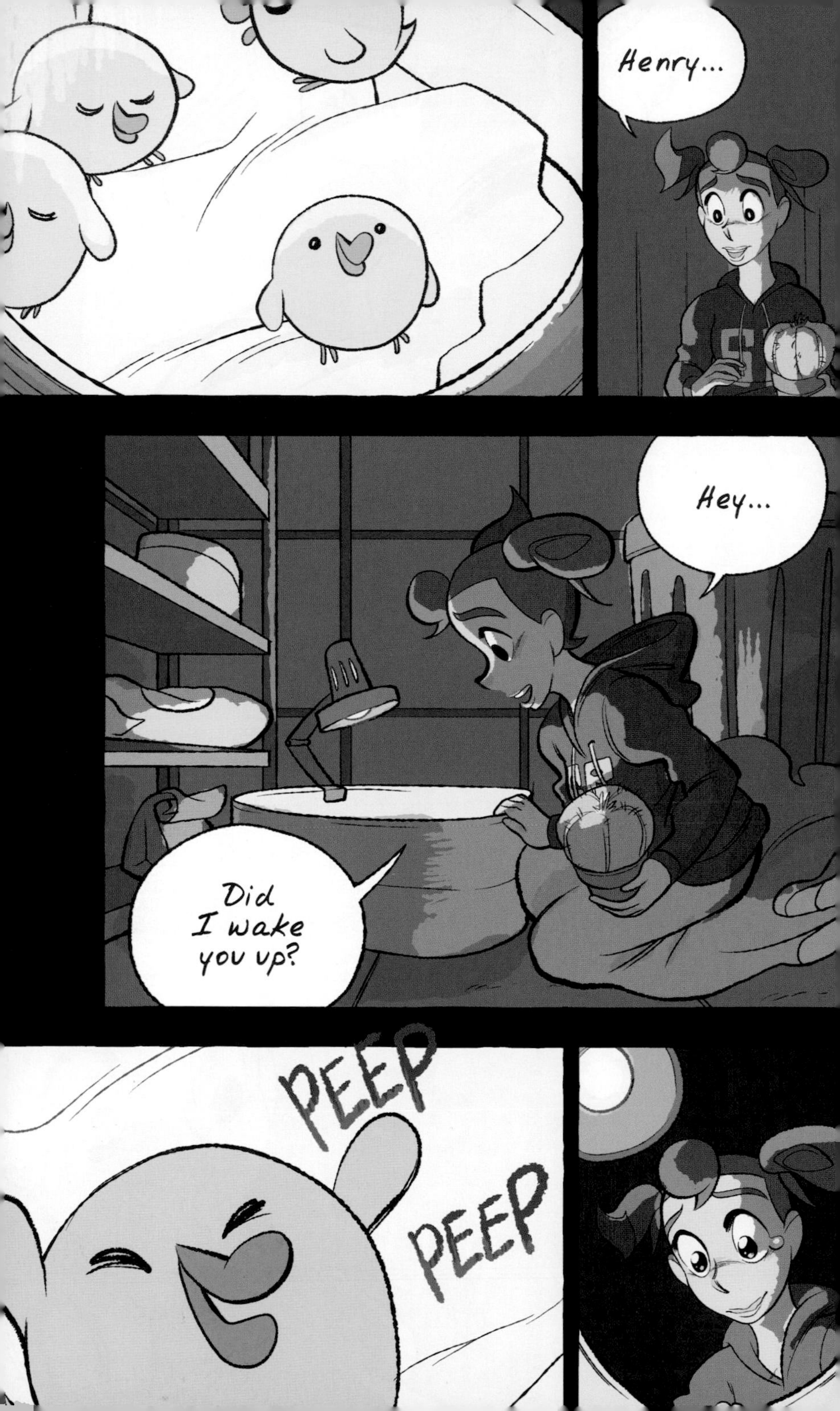

Henry...
Hey...
Did I wake you up?
PEEP
PEEP

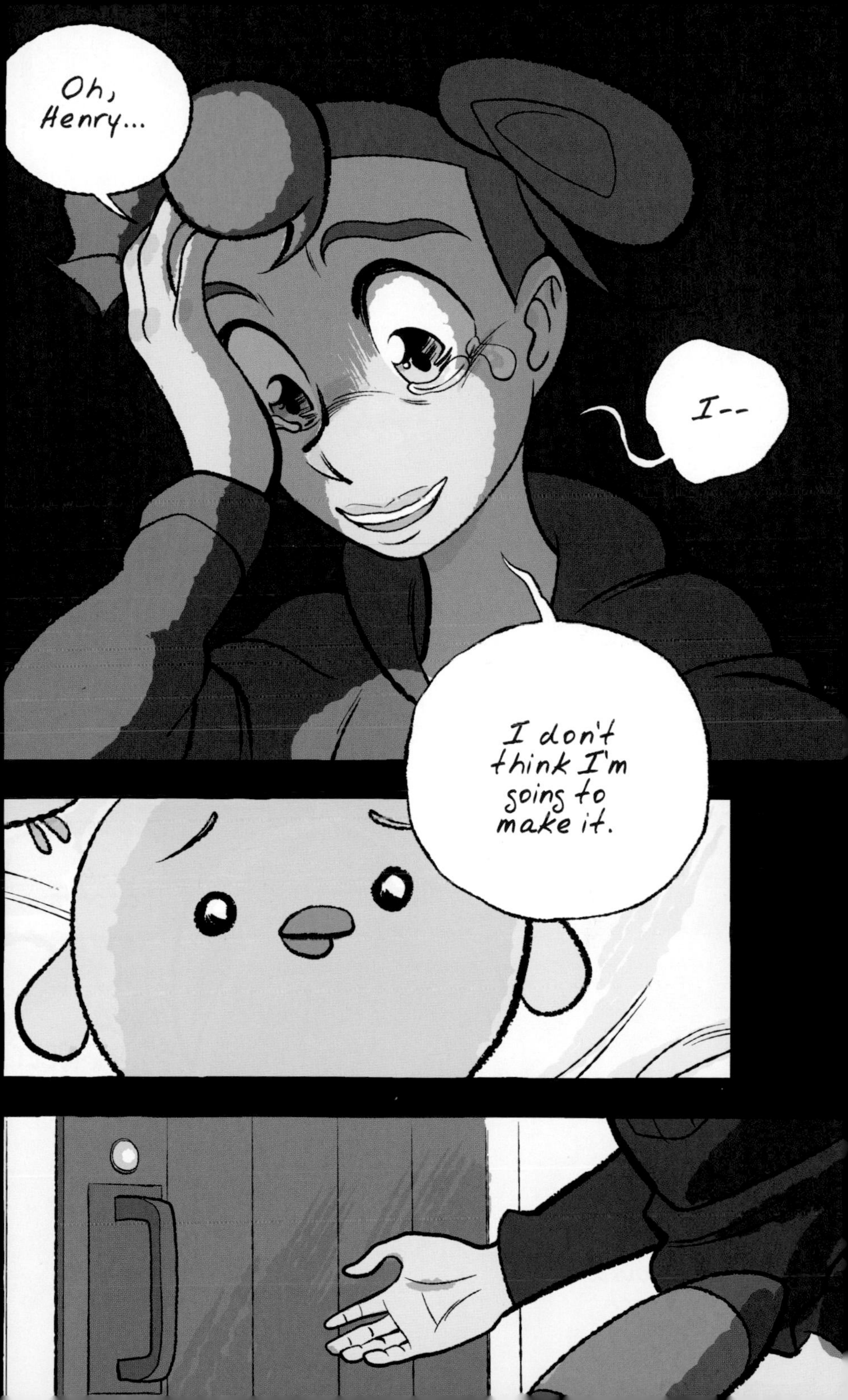
Oh, Henry...
I--
I don't think I'm goins to make it.

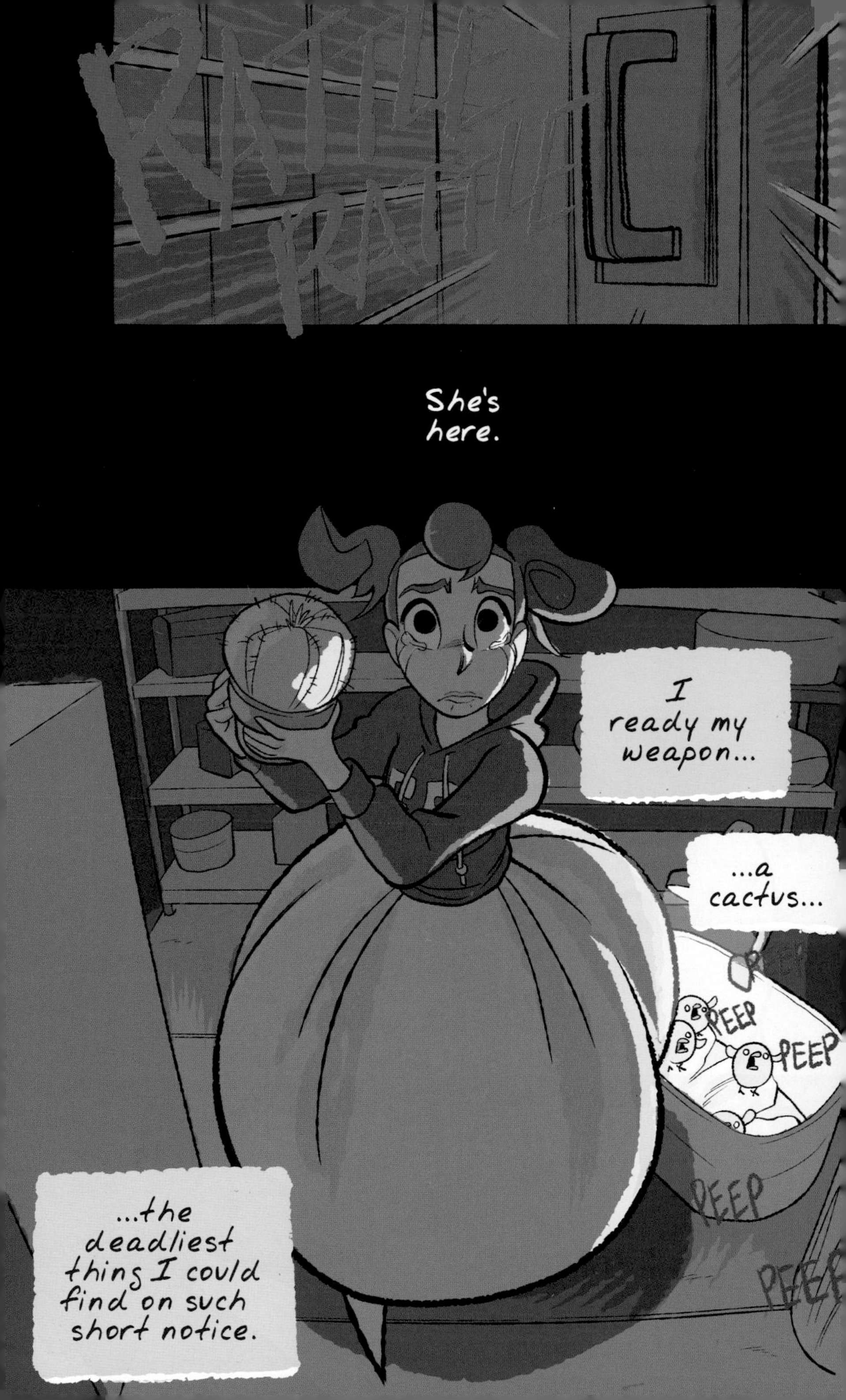
RATTLE RATTLE
She's here.
I ready my weapon...
...a cactus...
PEEP
PEEP
PEEP
PEEP
...the deadliest things I could find on such short notice.

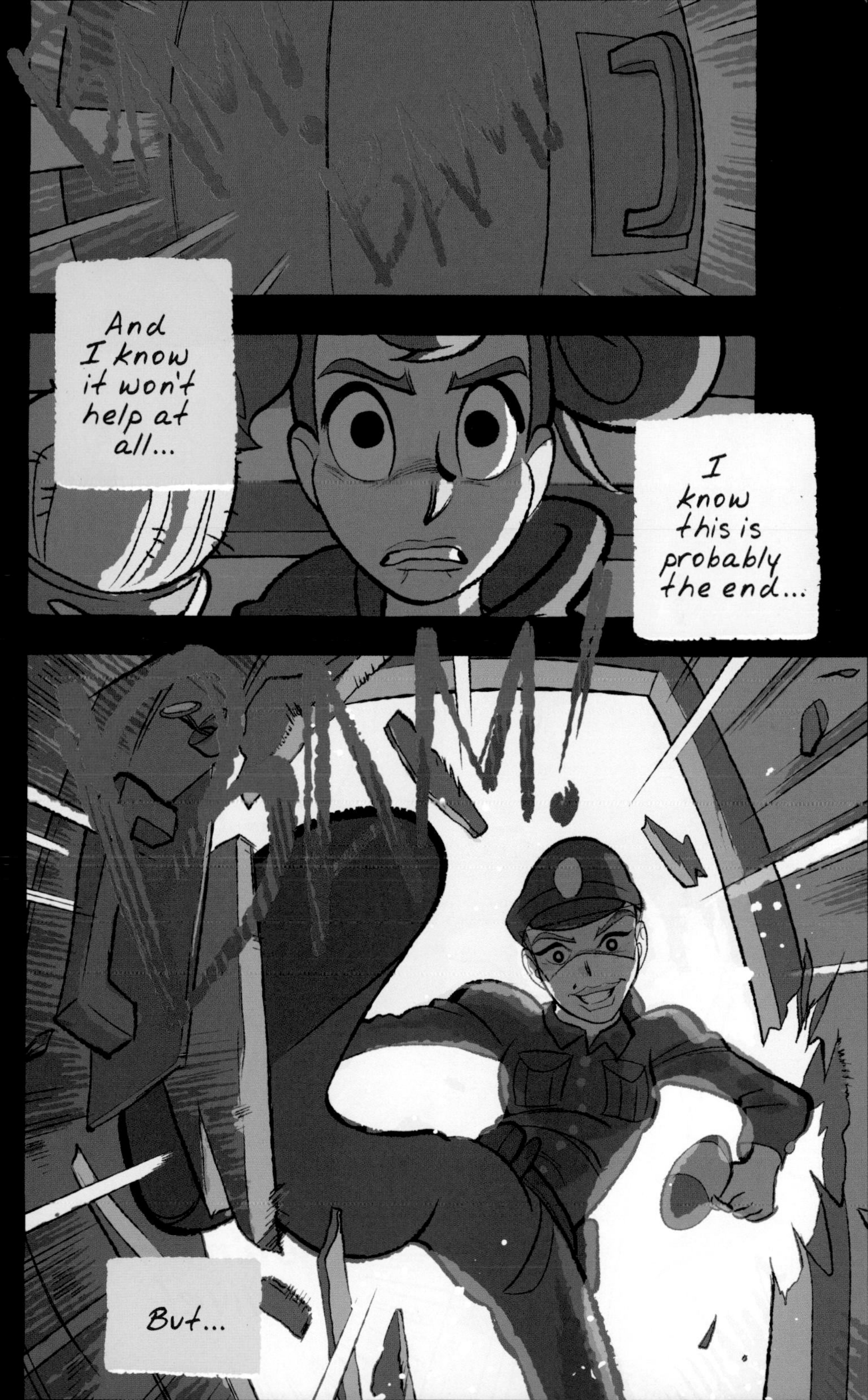
And I know it won't help at all...
I know this is probably the end...
But...

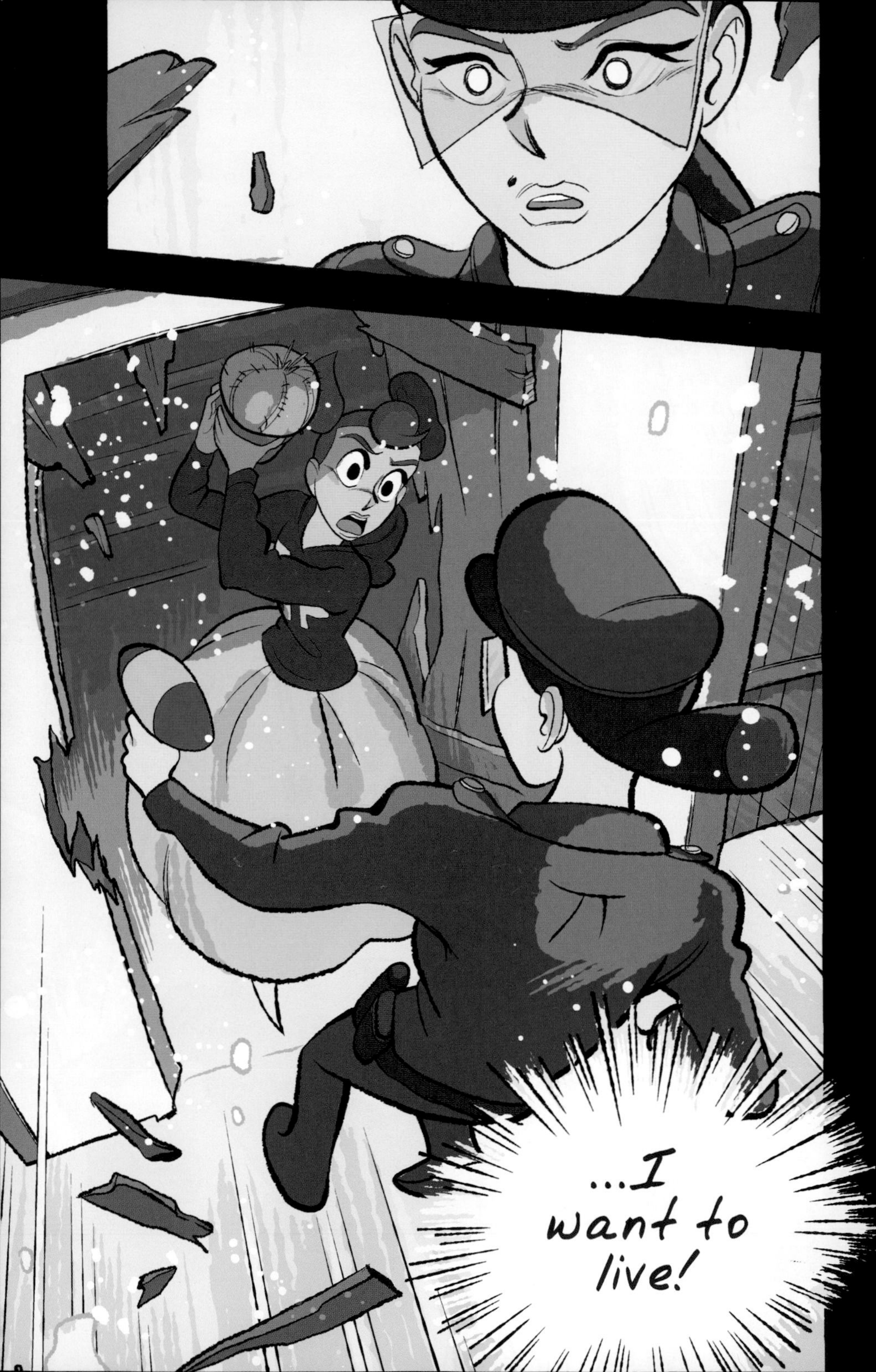
...I want to live!

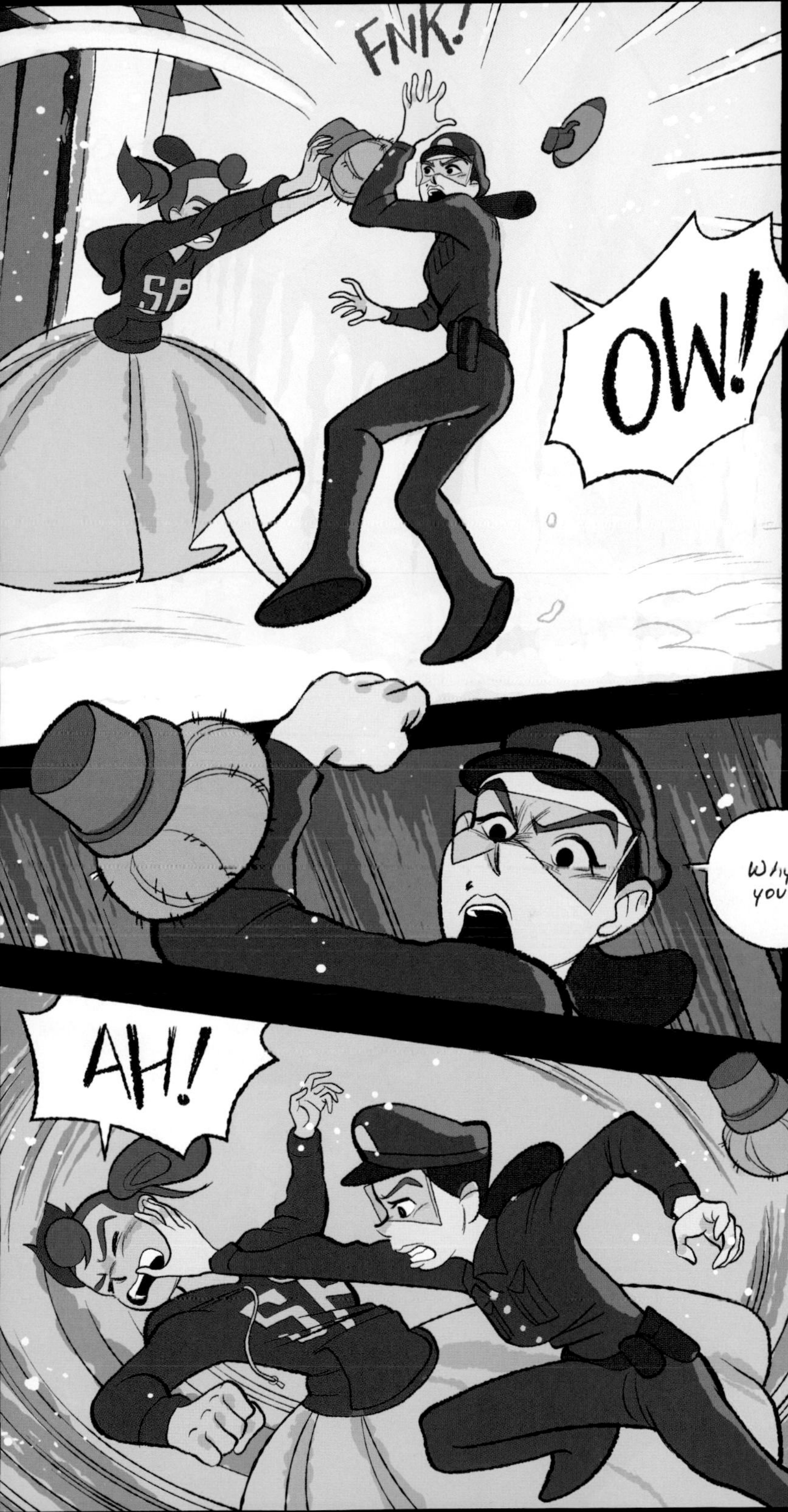
FNK!
OW!
Why,
you--
AH!

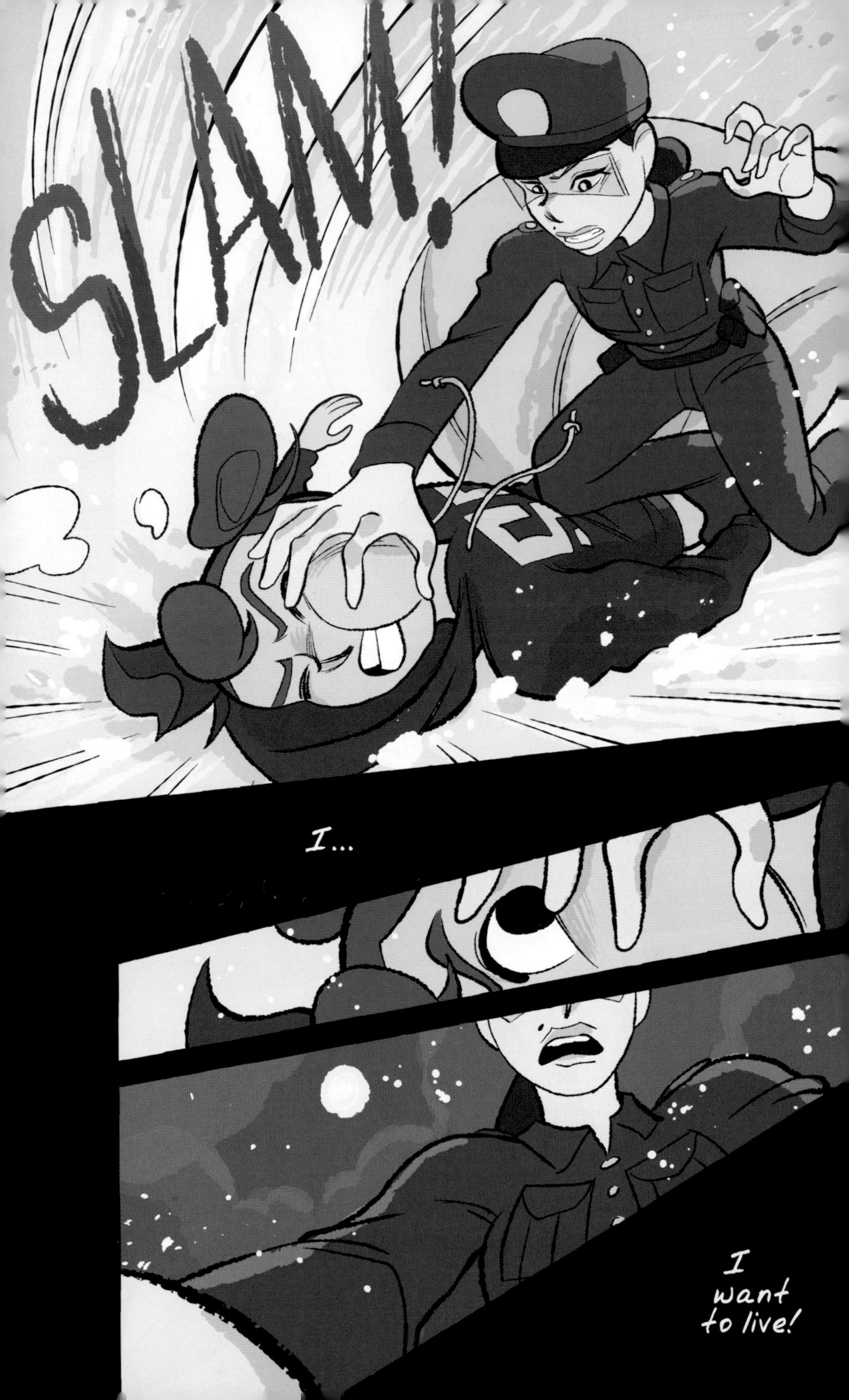
SLAM!
I...
I want to live!

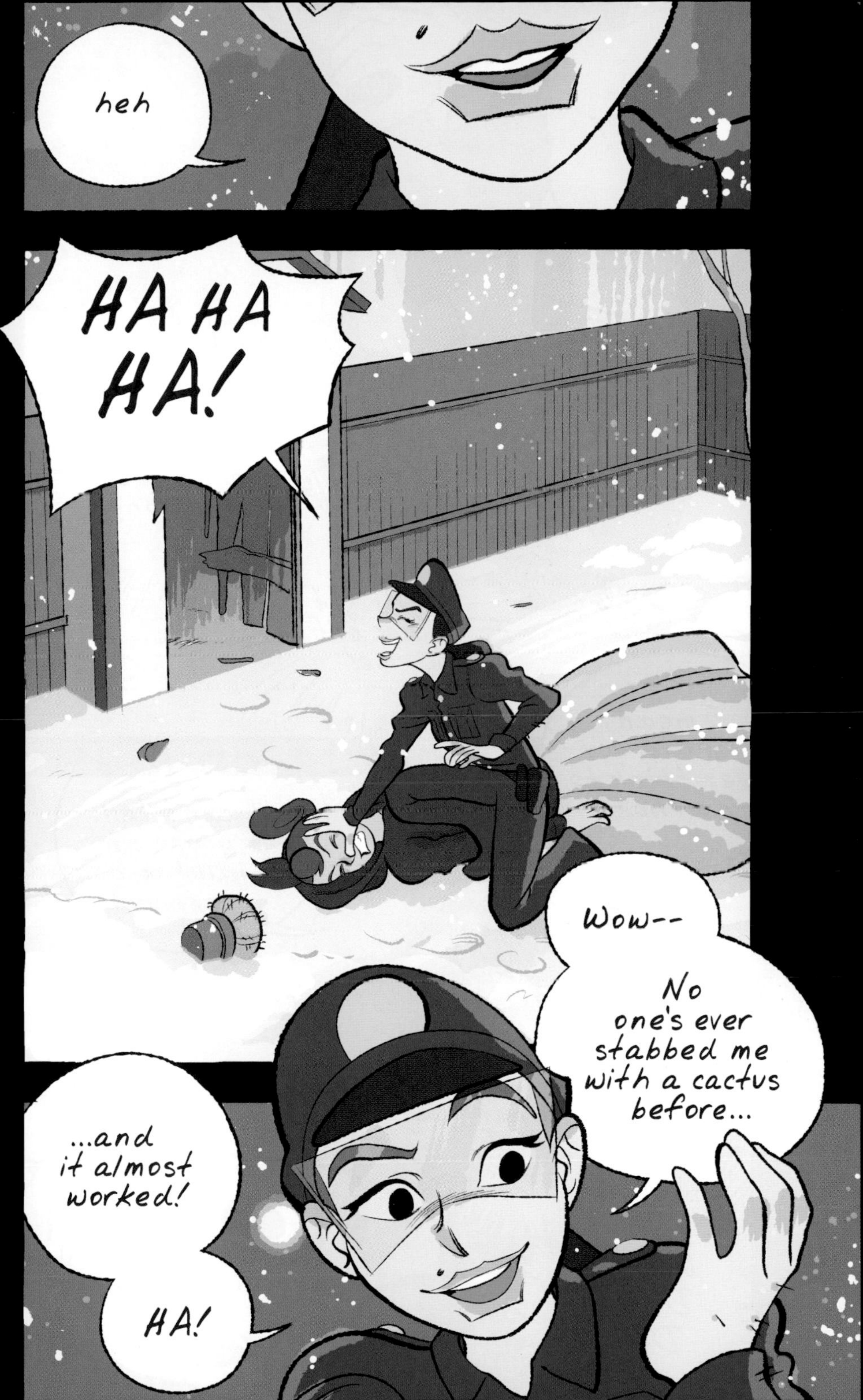
heh
HA HA HA HA!
Wow--
No one's ever stabbed me with a cactus before...
...and it almost worked!
HA!

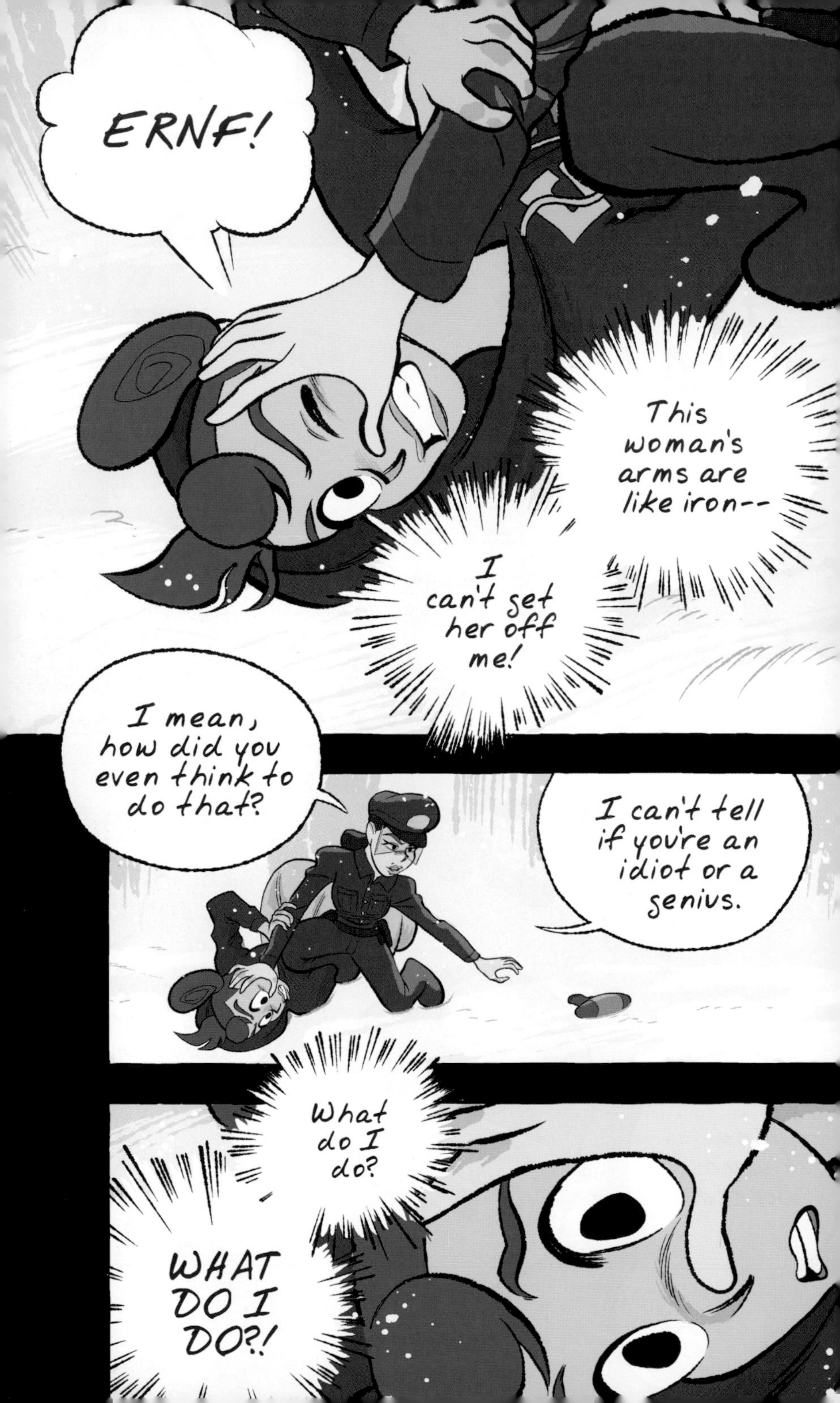
ERNF!
This woman's arms are like iron--
I can't get her off me!
I mean, how did you even think to do that?
I can't tell if you're an idiot or a genius.
What do I do?
WHAT DO I DO?!

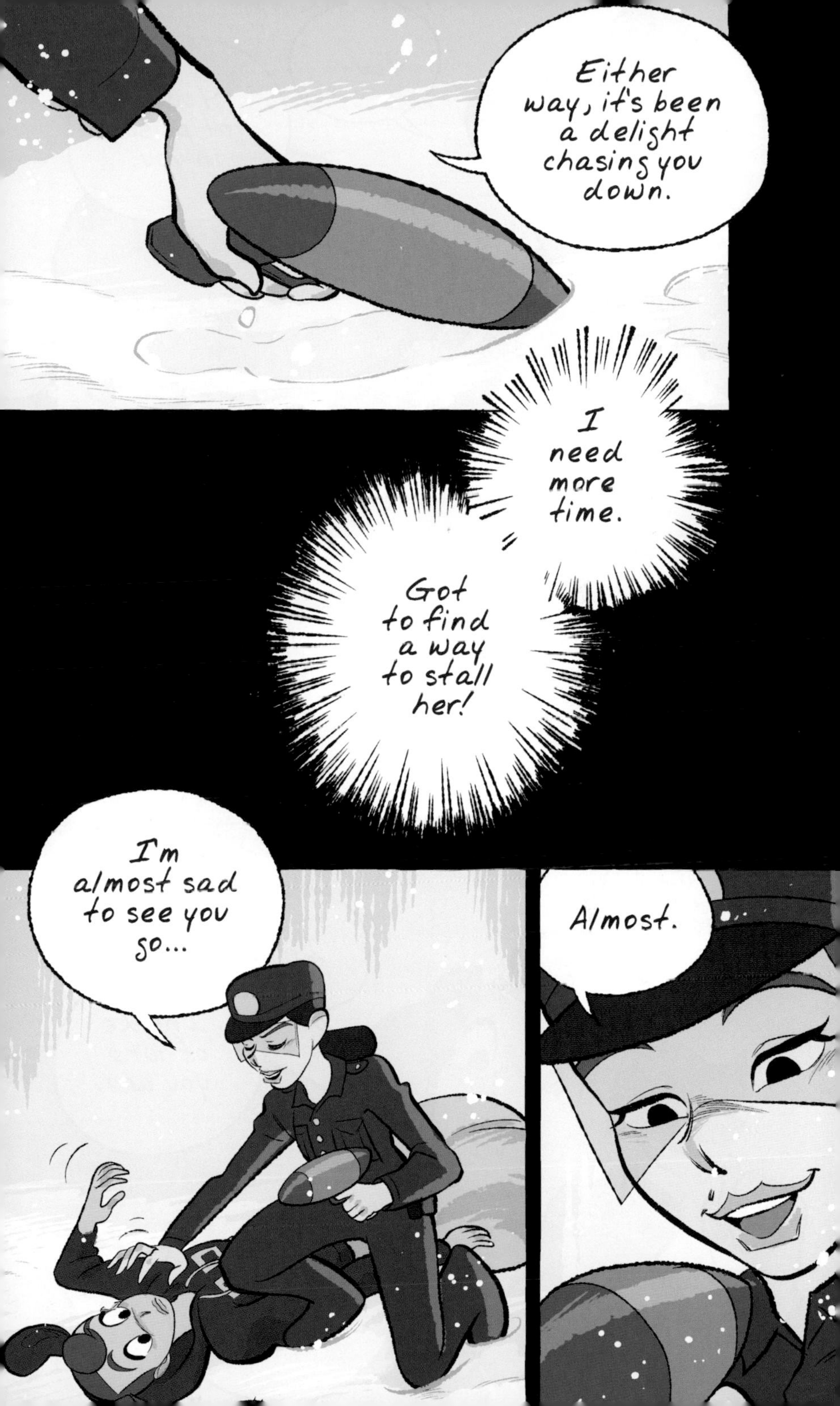
Either way, it's been a delight chasing you down.
I need more time.
Got to find a way to stall her!
I'm almost sad to see you go...
Almost.

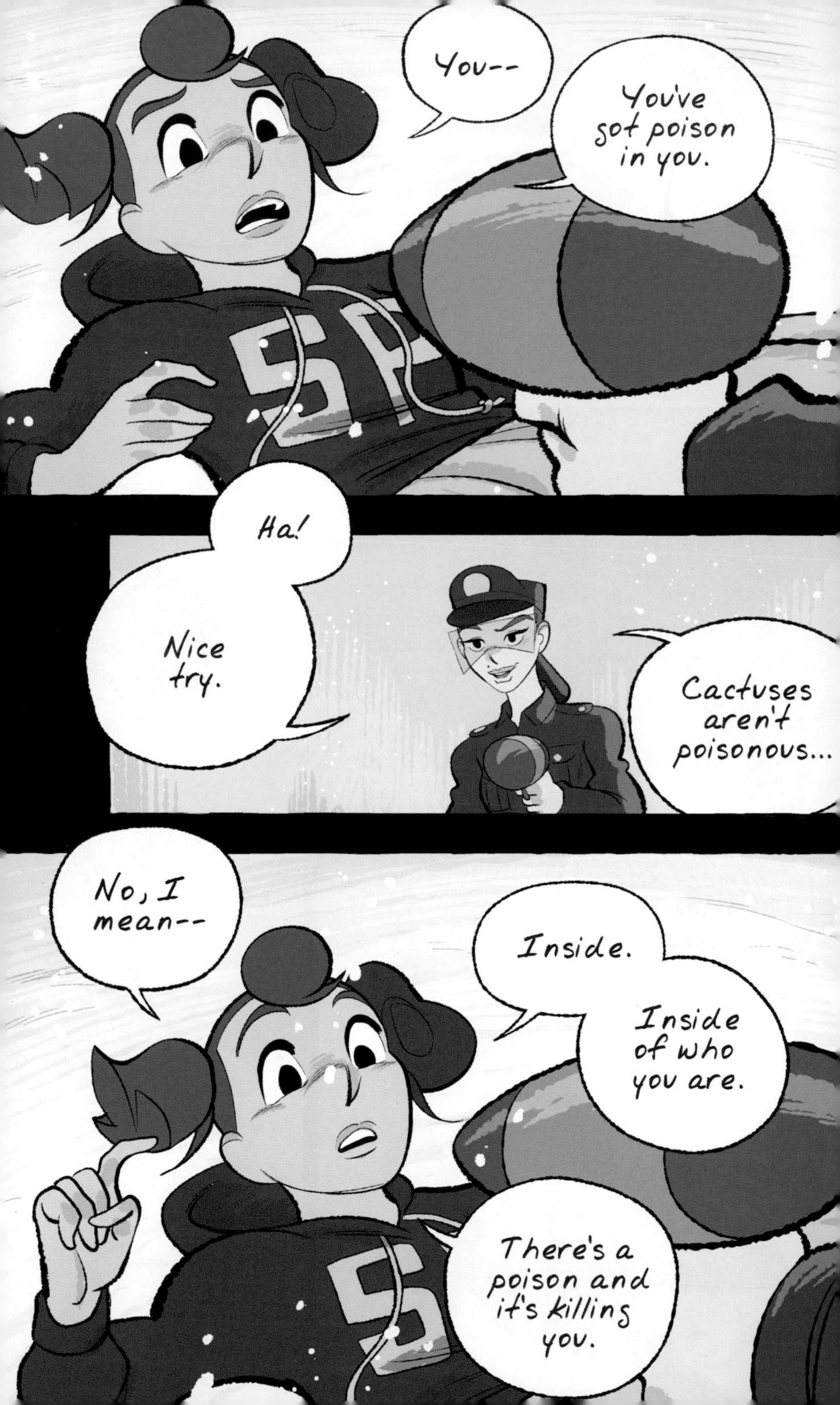

You--
You've got poison in you.
Ha!
Nice try.
Cactuses aren't poisonous...
No, I mean--
Inside.
Inside of who you are.
There's a poison and it's killing you.

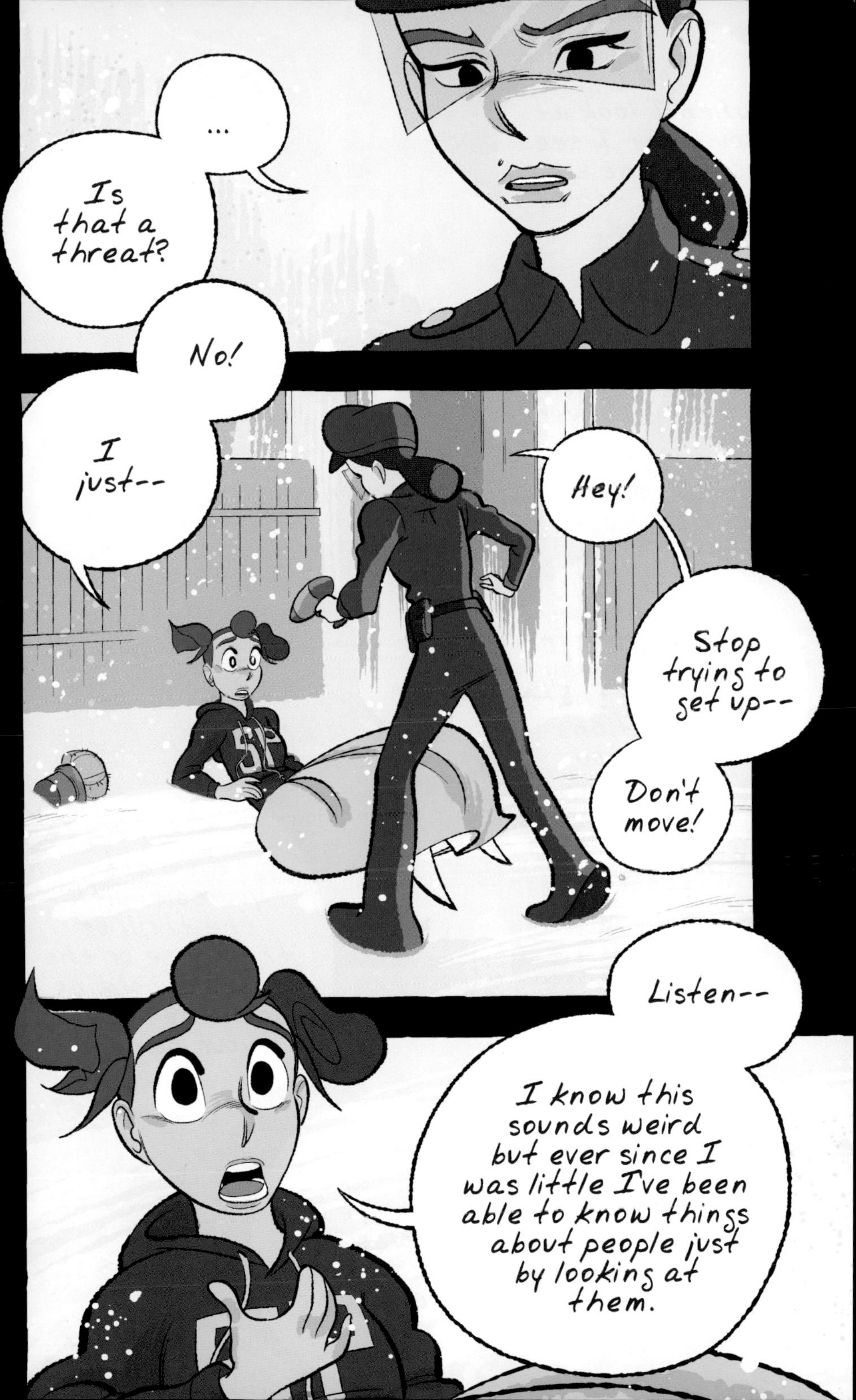
...
Is that a threat?
No!
I just--
Hey!
Stop trying to set up--
Don't move!
Listen--
I know this sounds weird but ever since I was little I've been able to know things about people just by looking at them.

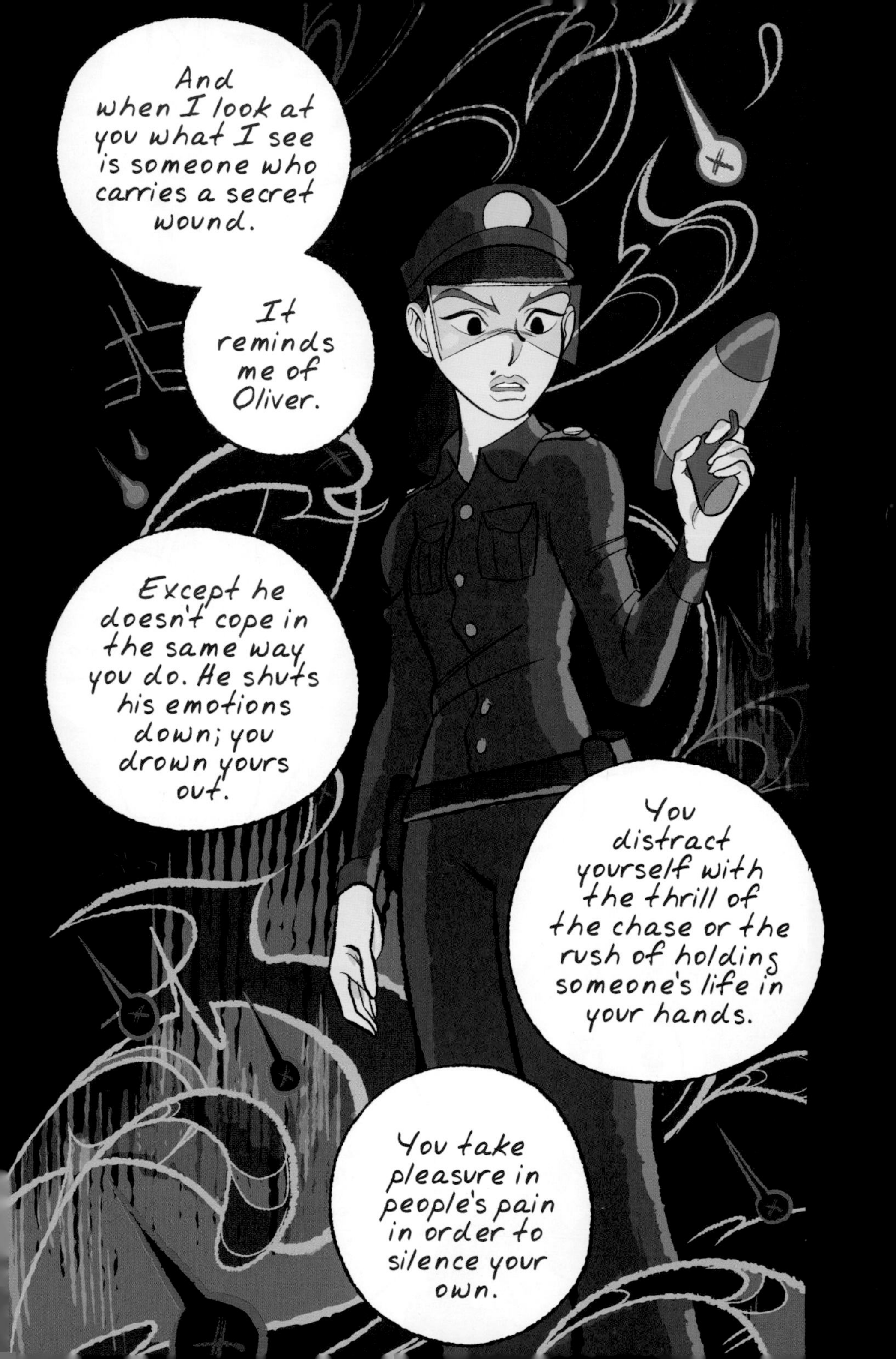
And when I look at you what I see is someone who carries a secret wound.
It reminds me of Oliver.
Except he doesn't cope in the same way you do. He shuts his emotions down; you drown yours out.
You distract yourself with the thrill of the chase or the rush of holding someone's life in your hands.
You take pleasure in people's pain in order to silence your own.

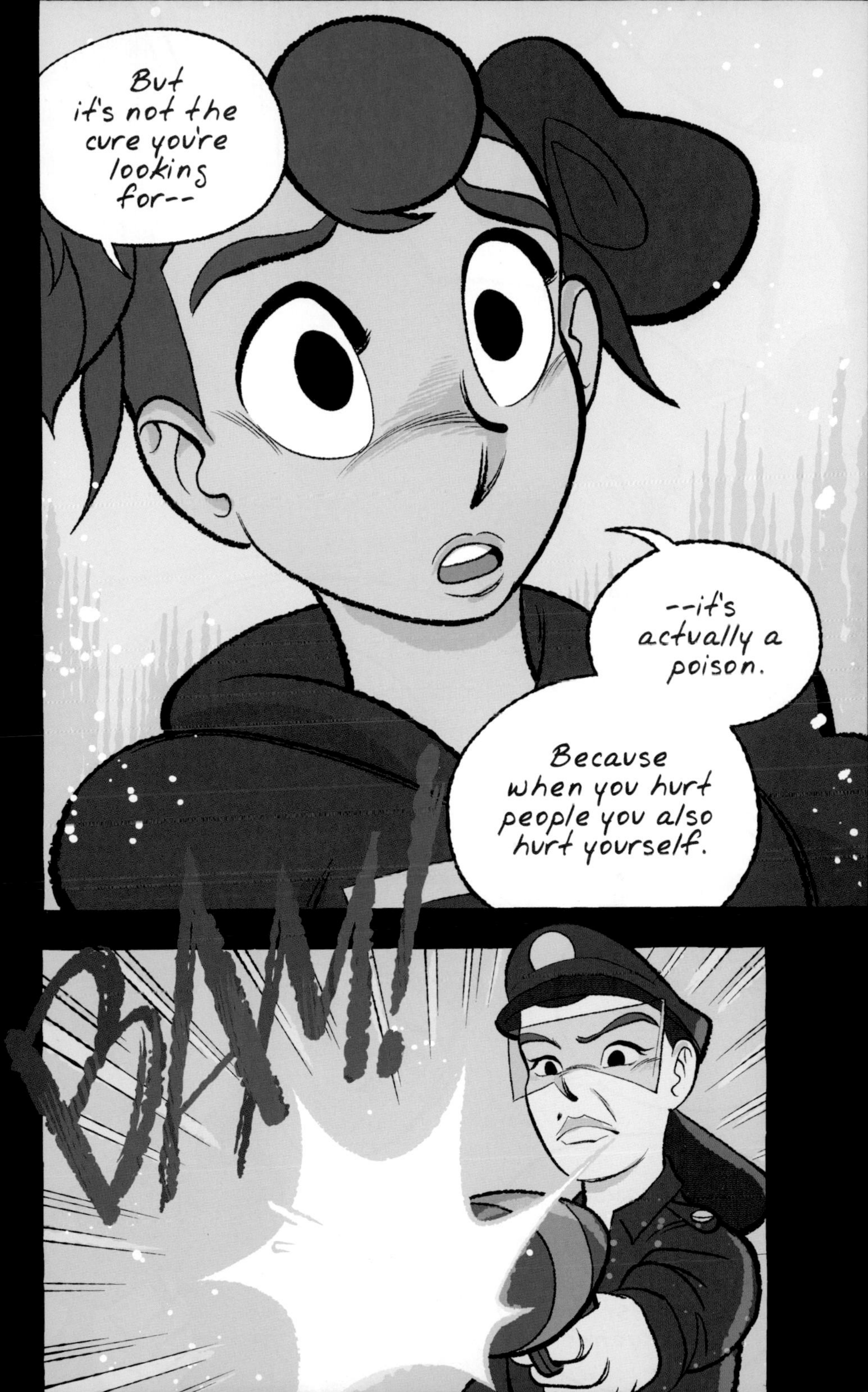

But it's not the cure you're looking for--
--it's actually a poison.
Because when you hurt people you also hurt yourself.
BAM!

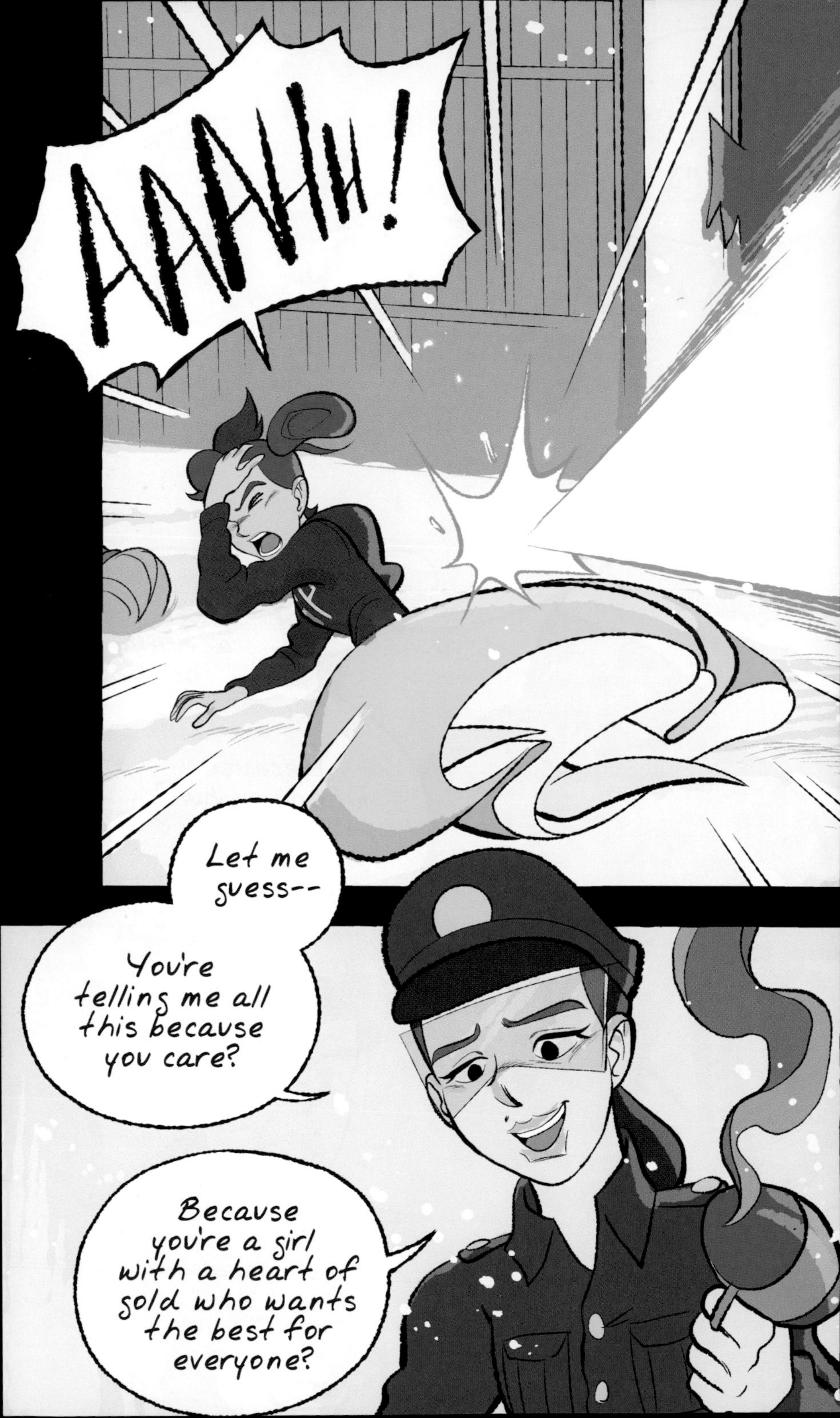
AAAHH!
Let me guess--
You're telling me all this because you care?
Because you're a girl with a heart of gold who wants the best for everyone?

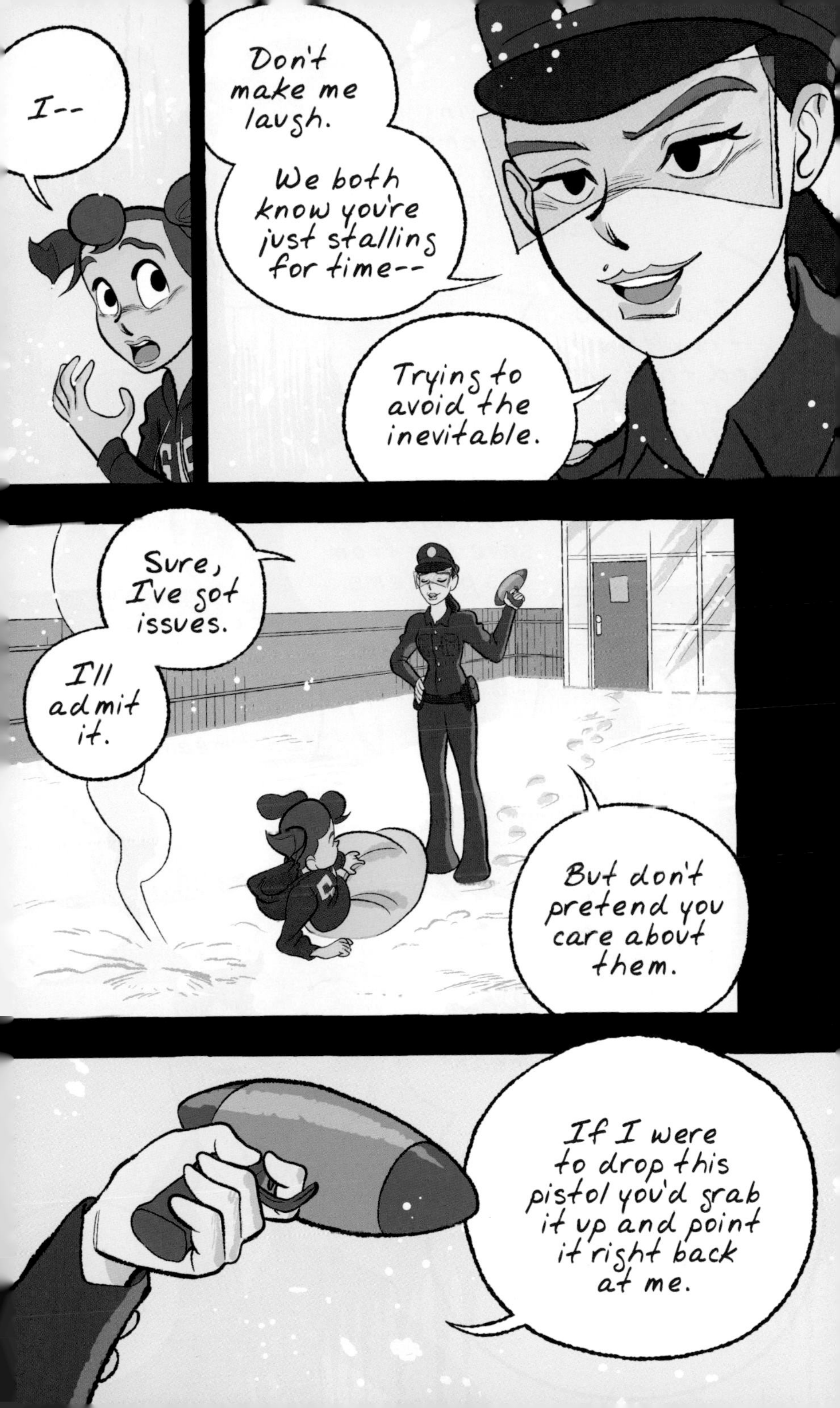

I--
Don't make me laugh.
We both know you're just stalling for time--
Trying to avoid the inevitable.
Sure, I've got issues.
I'll admit it.
But don't pretend you care about them.
If I were to drop this pistol you'd grab it up and point it right back at me.

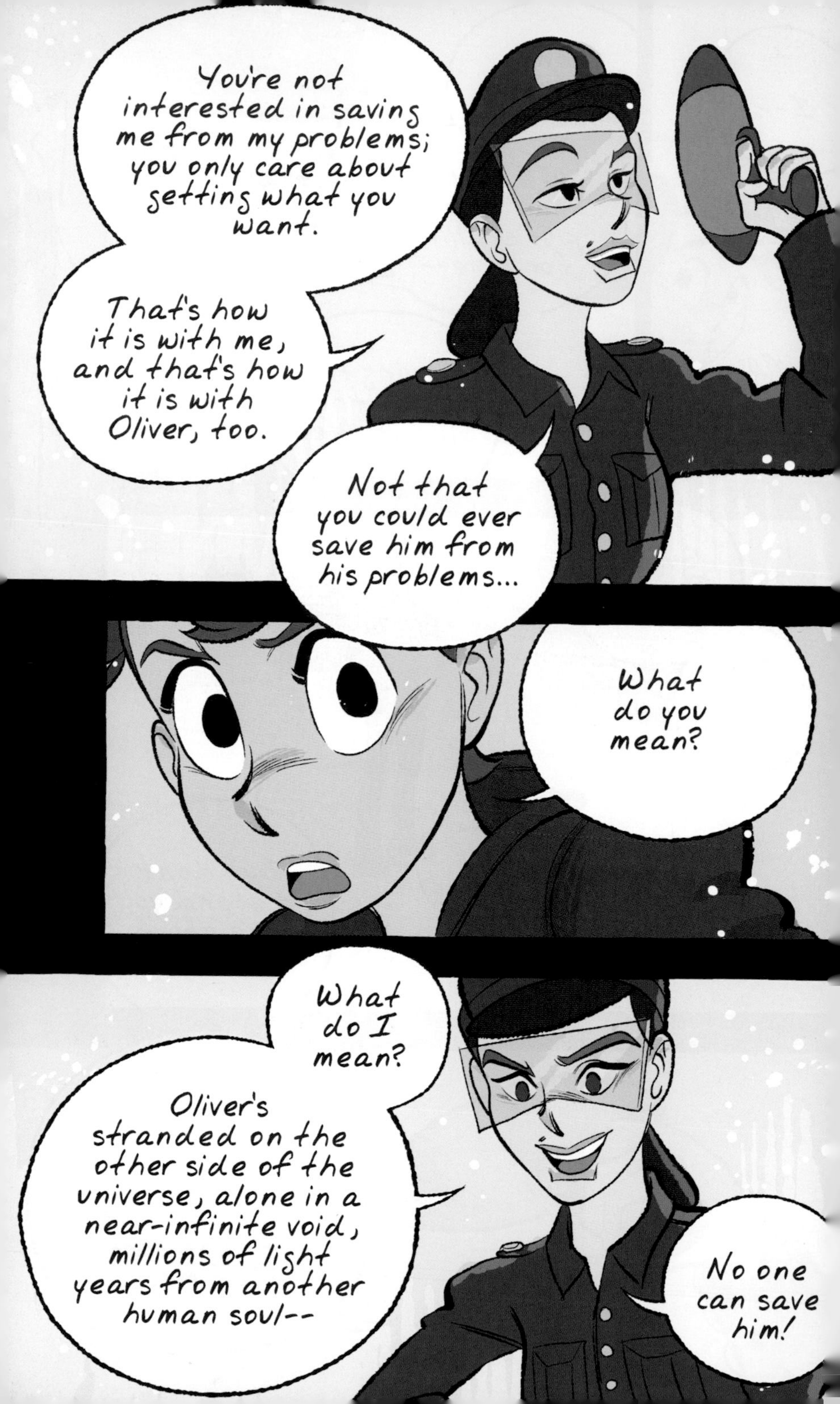
You're not interested in saving me from my problems; you only care about getting what you want.
That's how it is with me, and that's how it is with Oliver, too.
Not that you could ever save him from his problems...
What do you mean?
What do I mean?
Oliver's stranded on the other side of the universe, alone in a near-infinite void, millions of light years from another human soul--
No one can save him!

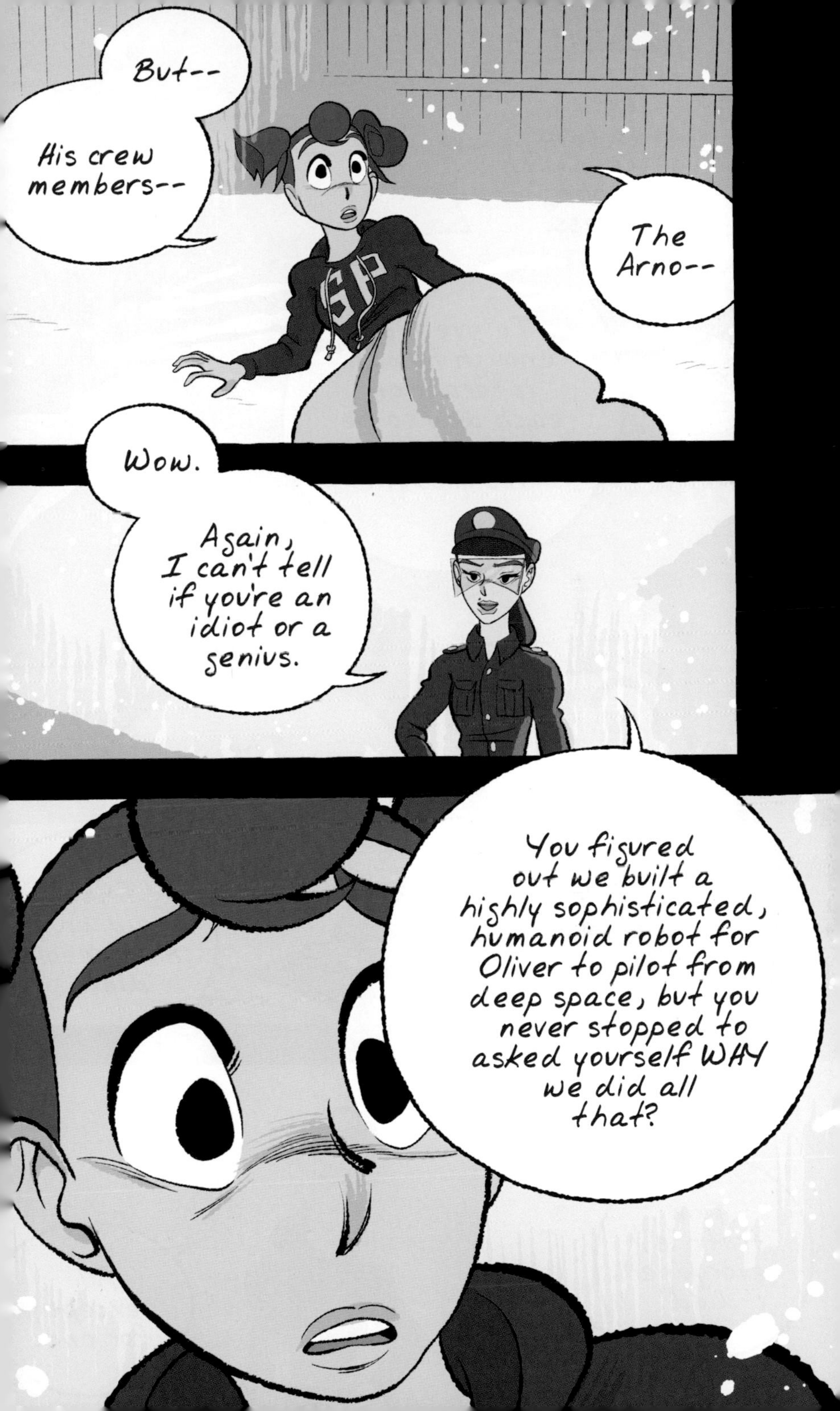
But--
His crew members--
The Arno--
Wow.
Again, I can't tell if you're an idiot or a genius.
You figured out we built a highly sophisticated, humanoid robot for Oliver to pilot from deep space, but you never stopped to asked yourself WHY we did all that?

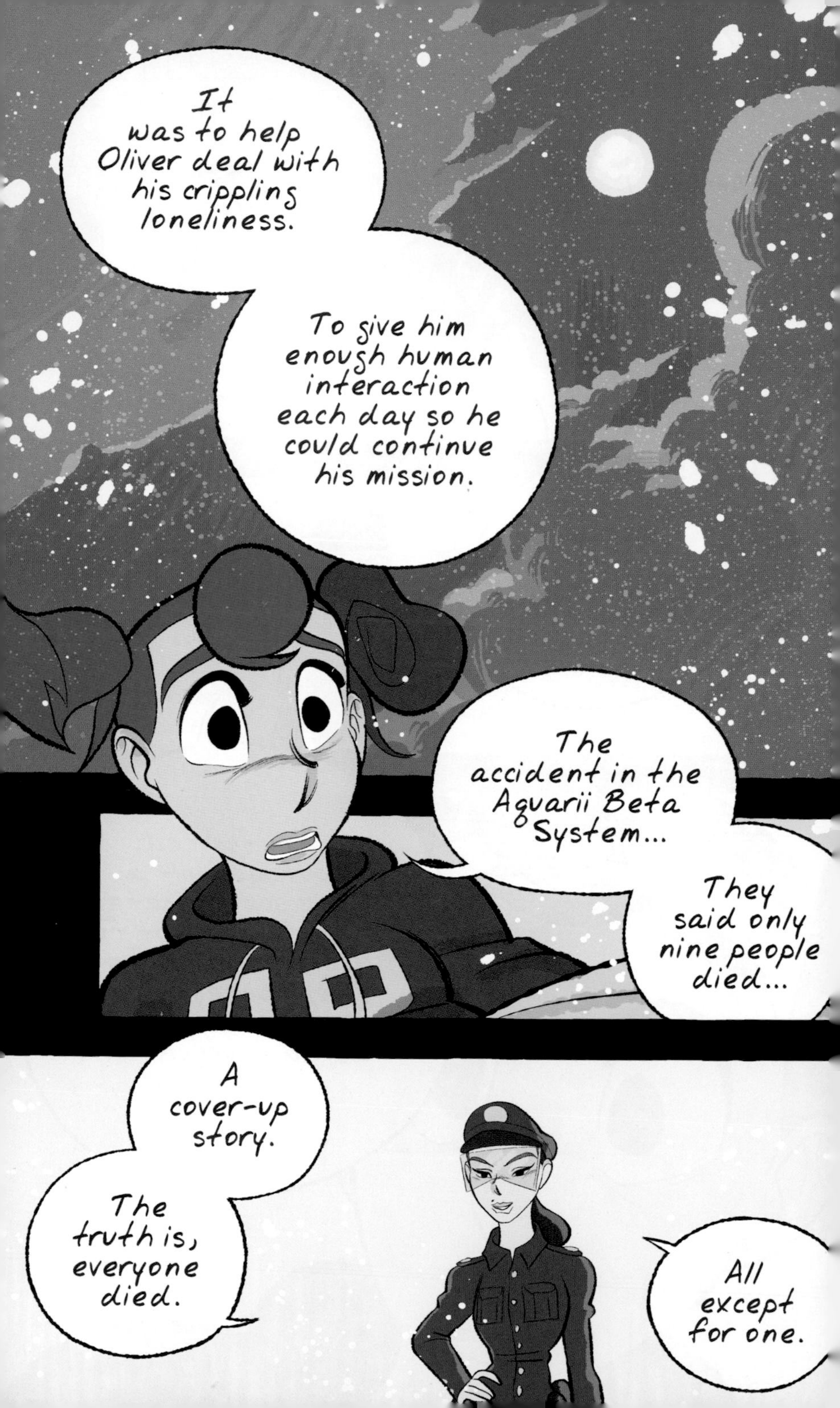
It was to help Oliver deal with his crippling loneliness.
To give him enough human interaction each day so he could continue his mission.
The accident in the Aquarii Beta System...
They said only nine people died...
A cover-up story.
The truth is, everyone died.
All except for one.

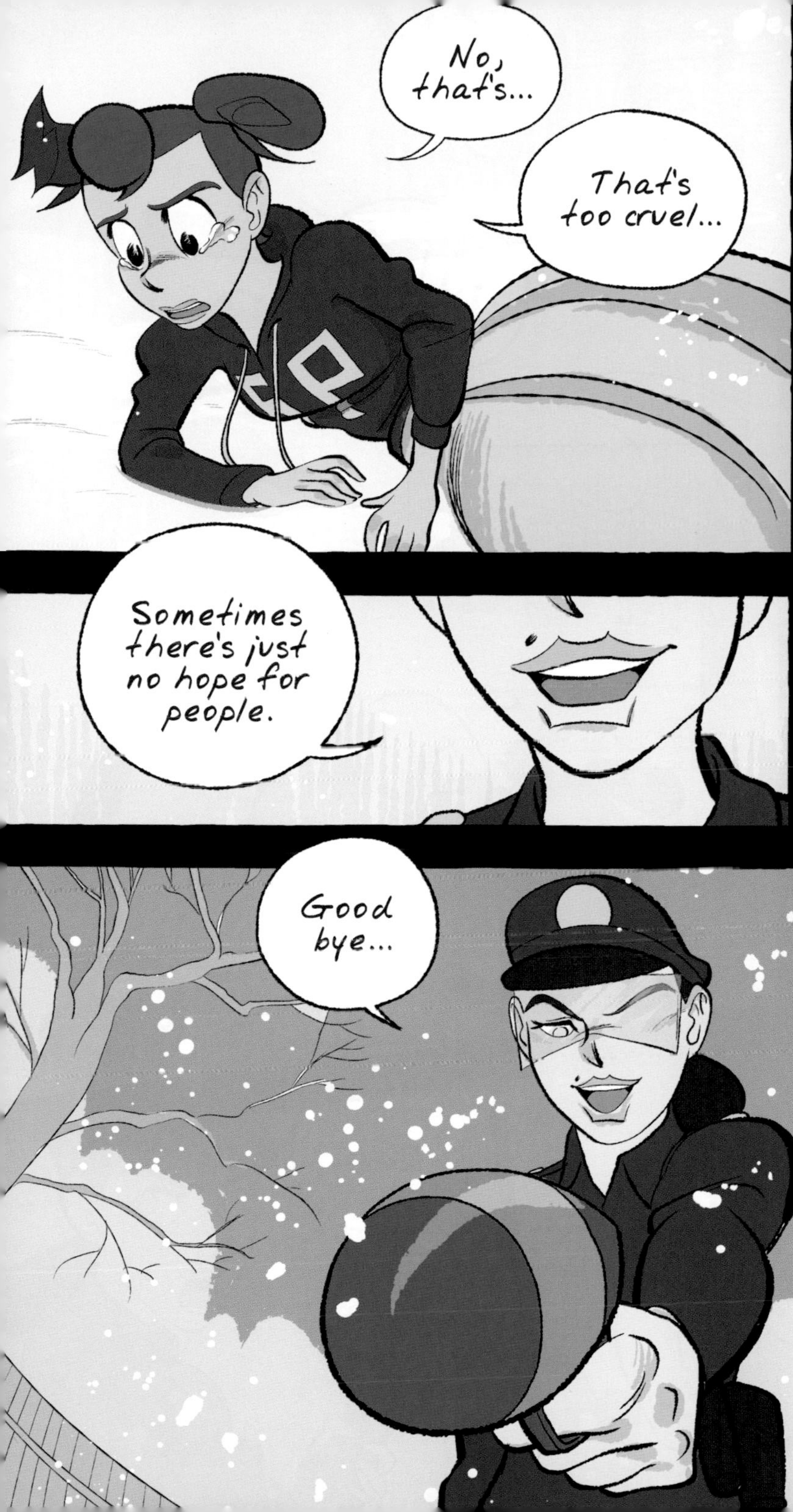
No, that's...
That's too cruel...
Sometimes there's just no hope for people.
Good bye...

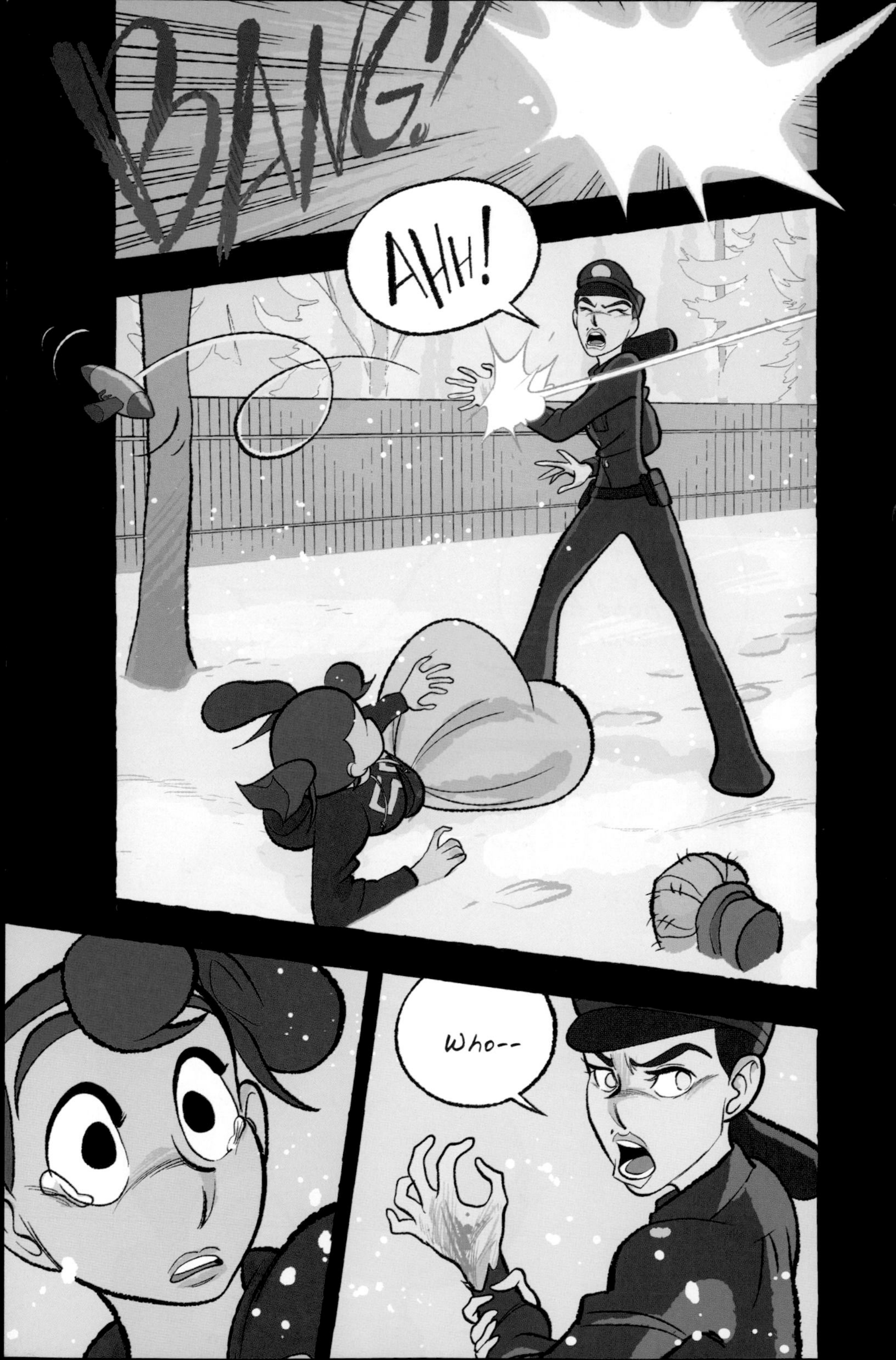
BANG!
AHH!
Who--

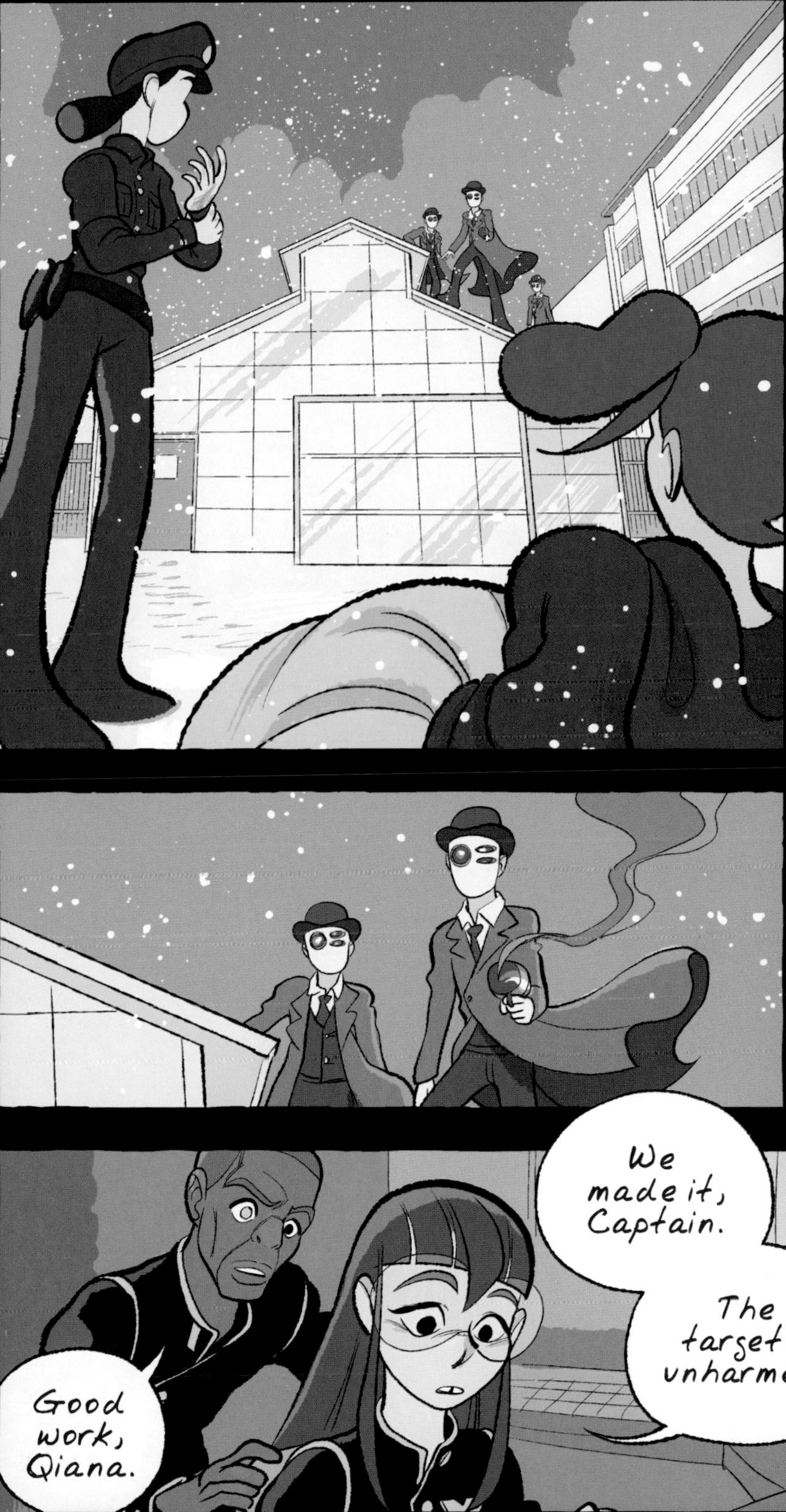
We made it, Captain.
The target is unharmed.
Good work, Qiana.

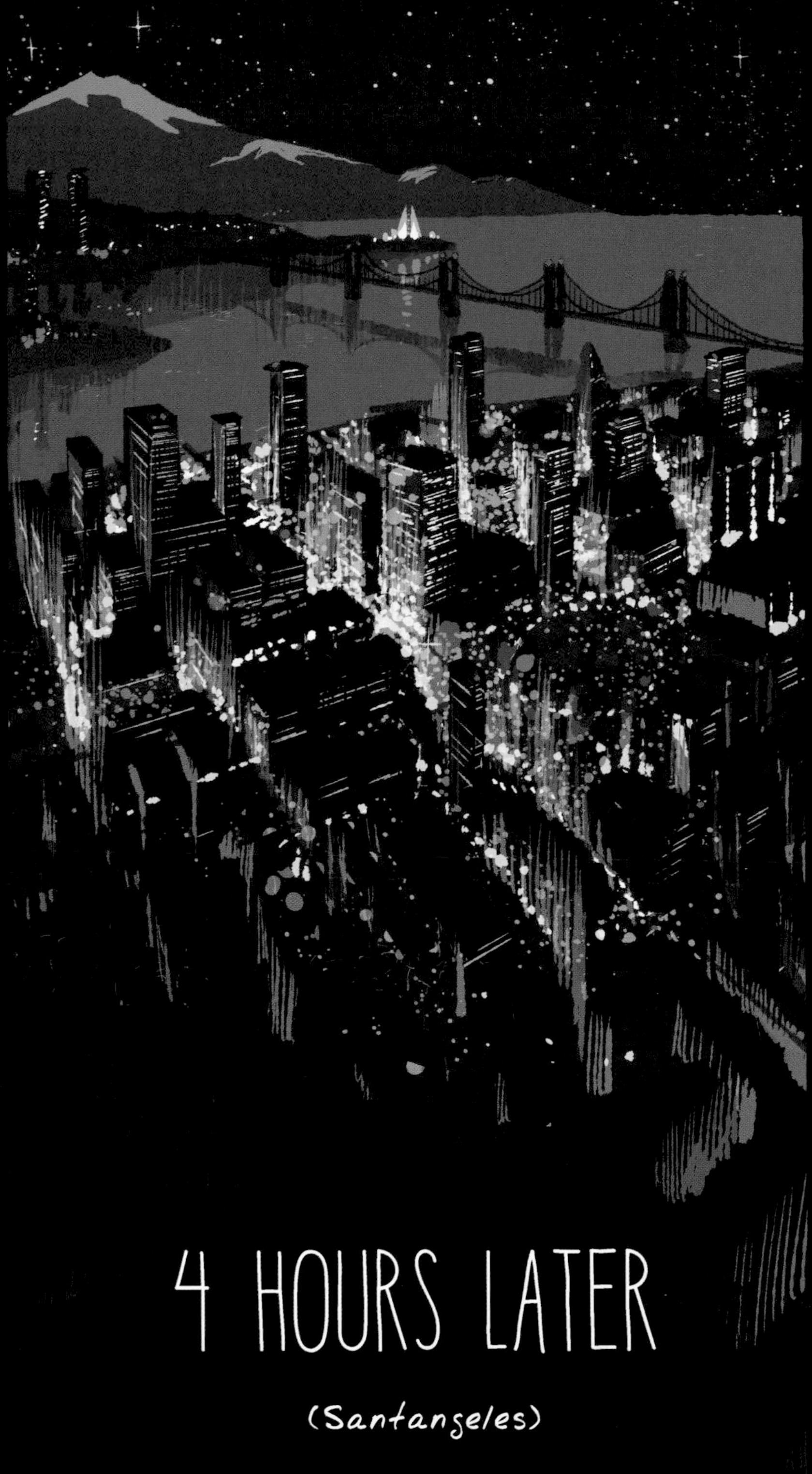
4 HOURS LATER
(Santangeles)

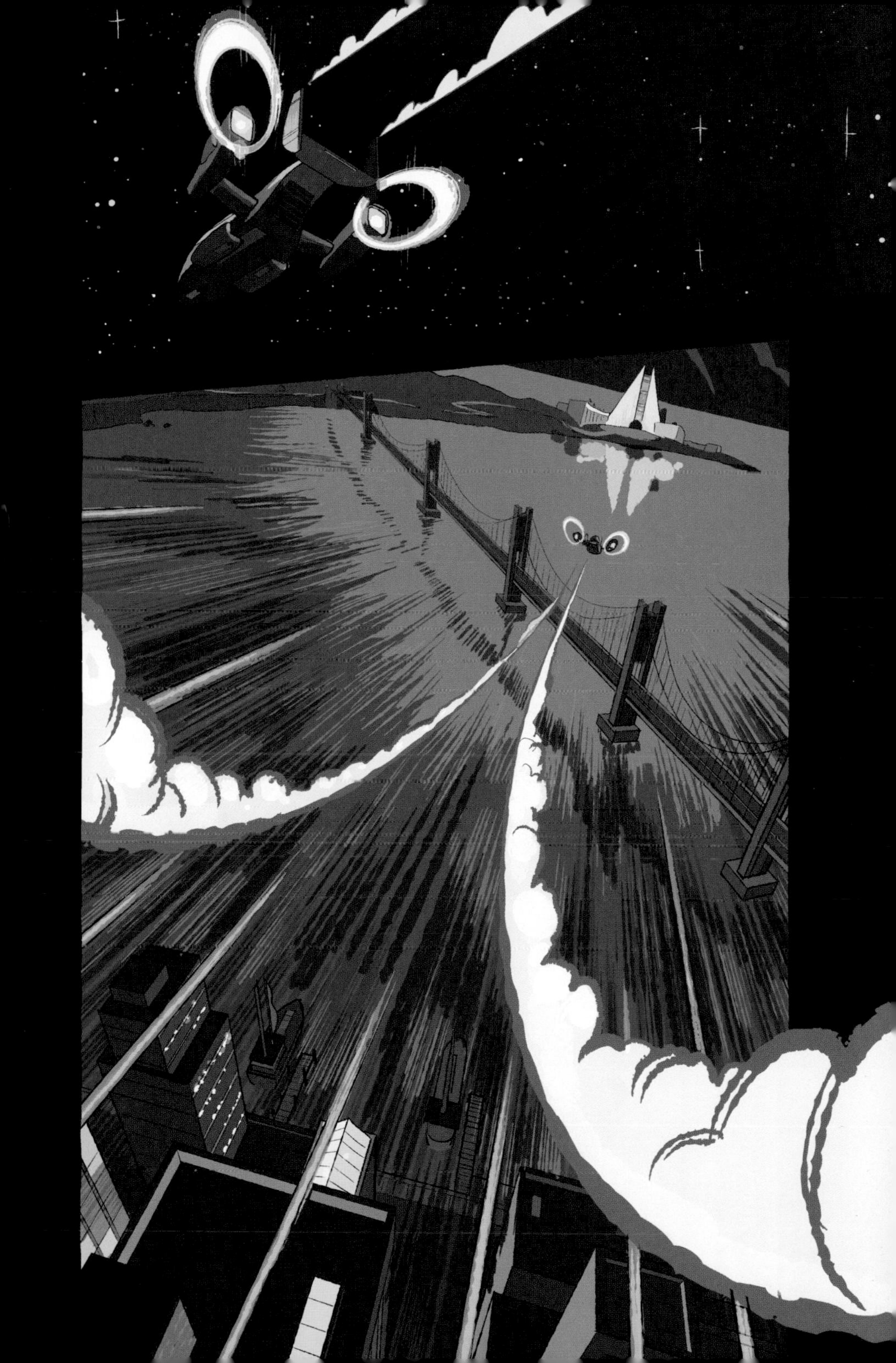

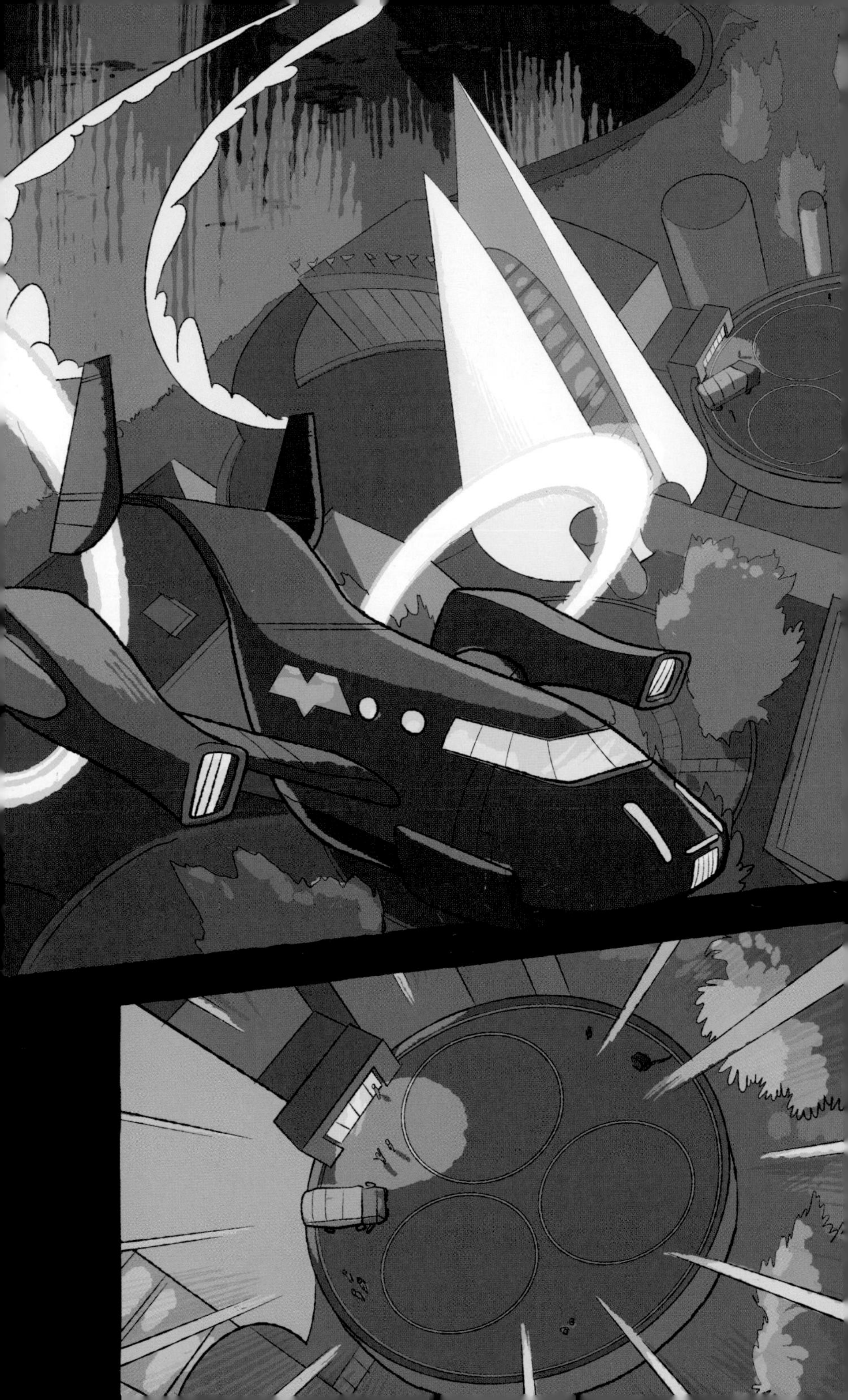

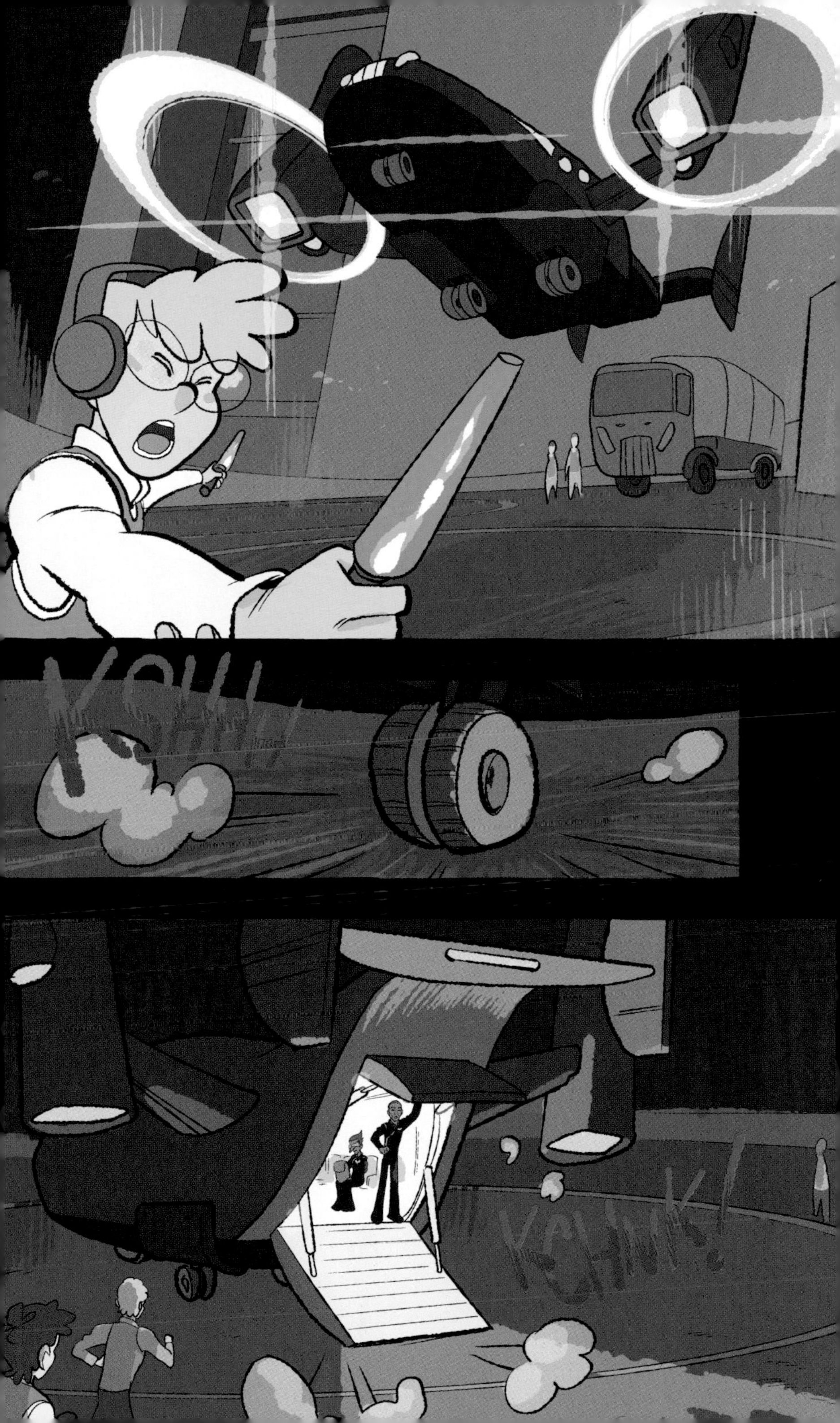
KSHH!
KCHUNK!

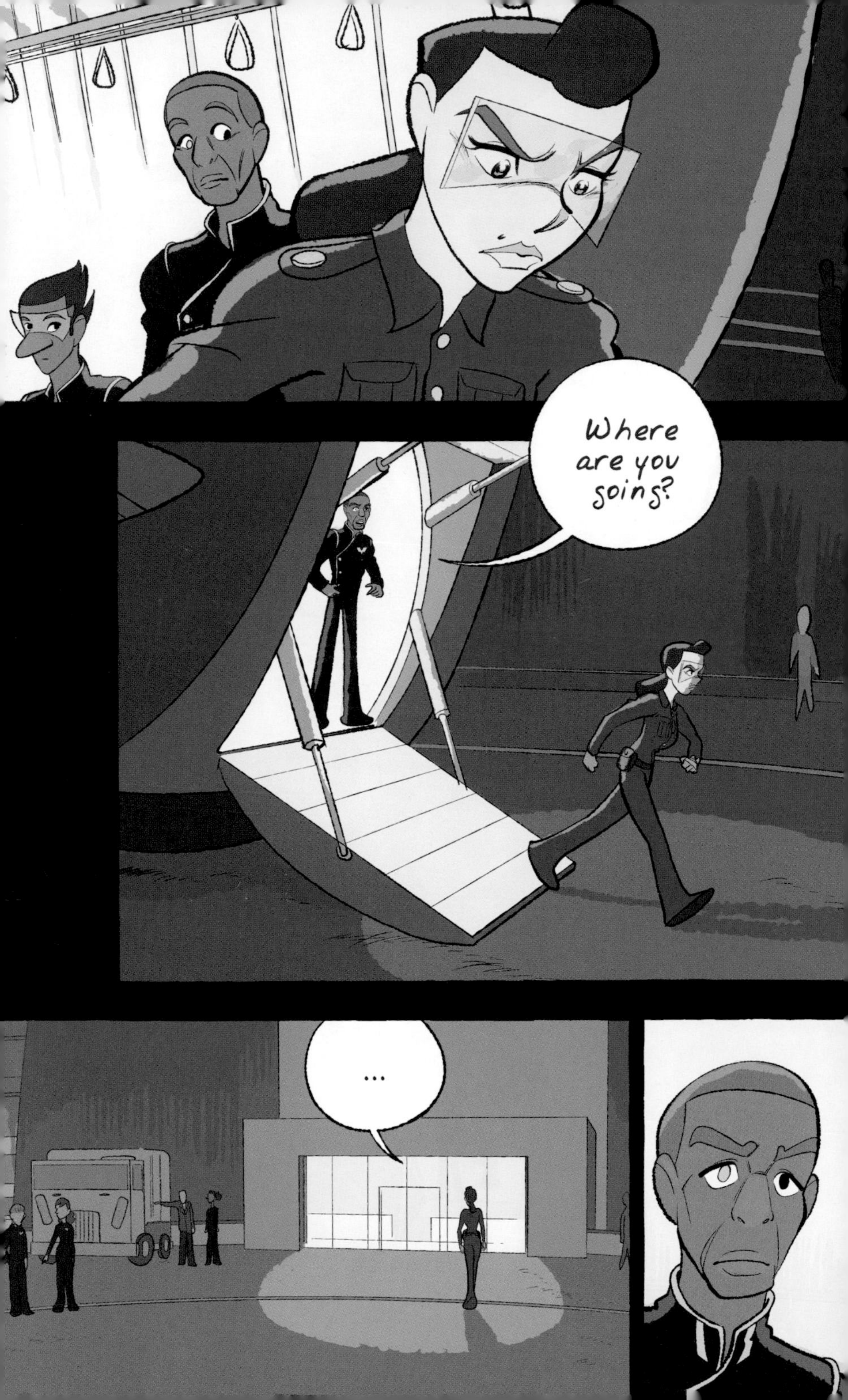
Where are you going?
...

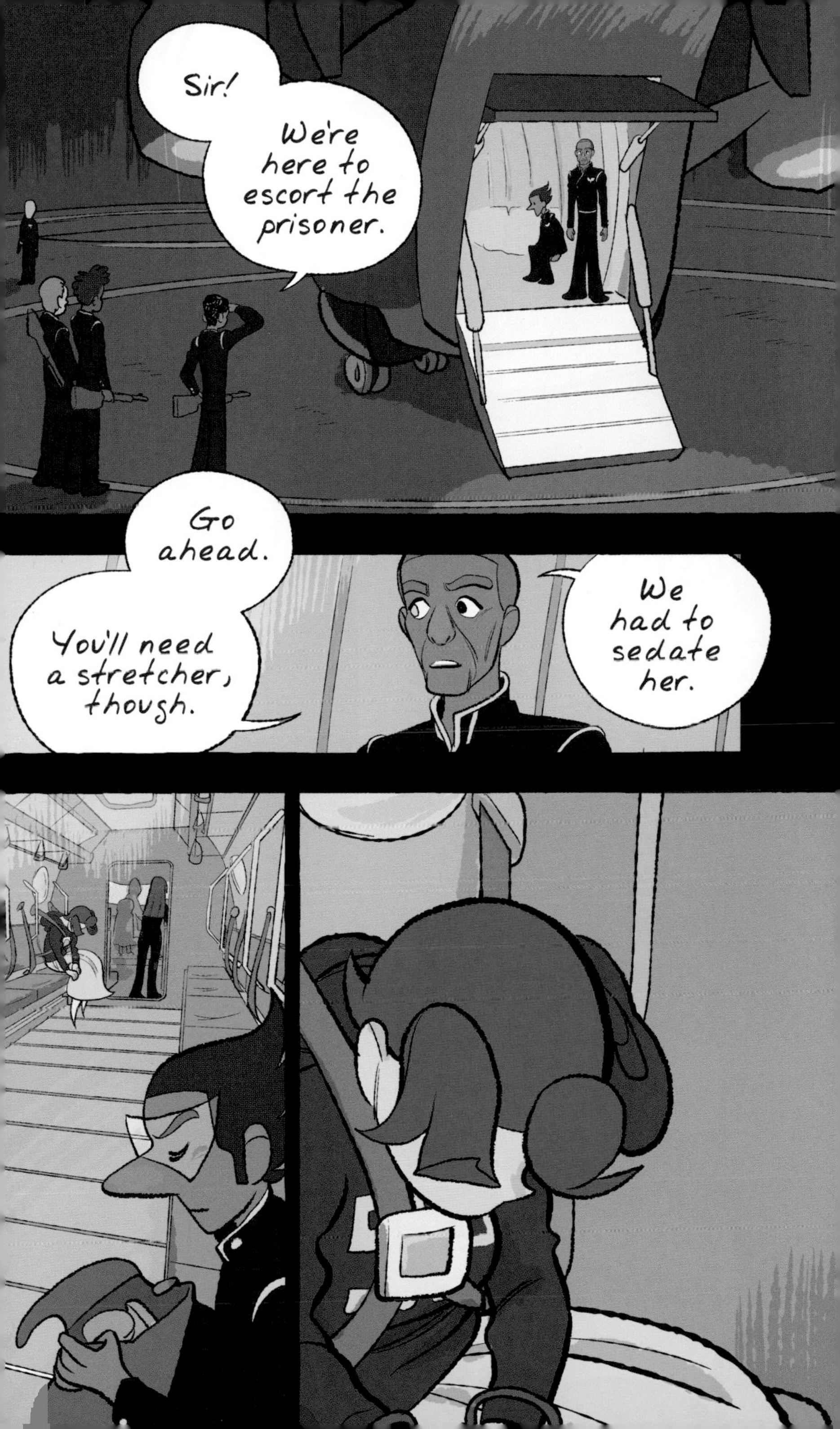
Sir!
We're here to escort the prisoner.
Go ahead.
You'll need a stretcher, though.
We had to sedate her.

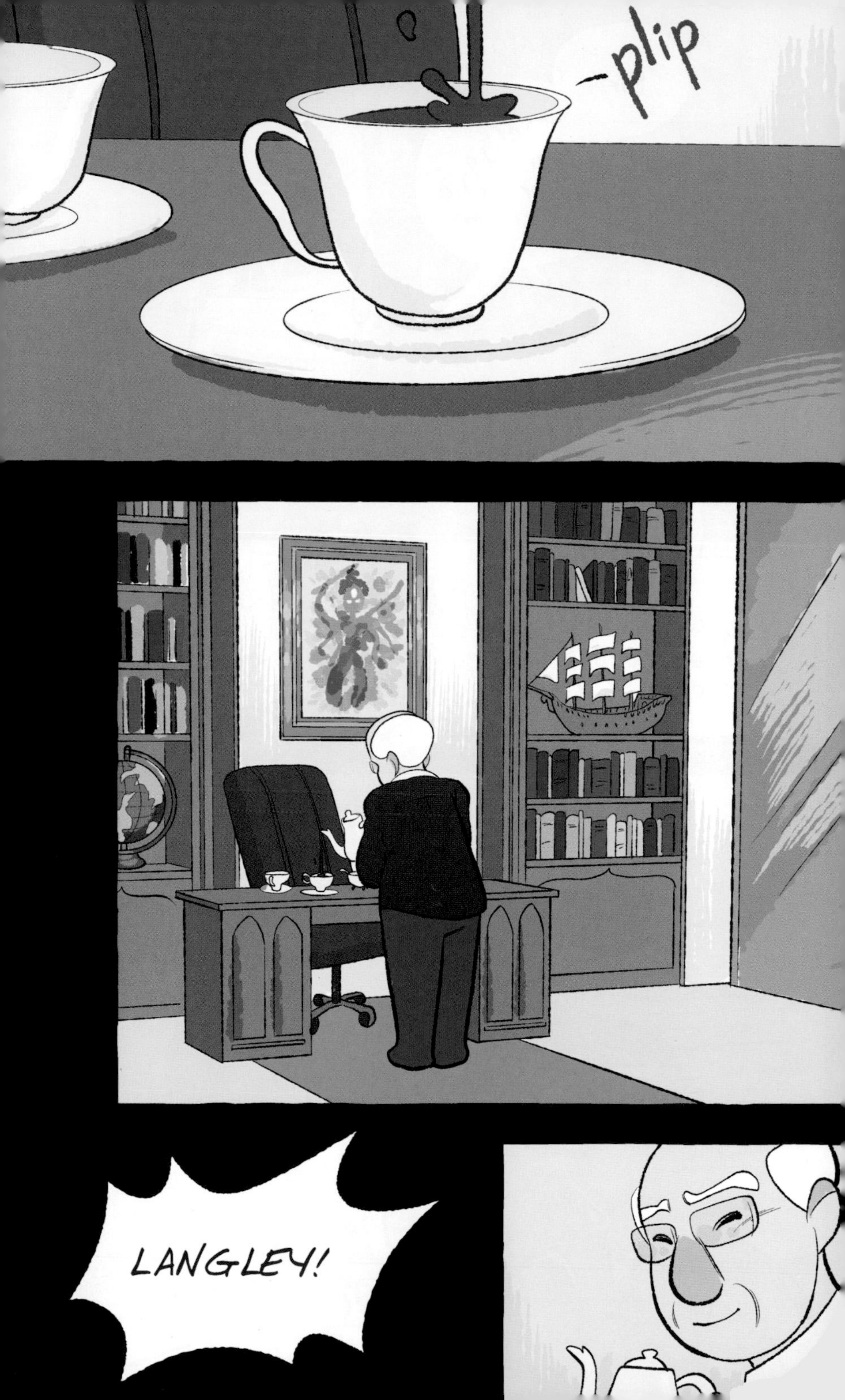
-plip
LANGLEY!

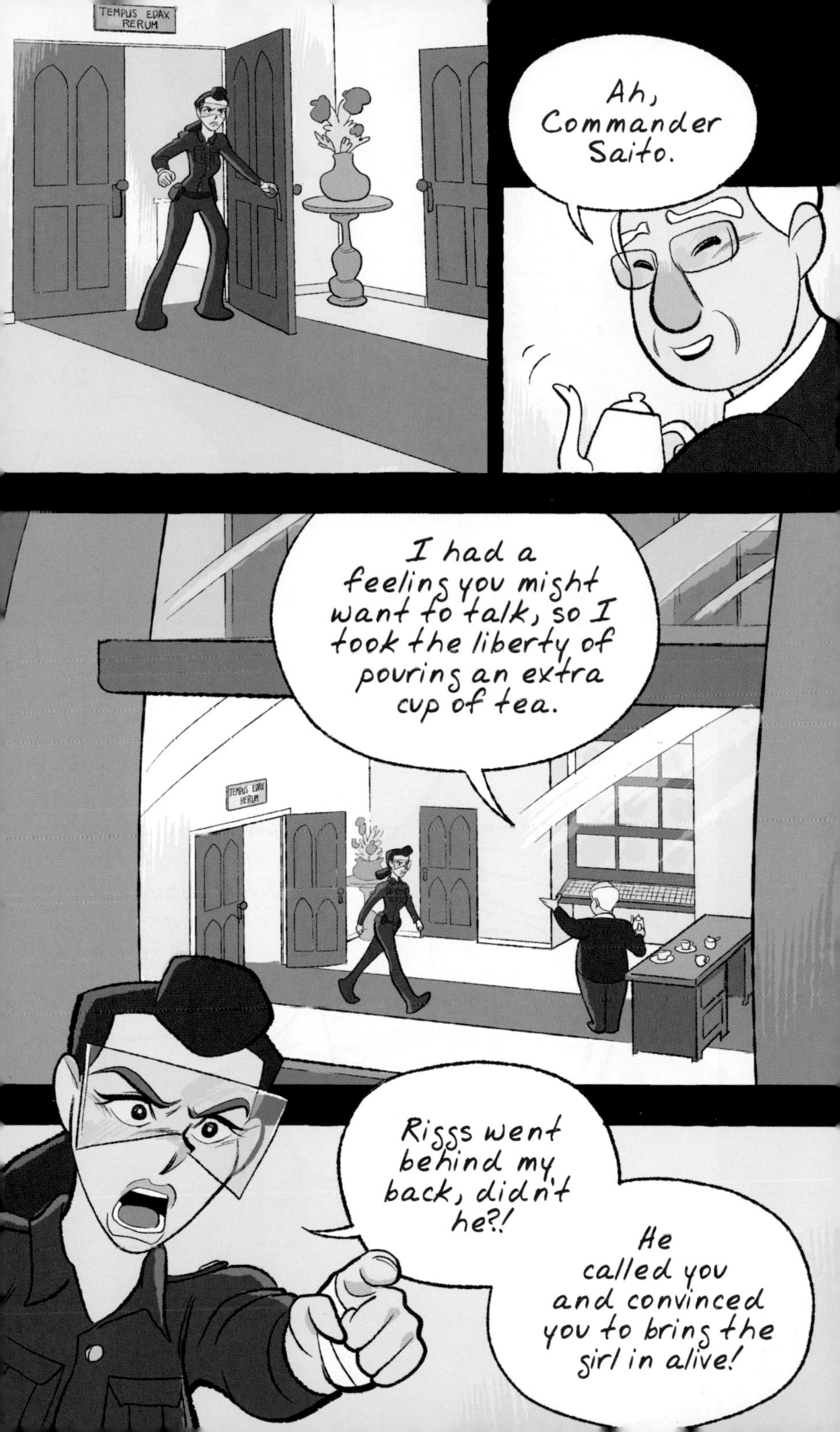
TEMPUS EDAX RERUM
Ah, Commander Saito.
I had a feeling you might want to talk, so I took the liberty of pouring an extra cup of tea.
TEMPUS EDAX RERUM
Riggs went behind my back, didn't he?!
He called you and convinced you to bring the girl in alive!

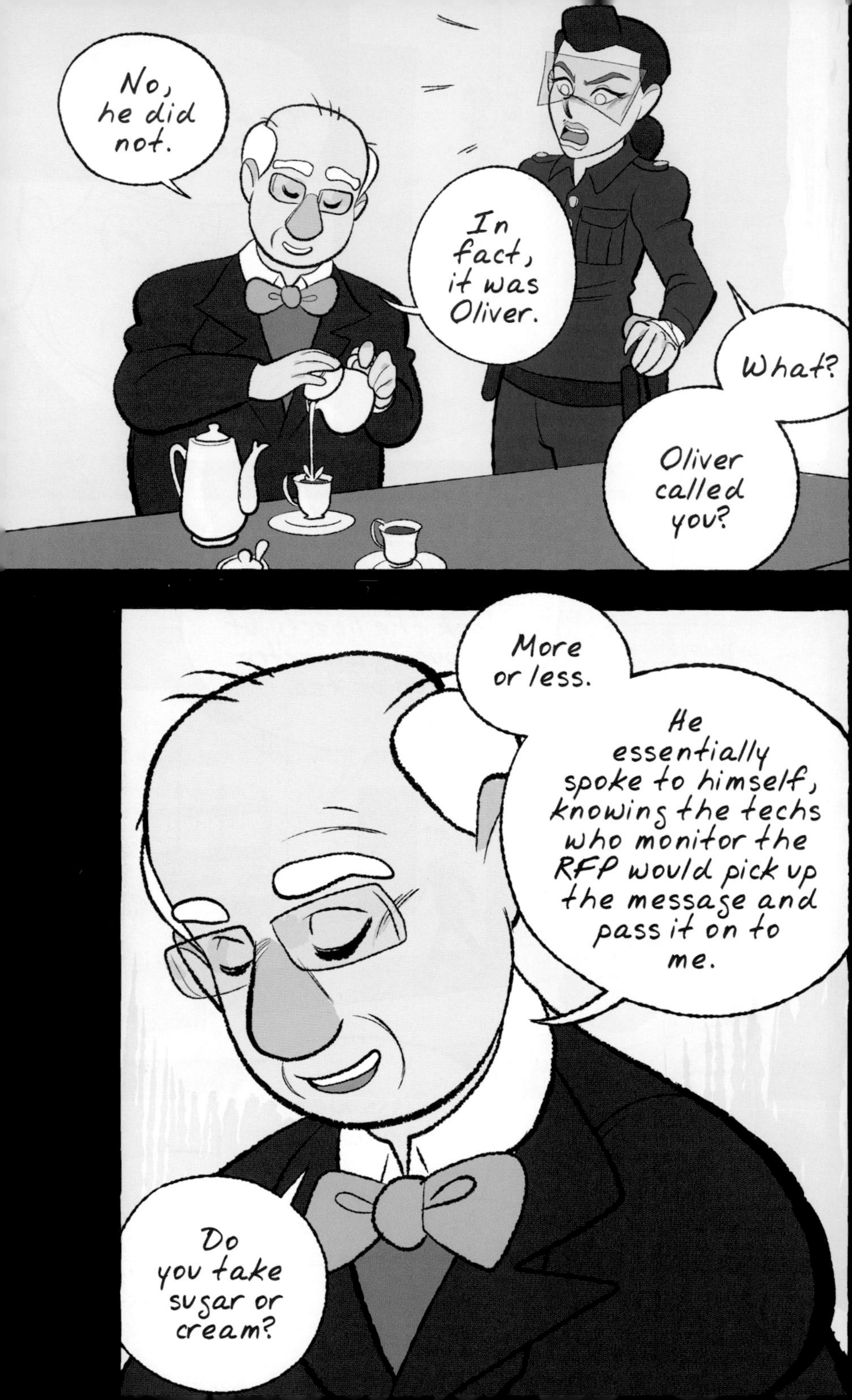
No, he did not.
In fact, it was Oliver.
What?
Oliver called you?
More or less.
He essentially spoke to himself, knowing the techs who monitor the RFP would pick up the message and pass it on to me.
Do you take sugar or cream?

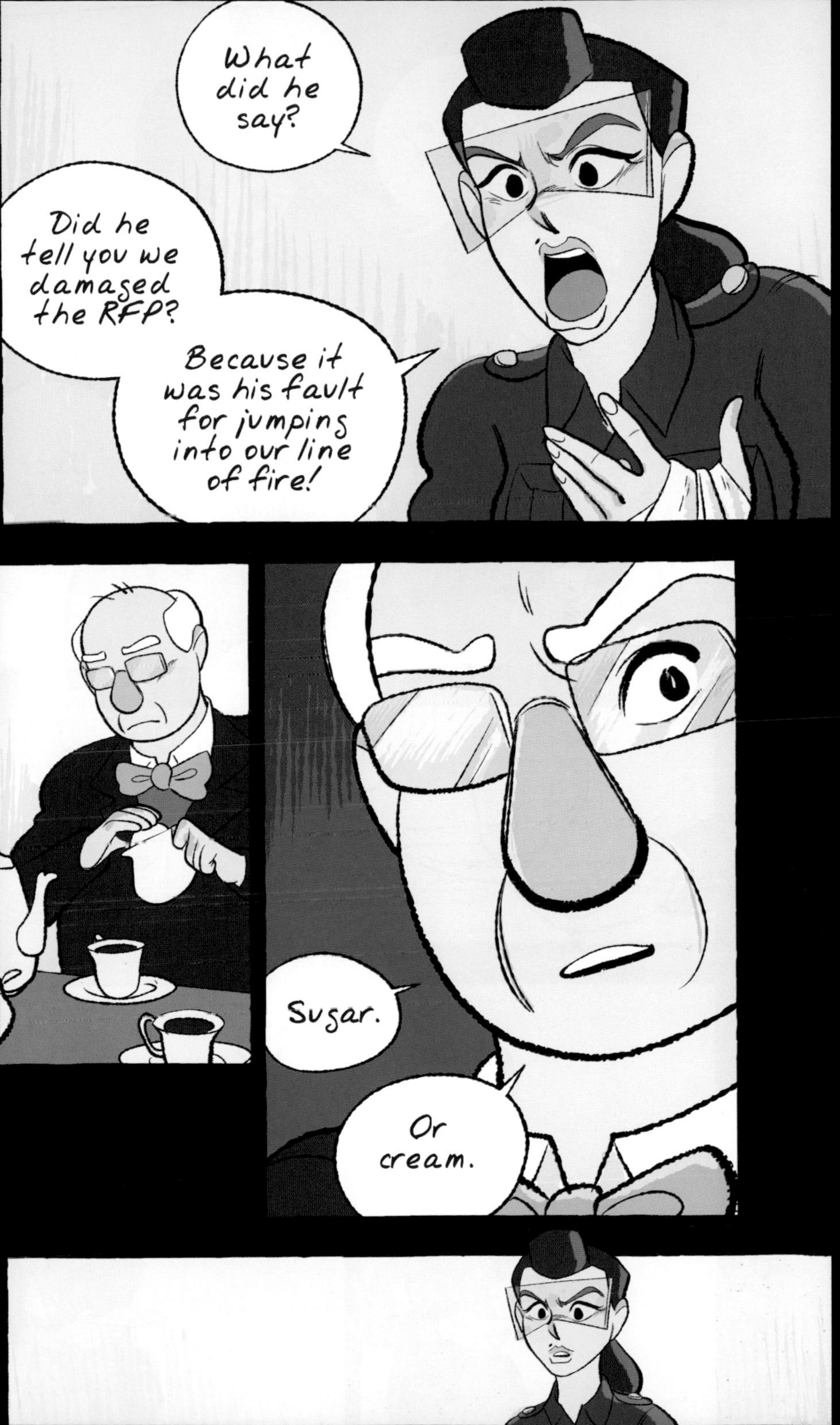
What did he say?
Did he tell you we damaged the RFP?
Because it was his fault for jumping into our line of fire!
Sugar.
Or cream.

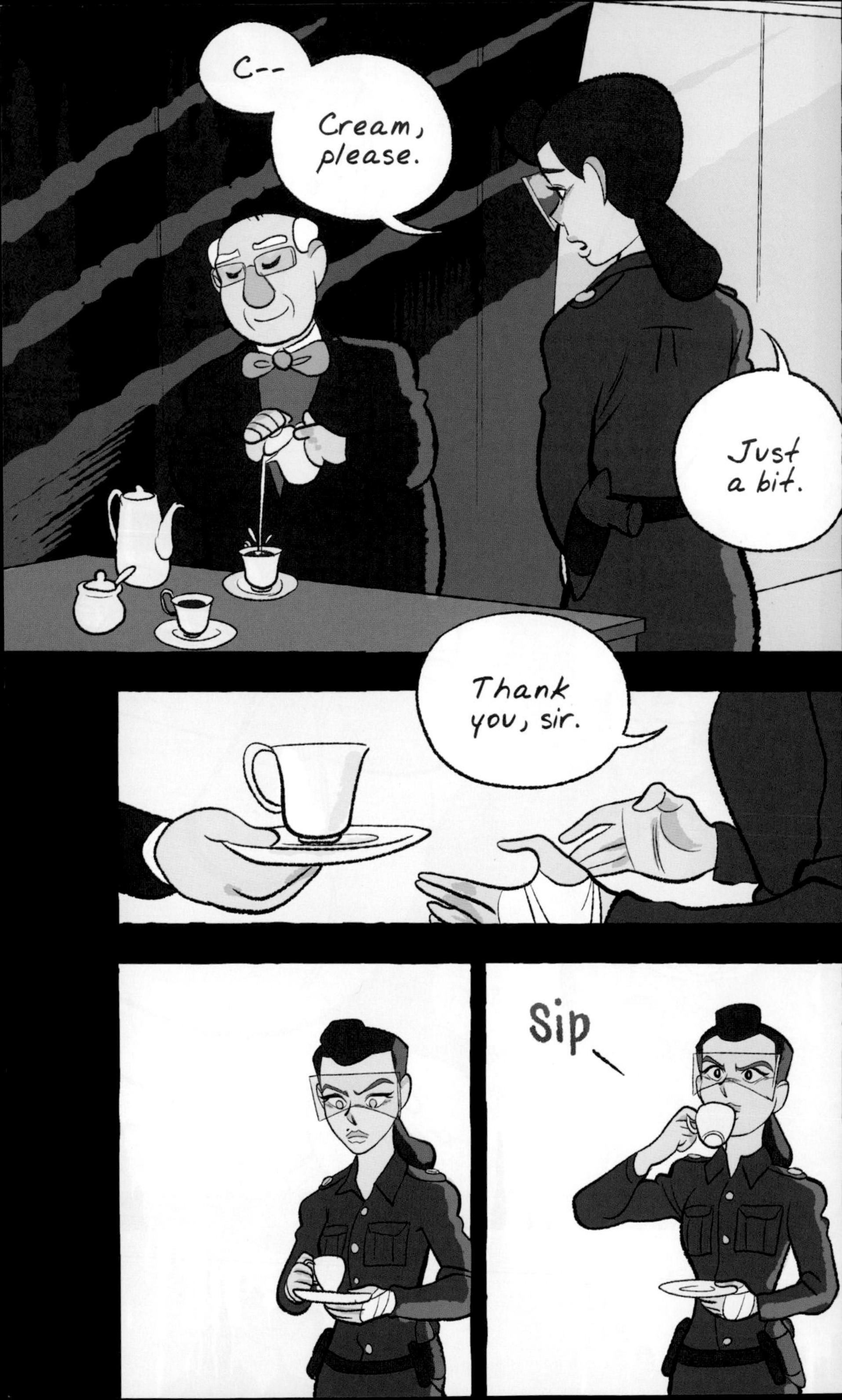
C--
Cream, please.
Just a bit.
Thank you, sir.
Sip

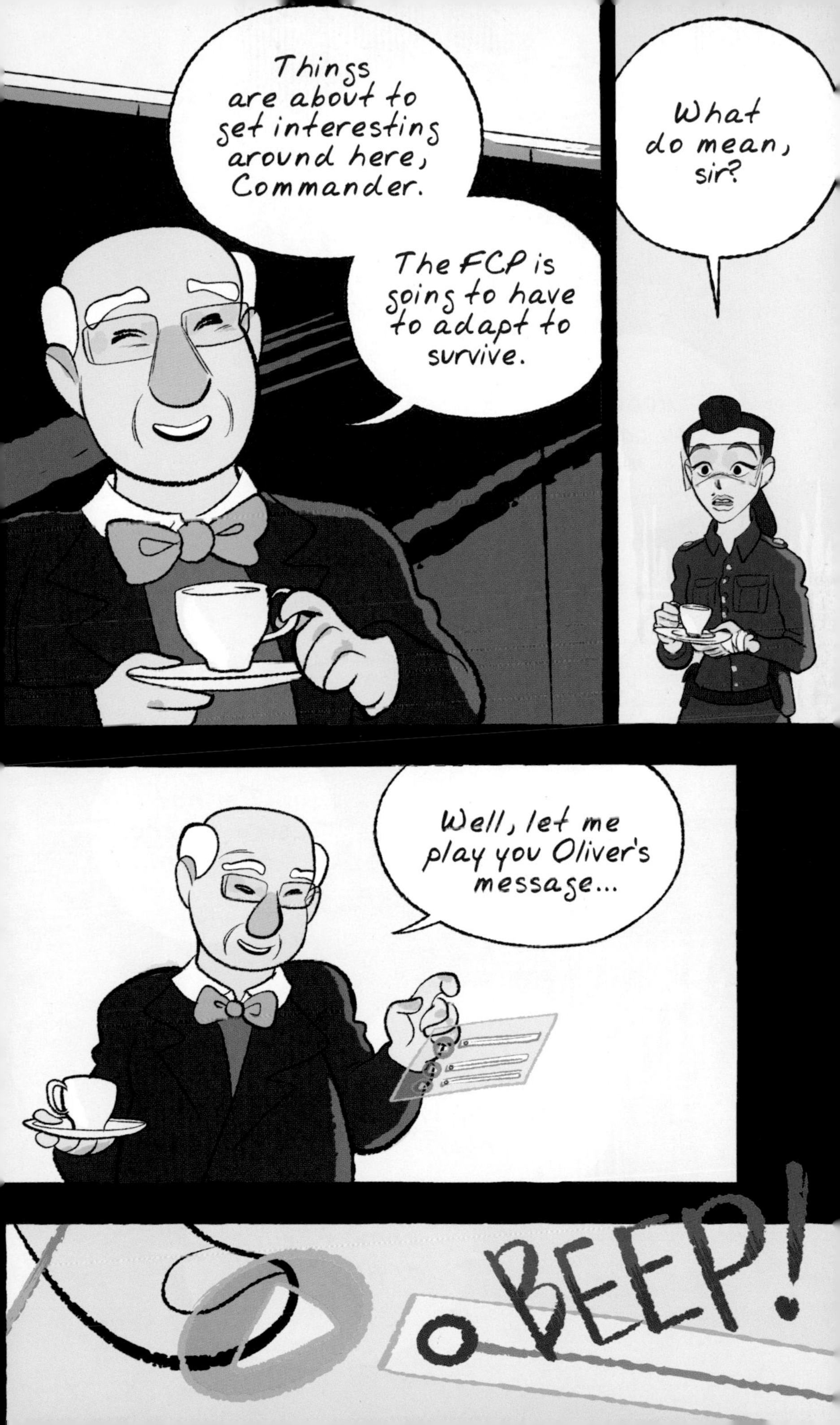
Things are about to get interesting around here, Commander.
The FCP is going to have to adapt to survive.
What do mean, sir?
Well, let me play you Oliver's message...
BEEP!

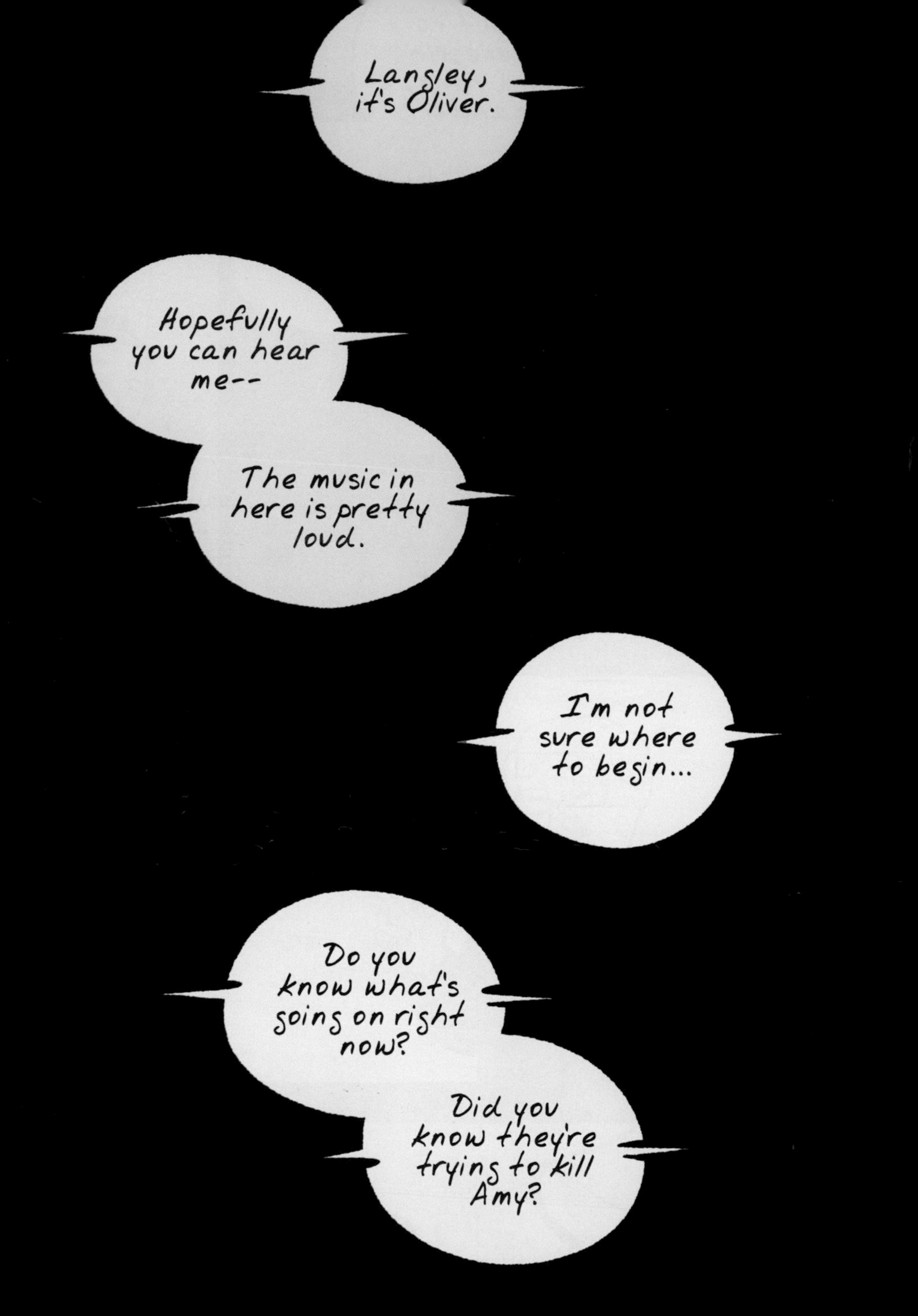
Langley, it's Oliver.
Hopefully you can hear me--
The music in here is pretty loud.
I'm not sure where to begin...
Do you know what's going on right now?
Did you know they're trying to kill Amy?

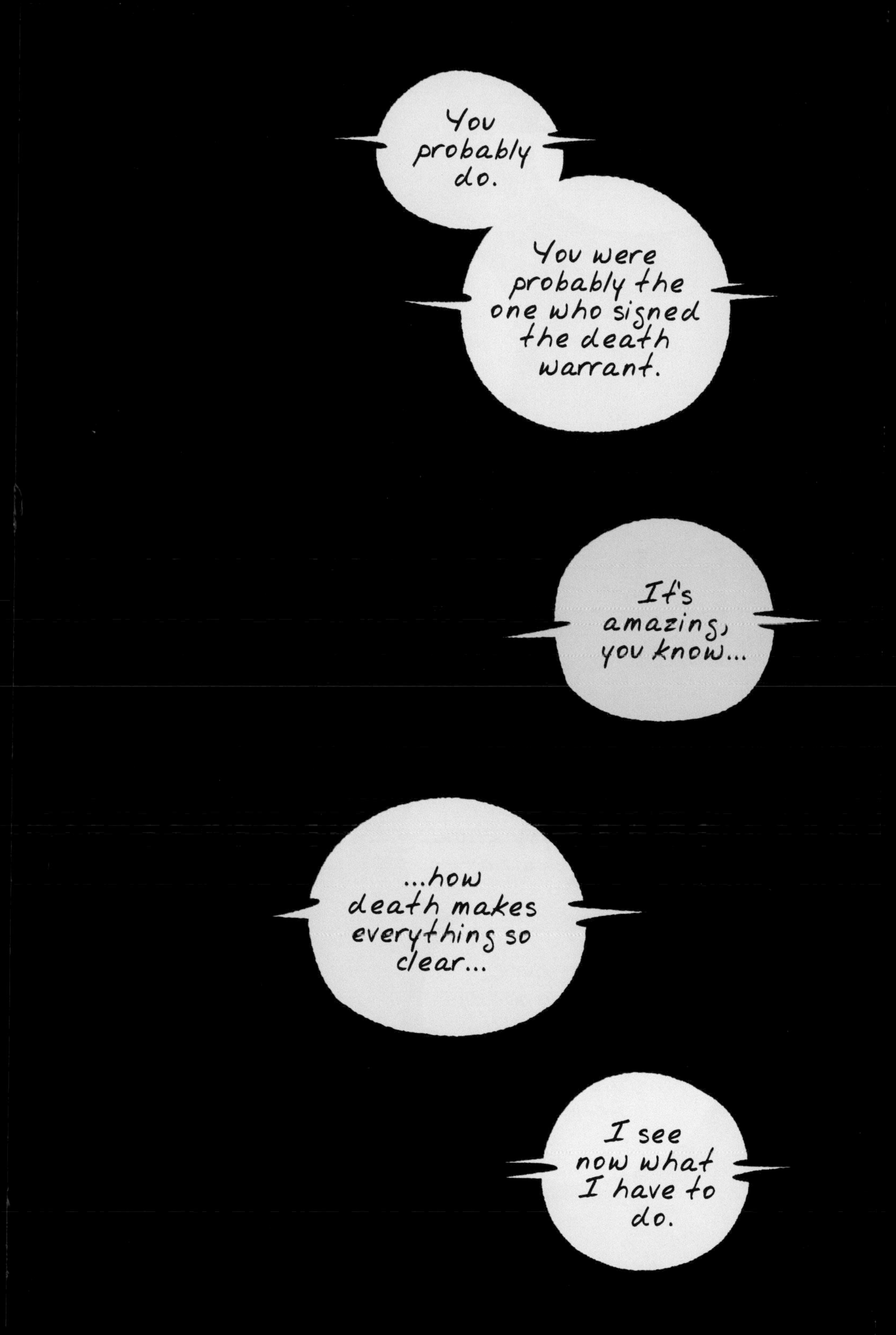
You probably do.
You were probably the one who signed the death warrant.
It's amazing, you know...
...how death makes everything so clear...
I see now what I have to do.

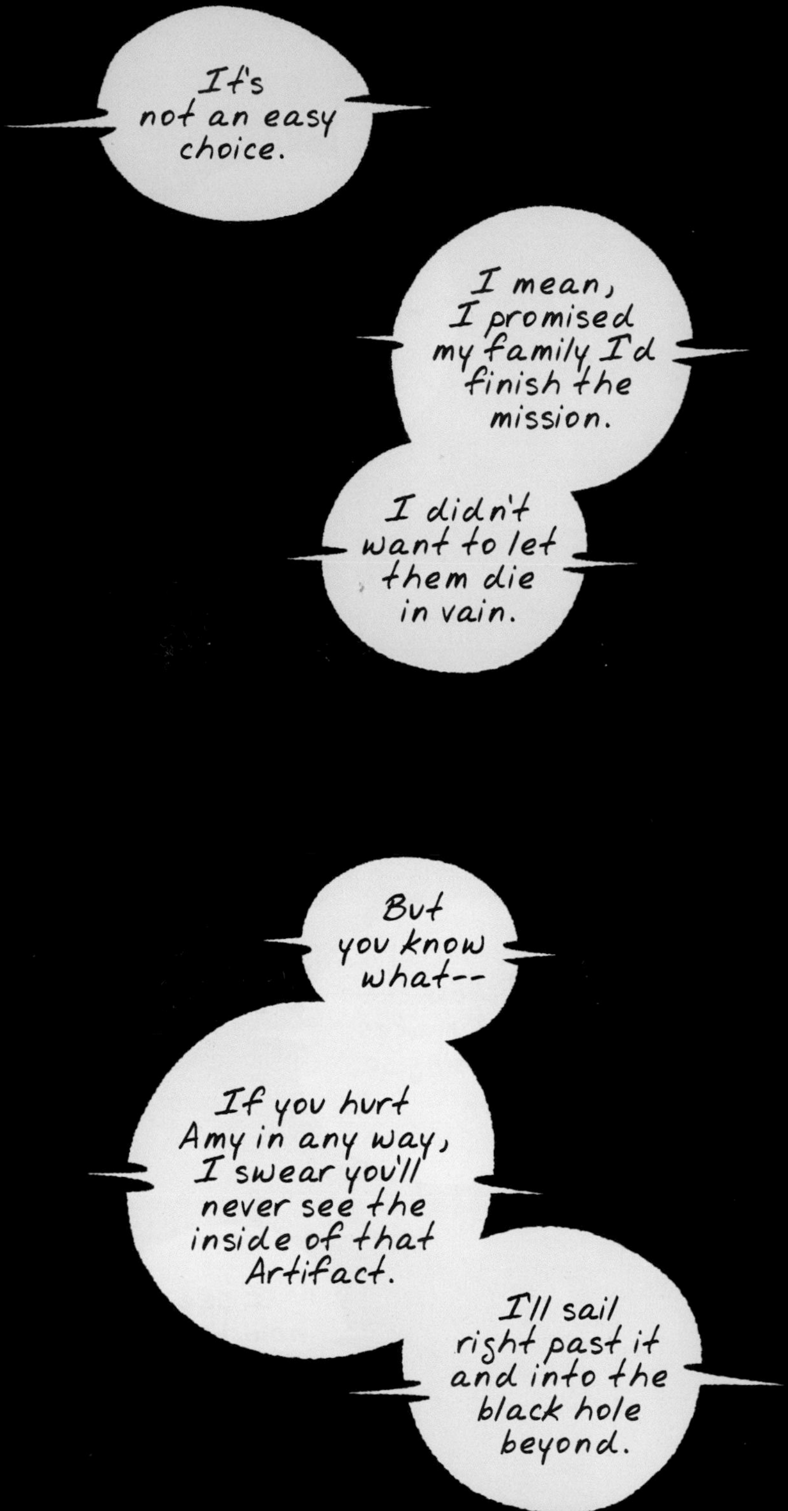
It's not an easy choice.
I mean, I promised my family I'd finish the mission.
I didn't want to let them die in vain.
But you know what--
If you hurt Amy in any way, I swear you'll never see the inside of that Artifact.
I'll sail right past it and into the black hole beyond.

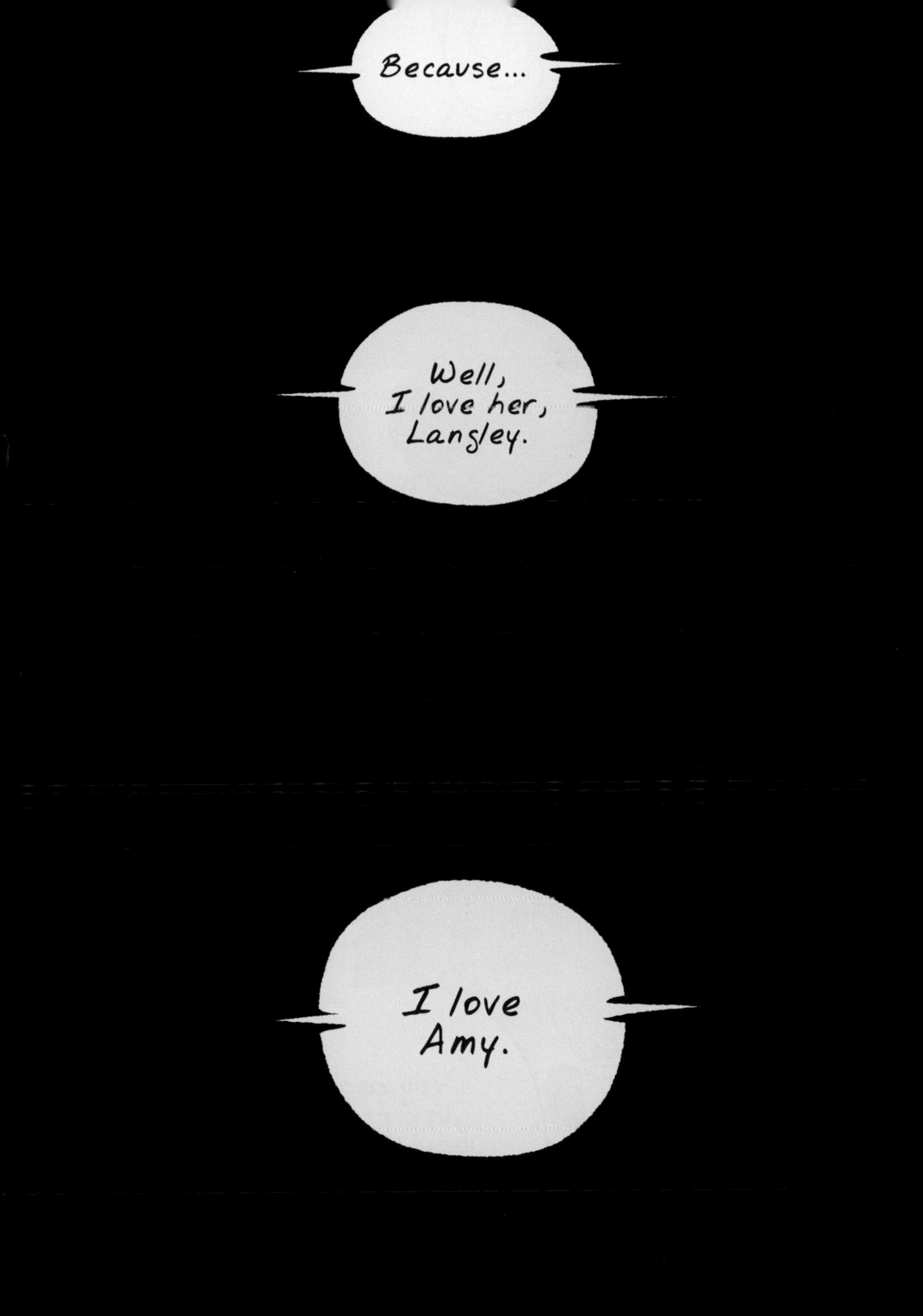
Because...
Well, I love her, Langley.
I love Amy.

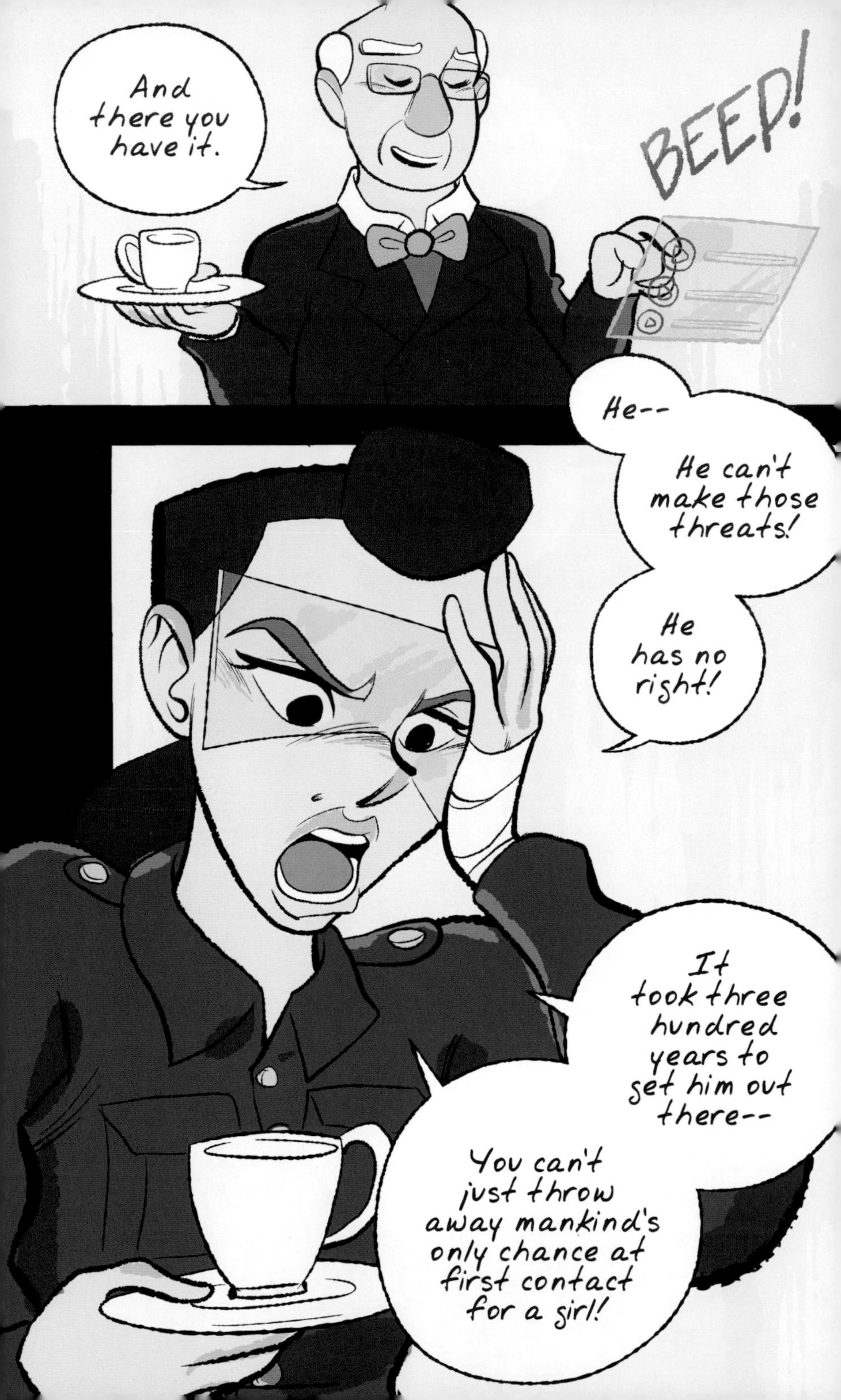
And there you have it.
BEEP!
He--
He can't make those threats!
He has no right!
It took three hundred years to set him out there--
You can't just throw away mankind's only chance at first contact for a girl!

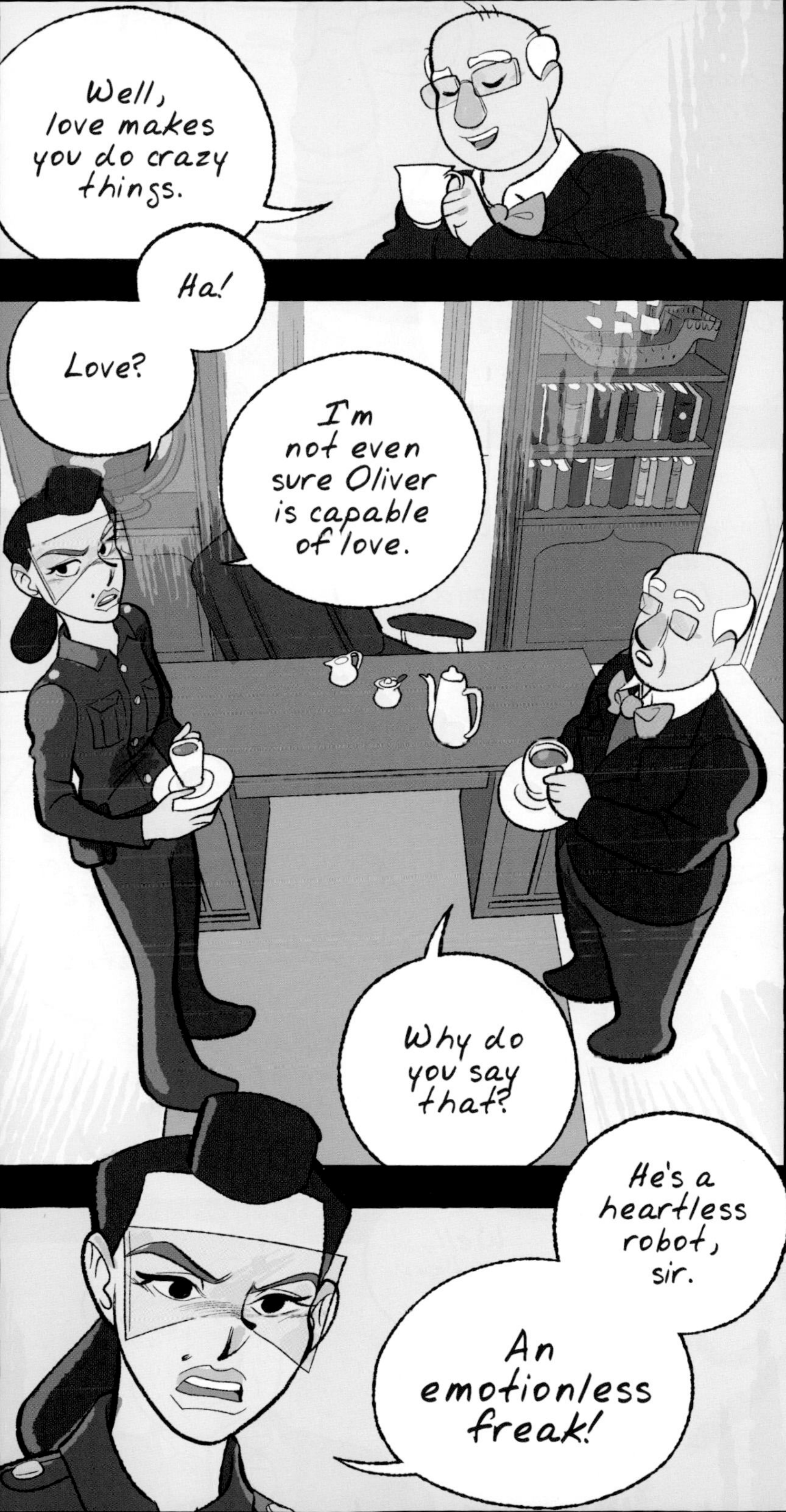

Well, love makes you do crazy things.
Ha!
Love?
I'm not even sure Oliver is capable of love.
Why do you say that?
He's a heartless robot, sir.
An emotionless freak!

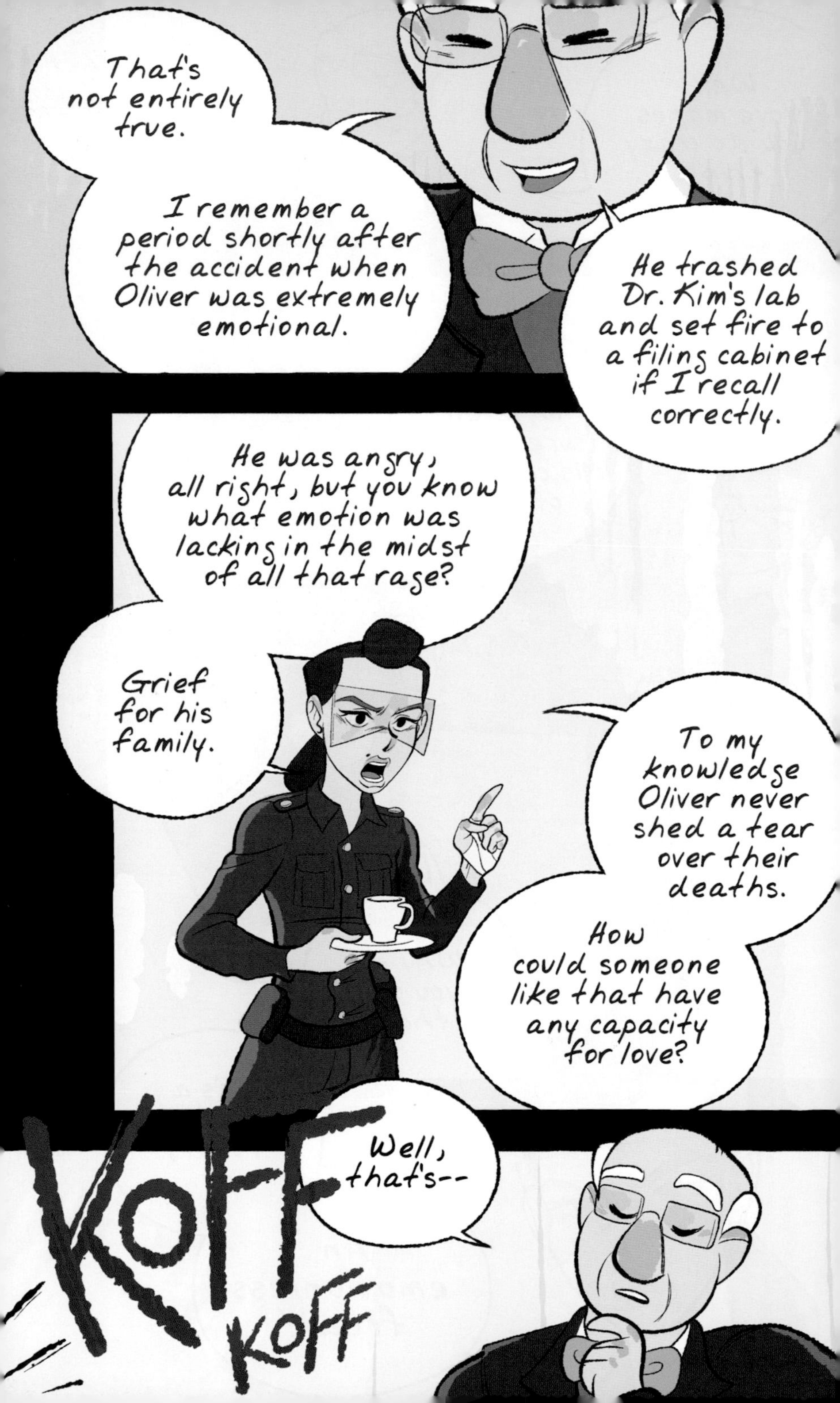
That's not entirely true.
I remember a period shortly after the accident when Oliver was extremely emotional.
He trashed Dr. Kim's lab and set fire to a filing cabinet if I recall correctly.
He was angry, all right, but you know what emotion was lacking in the midst of all that rage?
Grief for his family.
To my knowledge Oliver never shed a tear over their deaths.
How could someone like that have any capacity for love?
Well, that's--
KOFF
KOFF

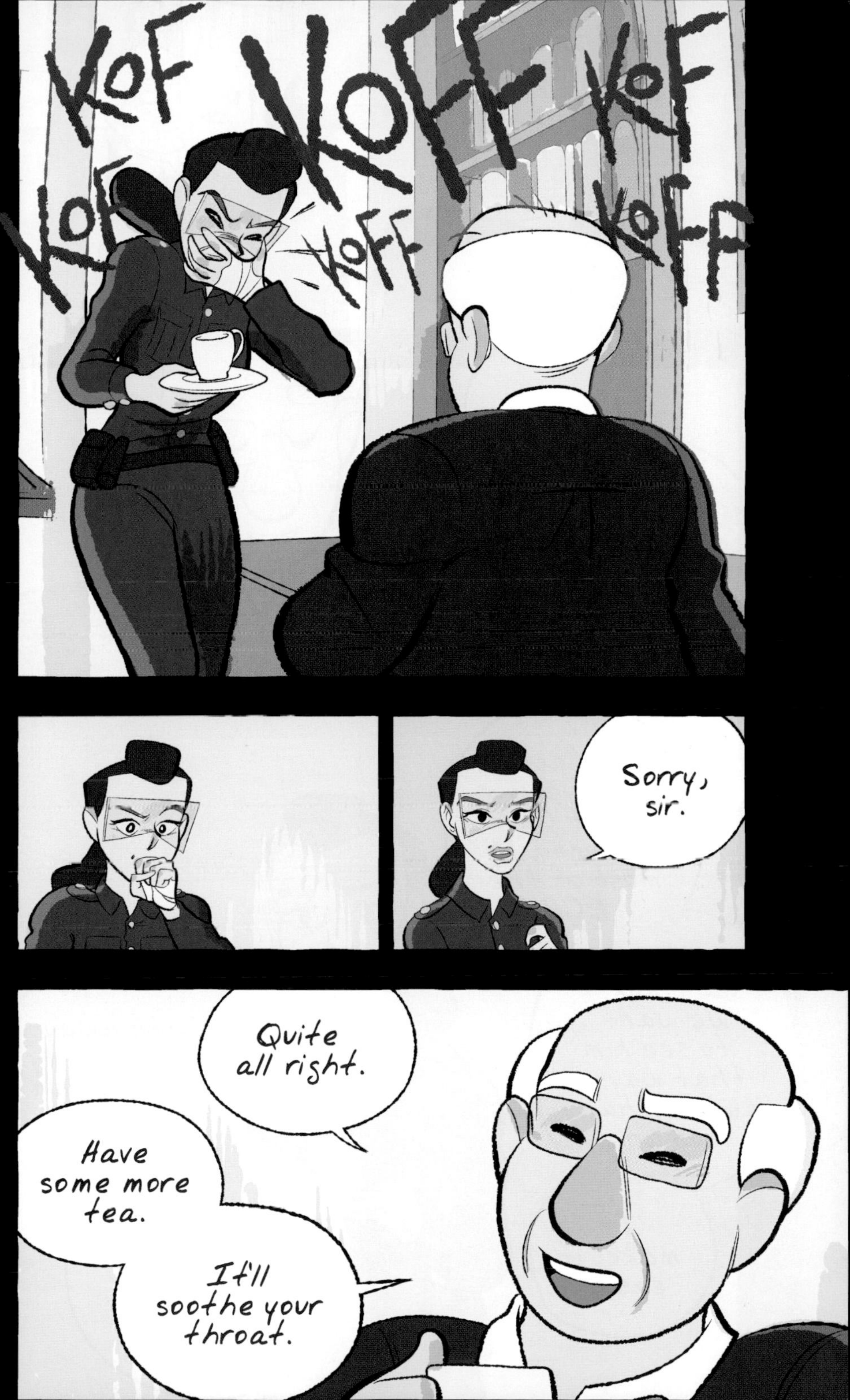
KOF
KOFF
KOF
KOF
KOFF
KOFF
Sorry, sir.
Quite all right.
Have some more tea.
It'll soothe your throat.

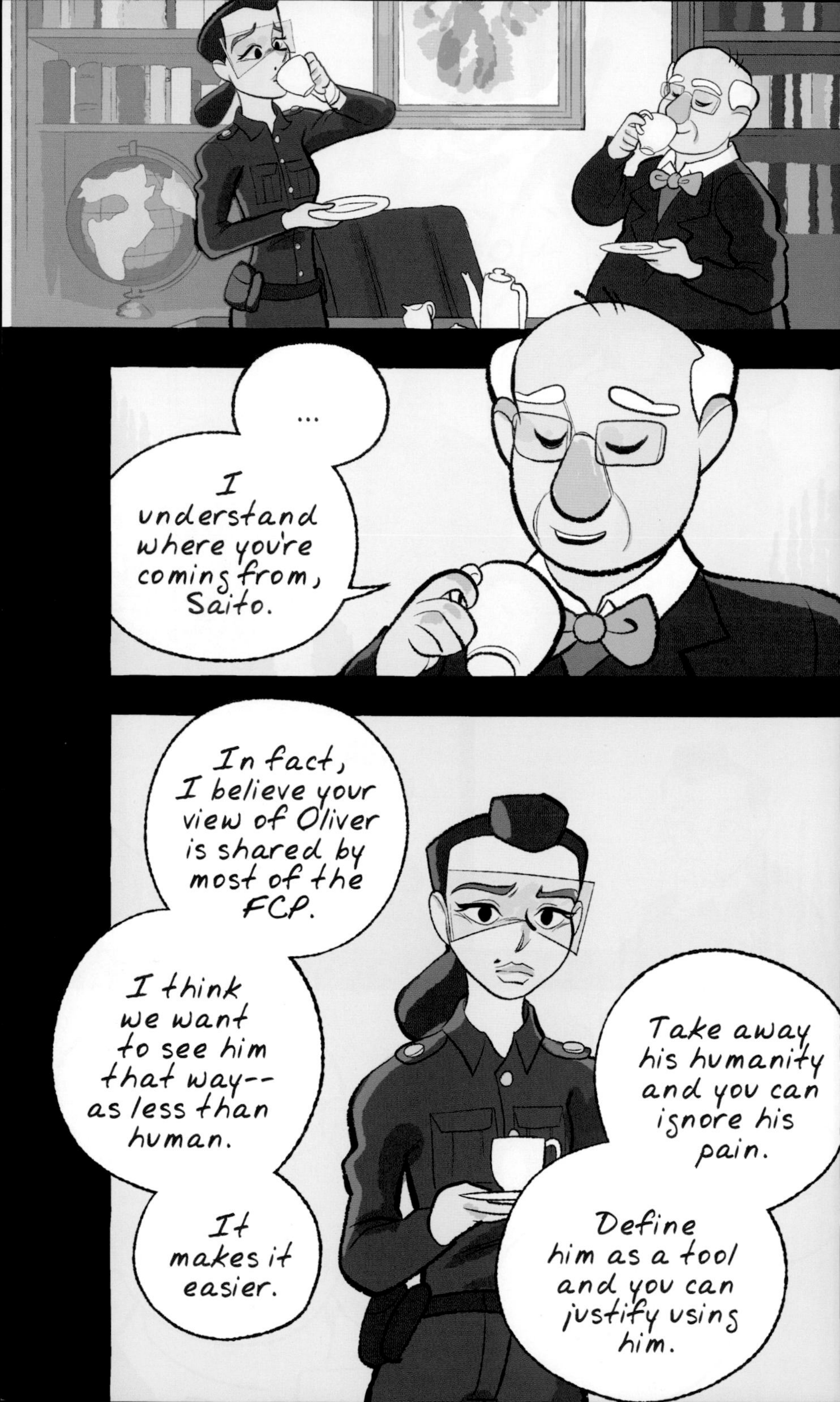
...
I understand where you're coming from, Saito.
In fact, I believe your view of Oliver is shared by most of the FCP.
I think we want to see him that way-- as less than human.
Take away his humanity and you can ignore his pain.
It makes it easier.
Define him as a tool and you can justify using him.

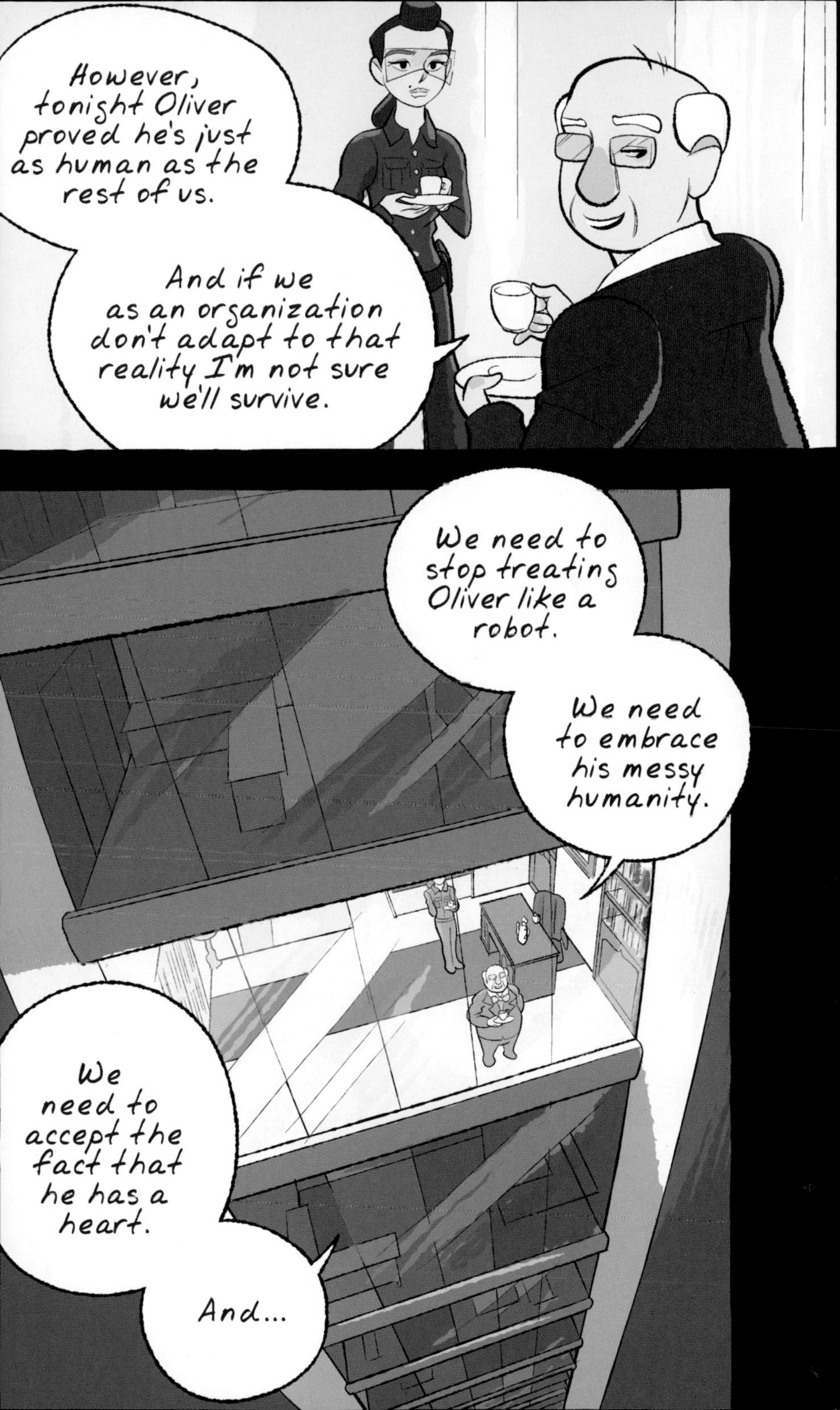
However, tonight Oliver proved he's just as human as the rest of us.
And if we as an organization don't adapt to that reality I'm not sure we'll survive.
We need to stop treating Oliver like a robot.
We need to embrace his messy humanity.
We need to accept the fact that he has a heart.
And...

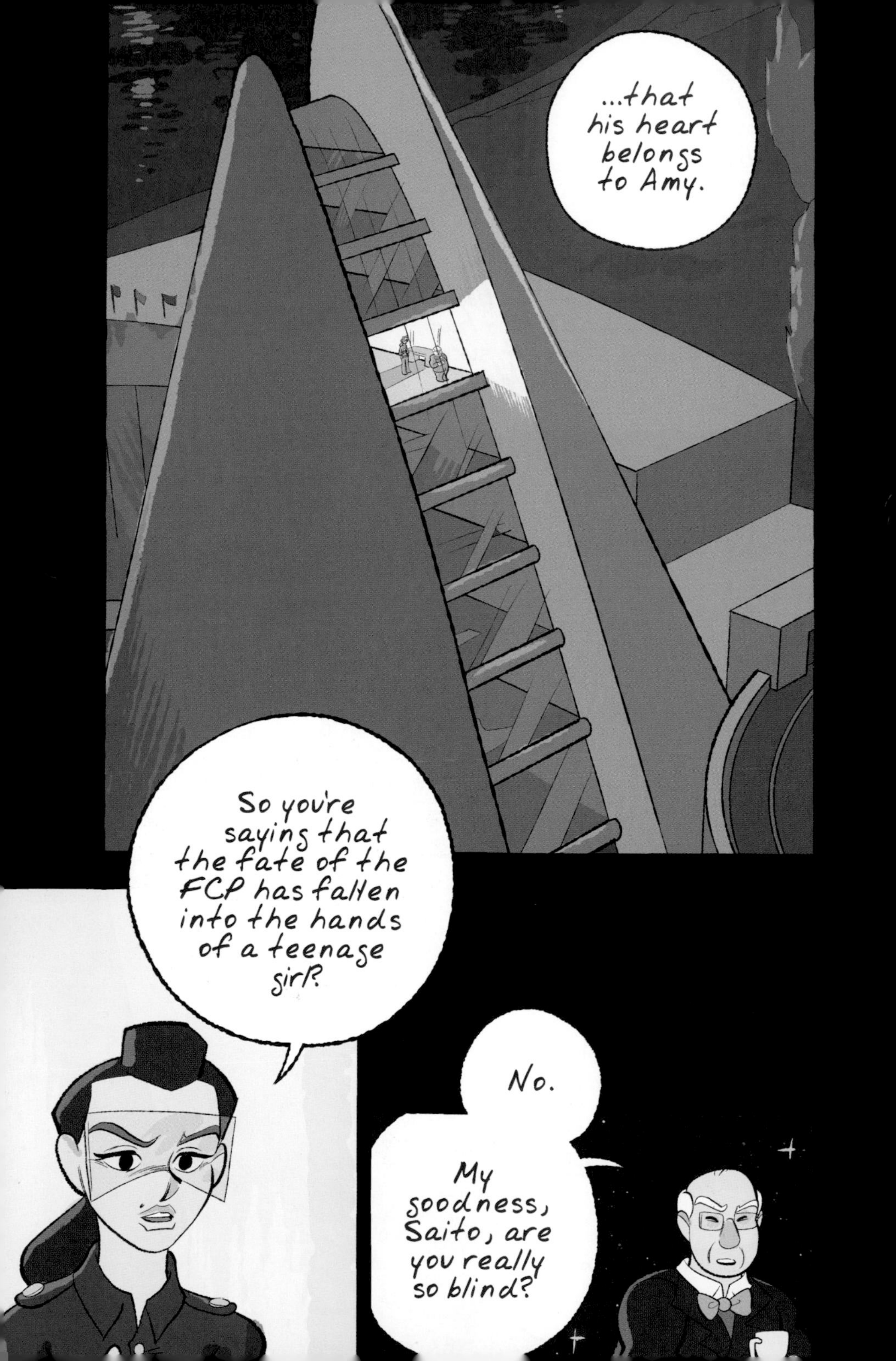
...that his heart belongs to Amy.
So you're saying that the fate of the FCP has fallen into the hands of a teenage girl?
No.
My goodness, Saito, are you really so blind?

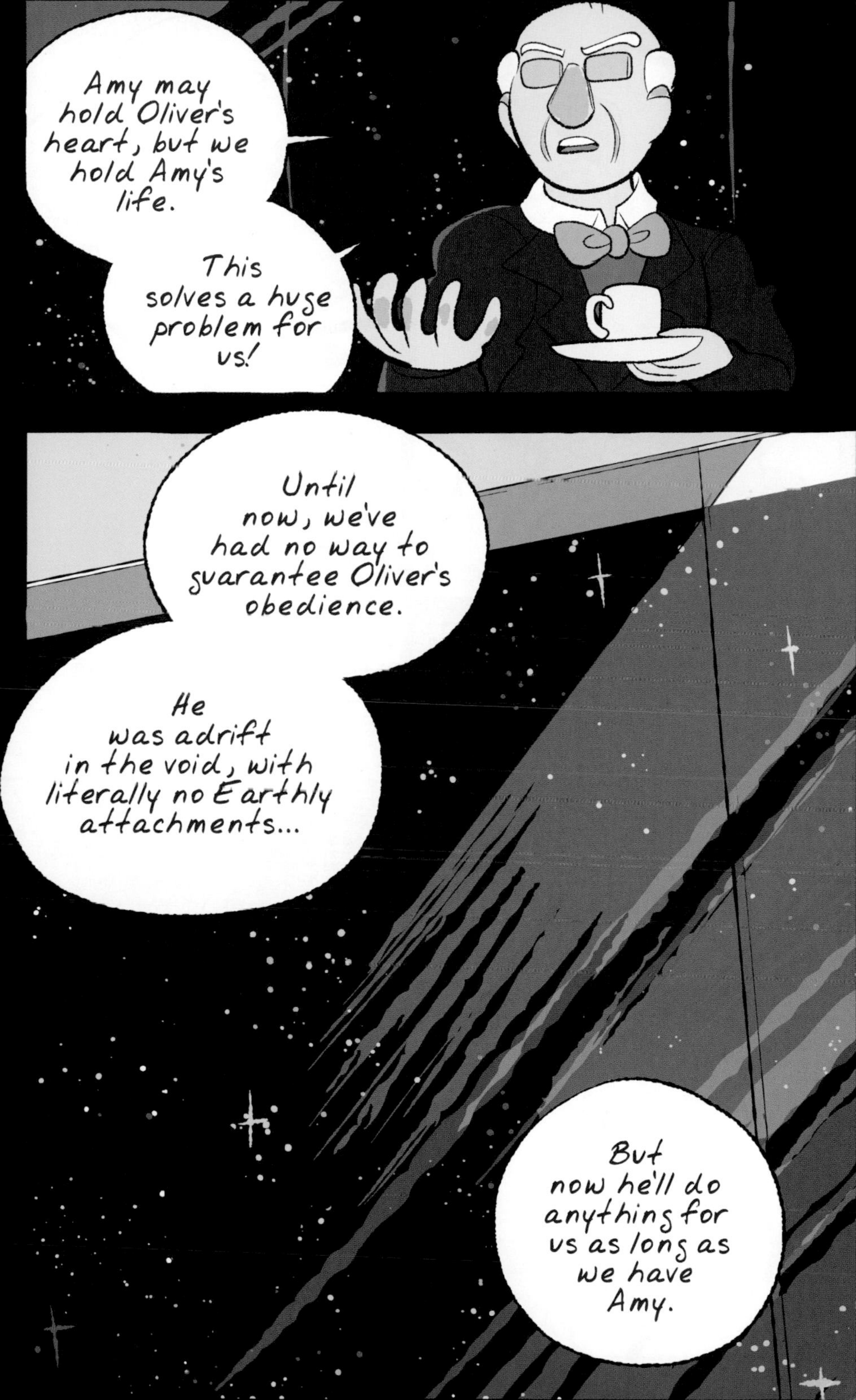
Amy may hold Oliver's heart, but we hold Amy's life.
This solves a huge problem for us!
Until now, we've had no way to guarantee Oliver's obedience.
He was adrift in the void, with literally no Earthly attachments...
But now he'll do anything for us as long as we have Amy.

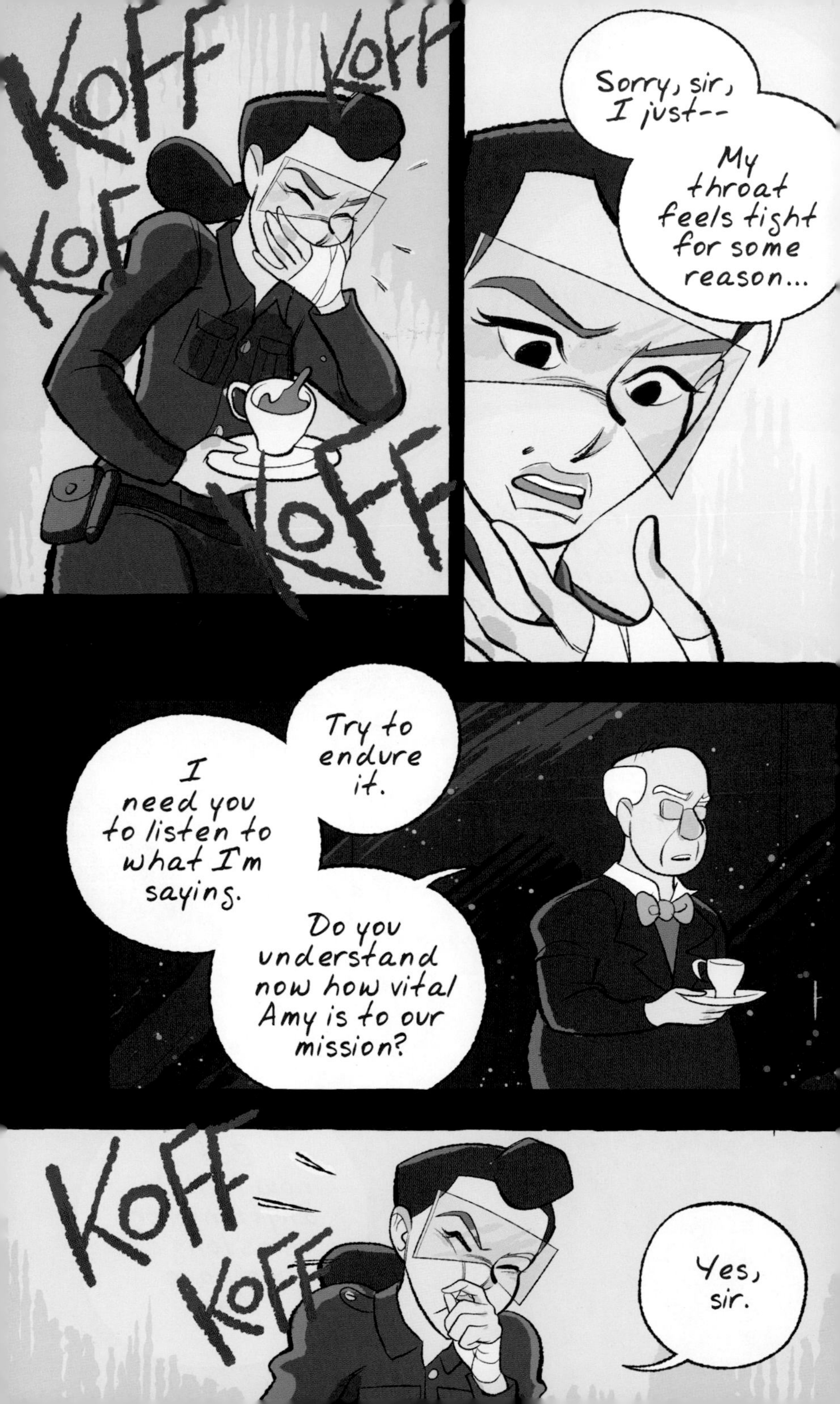
KOFF KOFF KOFF
KOFF
Sorry, sir, I just--
My throat feels tight for some reason...
Try to endure it.
I need you to listen to what I'm saying.
Do you understand now how vital Amy is to our mission?
KOFF KOFF
Yes, sir.

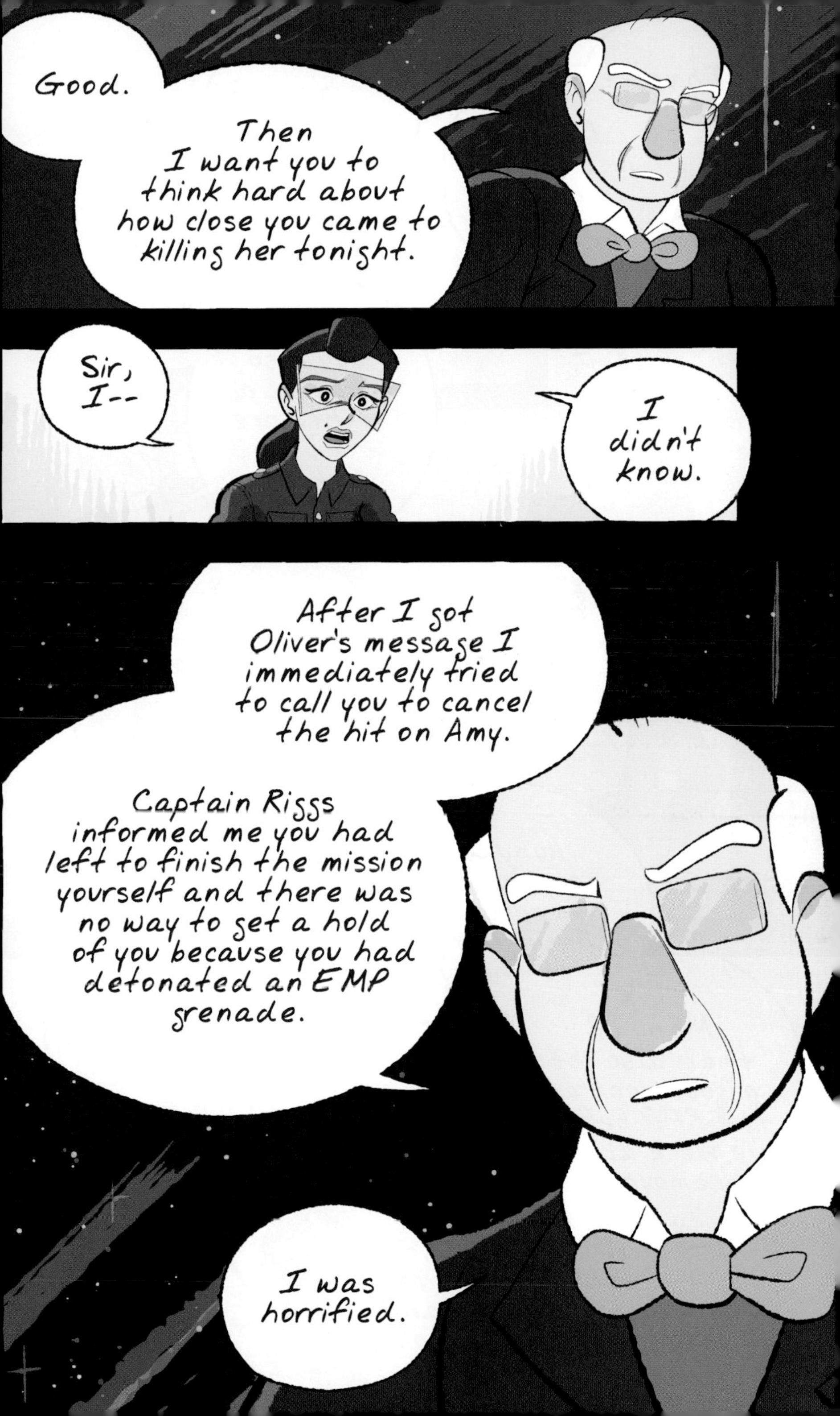
Good.
Then I want you to think hard about how close you came to killing her tonight.
Sir, I--
I didn't know.
After I got Oliver's message I immediately tried to call you to cancel the hit on Amy.
Captain Risss informed me you had left to finish the mission yourself and there was no way to get a hold of you because you had detonated an EMP grenade.
I was horrified.

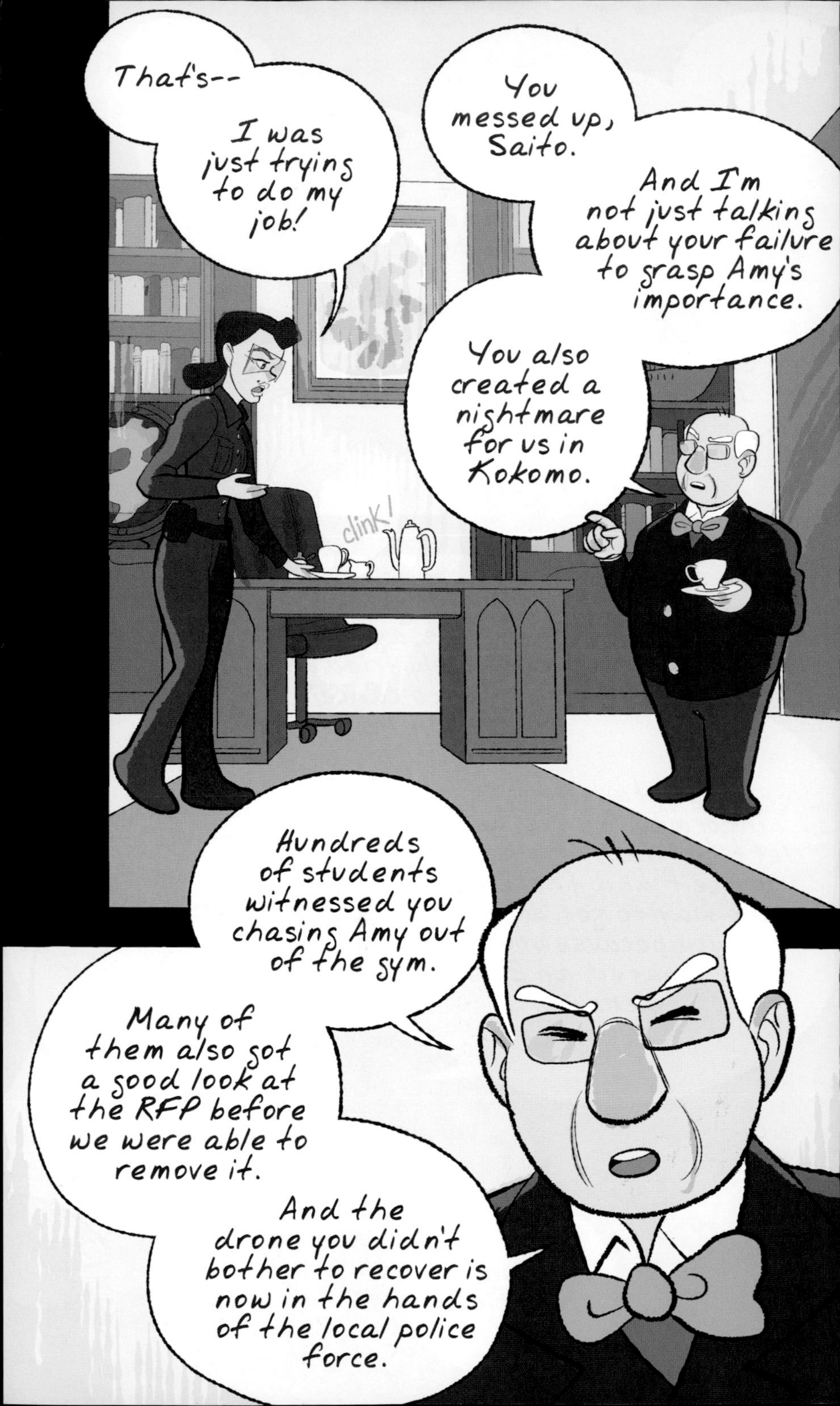

That's--
I was just trying to do my job!
You messed up, Saito.
And I'm not just talking about your failure to grasp Amy's importance.
You also created a nightmare for us in Kokomo.
clink!
Hundreds of students witnessed you chasing Amy out of the gym.
Many of them also got a good look at the RFP before we were able to remove it.
And the drone you didn't bother to recover is now in the hands of the local police force.

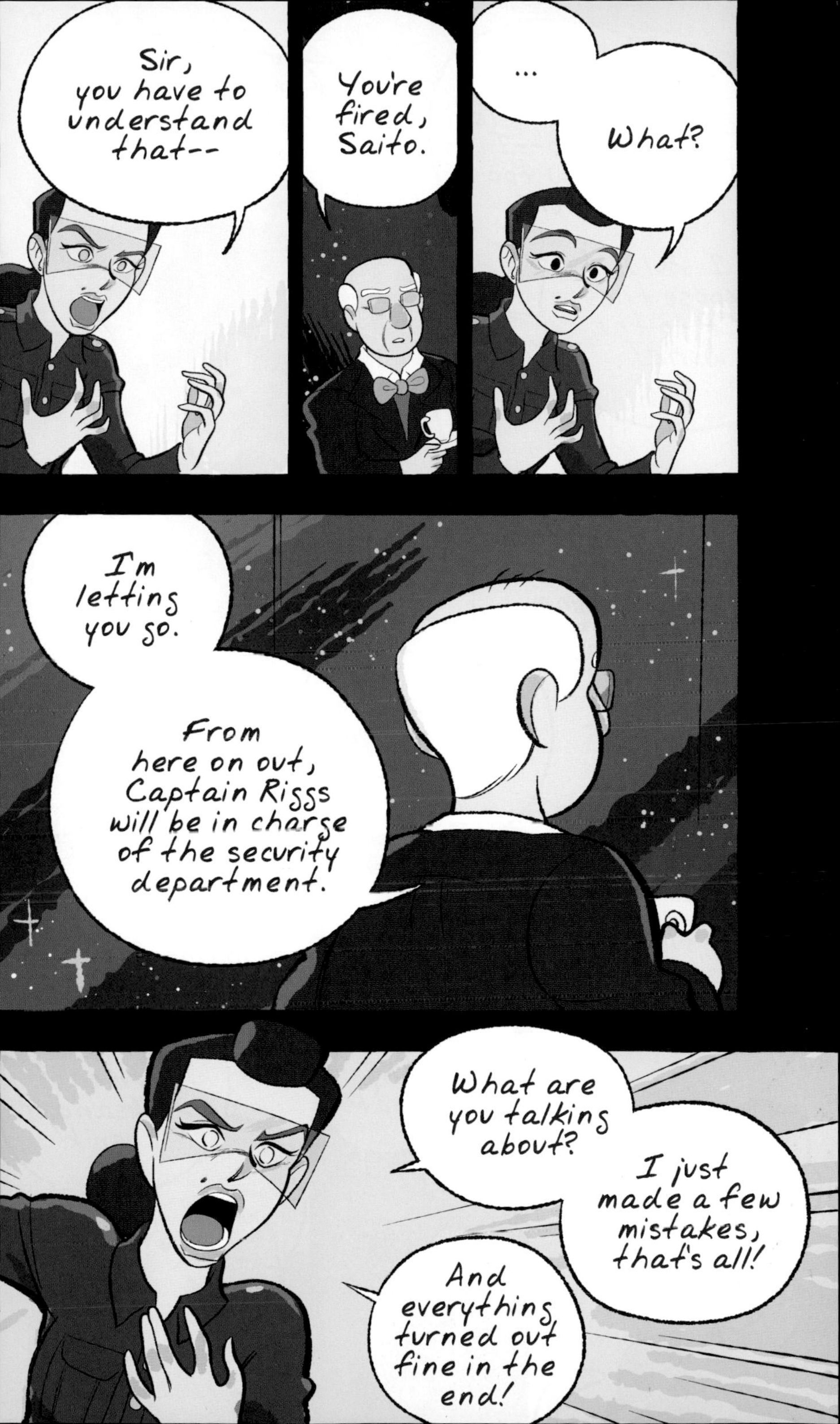

Sir, you have to understand that--
You're fired, Saito.
...
What?
I'm letting you go.
From here on out, Captain Riggs will be in charge of the security department.
What are you talking about?
I just made a few mistakes, that's all!
And everything turned out fine in the end!

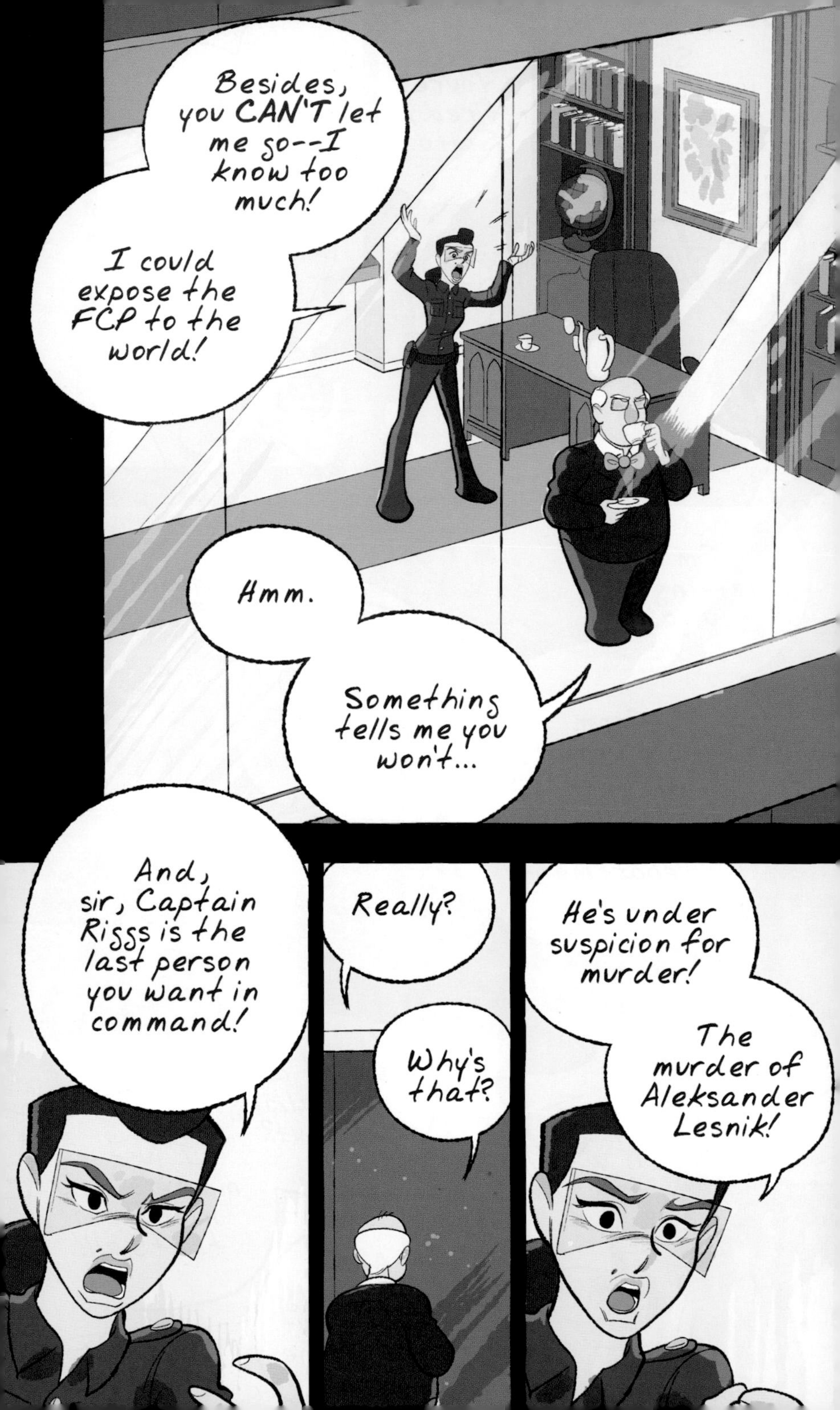
Besides, you CAN'T let me go--I know too much!
I could expose the FCP to the world!
Hmm.
Something tells me you won't...
And, sir, Captain Riggs is the last person you want in command!
Really?
Why's that?
He's under suspicion for murder!
The murder of Aleksander Lesnik!

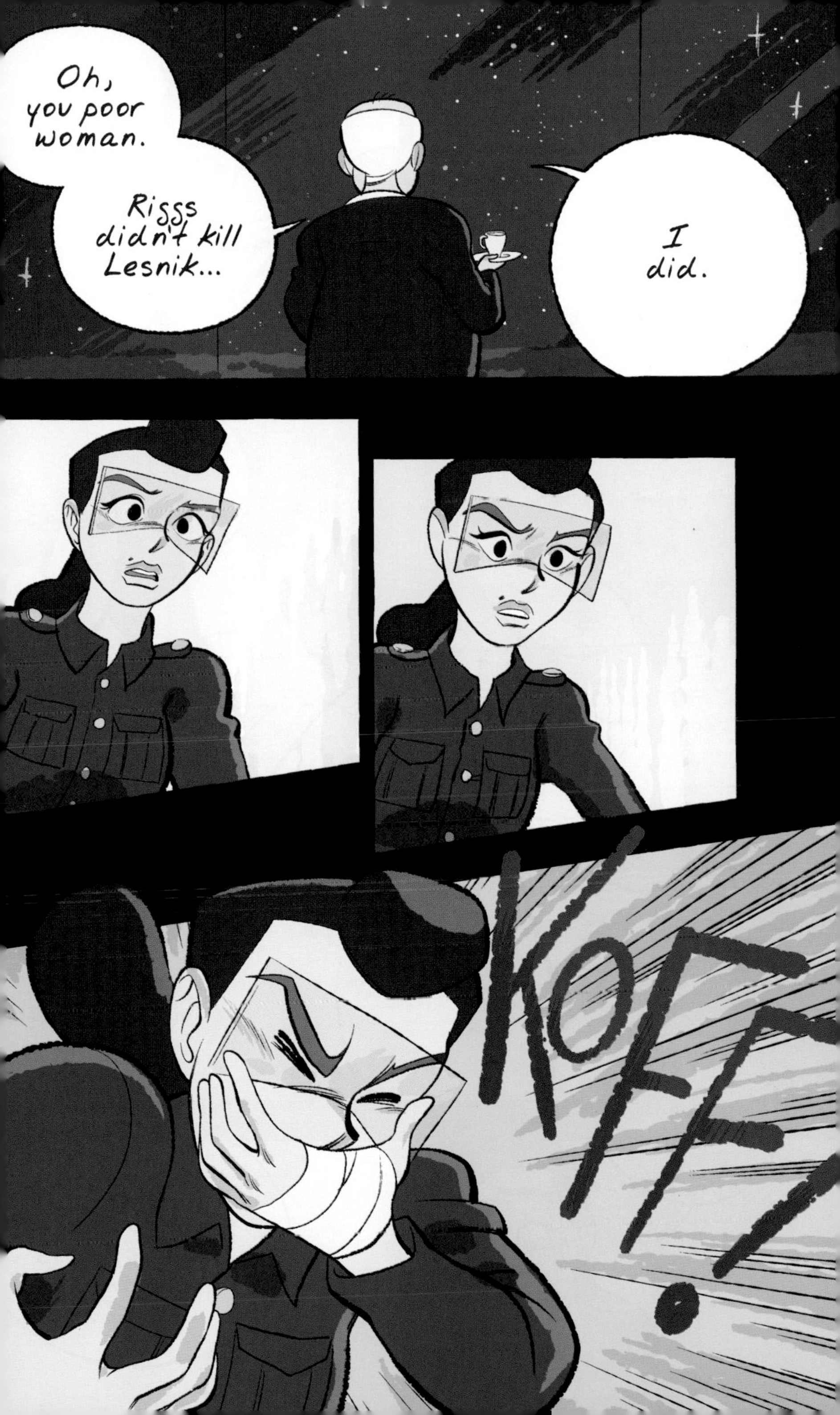
Oh, you poor woman.
Risss didn't kill Lesnik...
I did.
KOFF!

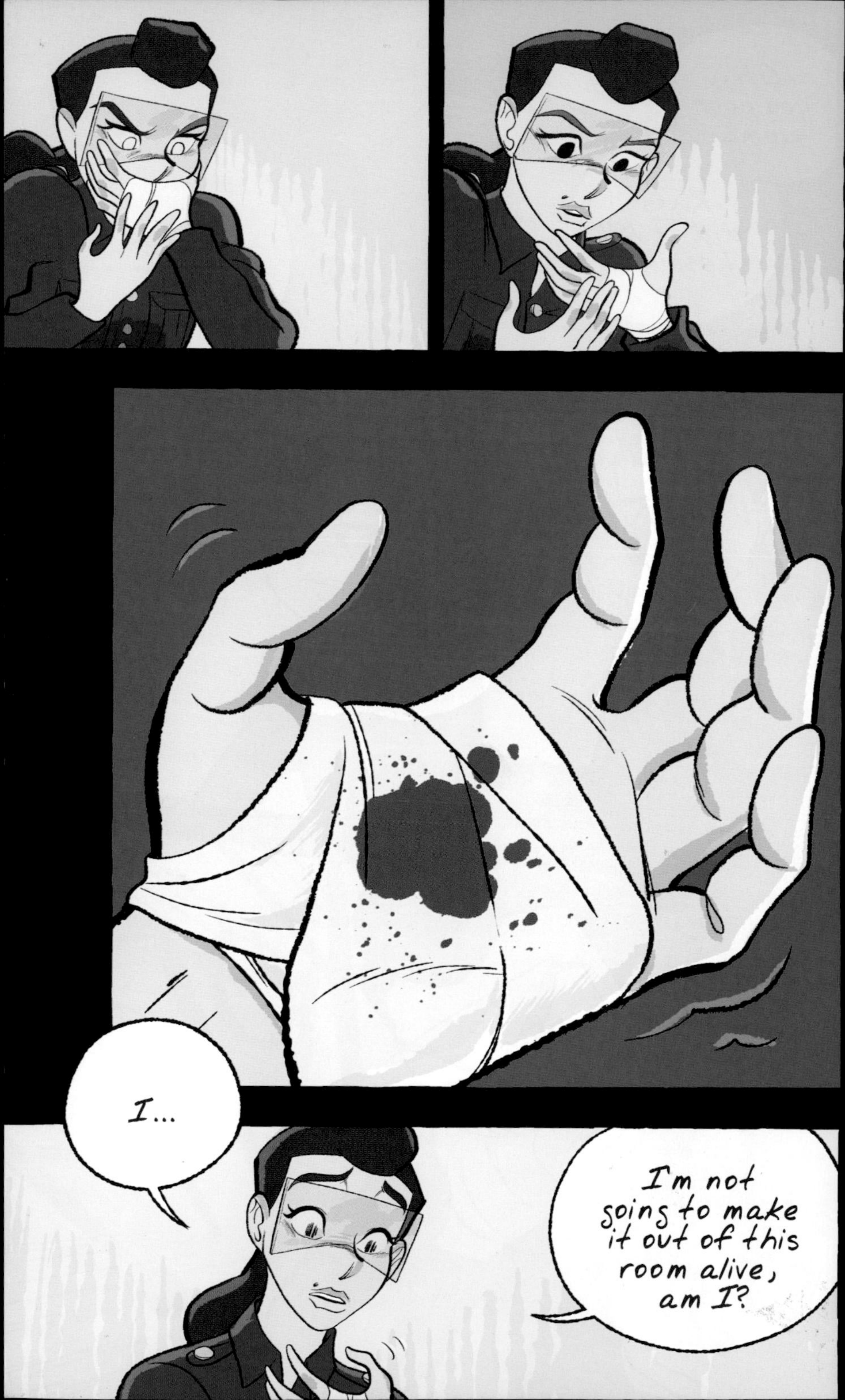
I...
I'm not going to make it out of this room alive, am I?

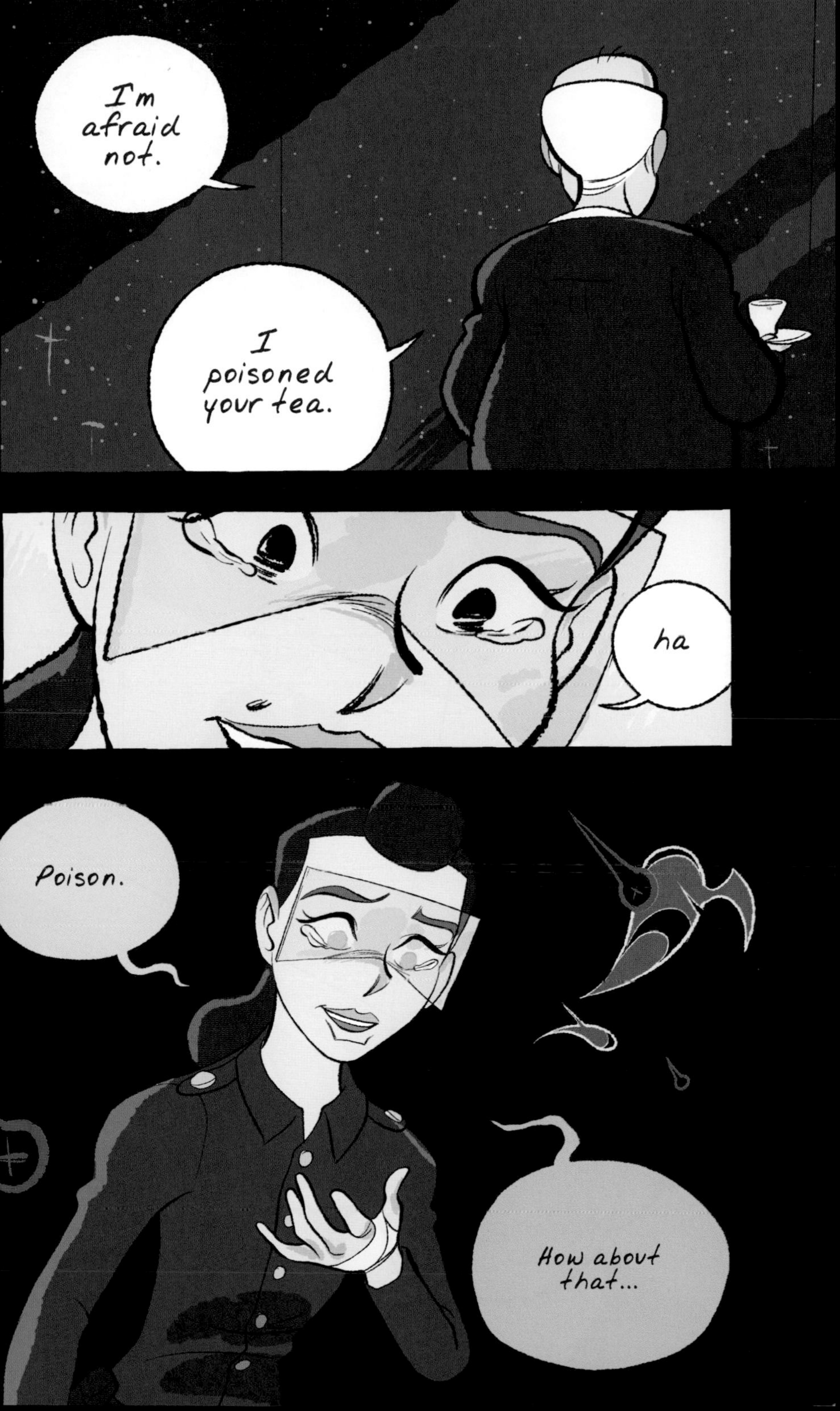
I'm afraid not.
I poisoned your tea.
ha
Poison.
How about that...

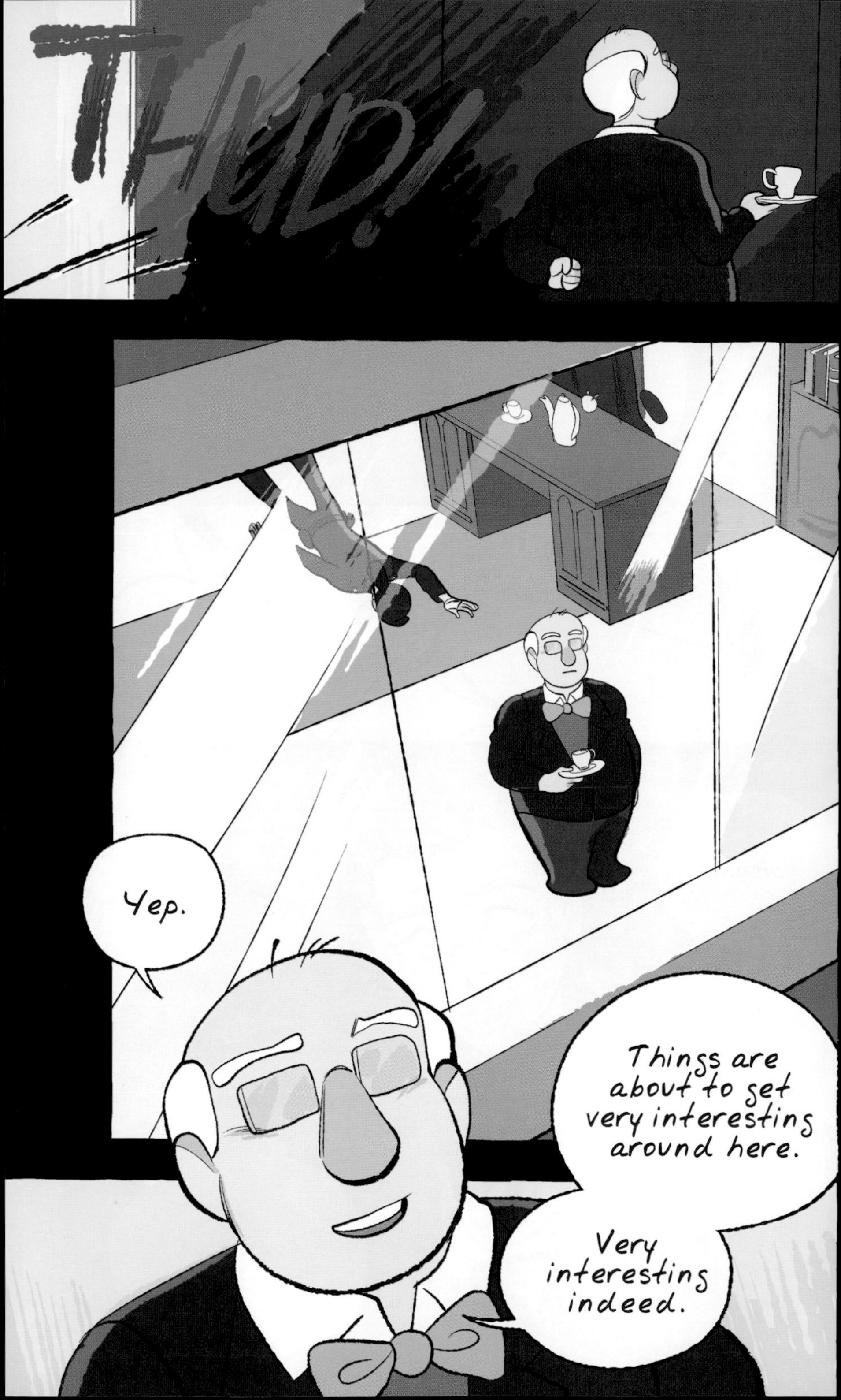
THUD!
Yep.
Things are about to get very interesting around here.
Very interesting indeed.

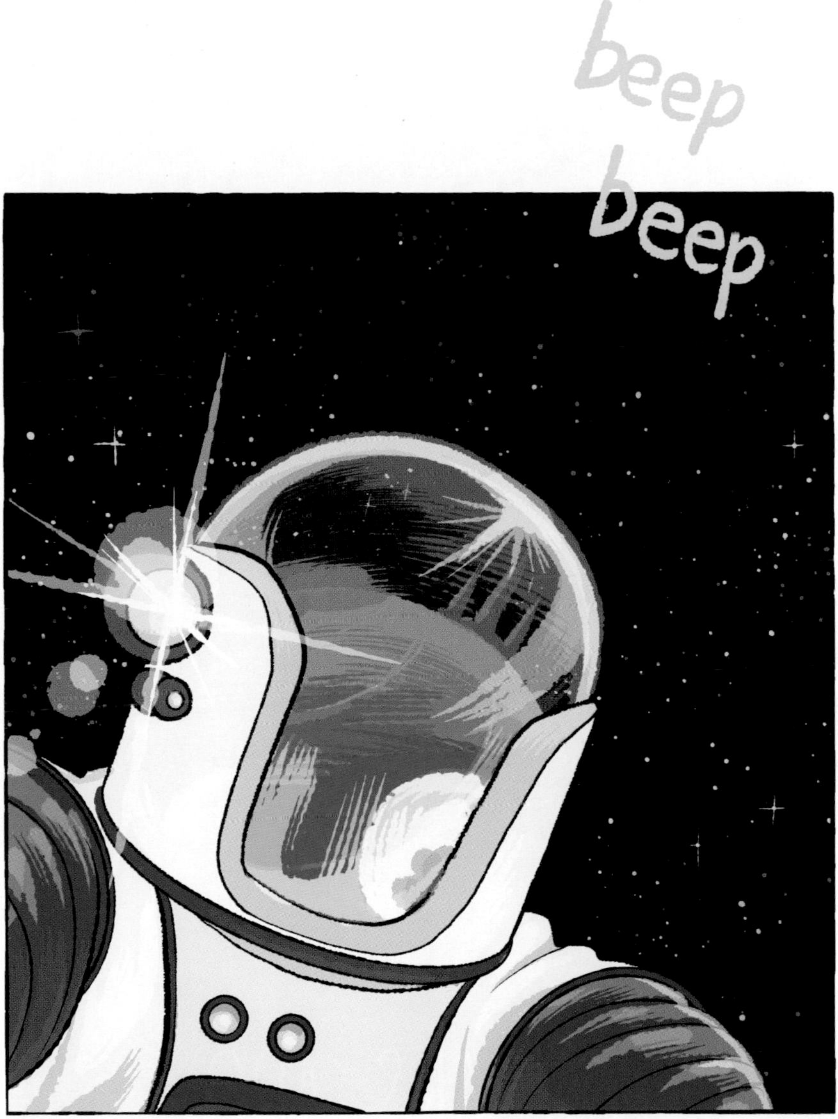
beep
beep

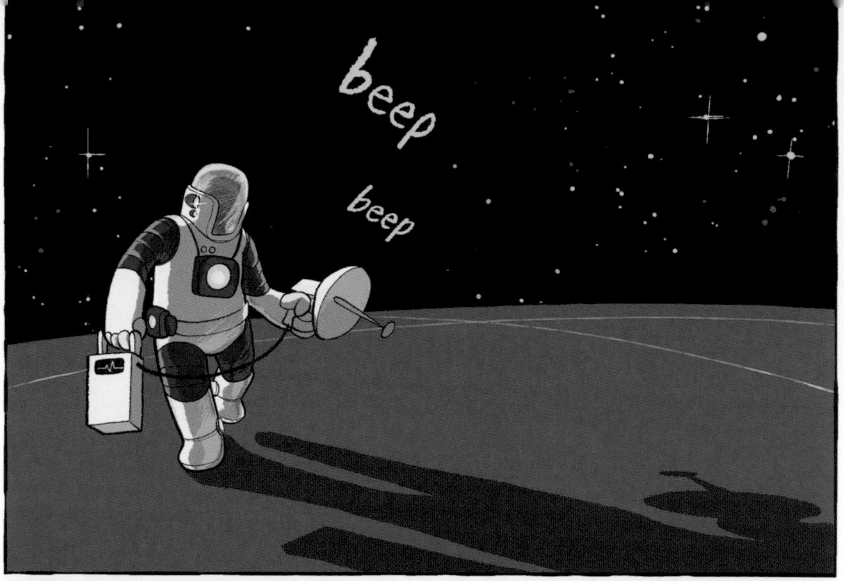
beep
beep

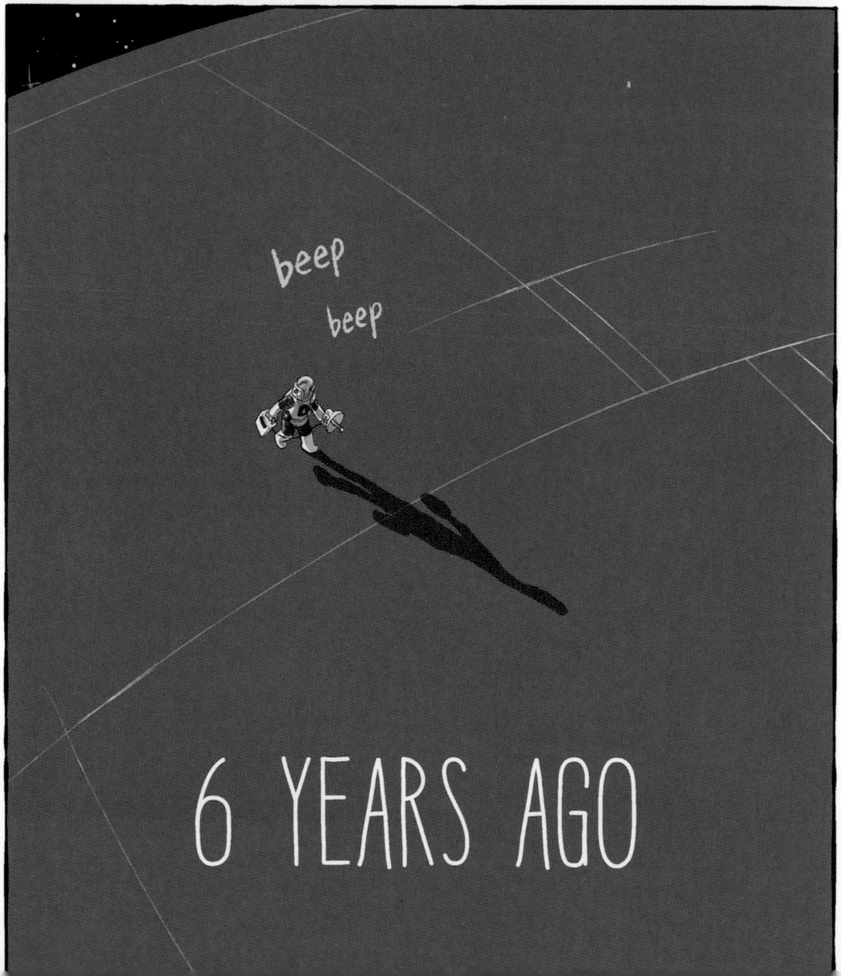
beep
beep
6 YEARS AGO

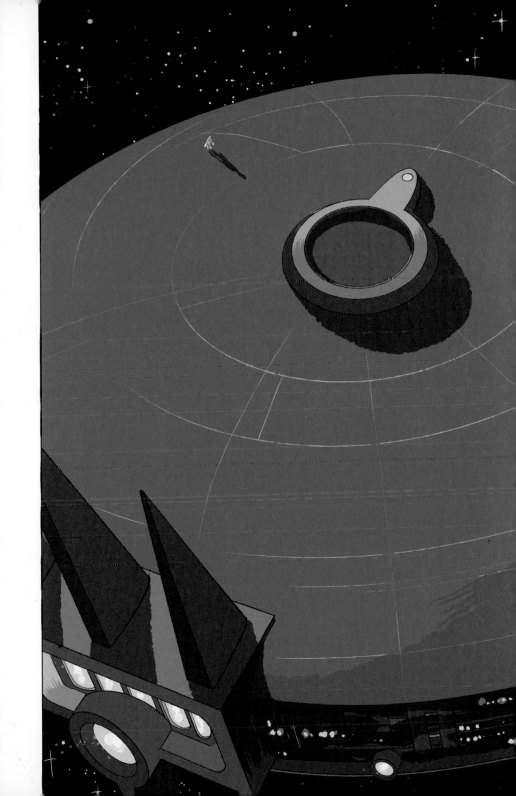

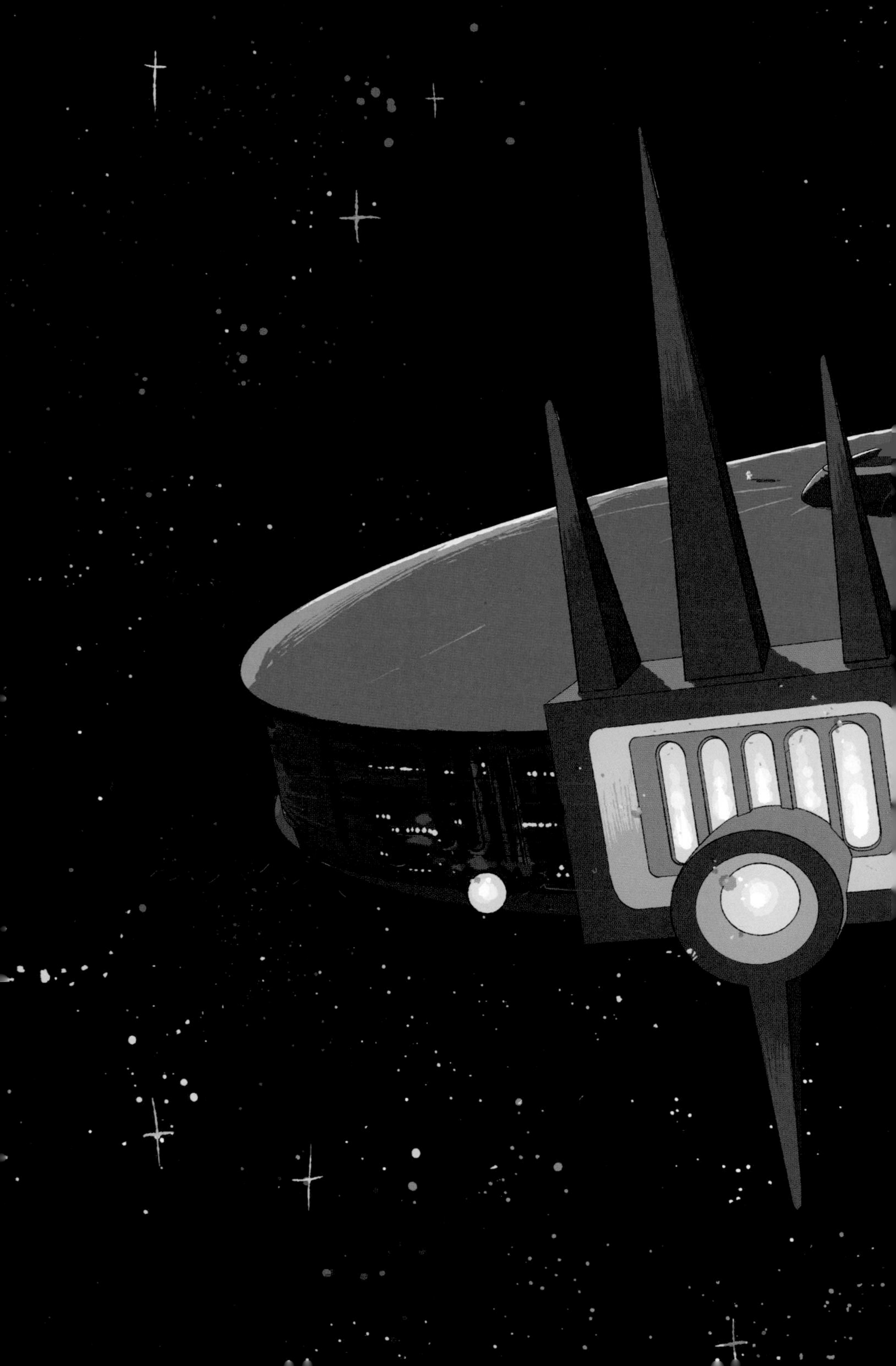

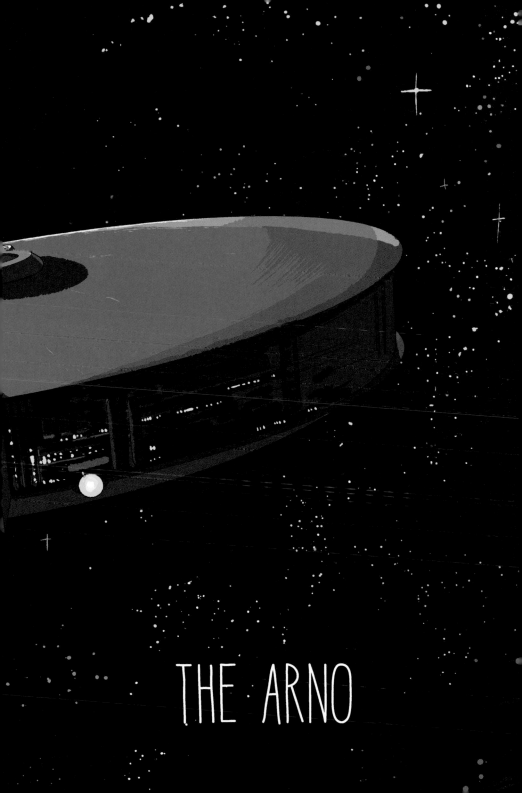

THE ARNO

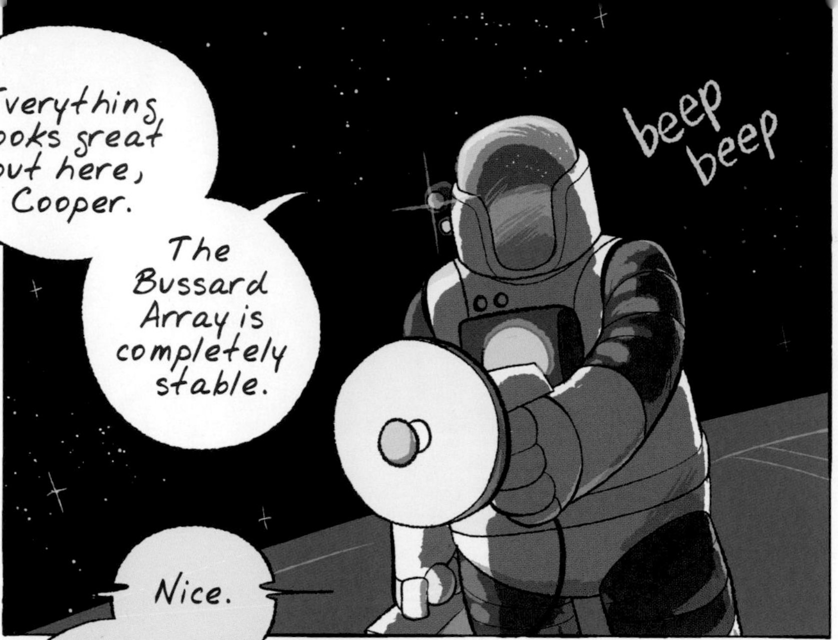
Everythinց looks ցreat out here, Cooper.
The Bussard Array is completely stable.
beep beep
Nice.

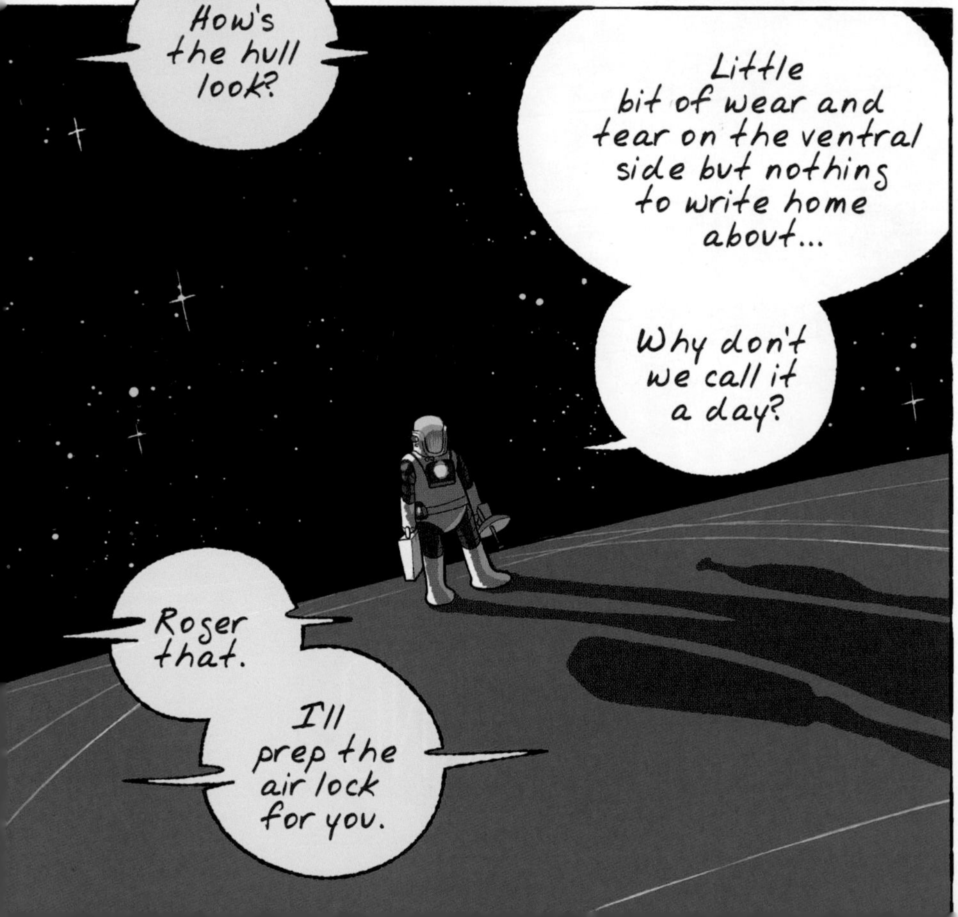
How's the hull look?
Little bit of wear and tear on the ventral side but nothinց to write home about...
Why don't we call it a day?
Roger that.
I'll prep the air lock for you.

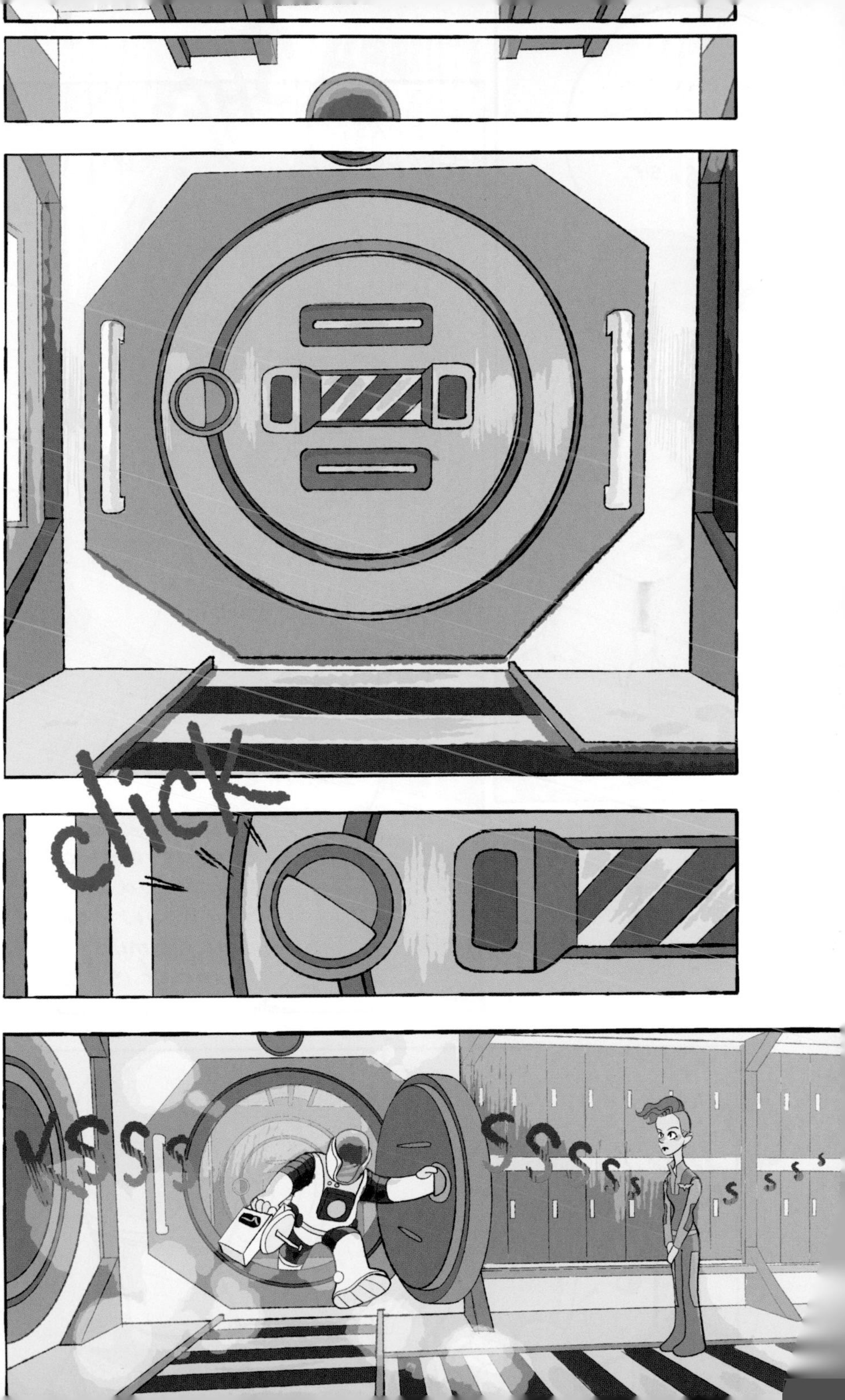
click

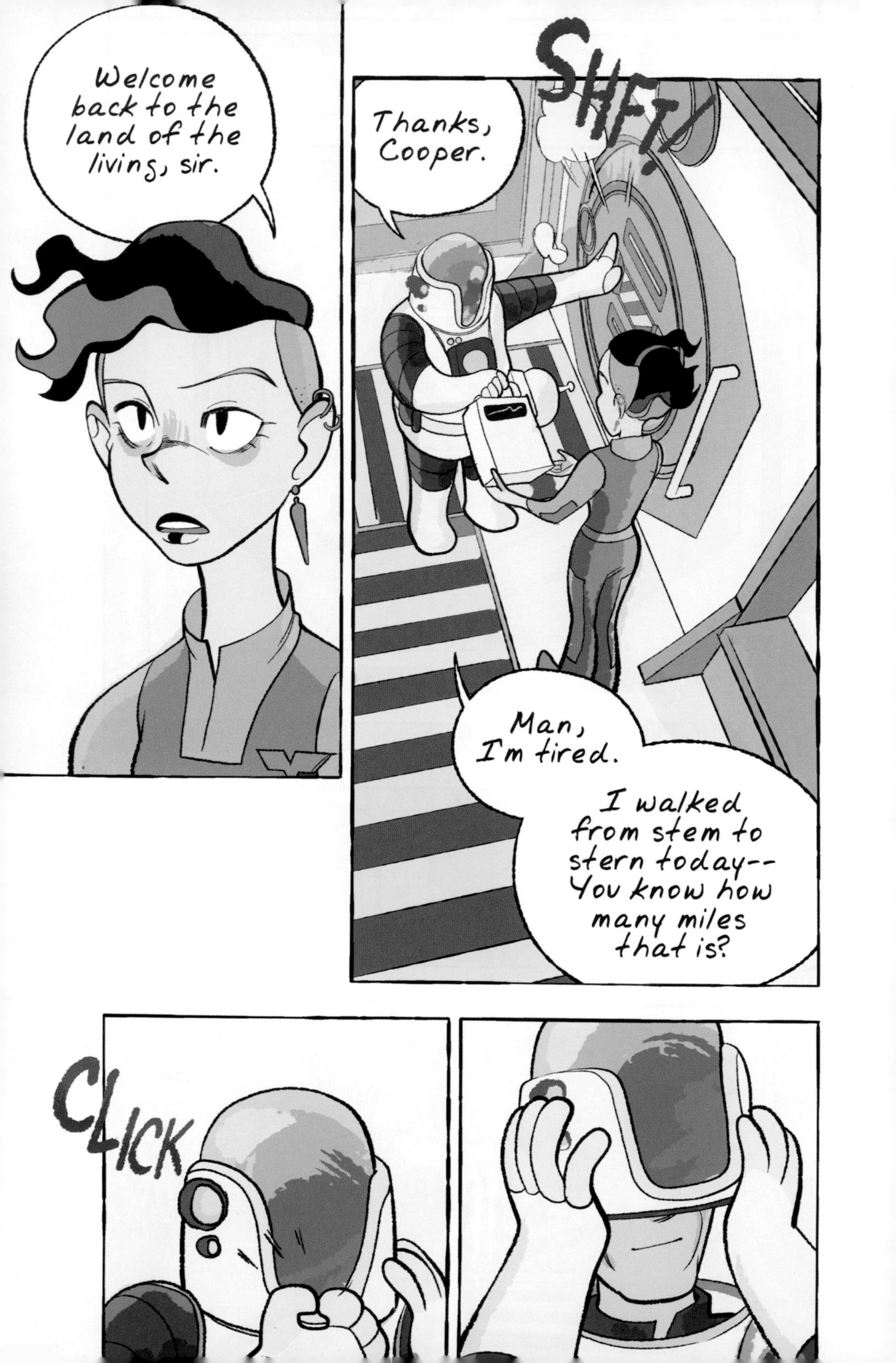
Welcome back to the land of the living, sir.
SHFT!
Thanks, Cooper.
Man, I'm tired.
I walked from stem to stern today-- You know how many miles that is?
CLICK

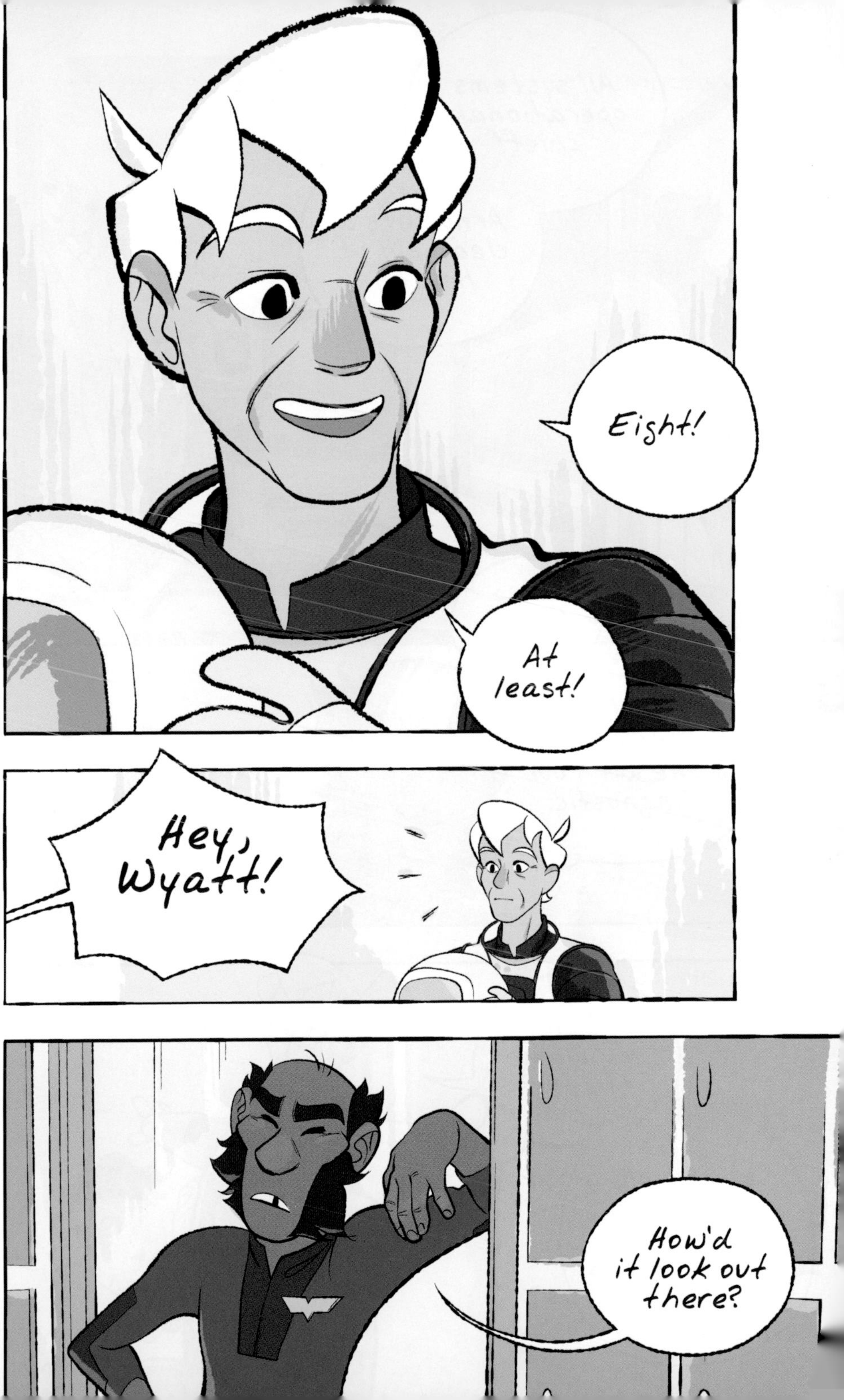

Eight!
At least!
Hey, Wyatt!
How'd it look out there?

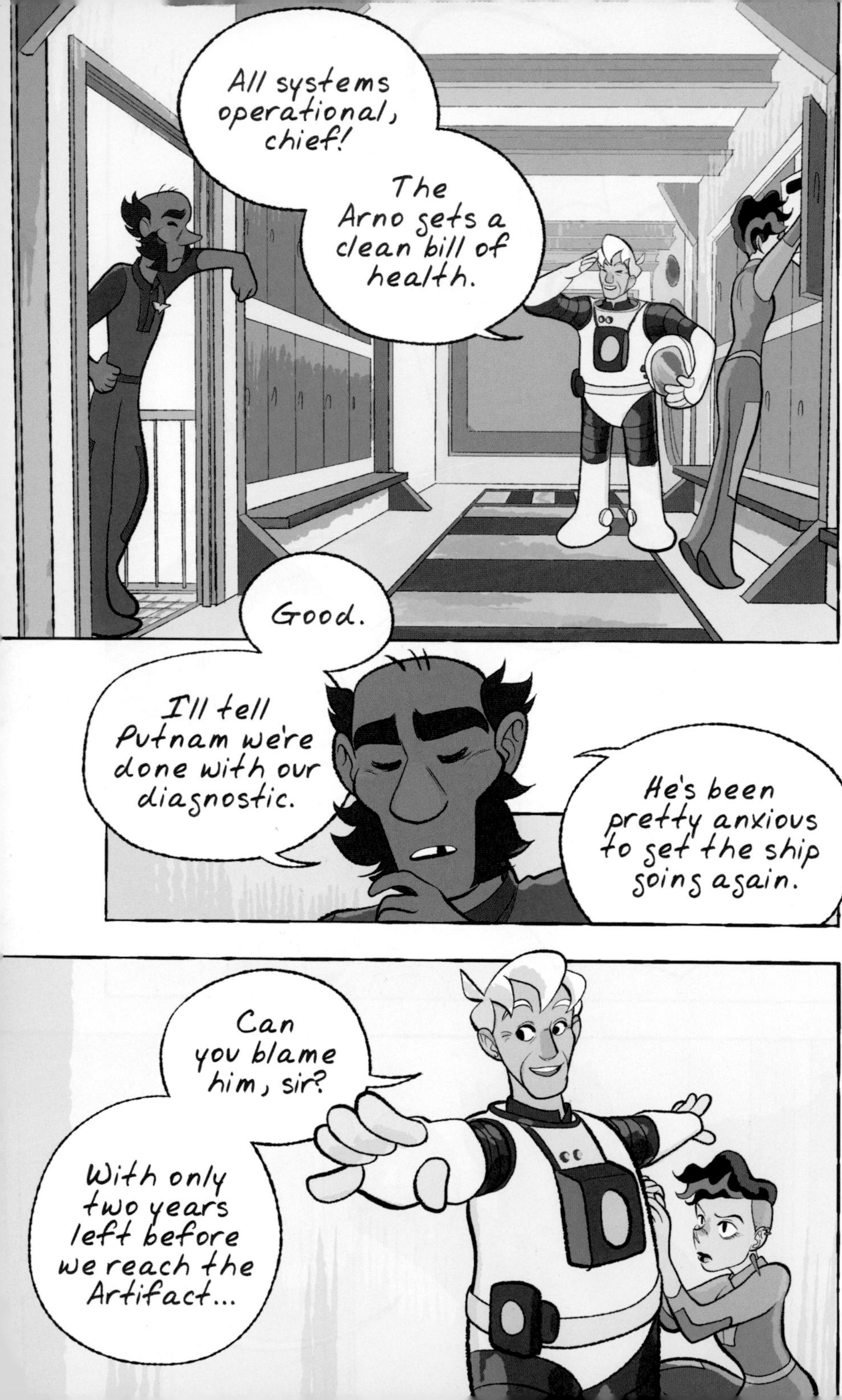
All systems operational, chief!
The Arno gets a clean bill of health.
Good.
I'll tell Putnam we're done with our diagnostic.
He's been pretty anxious to get the ship going again.
Can you blame him, sir?
With only two years left before we reach the Artifact...

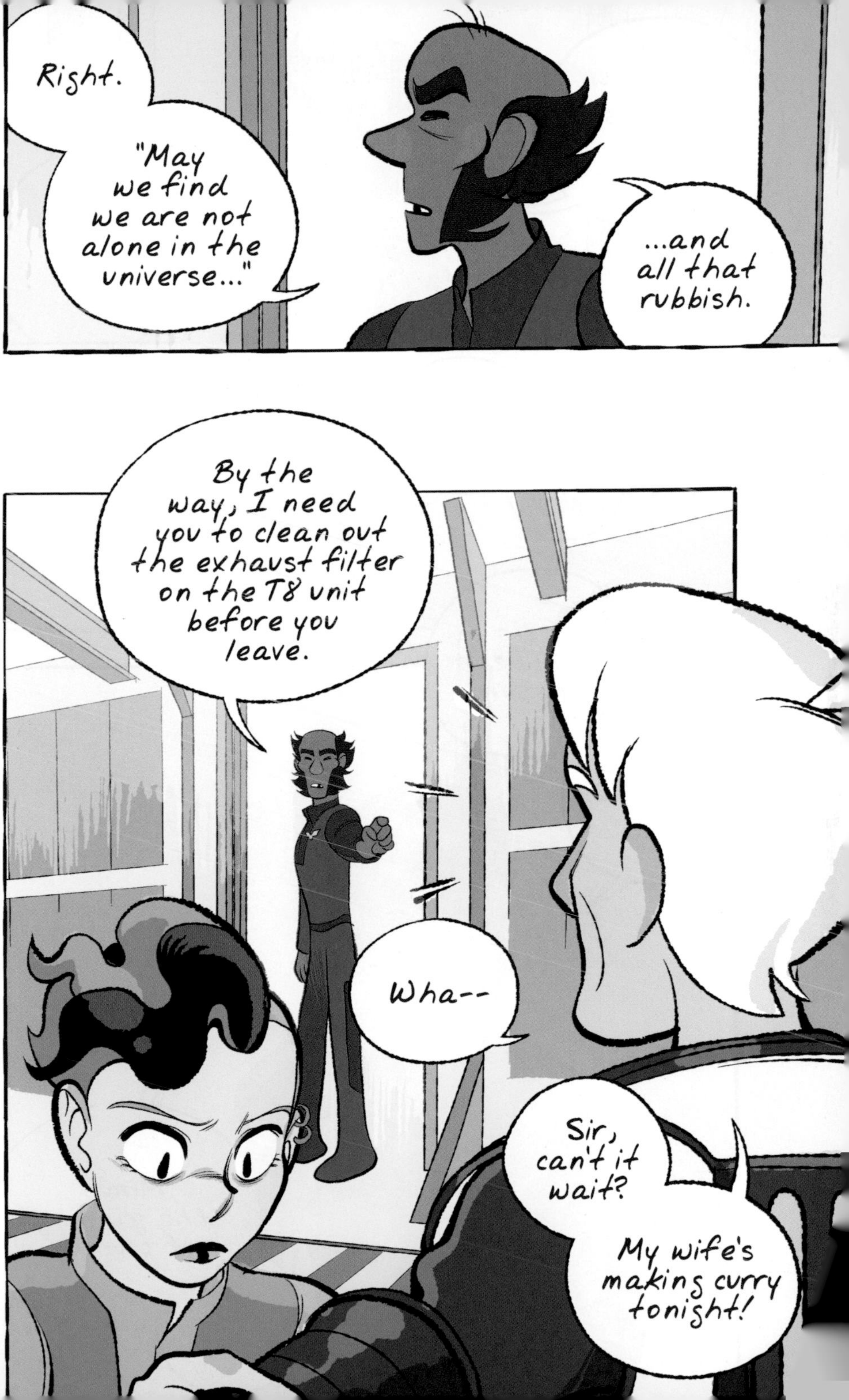
Right.
"May we find we are not alone in the universe..."
...and all that rubbish.
By the way, I need you to clean out the exhaust filter on the T8 unit before you leave.
Wha--
Sir, can't it wait?
My wife's making curry tonight!

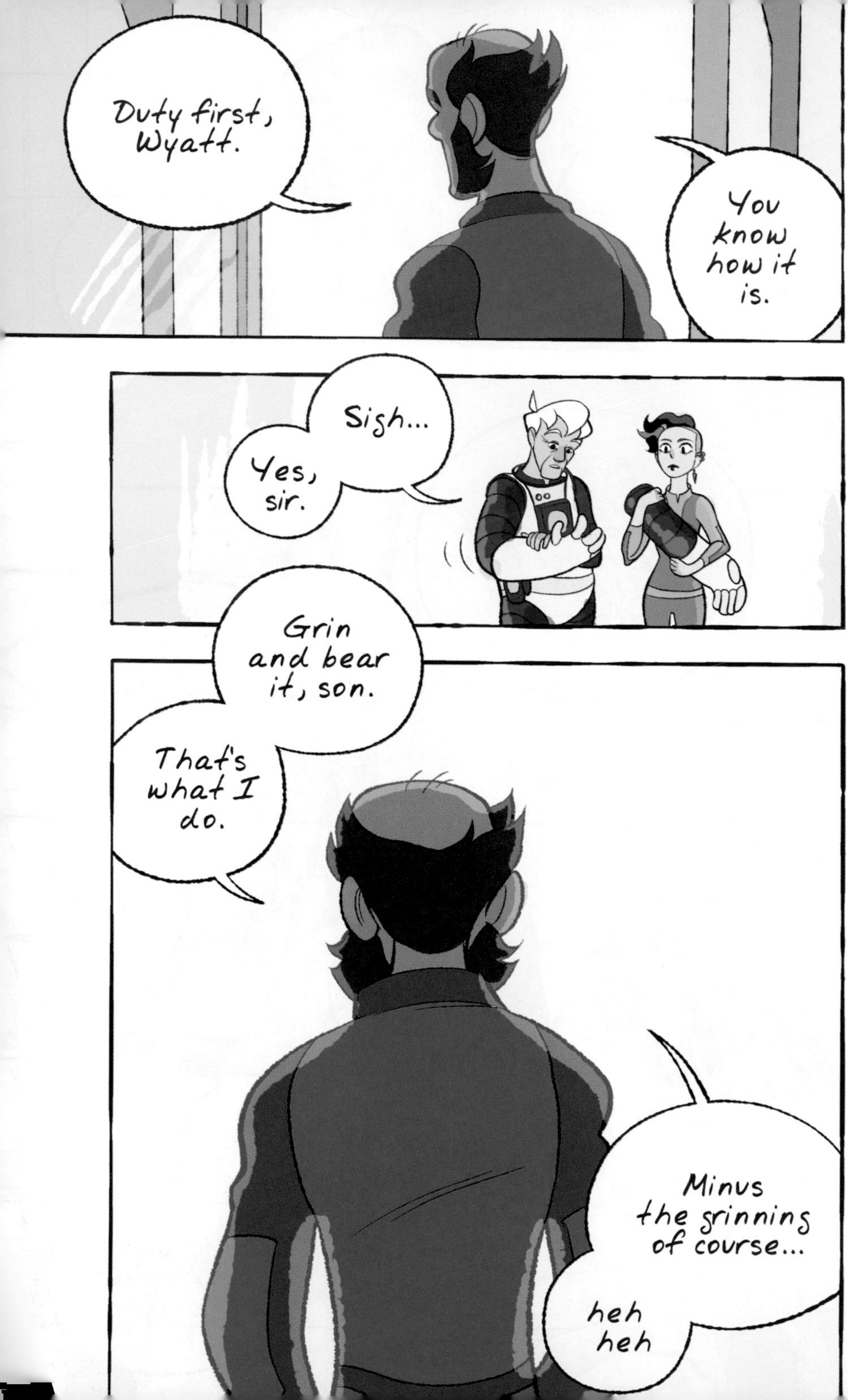
Duty first, Wyatt.
You know how it is.
Sigh...
Yes, sir.
Grin and bear it, son.
That's what I do.
Minus the grinning of course...
heh heh

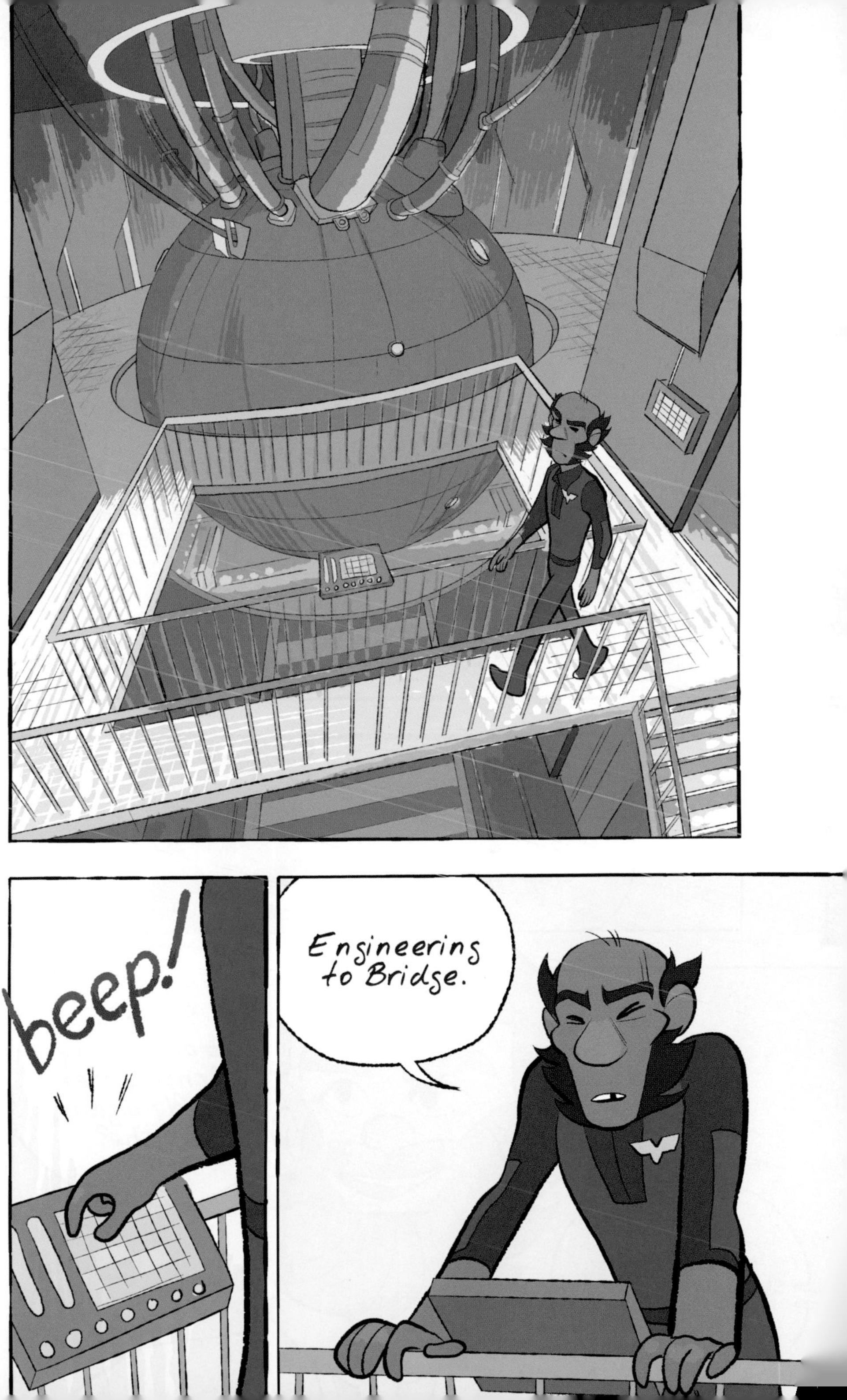
beep!
Engineering to Bridge.

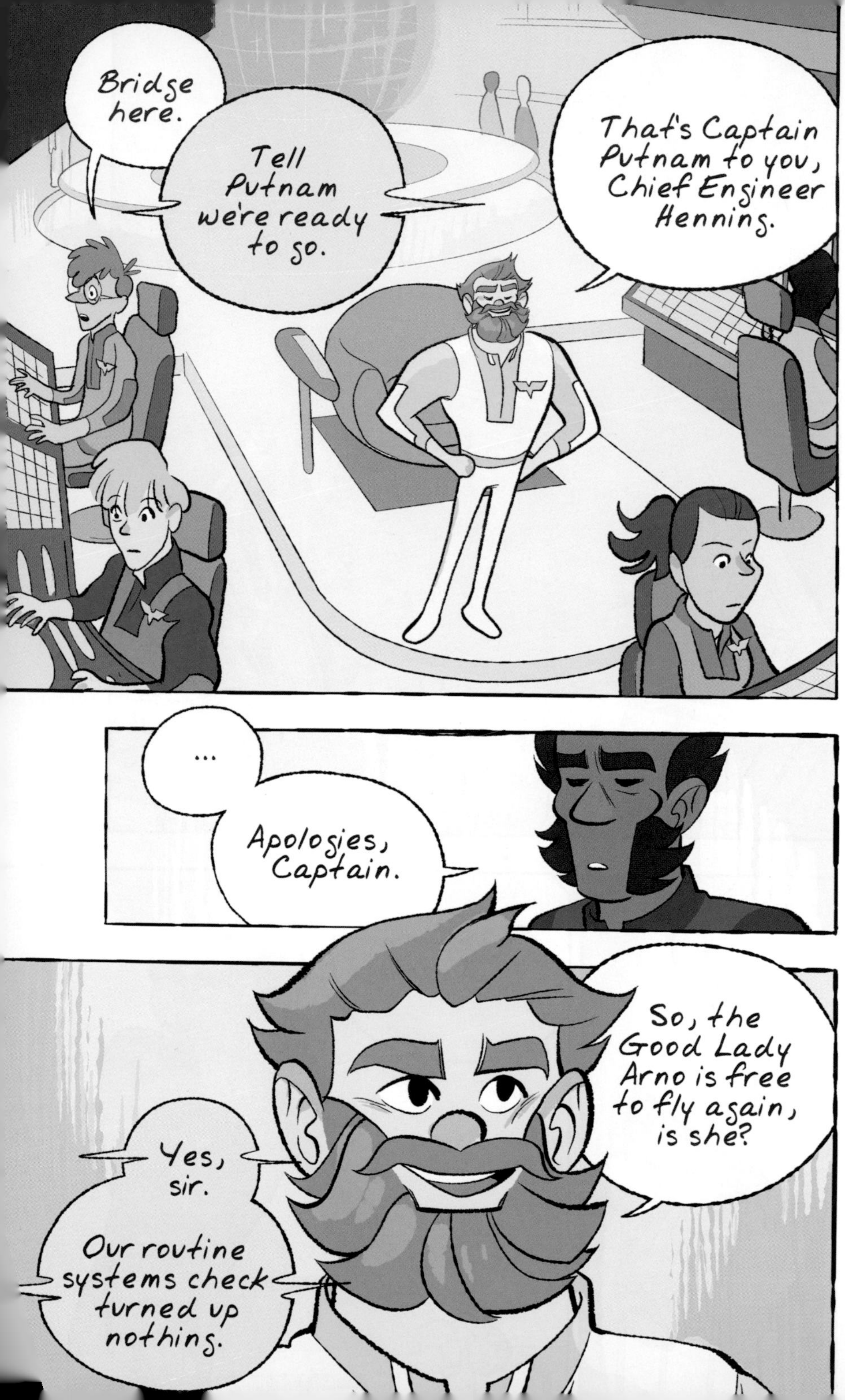
Bridge here.
Tell Putnam we're ready to go.
That's Captain Putnam to you, Chief Engineer Henning.
...
Apologies, Captain.
So, the Good Lady Arno is free to fly again, is she?
Yes, sir.
Our routine systems check turned up nothing.

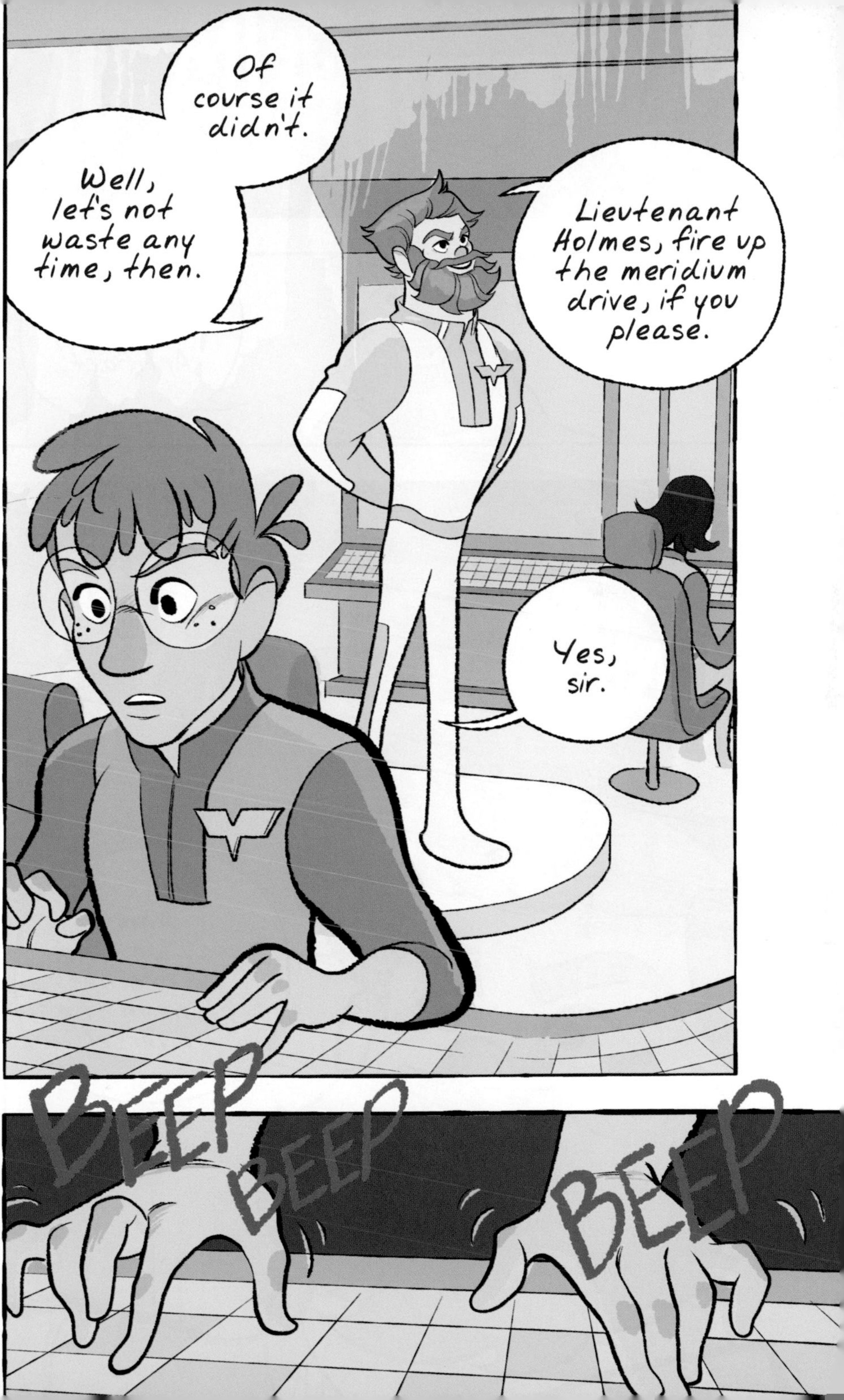
Of course it didn't.
Well, let's not waste any time, then.
Lieutenant Holmes, fire up the meridium drive, if you please.
Yes, sir.
BEEP
BEEP
BEEP

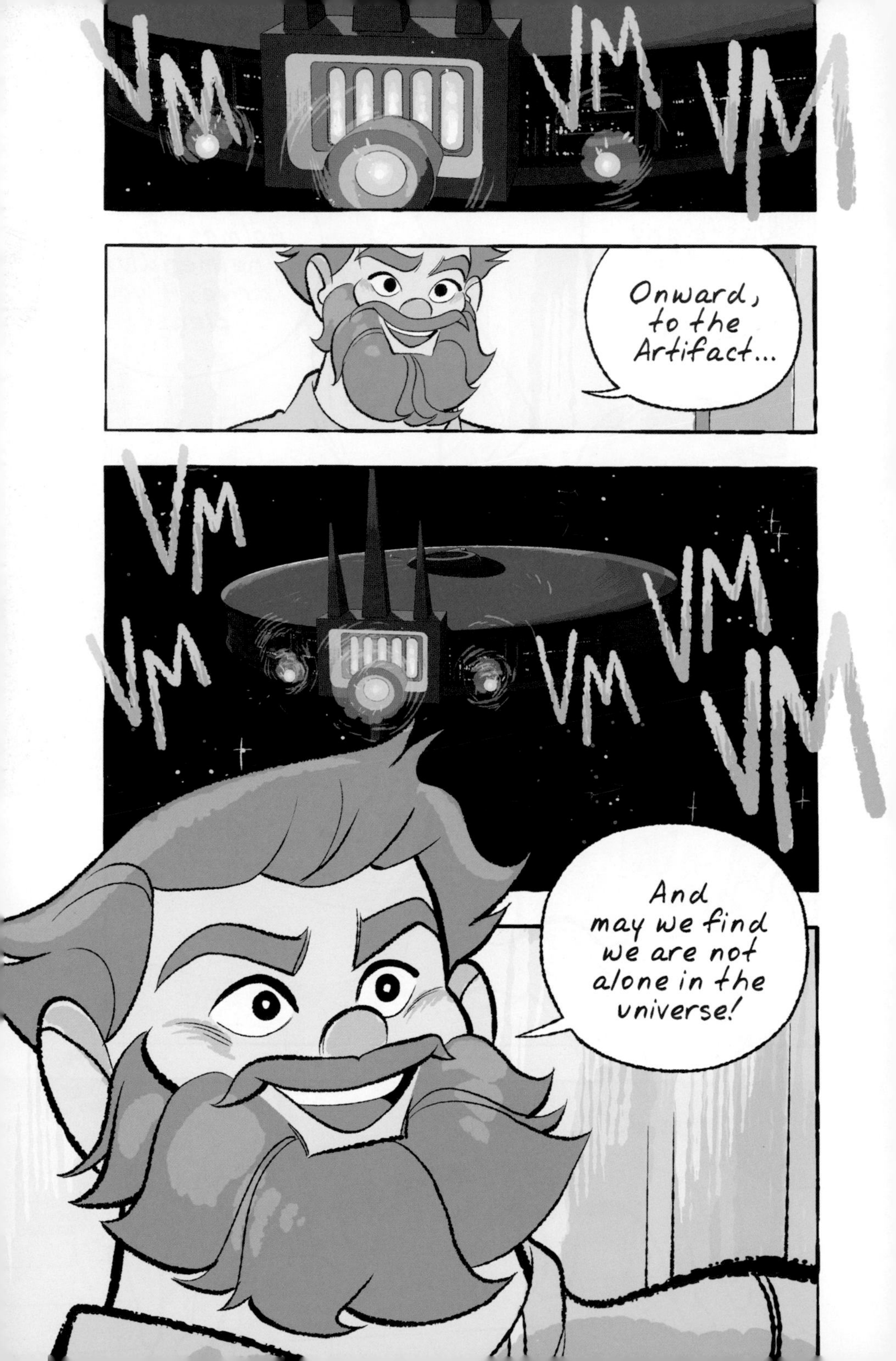
VM VM VM
Onward, to the Artifact...
VM VM VM VM VM
And may we find we are not alone in the universe!

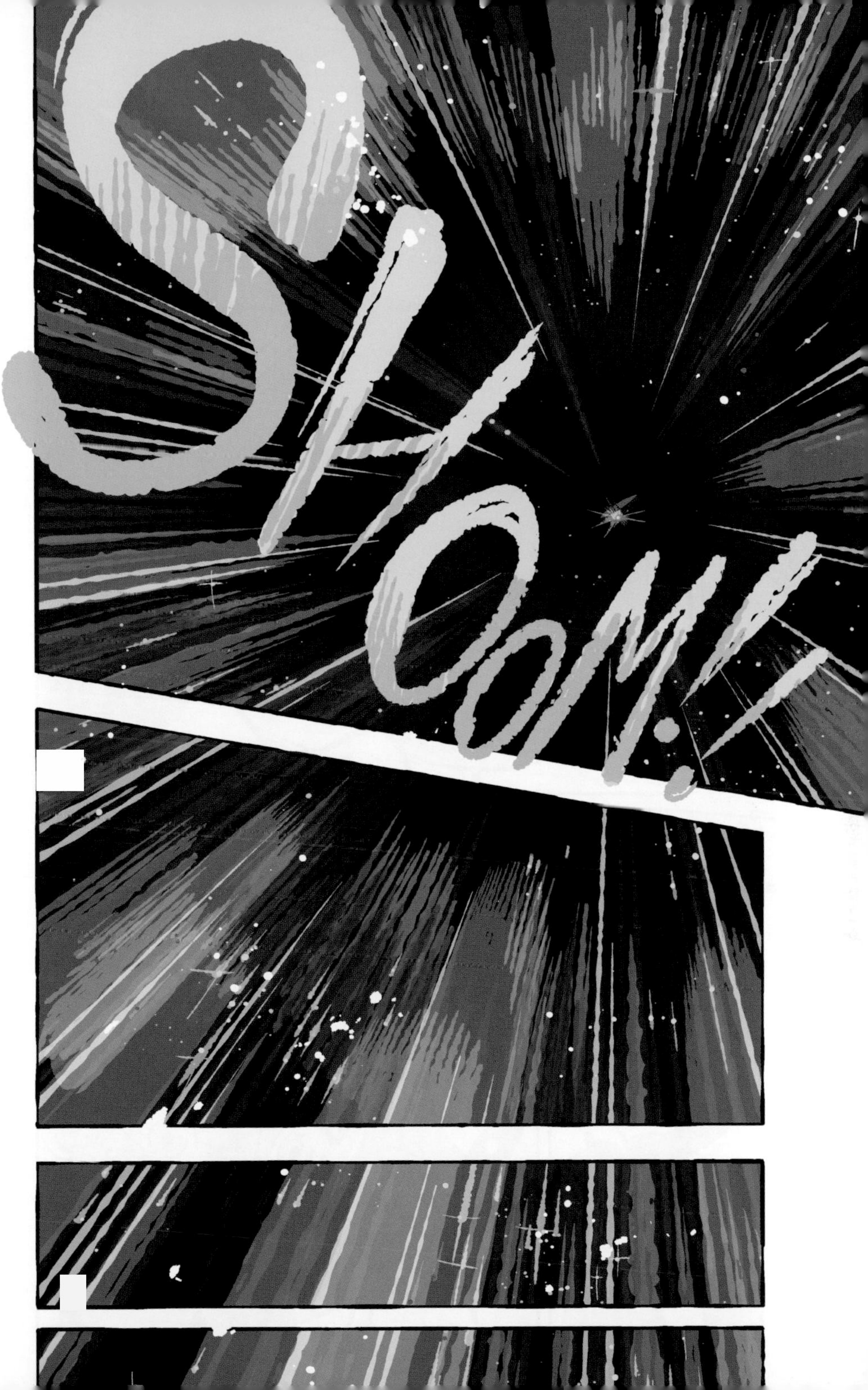
SHOOM!!

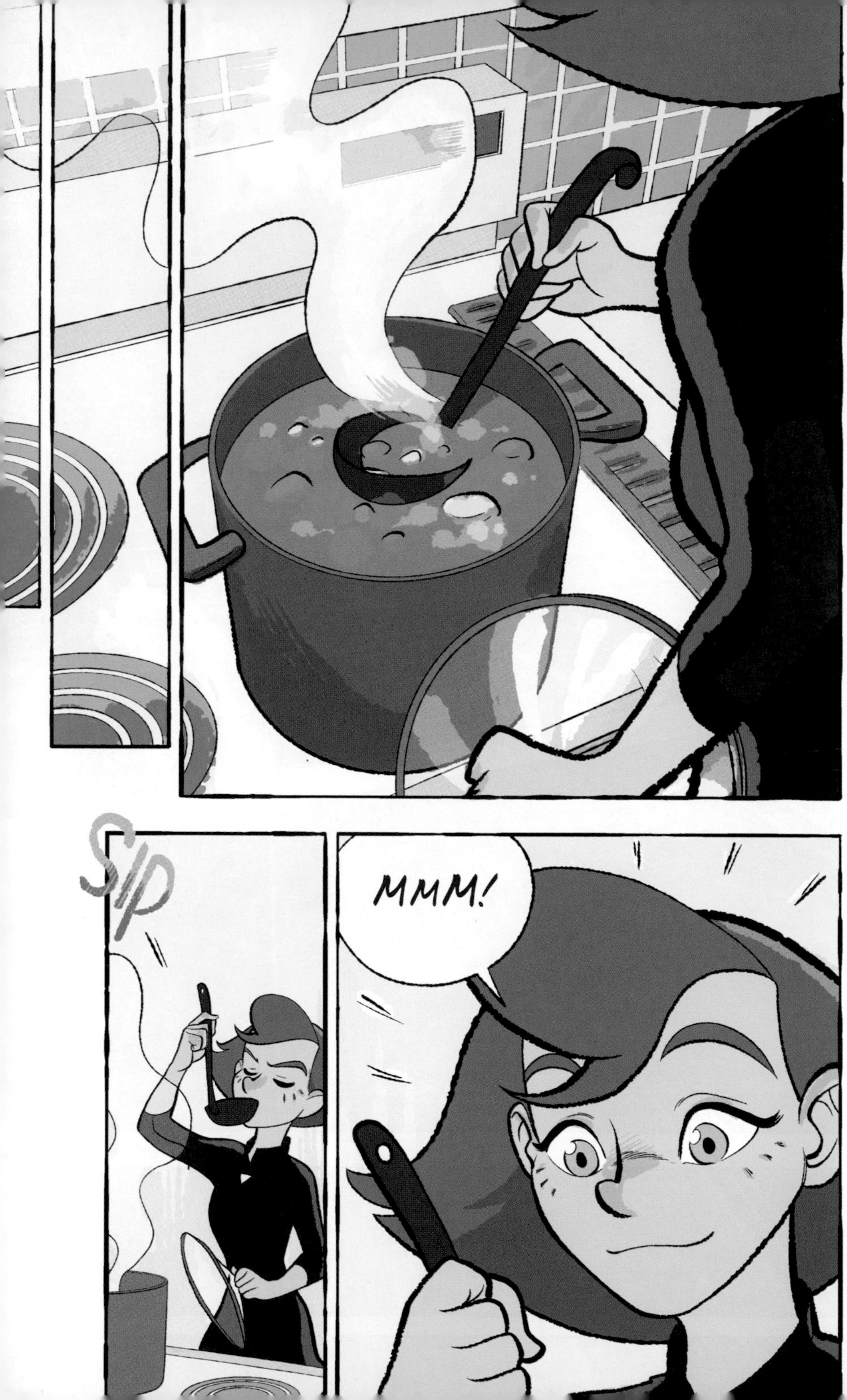
SIP
MMM!

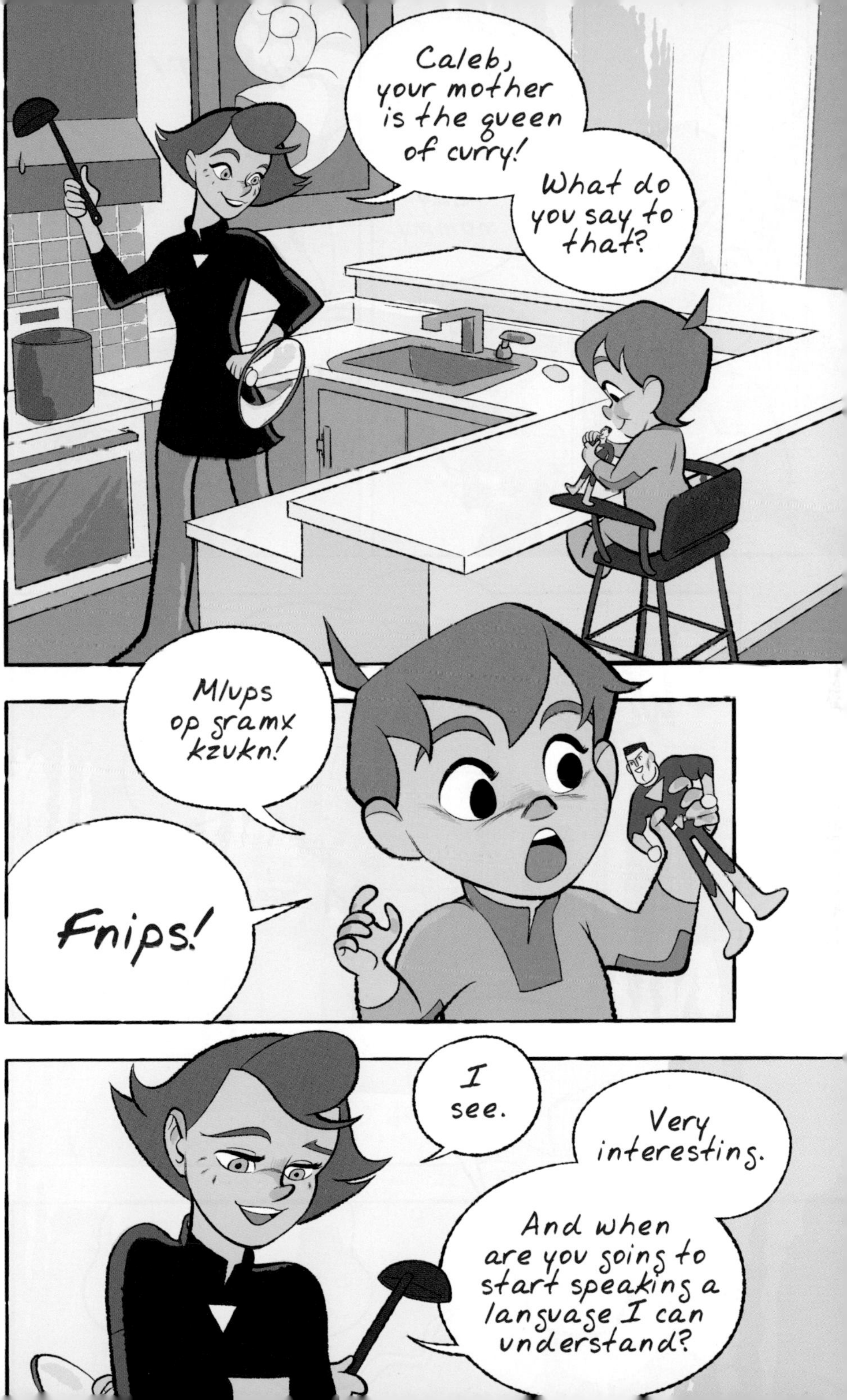
Caleb, your mother is the queen of curry!
What do you say to that?
Mlups op gramx kzukn!
Fnips!
I see.
Very interesting.
And when are you going to start speaking a language I can understand?

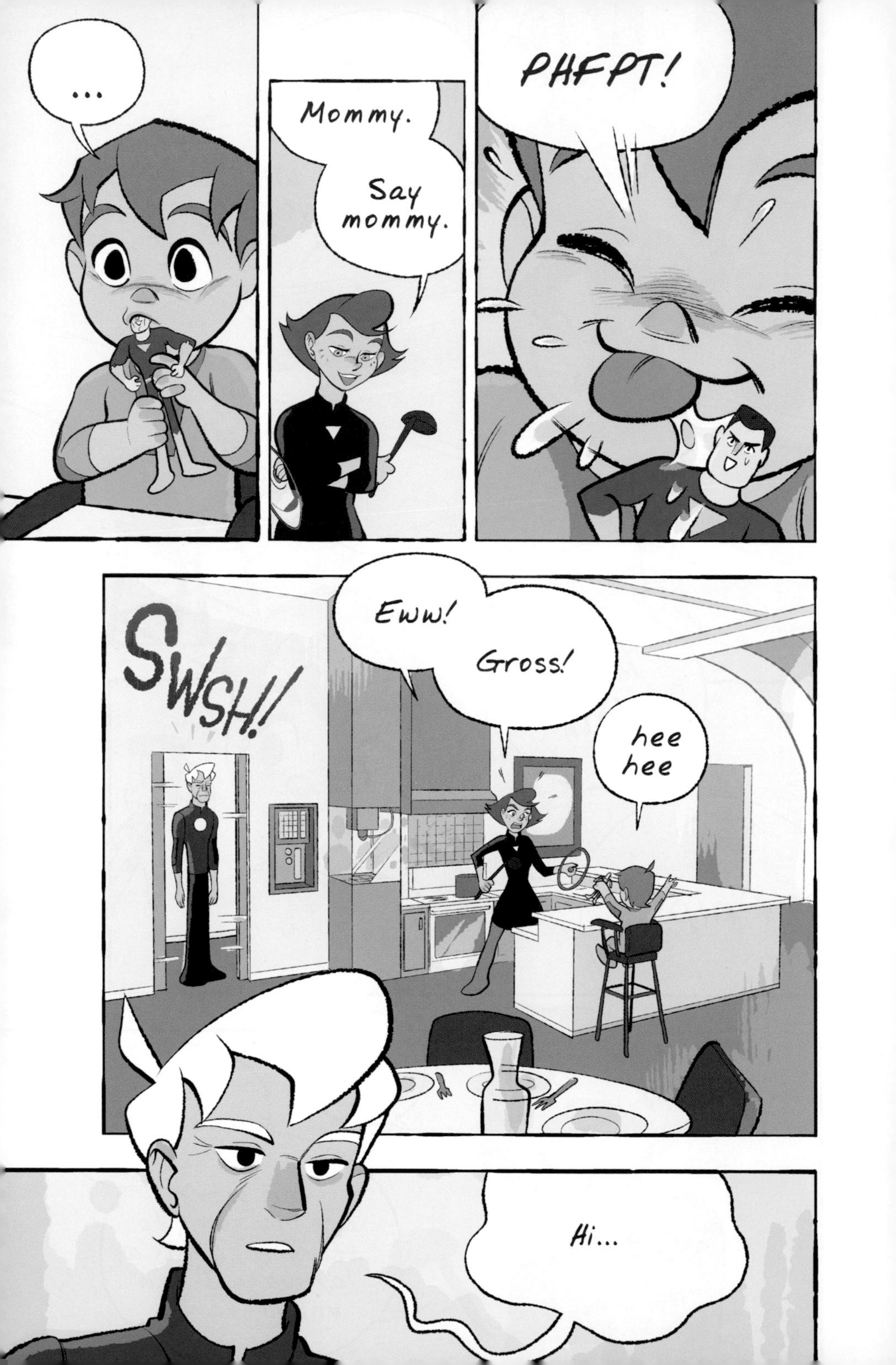
...
Mommy.
Say mommy.
PHFPT!
SWSH!!
Eww!
Gross!
hee hee
Hi...

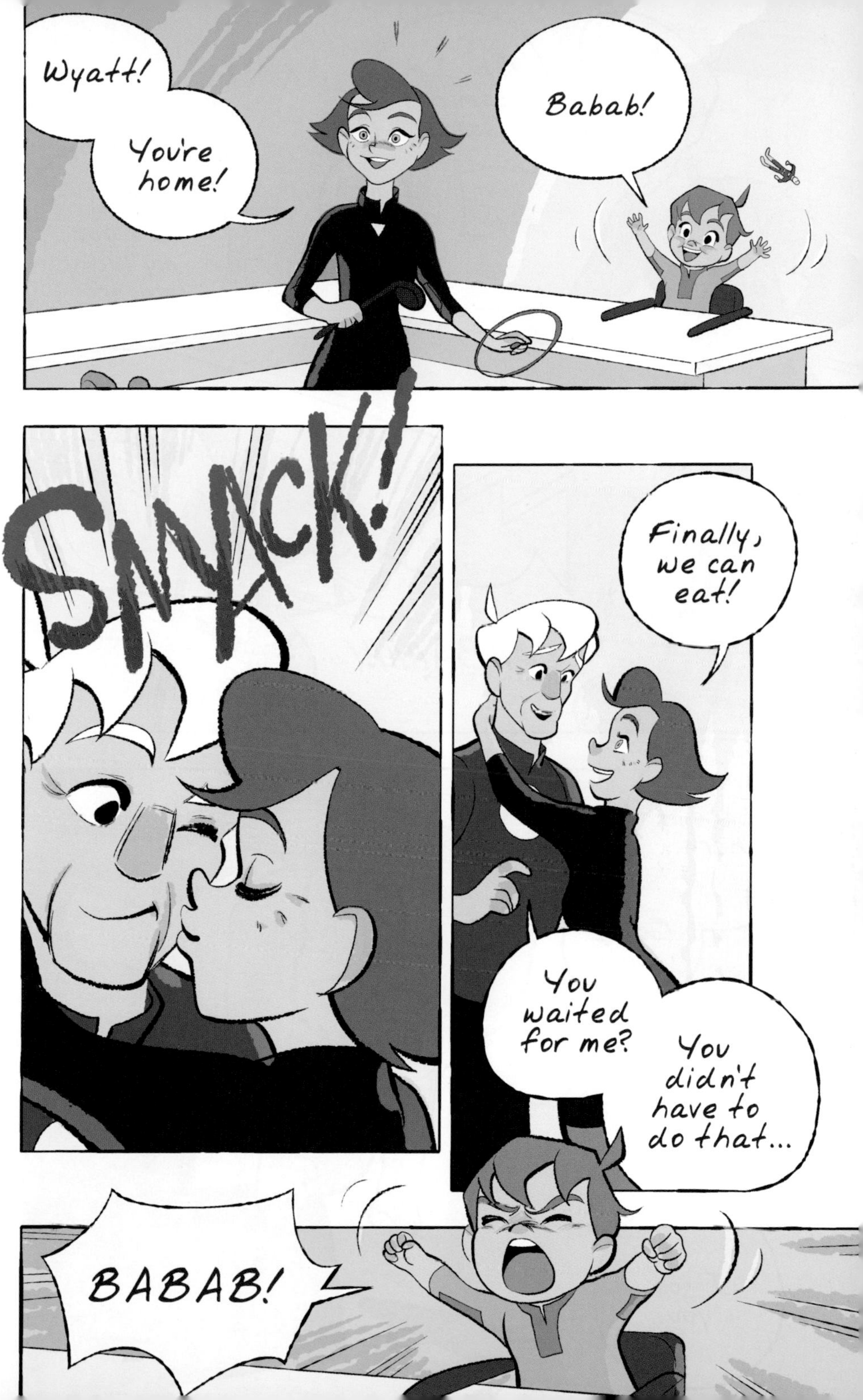
Wyatt!
You're home!
Babab!
SMACK!
Finally, we can eat!
You waited for me?
You didn't have to do that...
BABAB!

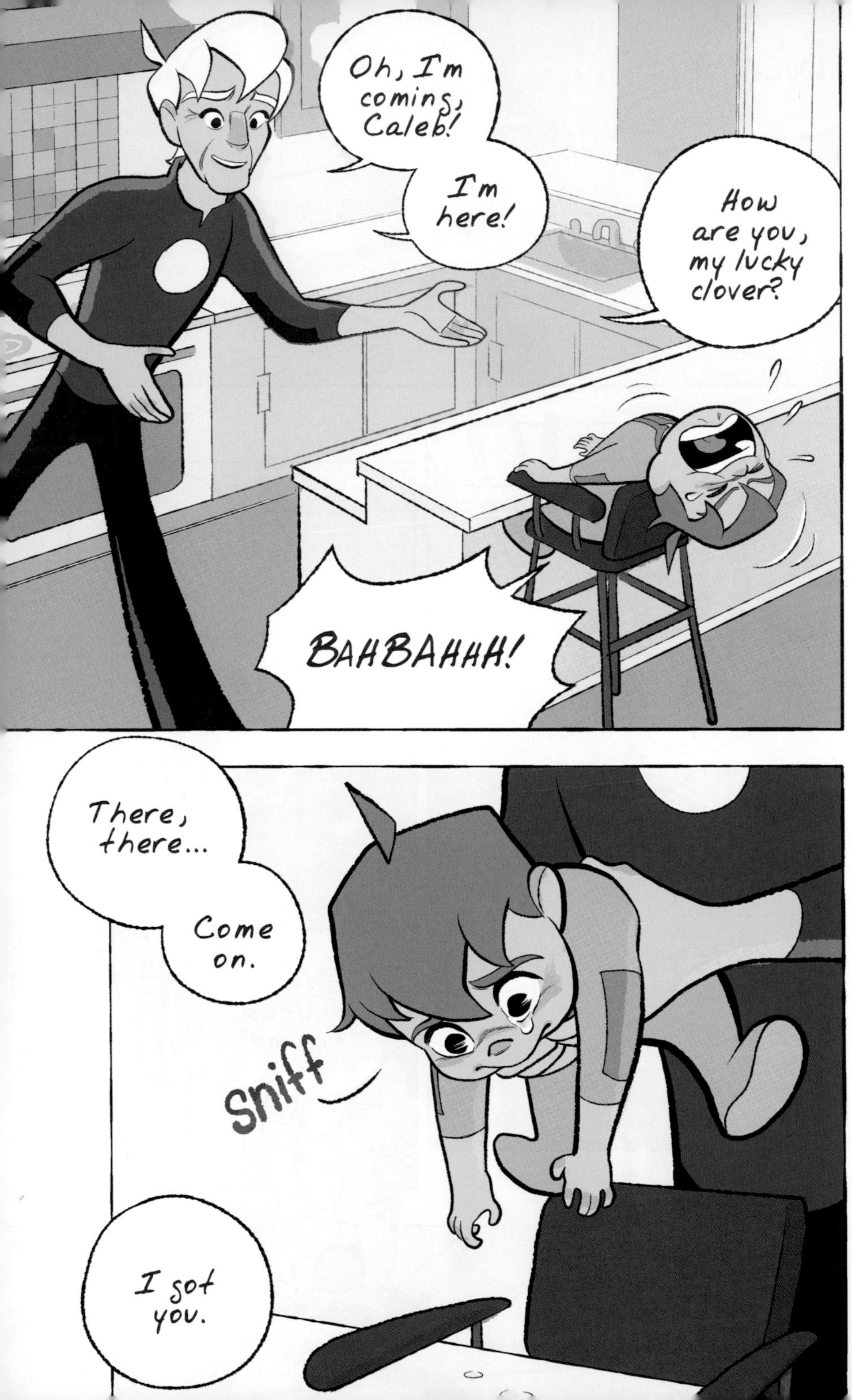
Oh, I'm coming, Caleb!
I'm here!
How are you, my lucky clover?
BAHBAHHH!
There, there...
Come on.
Sniff
I got you.

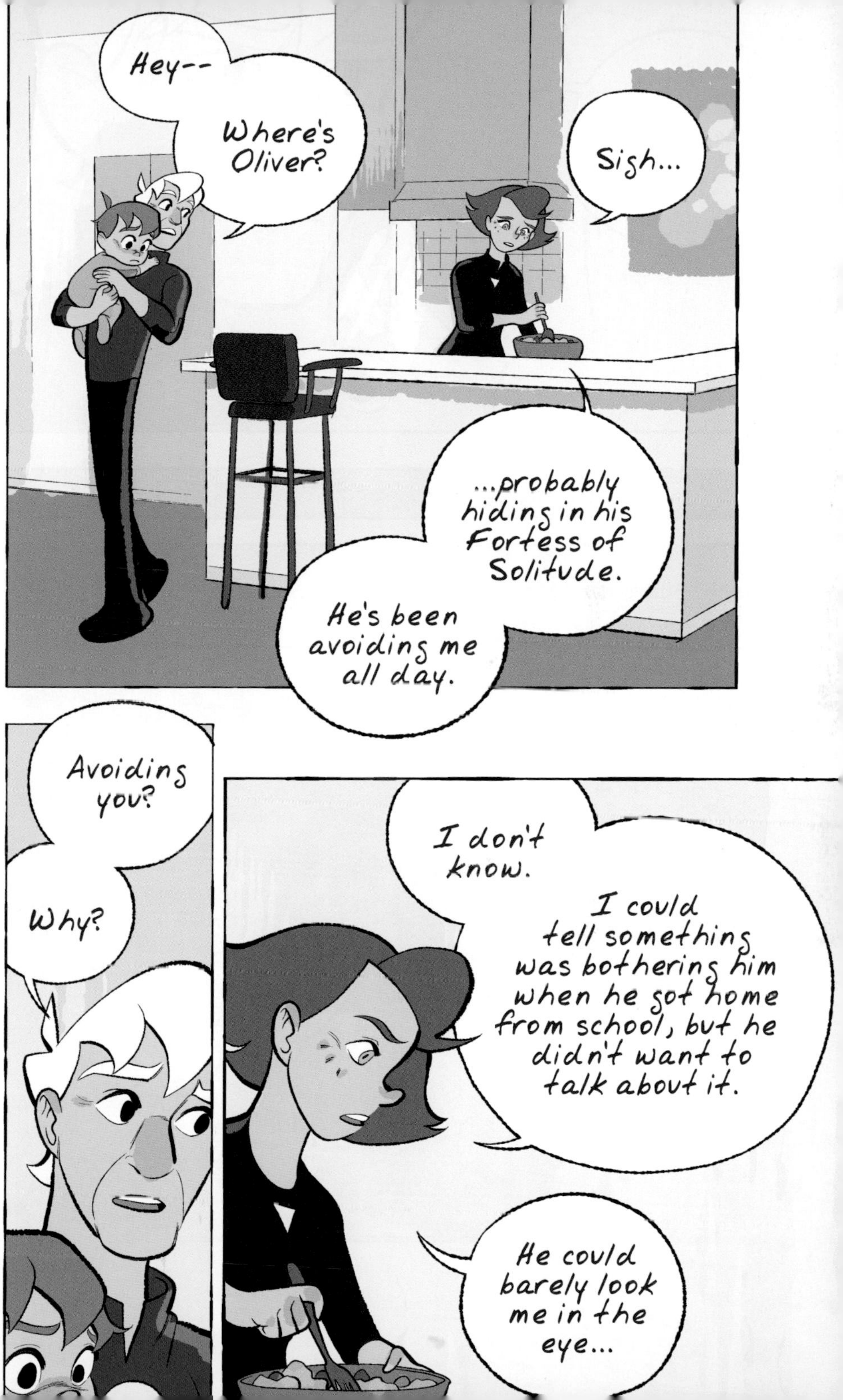
Hey--
Where's Oliver?
Sigh...
...probably hiding in his Fortess of Solitude.
He's been avoiding me all day.
Avoiding you?
Why?
I don't know.
I could tell something was bothering him when he got home from school, but he didn't want to talk about it.
He could barely look me in the eye...

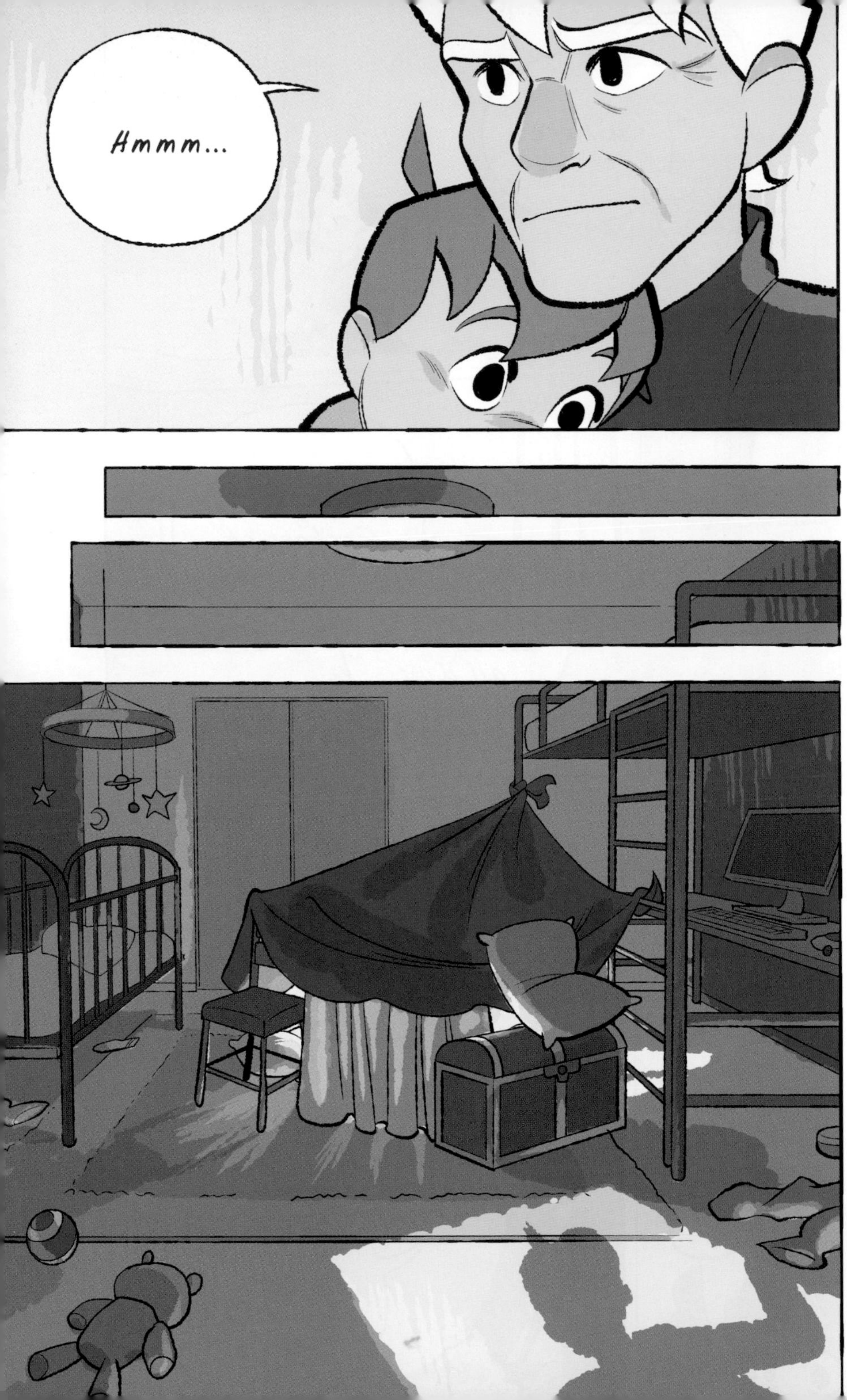
Hmmm...

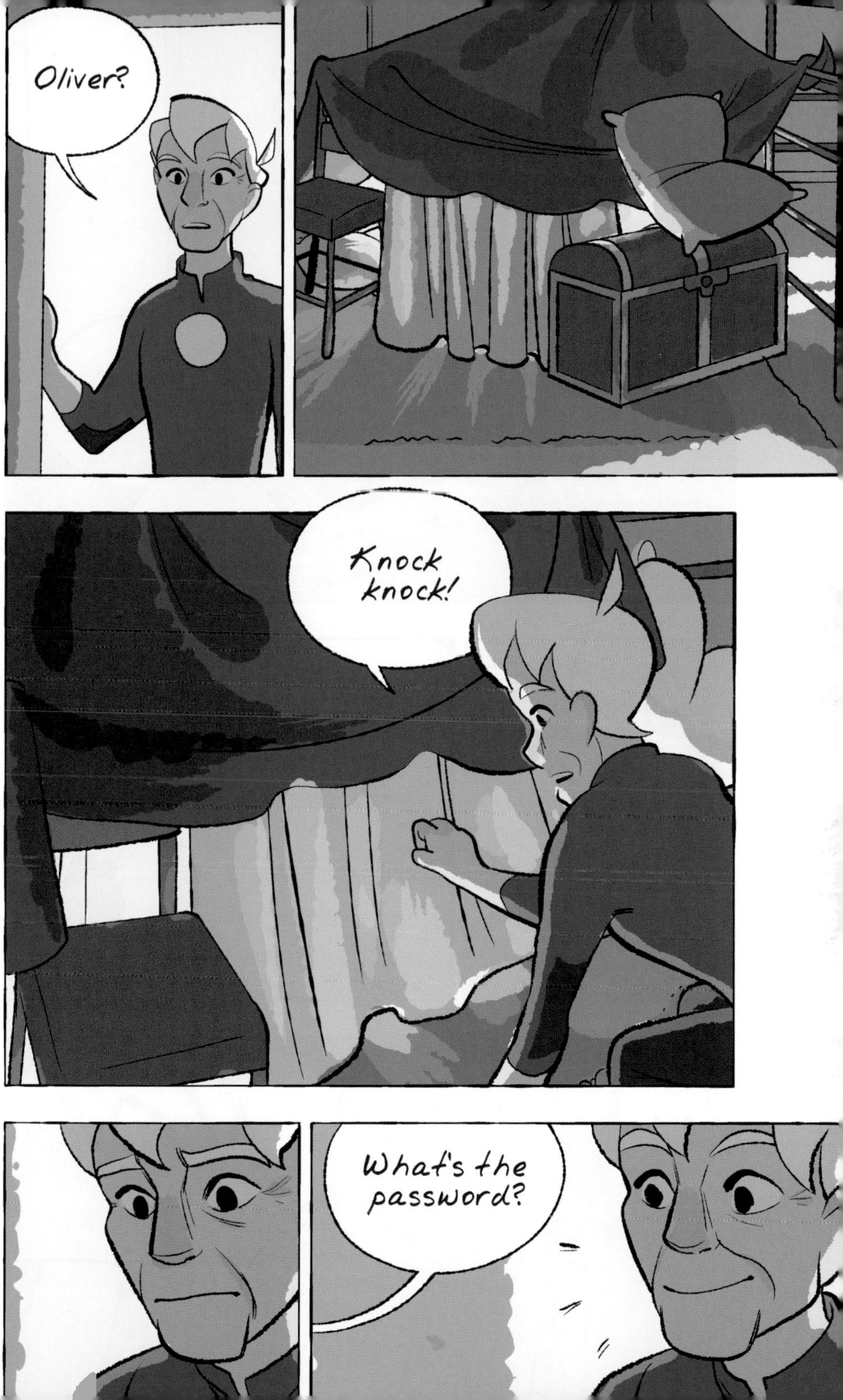
Oliver?
Knock knock!
What's the password?

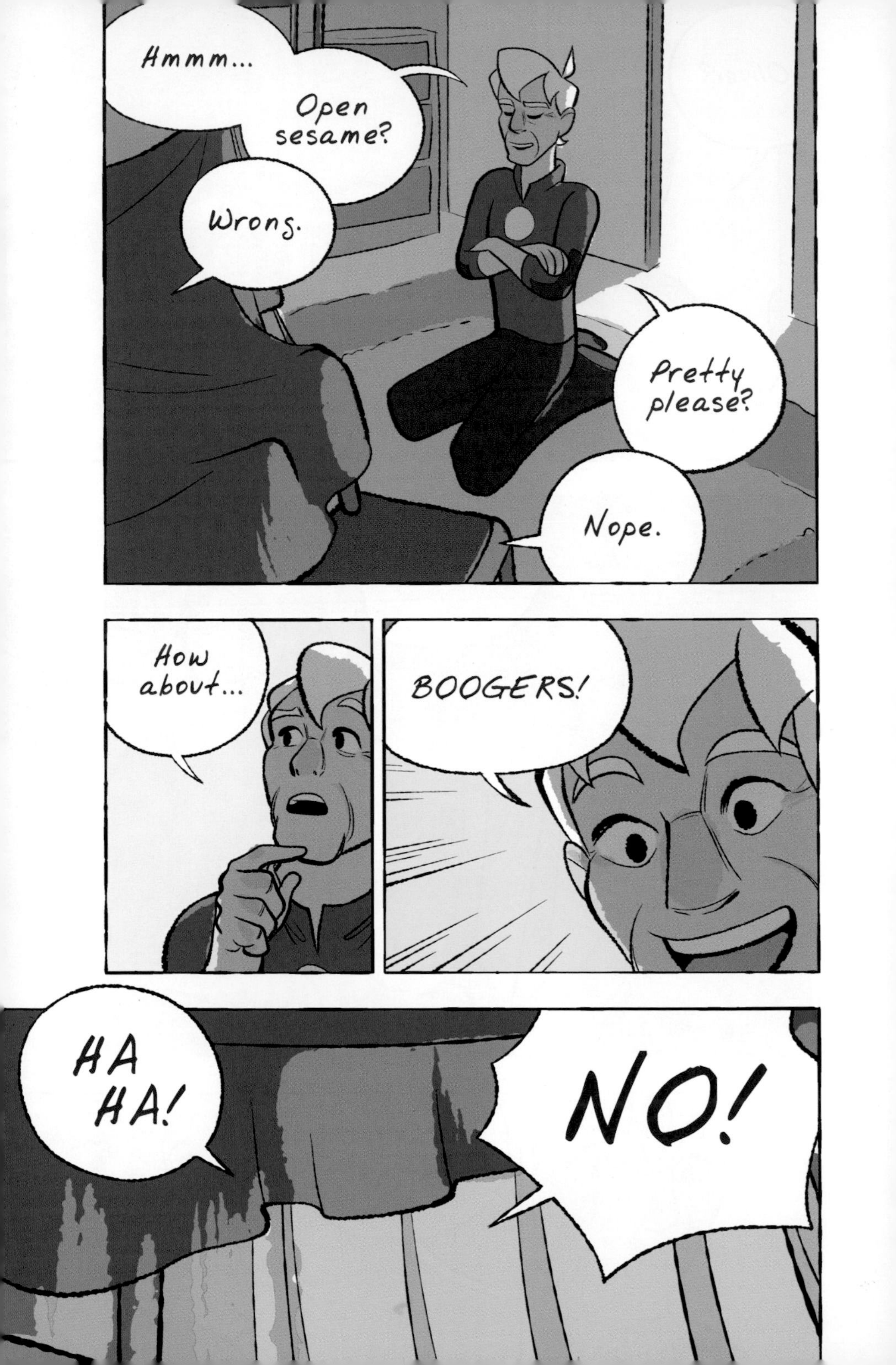
Hmmm...
Open sesame?
Wrong.
Pretty please?
Nope.
How about...
BOOGERS!
HA HA!
NO!

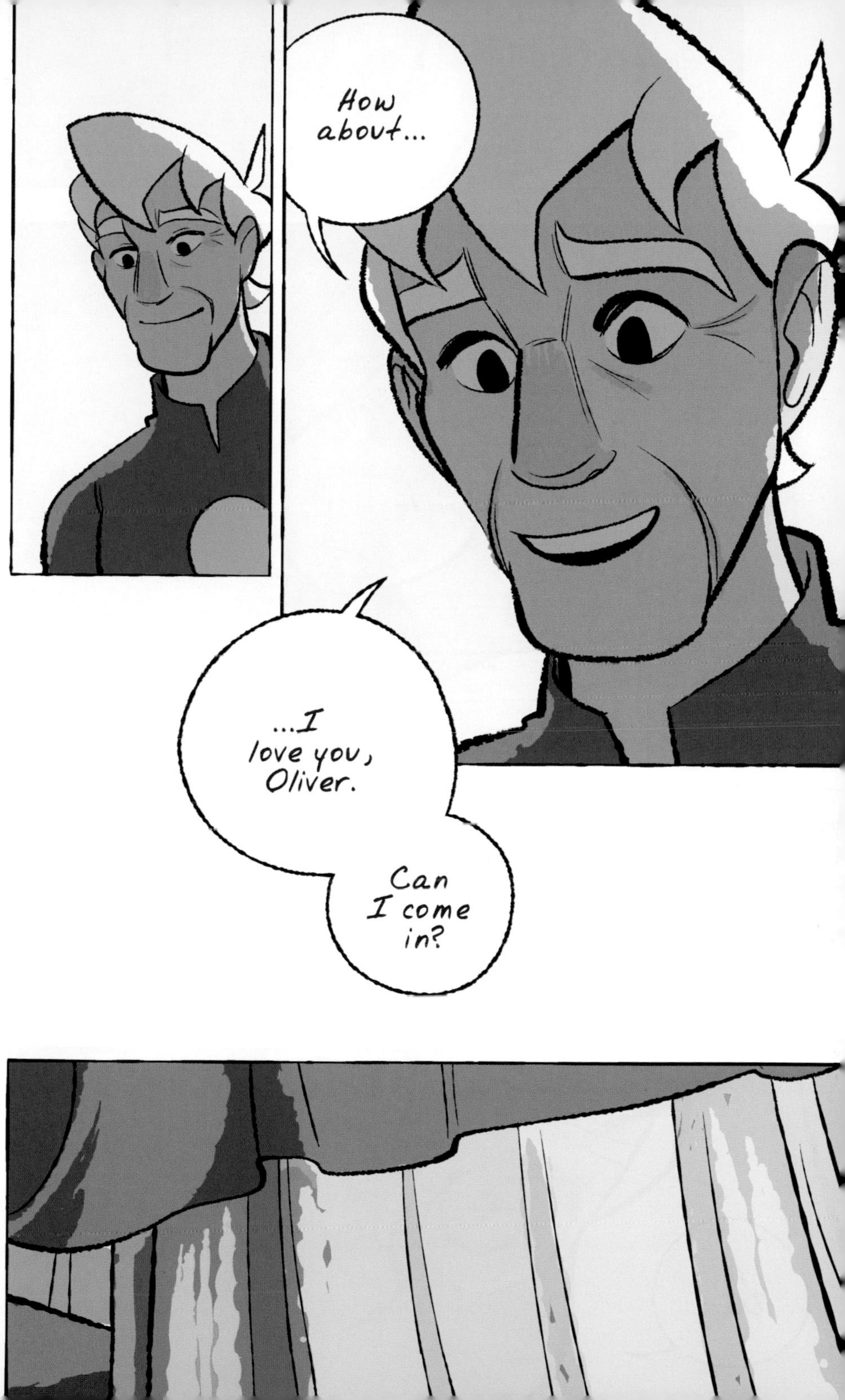
How about...
...I love you, Oliver.
Can I come in?

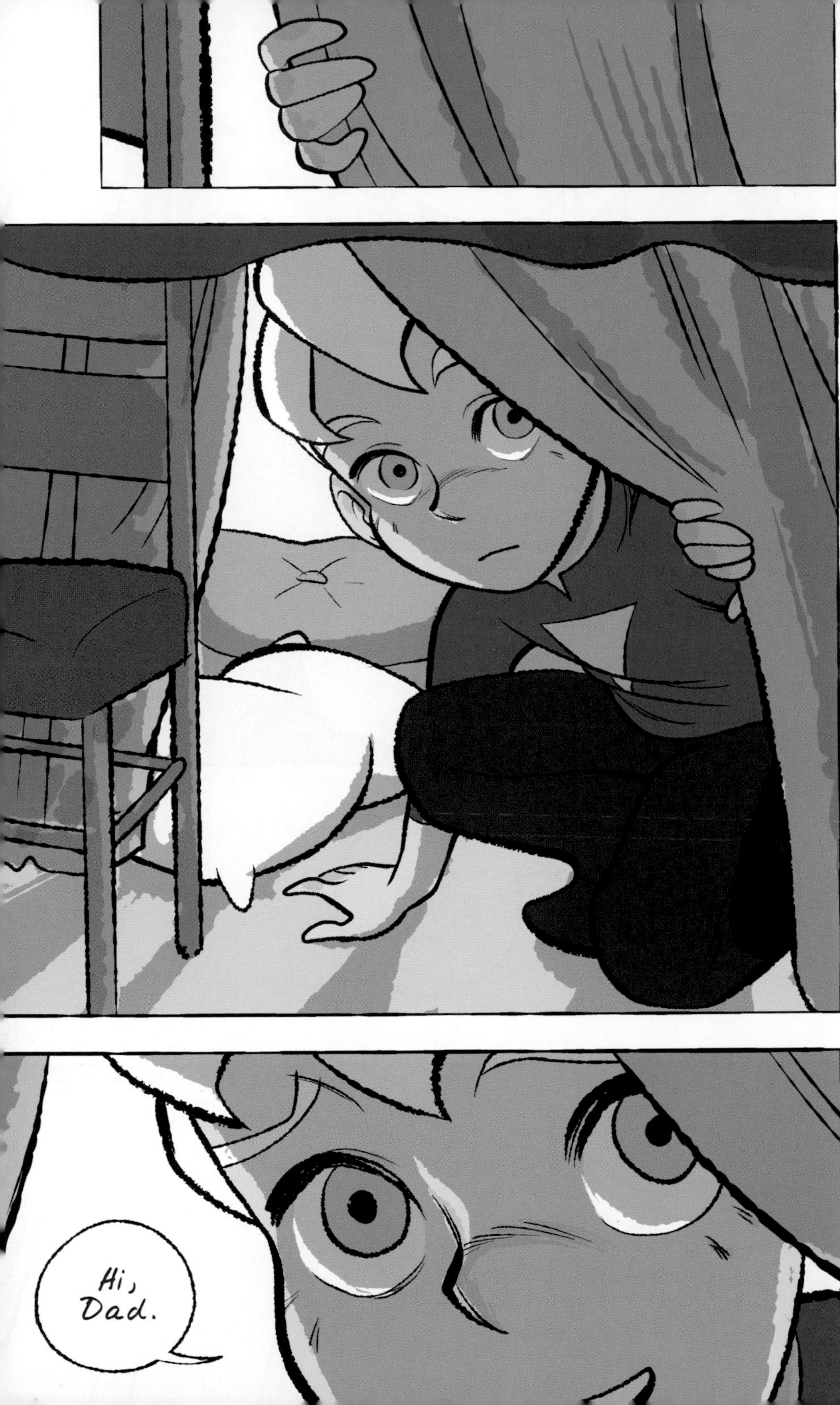
Hi, Dad.

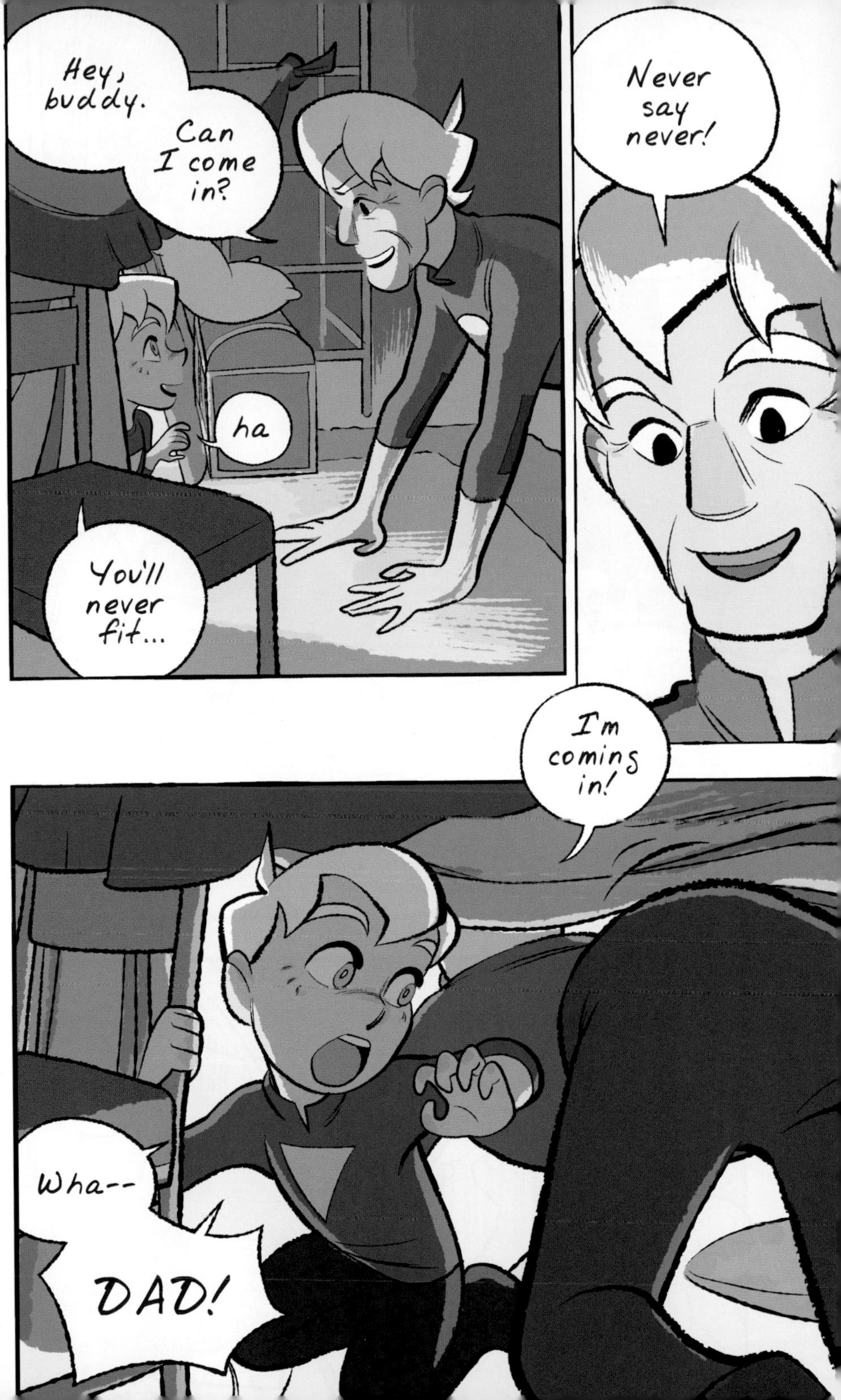
Hey, buddy.
Can I come in?
ha
You'll never fit...
Never say never!
I'm comins in!
Wha--
DAD!

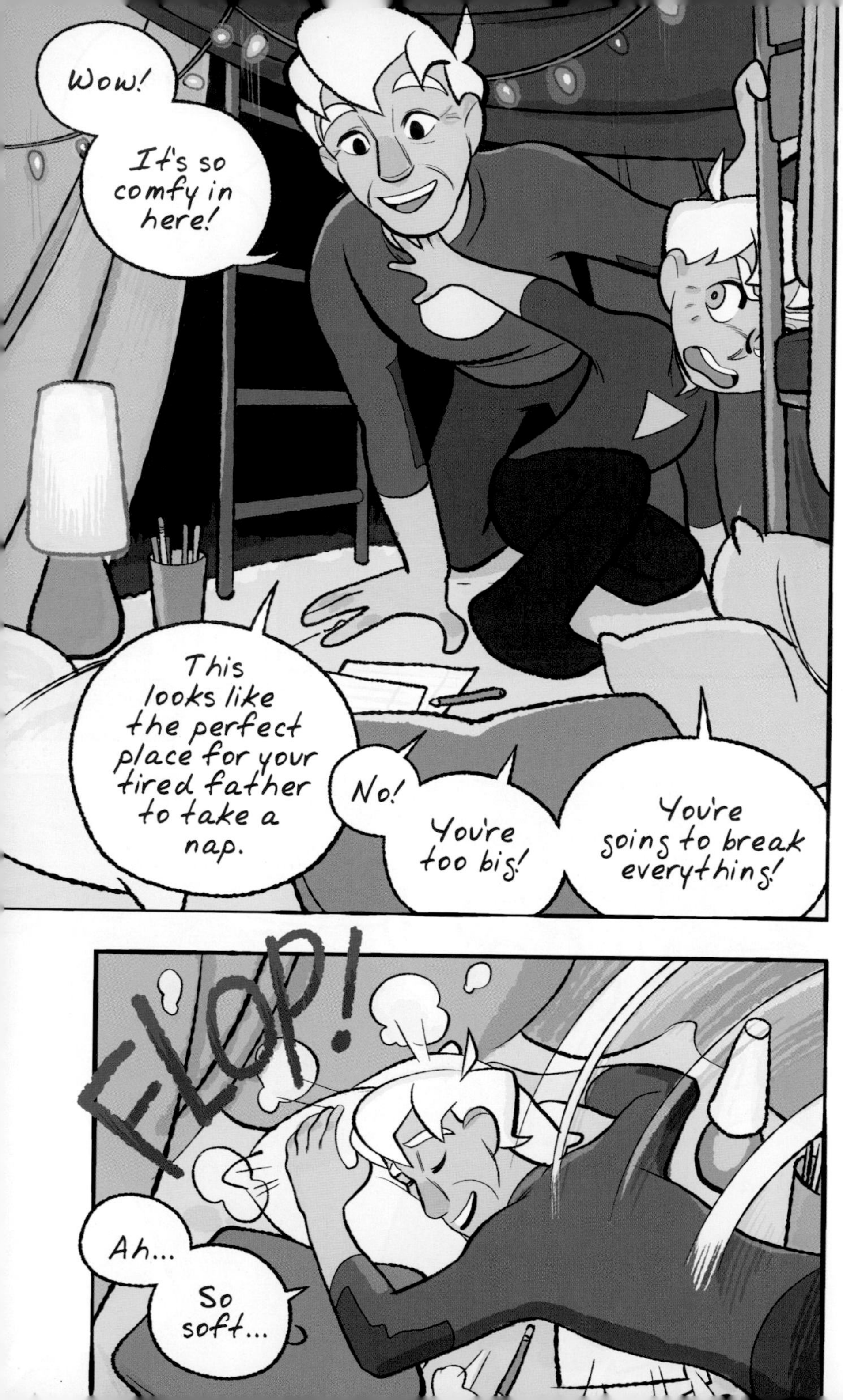
Wow!
It's so comfy in here!
This looks like the perfect place for your tired father to take a nap.
No!
You're too big!
You're going to break everything!
FLOP!
Ah...
So soft...

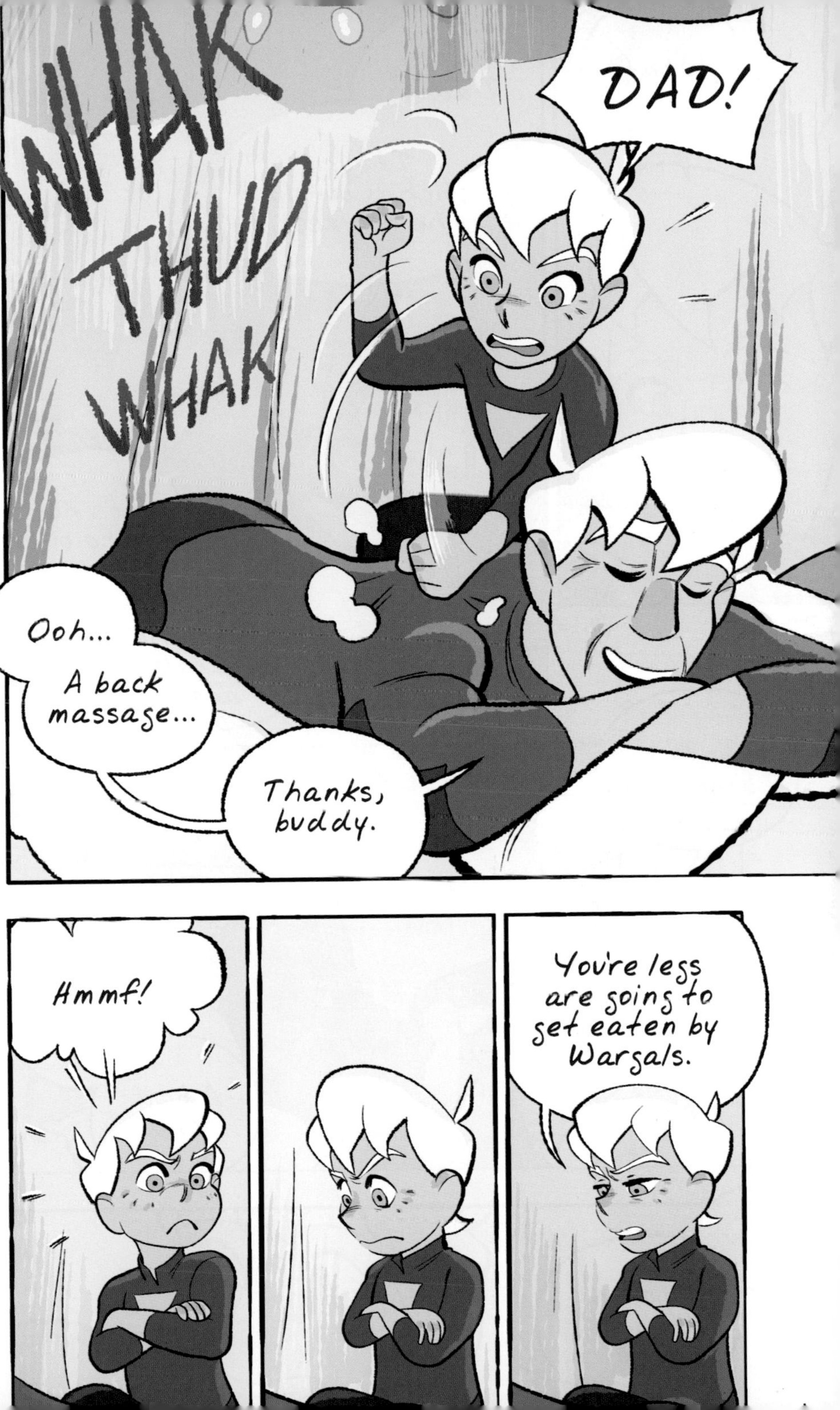
WHAK
THUD
WHAK
DAD!
Ooh...
A back massage...
Thanks, buddy.
Hmmf!
You're less are going to get eaten by Wargals.

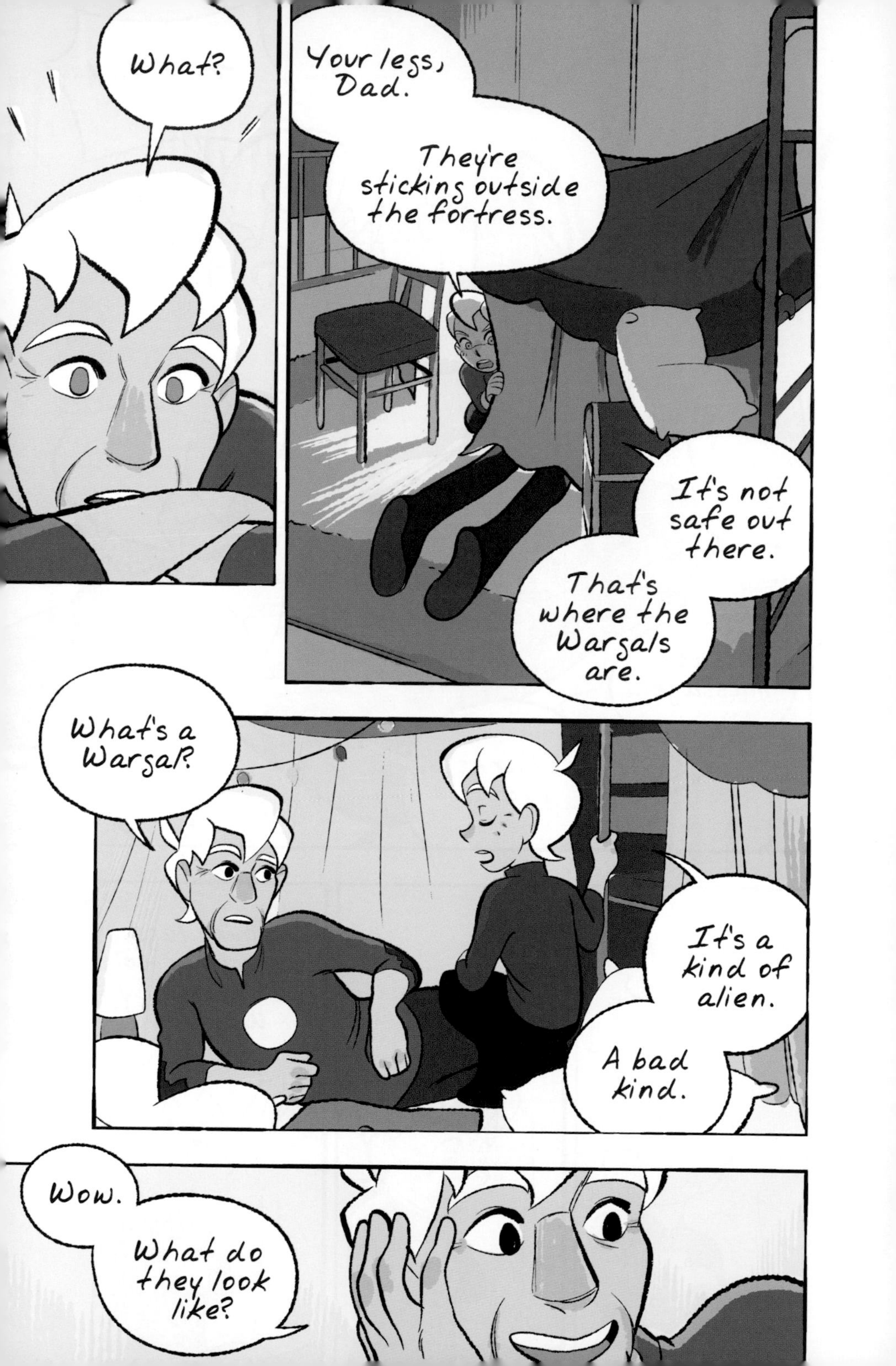
What?
Your legs, Dad.
They're sticking outside the fortress.
It's not safe out there.
That's where the Wargals are.
What's a Wargal?
It's a kind of alien.
A bad kind.
Wow.
What do they look like?

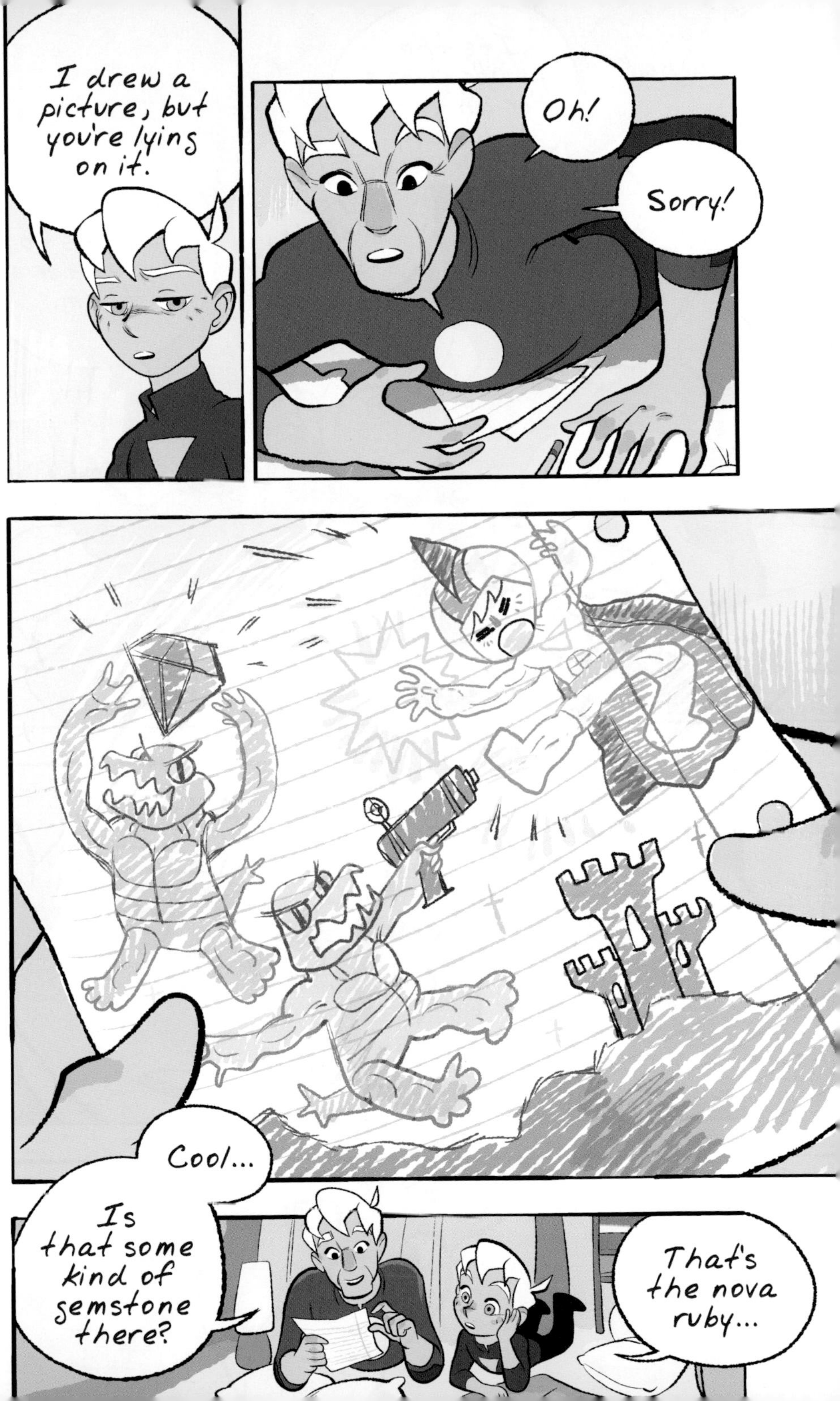
I drew a picture, but you're lying on it.
Oh!
Sorry!
Cool...
Is that some kind of gemstone there?
That's the nova ruby...

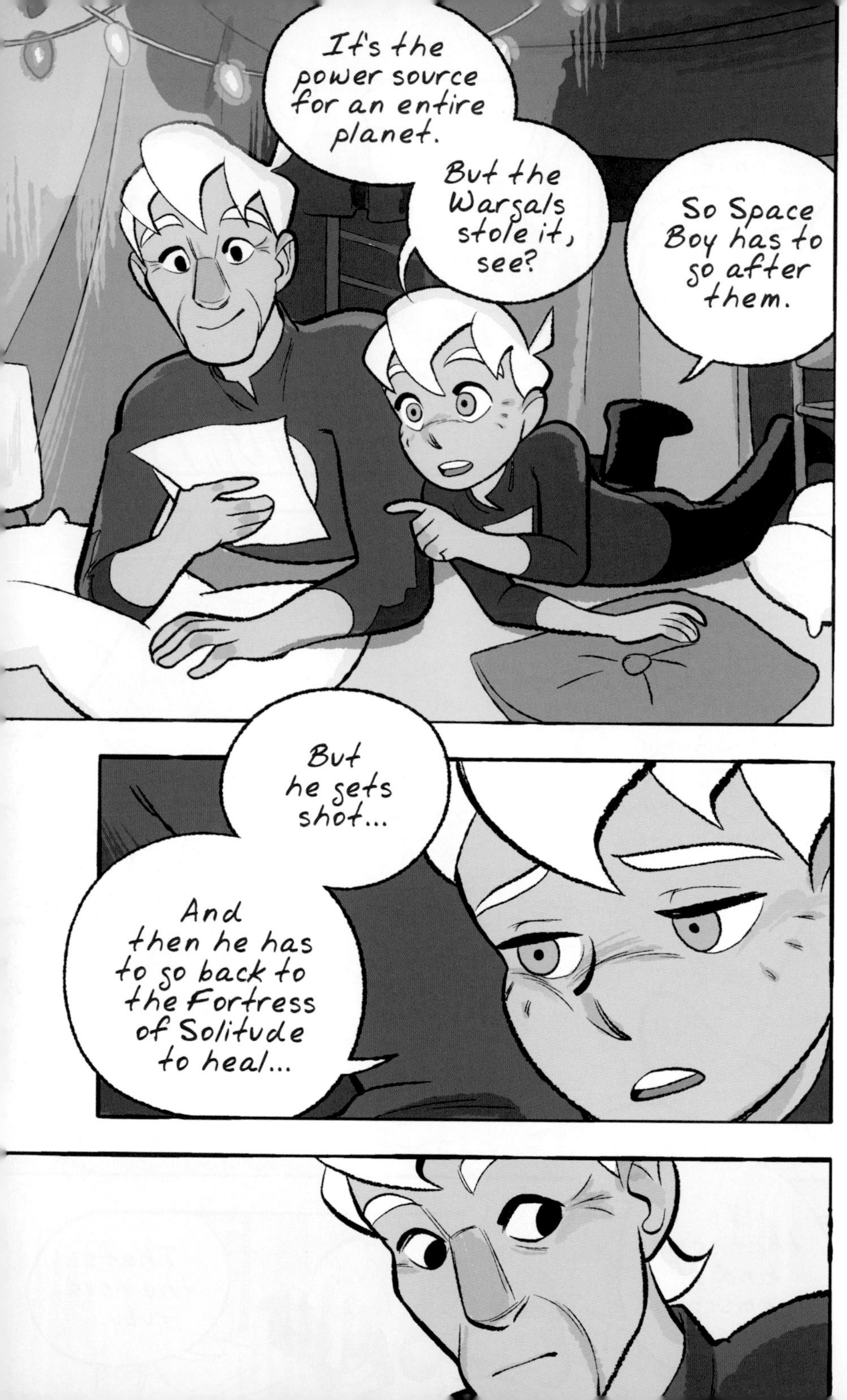
It's the power source for an entire planet.
But the Wargals stole it, see?
So Space Boy has to go after them.
But he gets shot...
And then he has to go back to the Fortress of Solitude to heal...

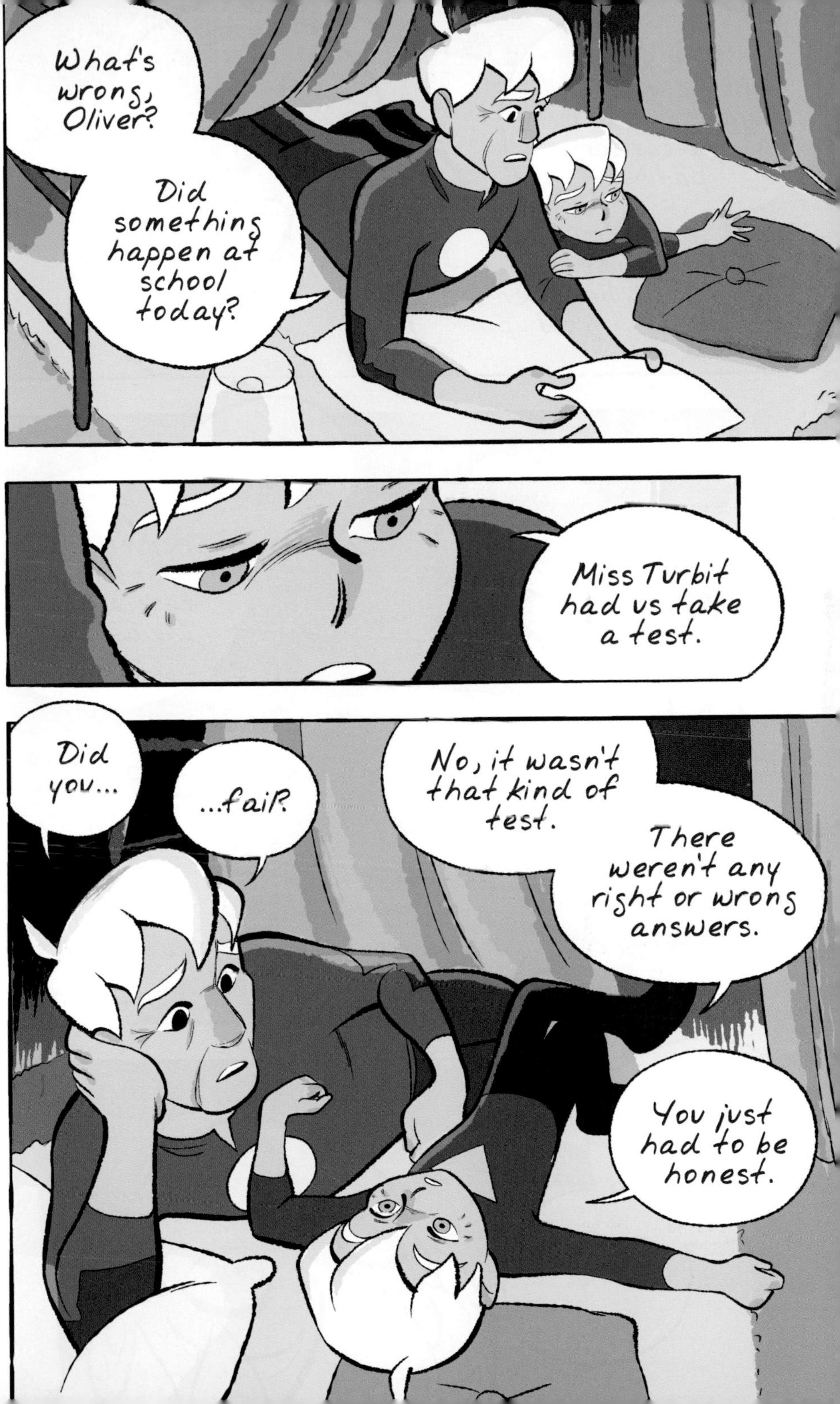
What's wrong, Oliver?
Did something happen at school today?
Miss Turbit had us take a test.
Did you...
...fail?
No, it wasn't that kind of test.
There weren't any right or wrong answers.
You just had to be honest.

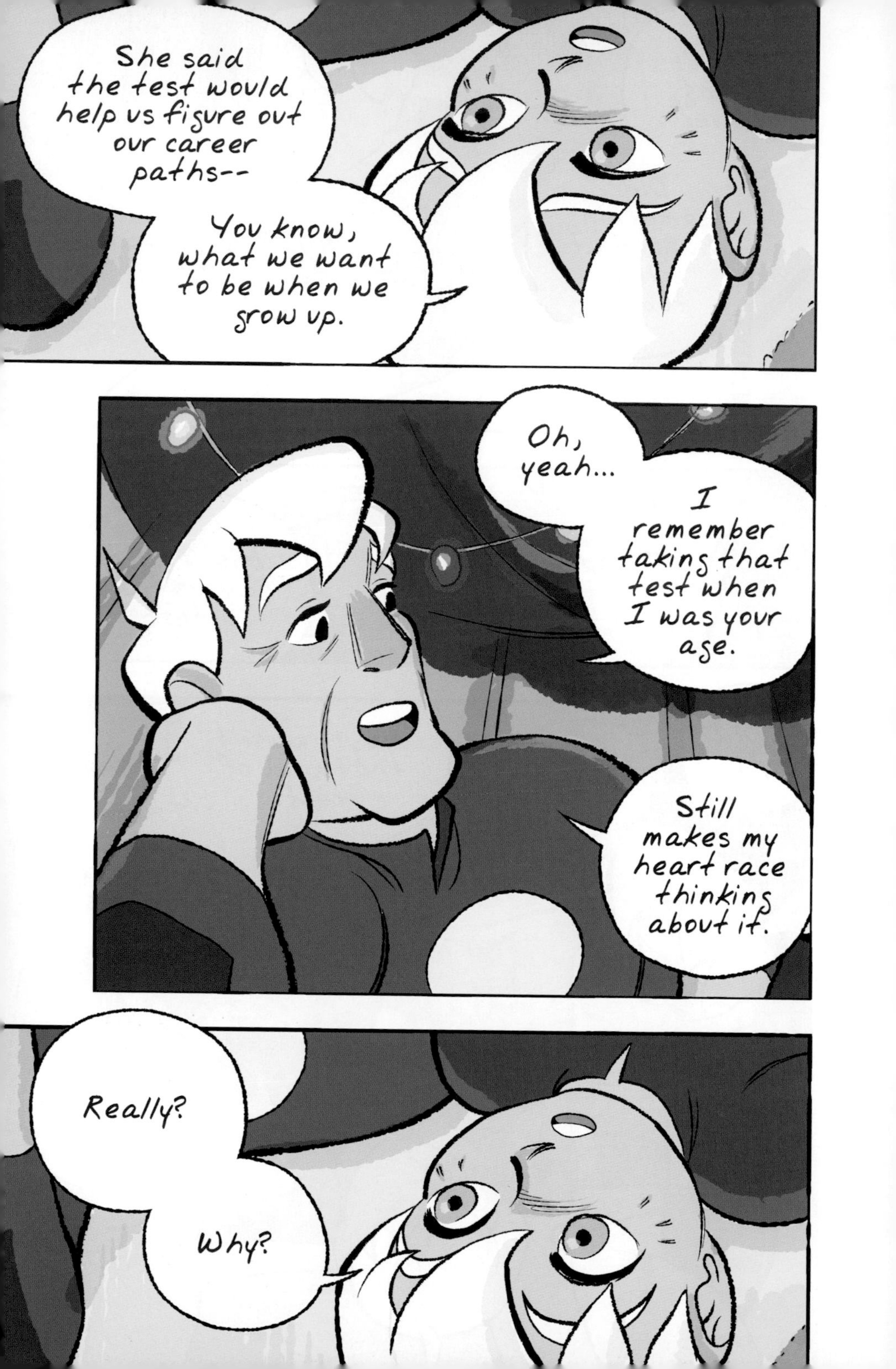
She said the test would help us figure out our career paths--
You know, what we want to be when we grow up.
Oh, yeah...
I remember taking that test when I was your age.
Still makes my heart race thinking about it.
Really?
Why?

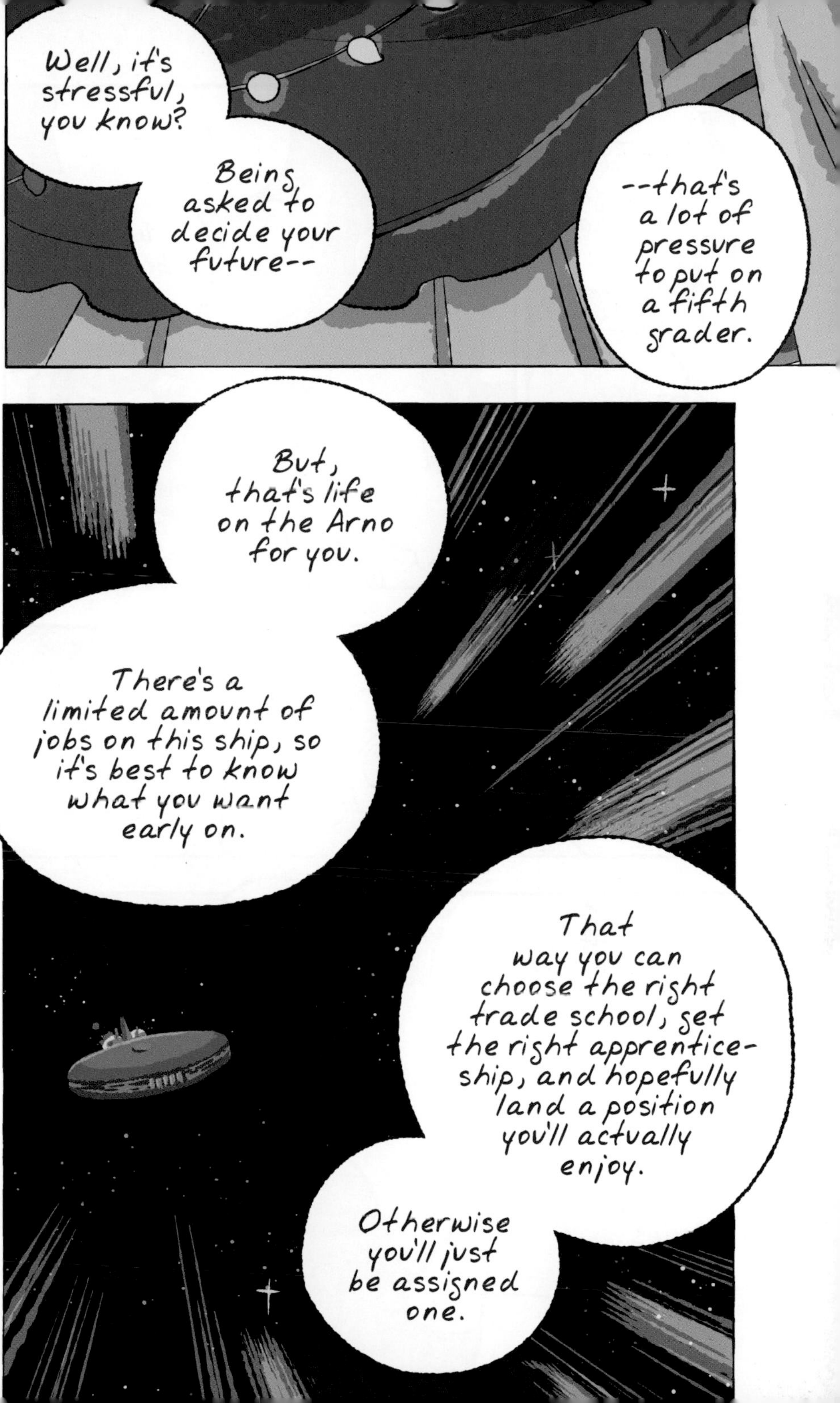
Well, it's stressful, you know?
Being asked to decide your future--
--that's a lot of pressure to put on a fifth grader.
But, that's life on the Arno for you.
There's a limited amount of jobs on this ship, so it's best to know what you want early on.
That way you can choose the right trade school, get the right apprentice-ship, and hopefully land a position you'll actually enjoy.
Otherwise you'll just be assigned one.

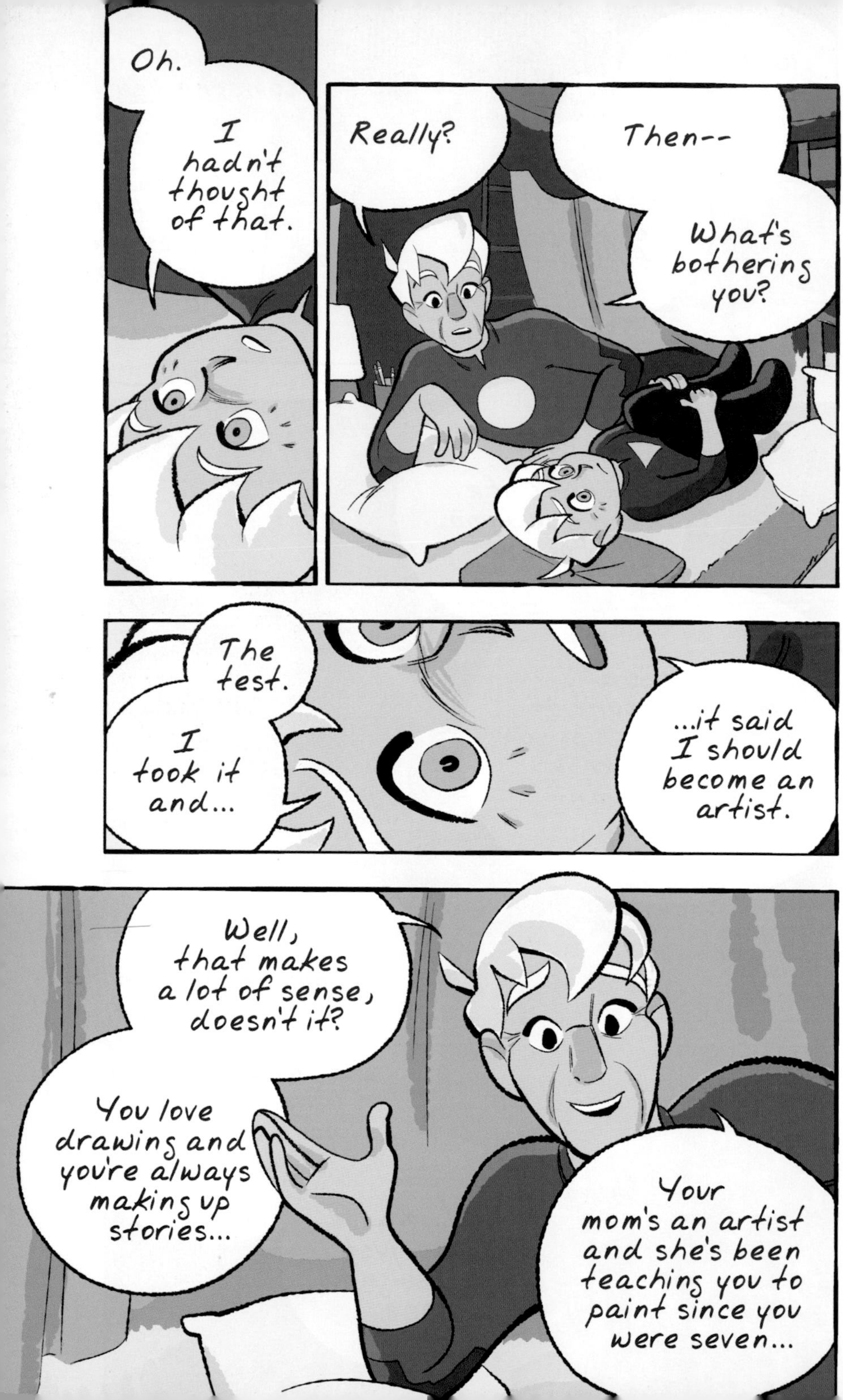
Oh.
I hadn't thought of that.
Really?
Then--
What's bothering you?
The test.
I took it and...
...it said I should become an artist.
Well, that makes a lot of sense, doesn't it?
You love drawing and you're always making up stories...
Your mom's an artist and she's been teaching you to paint since you were seven...

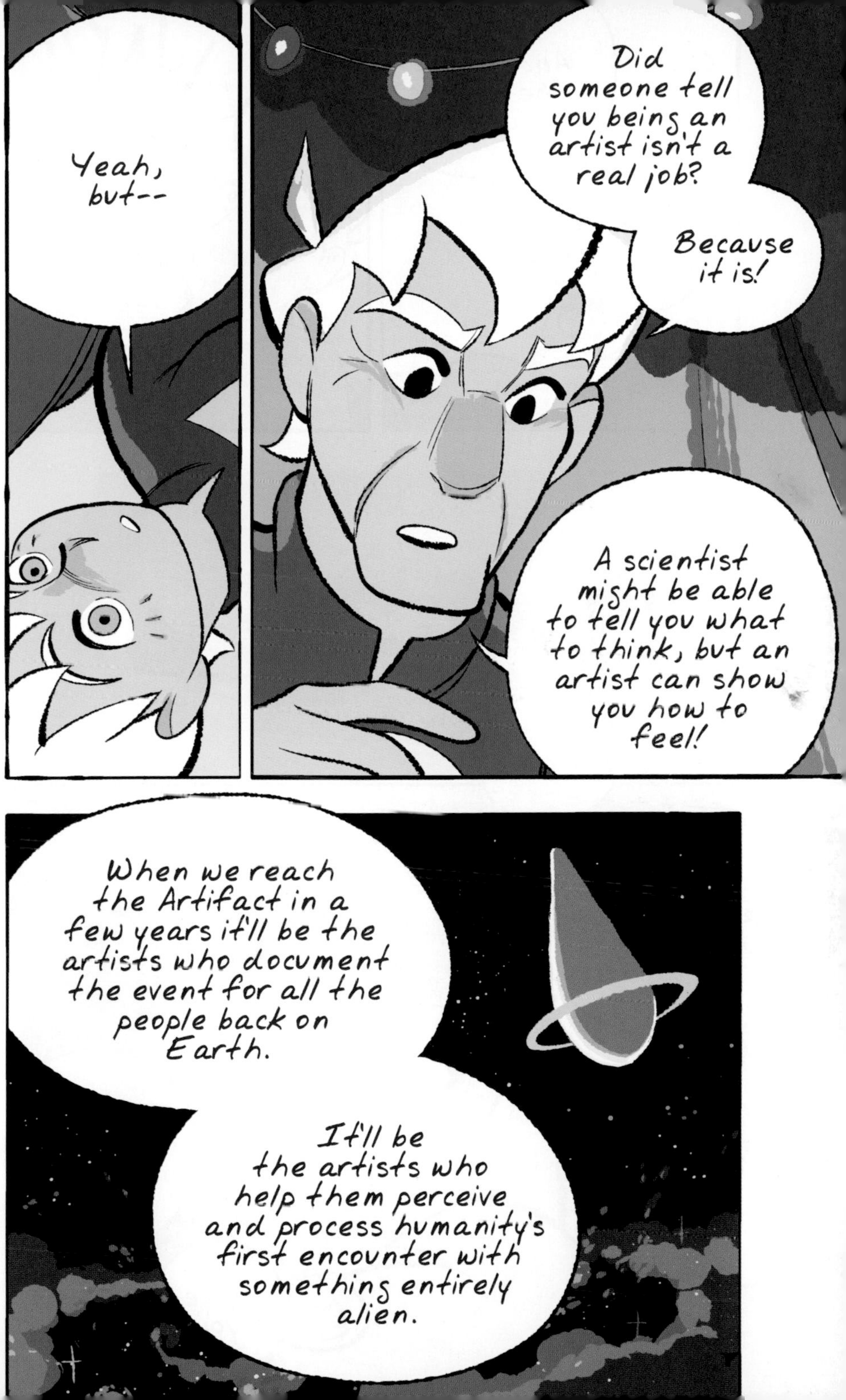
Yeah, but--
Did someone tell you being an artist isn't a real job?
Because it is!
A scientist might be able to tell you what to think, but an artist can show you how to feel!
When we reach the Artifact in a few years it'll be the artists who document the event for all the people back on Earth.
It'll be the artists who help them perceive and process humanity's first encounter with something entirely alien.

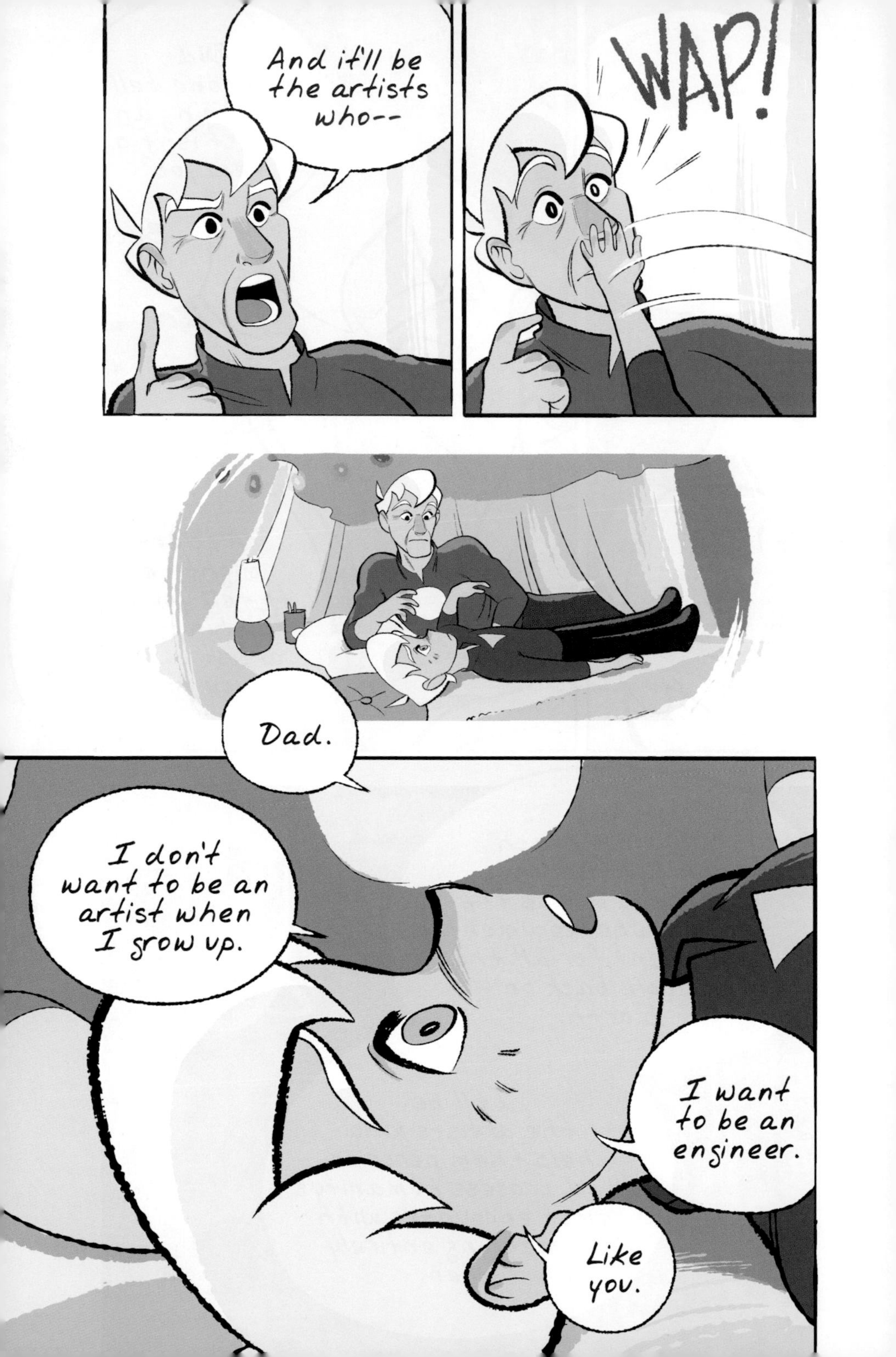
And it'll be the artists who--
WAP!
Dad.
I don't want to be an artist when I grow up.
I want to be an engineer.
Like you.

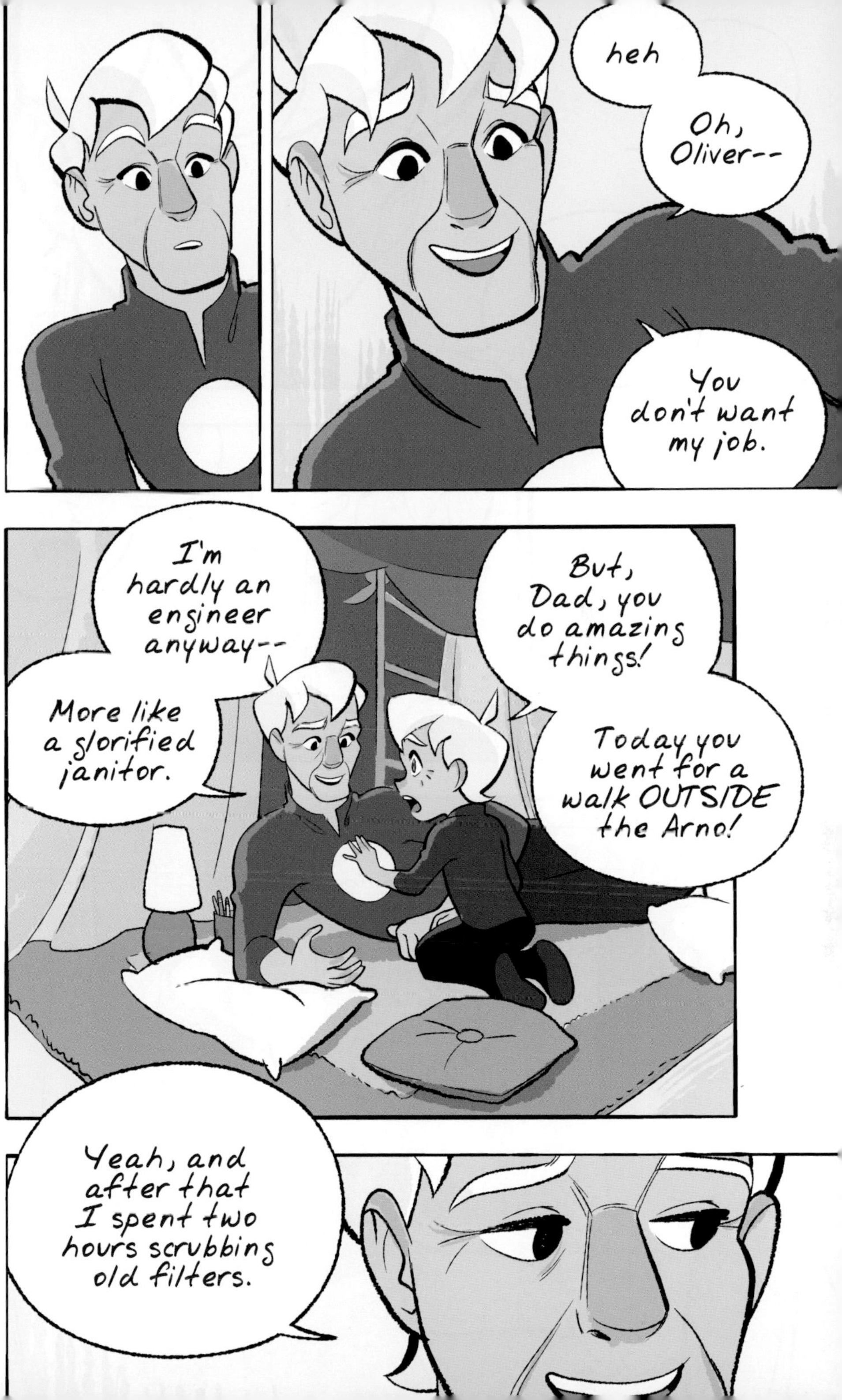
heh
Oh, Oliver--
You don't want my job.
I'm hardly an engineer anyway--
More like a glorified janitor.
But, Dad, you do amazing things!
Today you went for a walk OUTSIDE the Arno!
Yeah, and after that I spent two hours scrubbing old filters.

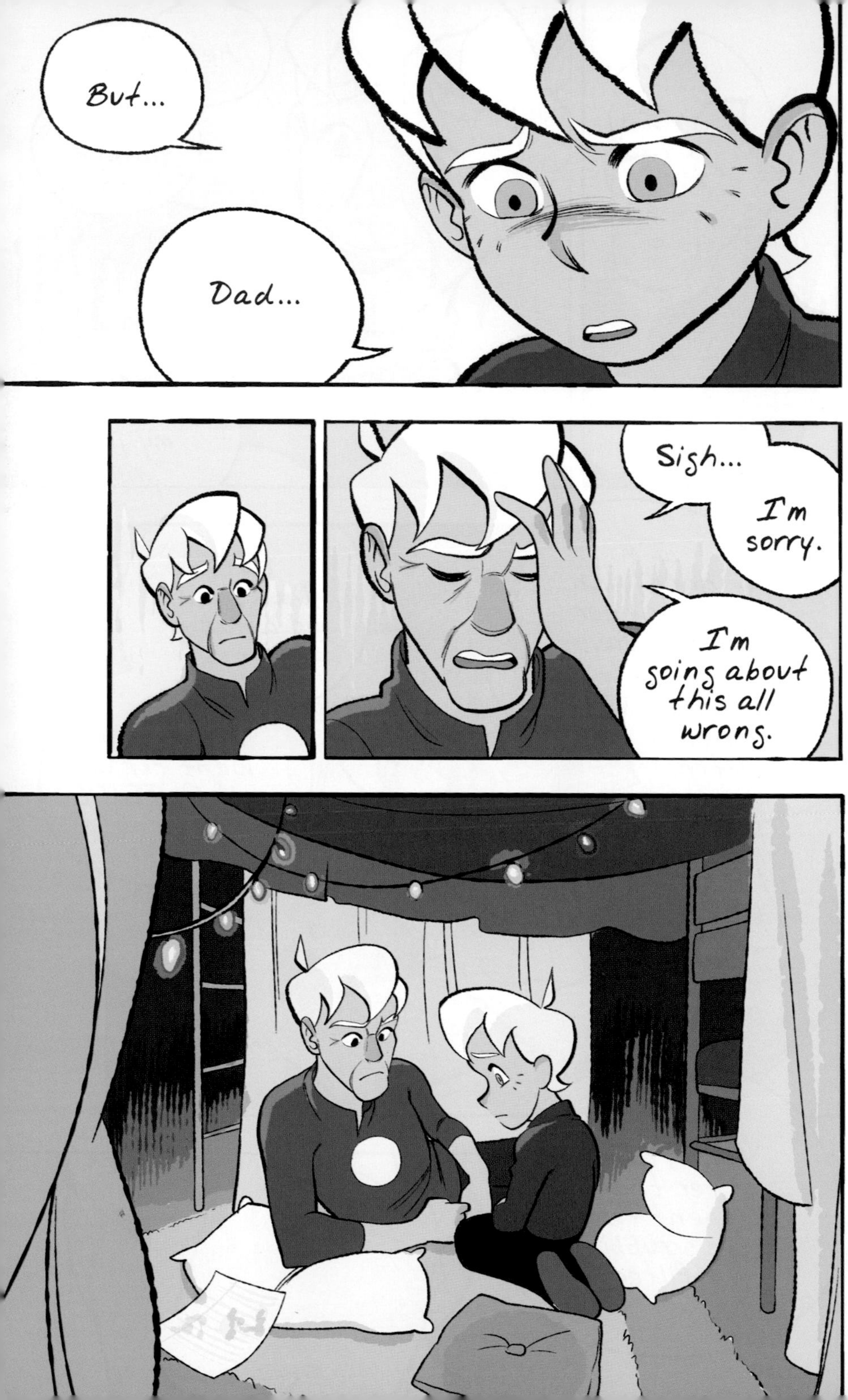
But...
Dad...
Sigh...
I'm sorry.
I'm going about this all wrong.

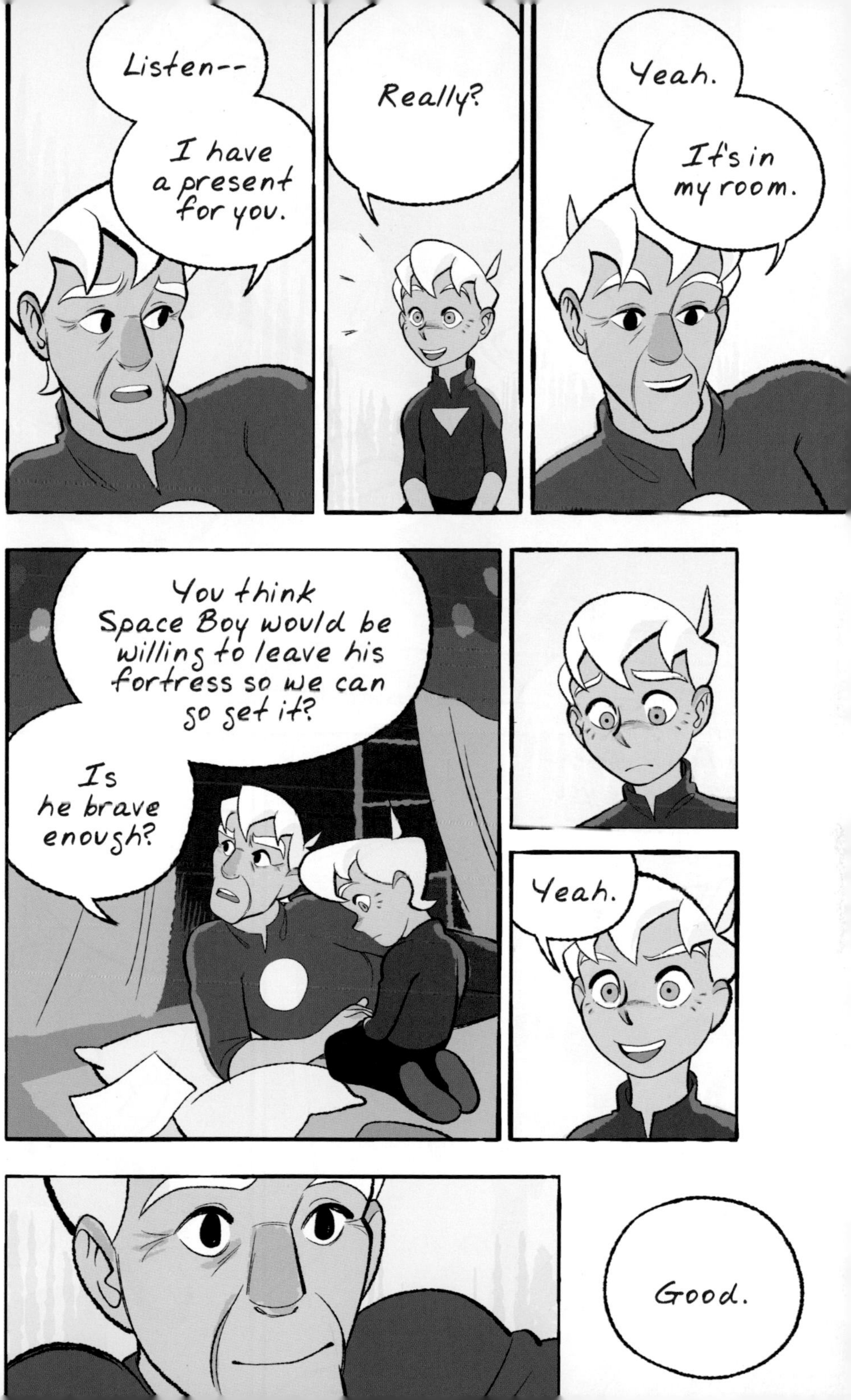
Listen--
I have a present for you.
Really?
Yeah.
It's in my room.
You think Space Boy would be willing to leave his fortress so we can go get it?
Is he brave enough?
Yeah.
Good.

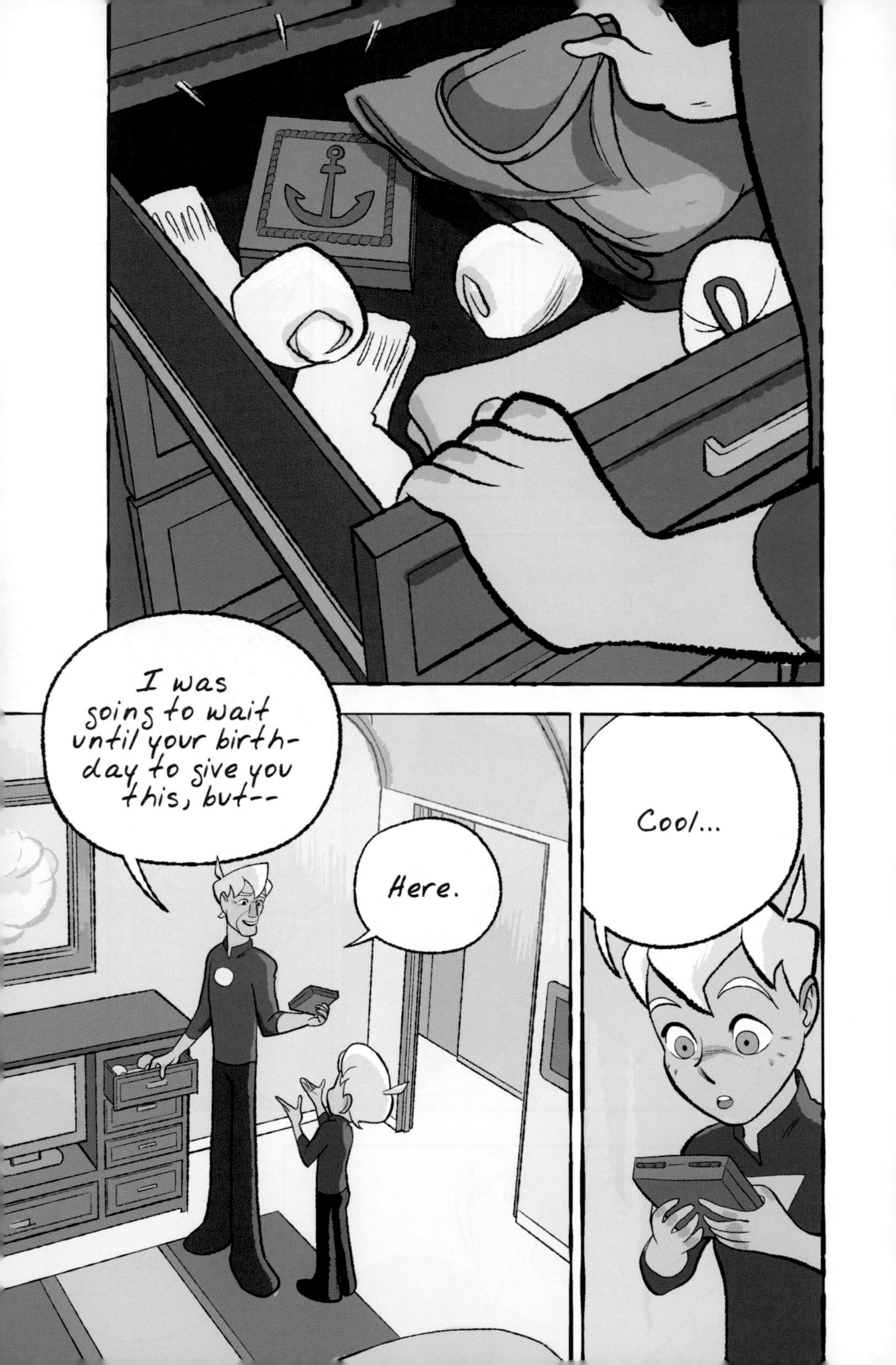
I was going to wait until your birthday to give you this, but--
Here.
Cool...

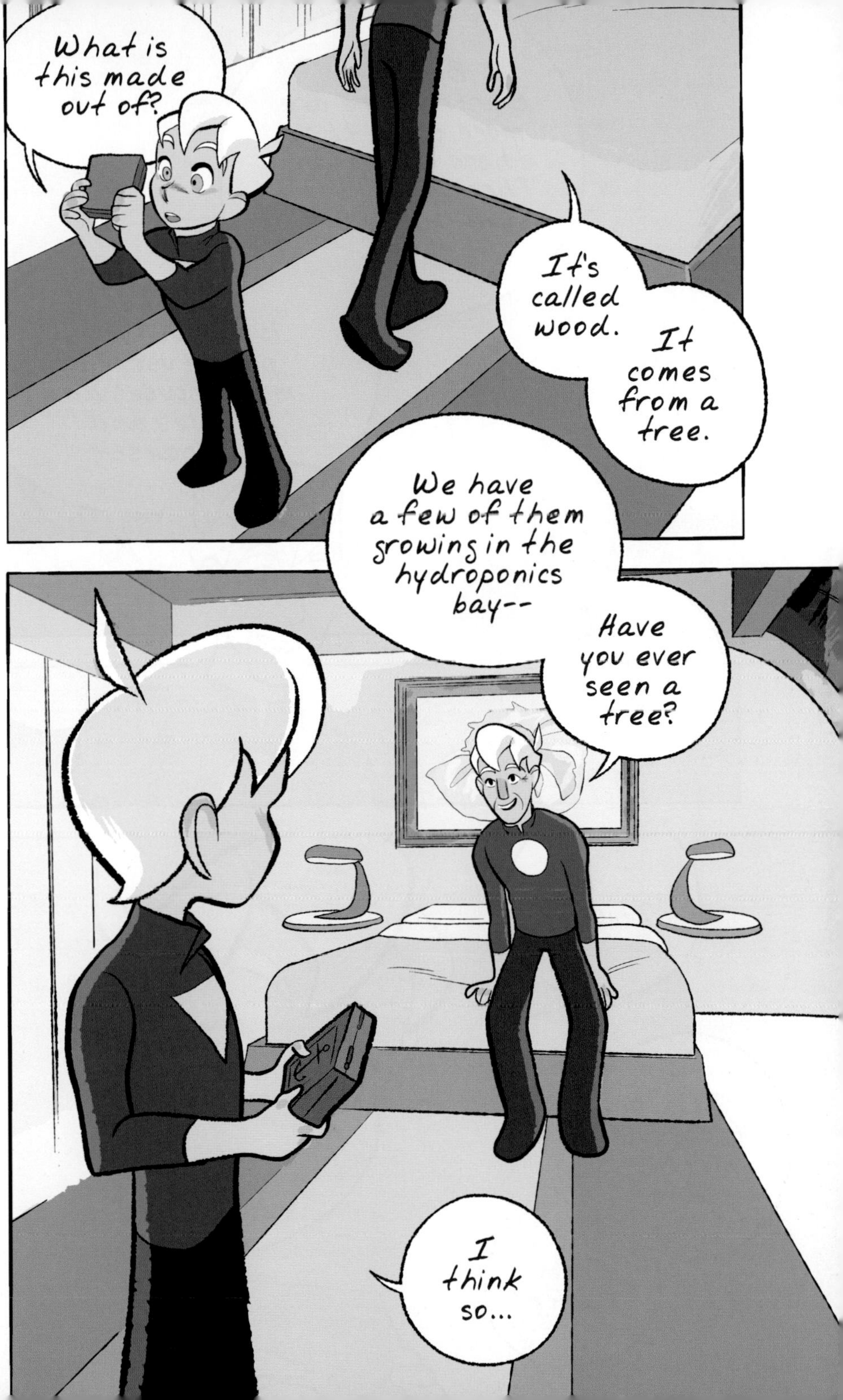
What is this made out of?
It's called wood.
It comes from a tree.
We have a few of them growing in the hydroponics bay--
Have you ever seen a tree?
I think so...

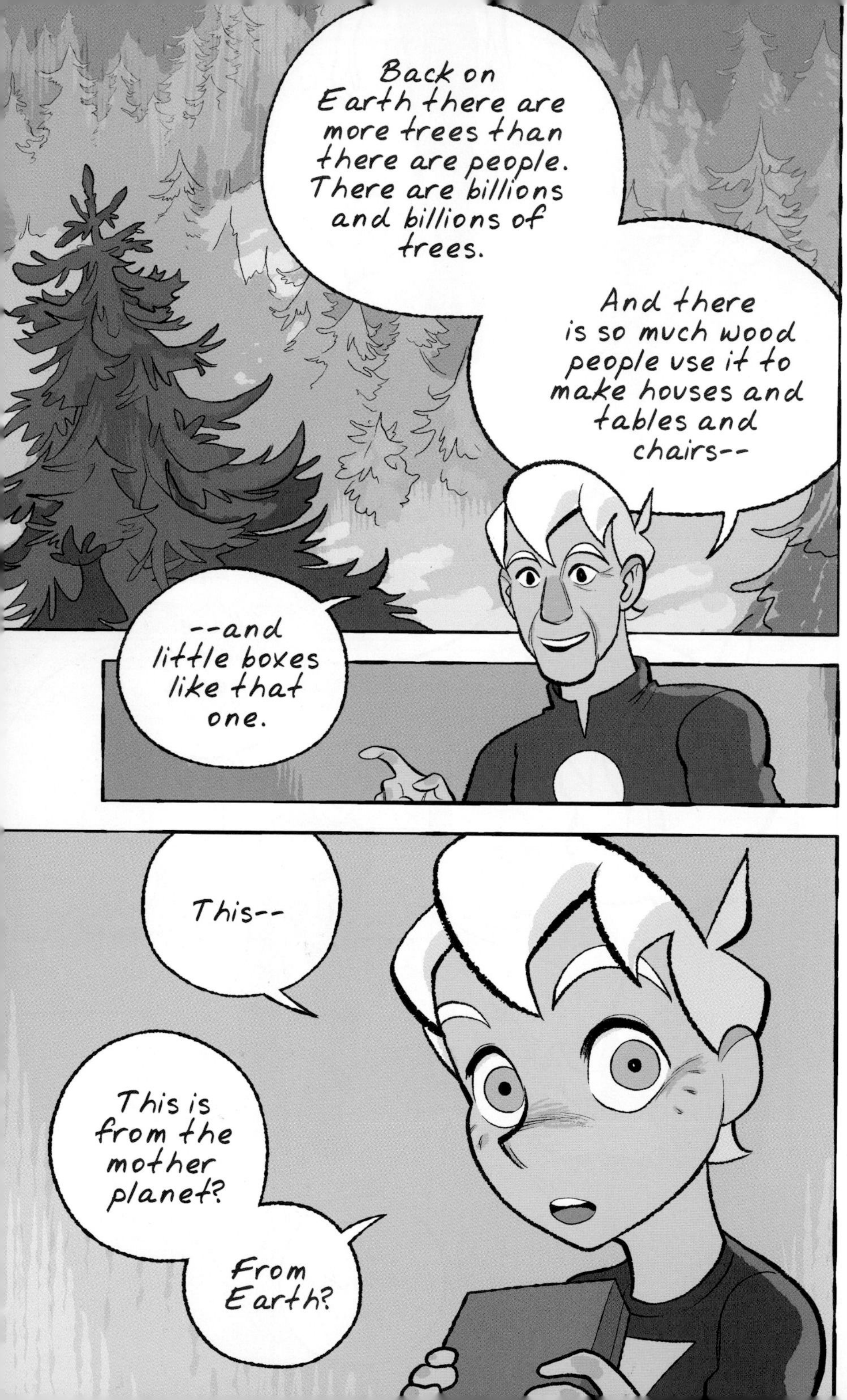
Back on Earth there are more trees than there are people. There are billions and billions of trees.
And there is so much wood people use it to make houses and tables and chairs--
--and little boxes like that one.
This--
This is from the mother planet?
From Earth?

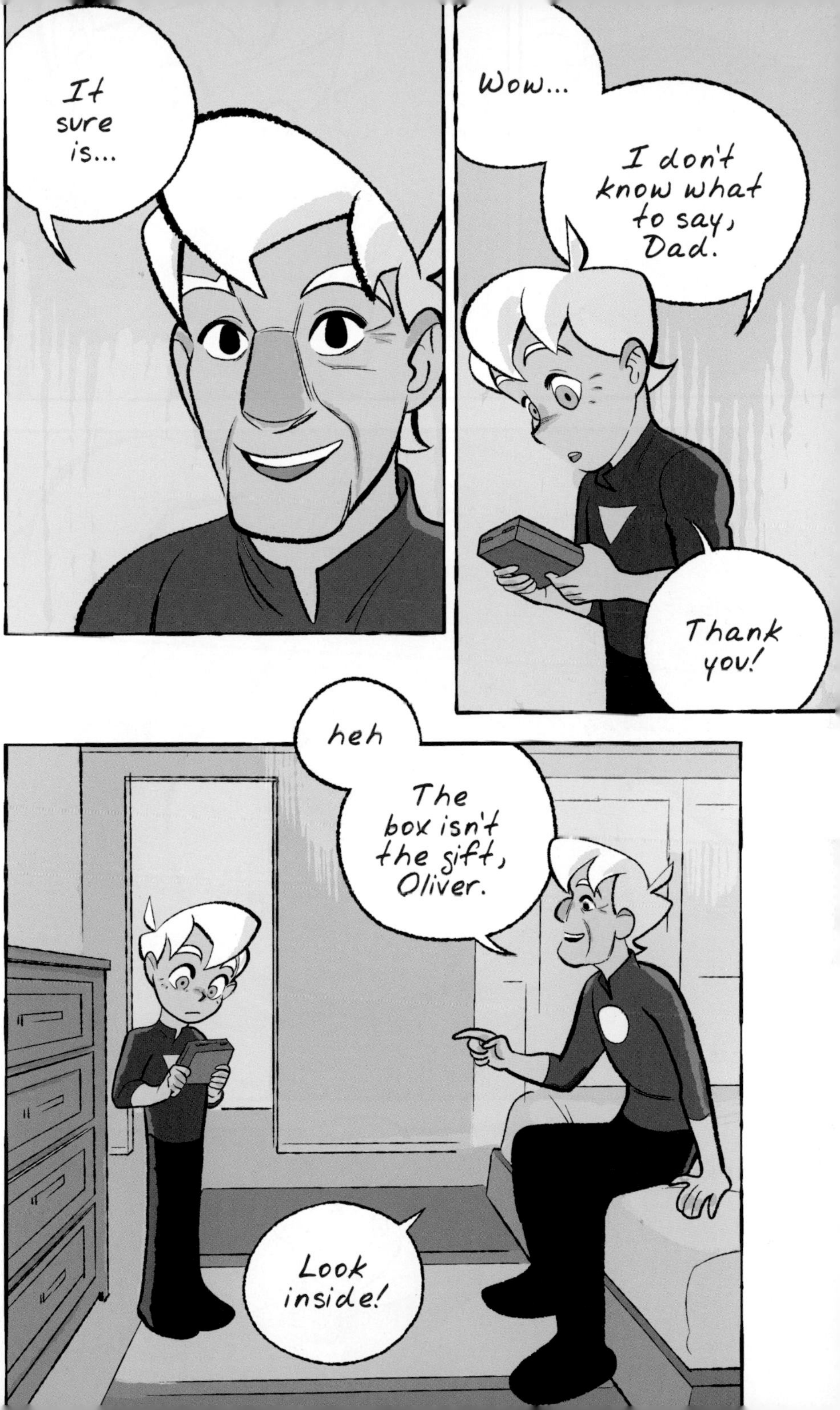
It sure is...
Wow...
I don't know what to say, Dad.
Thank you!
heh
The box isn't the gift, Oliver.
Look inside!

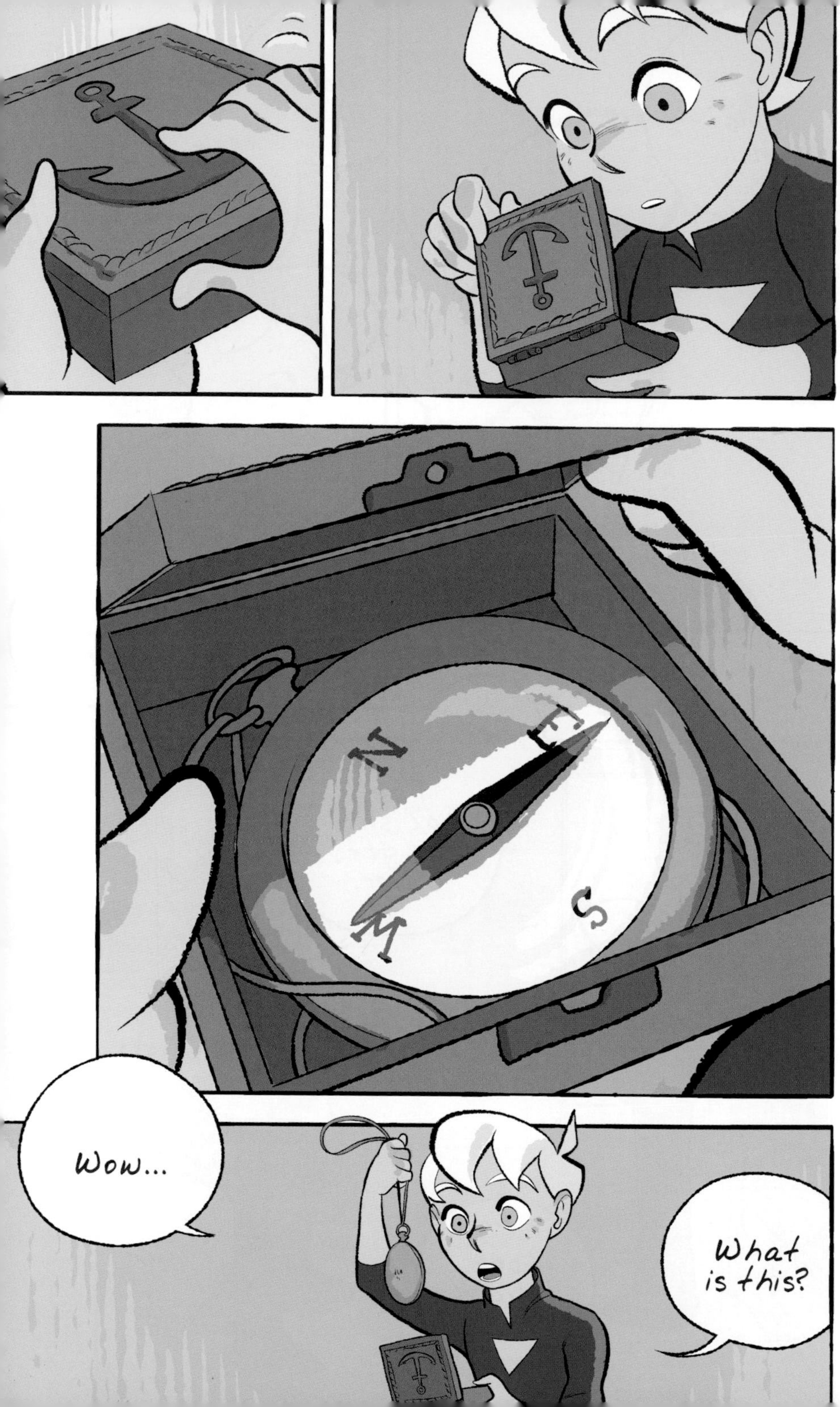
N
E
S
W
Wow...
What is this?

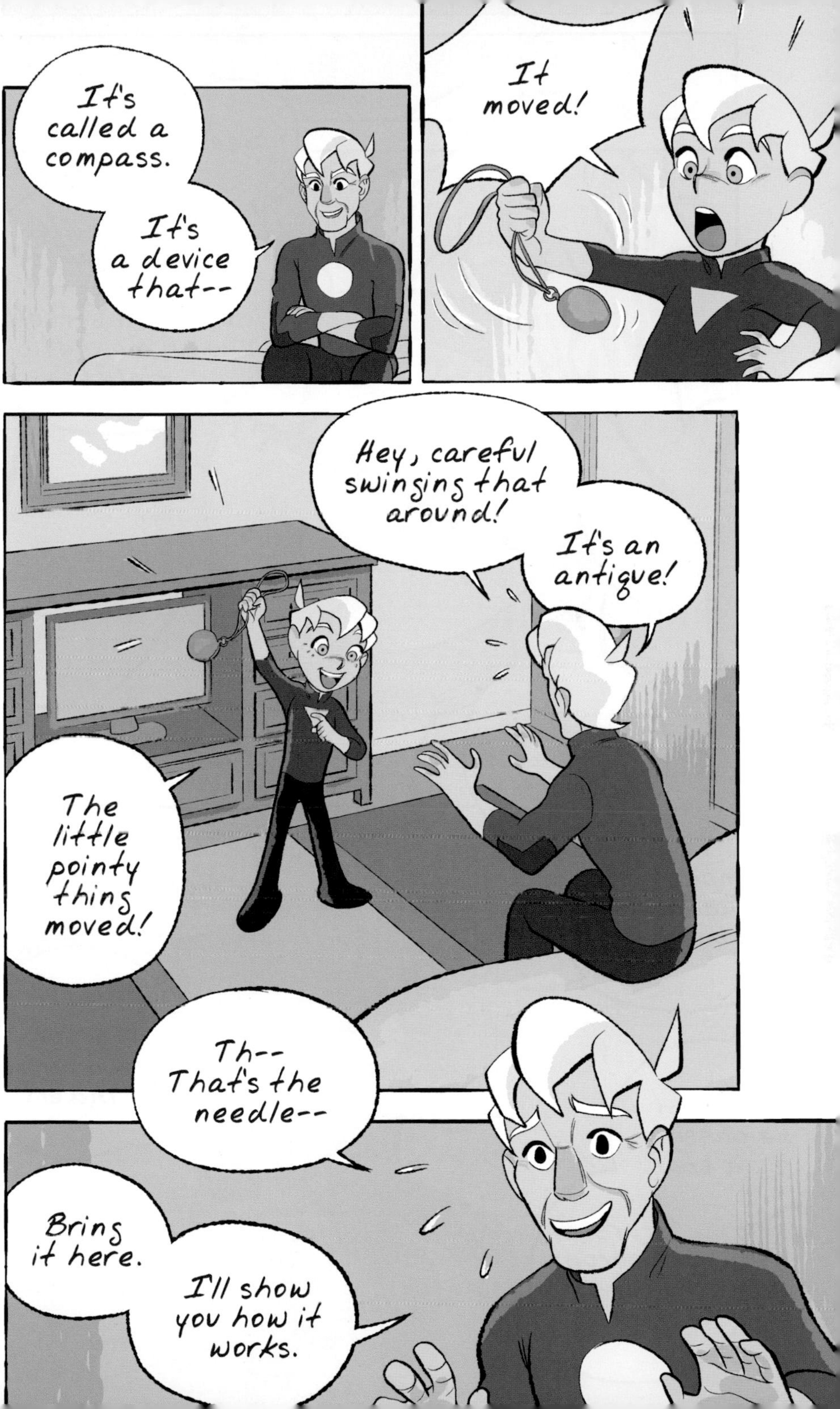
It's called a compass.
It's a device that--
It moved!
Hey, careful swinging that around!
It's an antique!
The little pointy thing moved!
Th-- That's the needle--
Bring it here.
I'll show you how it works.

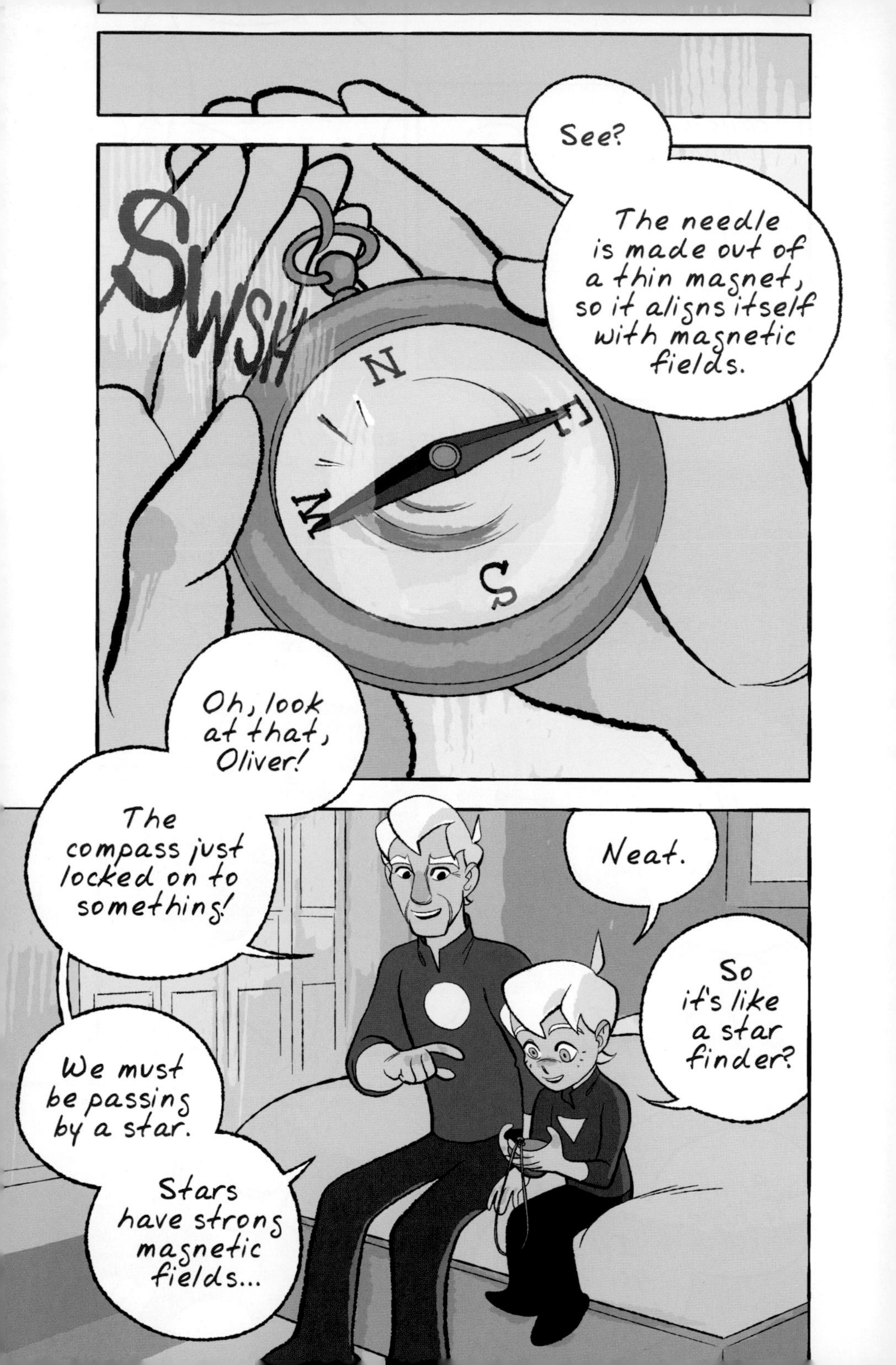
SWSH
See?
The needle is made out of a thin magnet, so it aligns itself with magnetic fields.
N
E
S
W
Oh, look at that, Oliver!
The compass just locked on to something!
Neat.
So it's like a star finder?
We must be passing by a star.
Stars have strong magnetic fields...

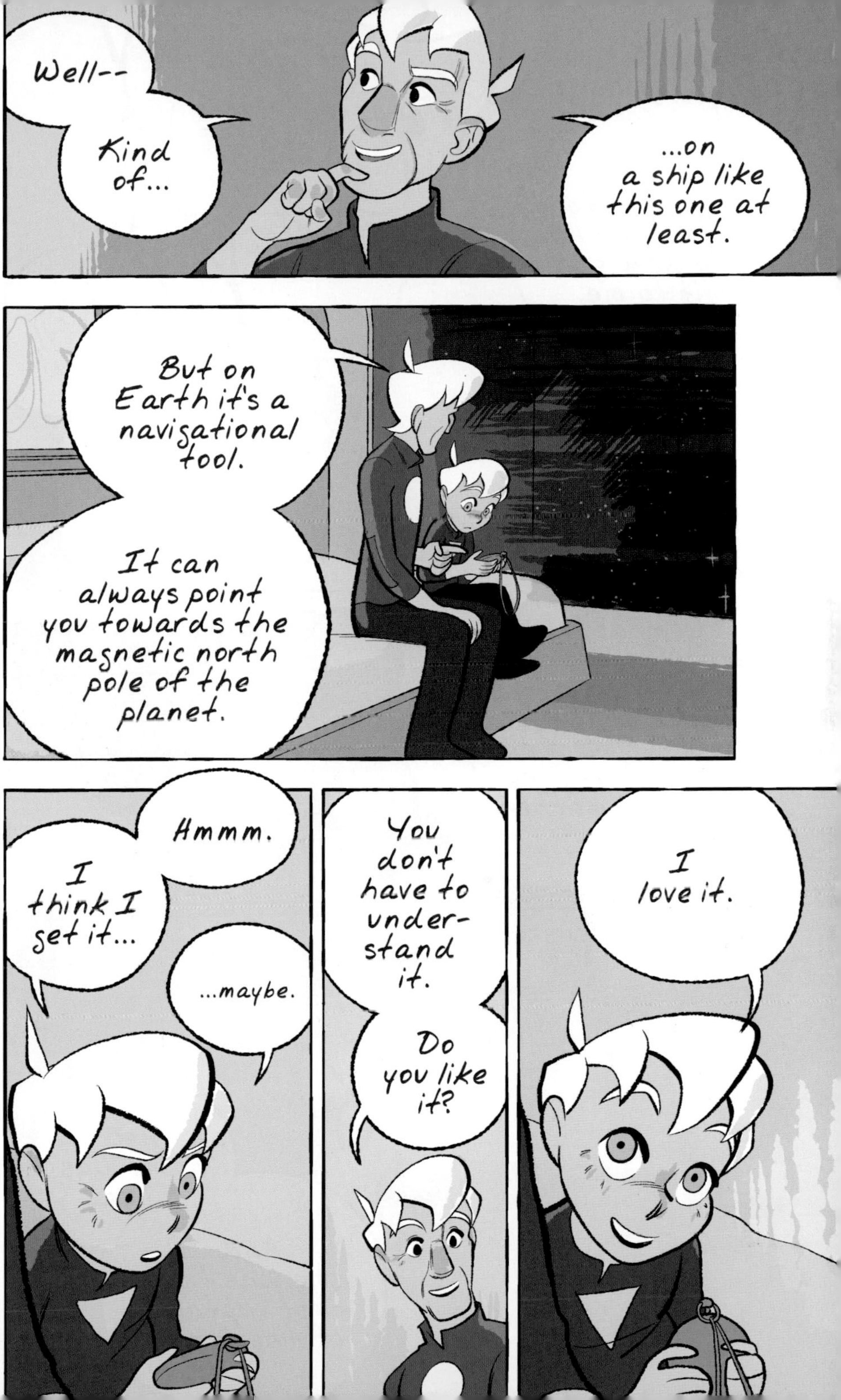
Well--
Kind of...
...on a ship like this one at least.
But on Earth it's a navigational tool.
It can always point you towards the magnetic north pole of the planet.
Hmmm.
I think I get it...
...maybe.
You don't have to under-stand it.
Do you like it?
I love it.

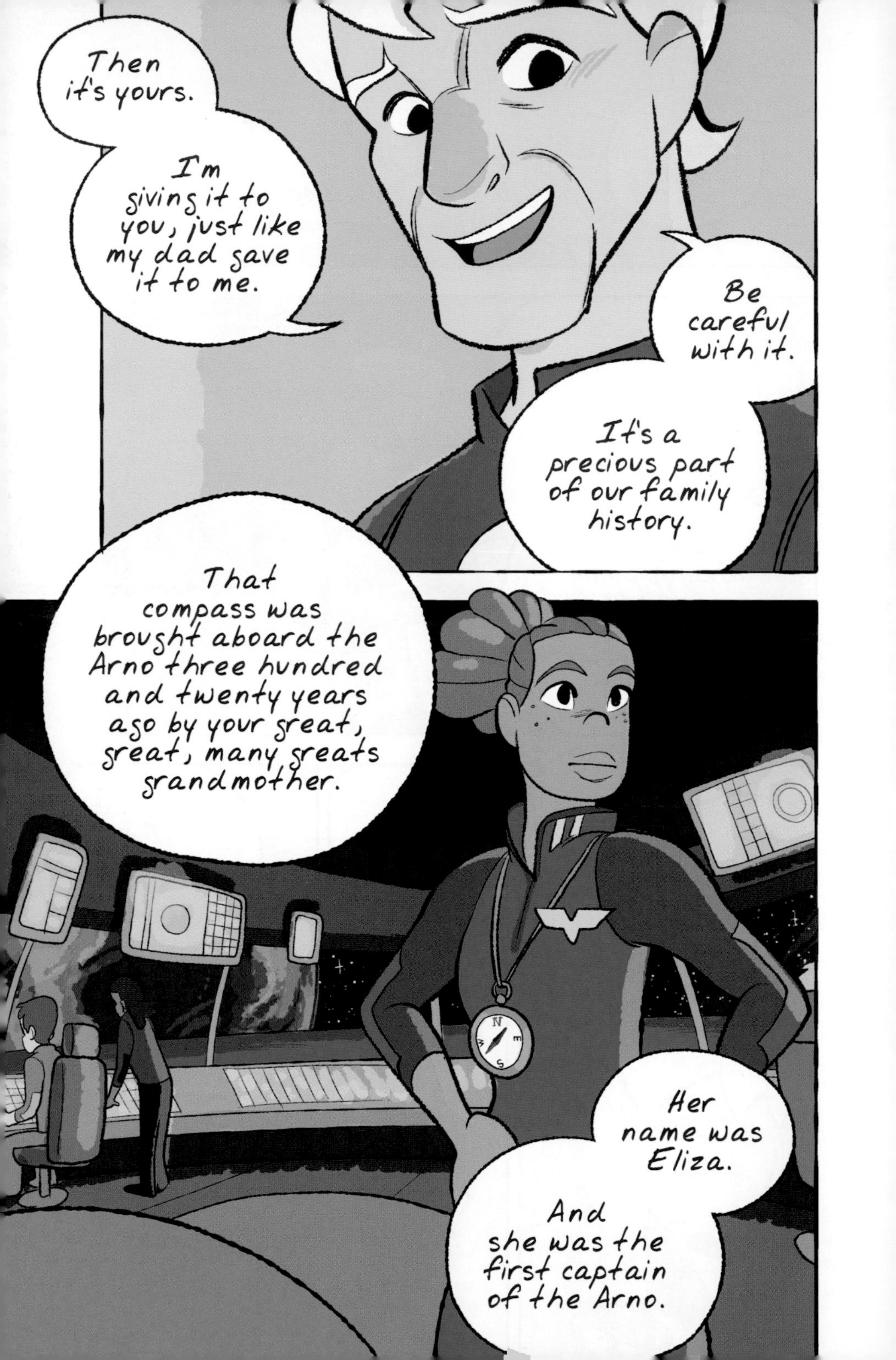
Then it's yours.
I'm giving it to you, just like my dad gave it to me.
Be careful with it.
It's a precious part of our family history.
That compass was brought aboard the Arno three hundred and twenty years ago by your great, great, many greats grandmother.
Her name was Eliza.
And she was the first captain of the Arno.
N
E
S
W

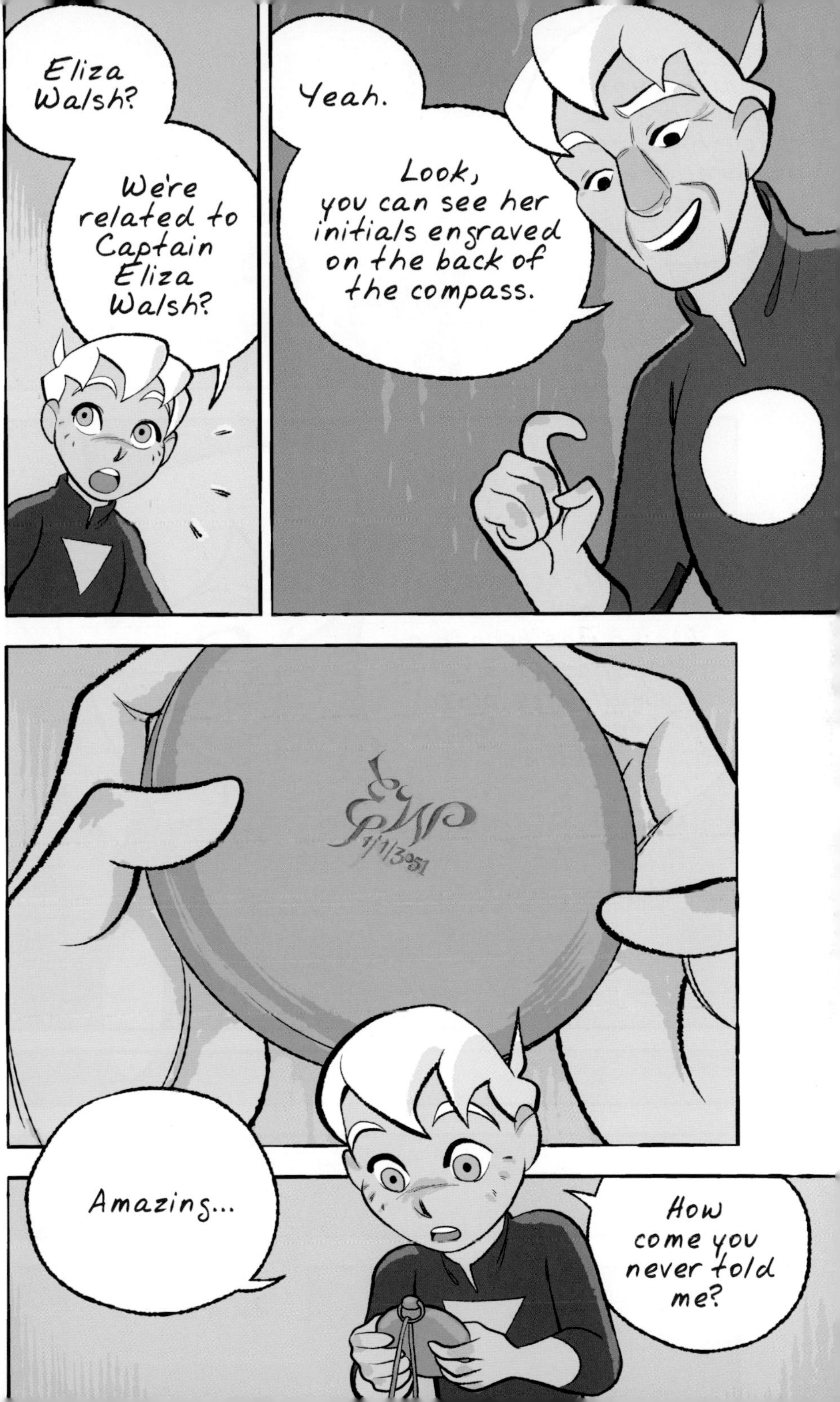
Eliza Walsh?
We're related to Captain Eliza Walsh?
Yeah.
Look, you can see her initials engraved on the back of the compass.
EW
1/1/3051
Amazing...
How come you never told me?

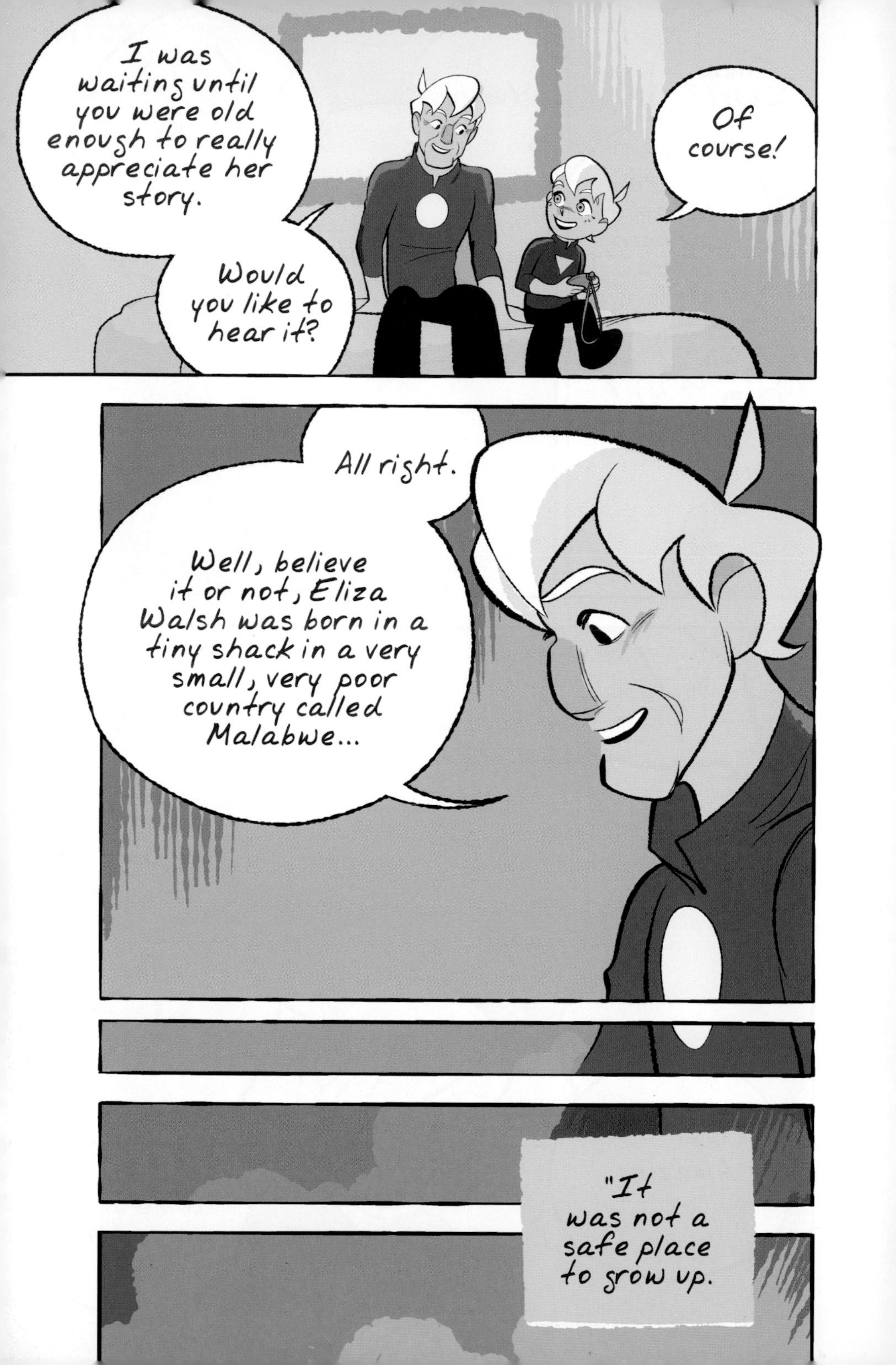

I was waiting until you were old enough to really appreciate her story.
Would you like to hear it?
Of course!
All right.
Well, believe it or not, Eliza Walsh was born in a tiny shack in a very small, very poor country called Malabwe...
"It was not a safe place to grow up.

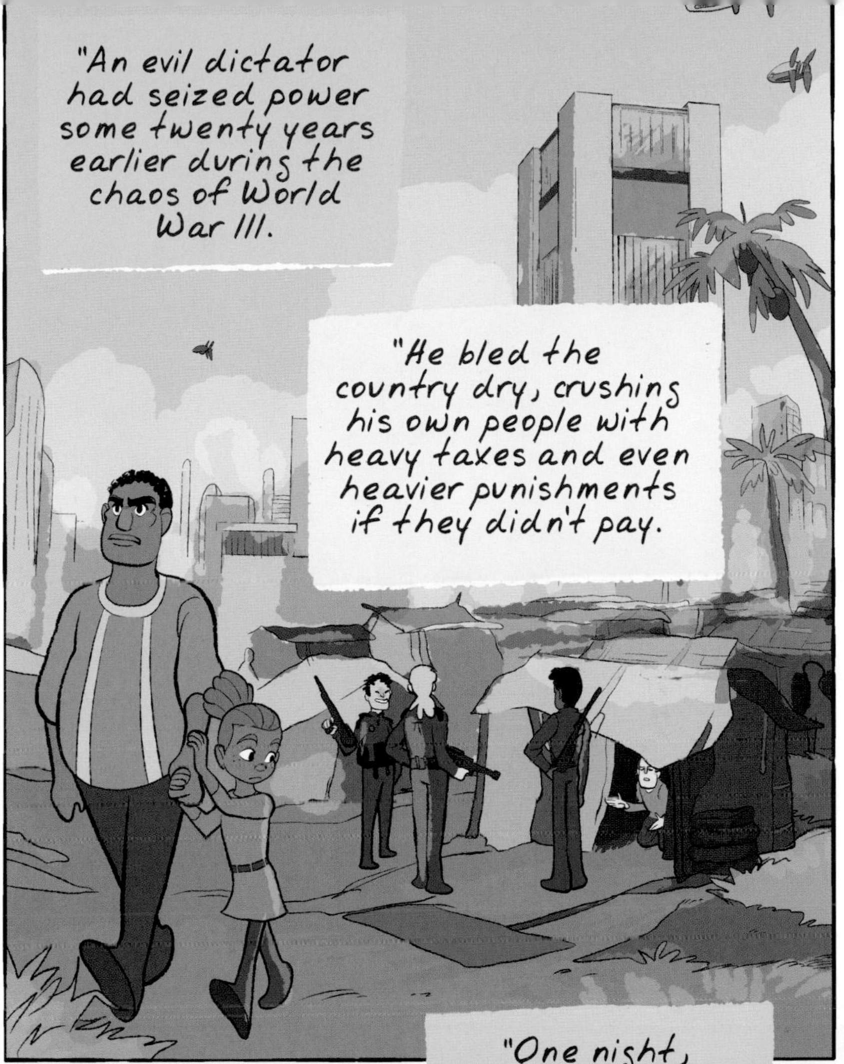
"An evil dictator had seized power some twenty years earlier during the chaos of World War III.
"He bled the country dry, crushing his own people with heavy taxes and even heavier punishments if they didn't pay.

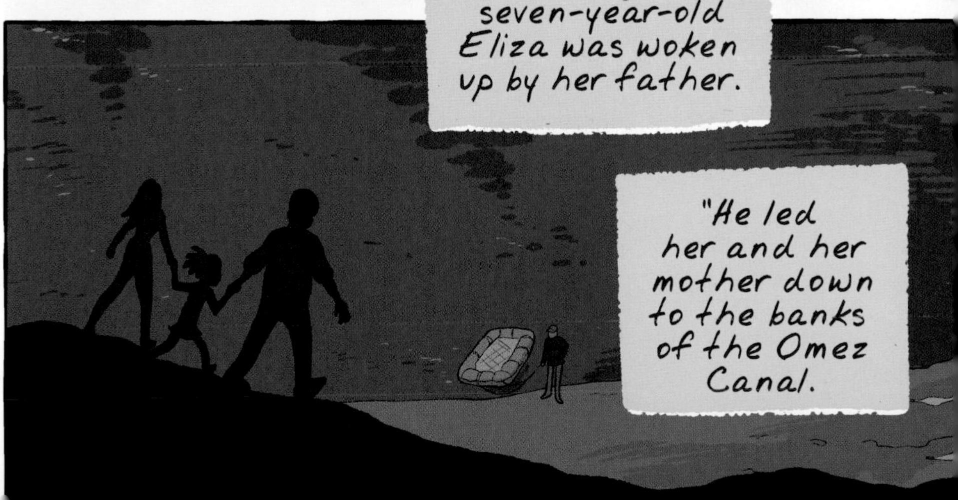
"One night, seven-year-old Eliza was woken up by her father.
"He led her and her mother down to the banks of the Omez Canal.

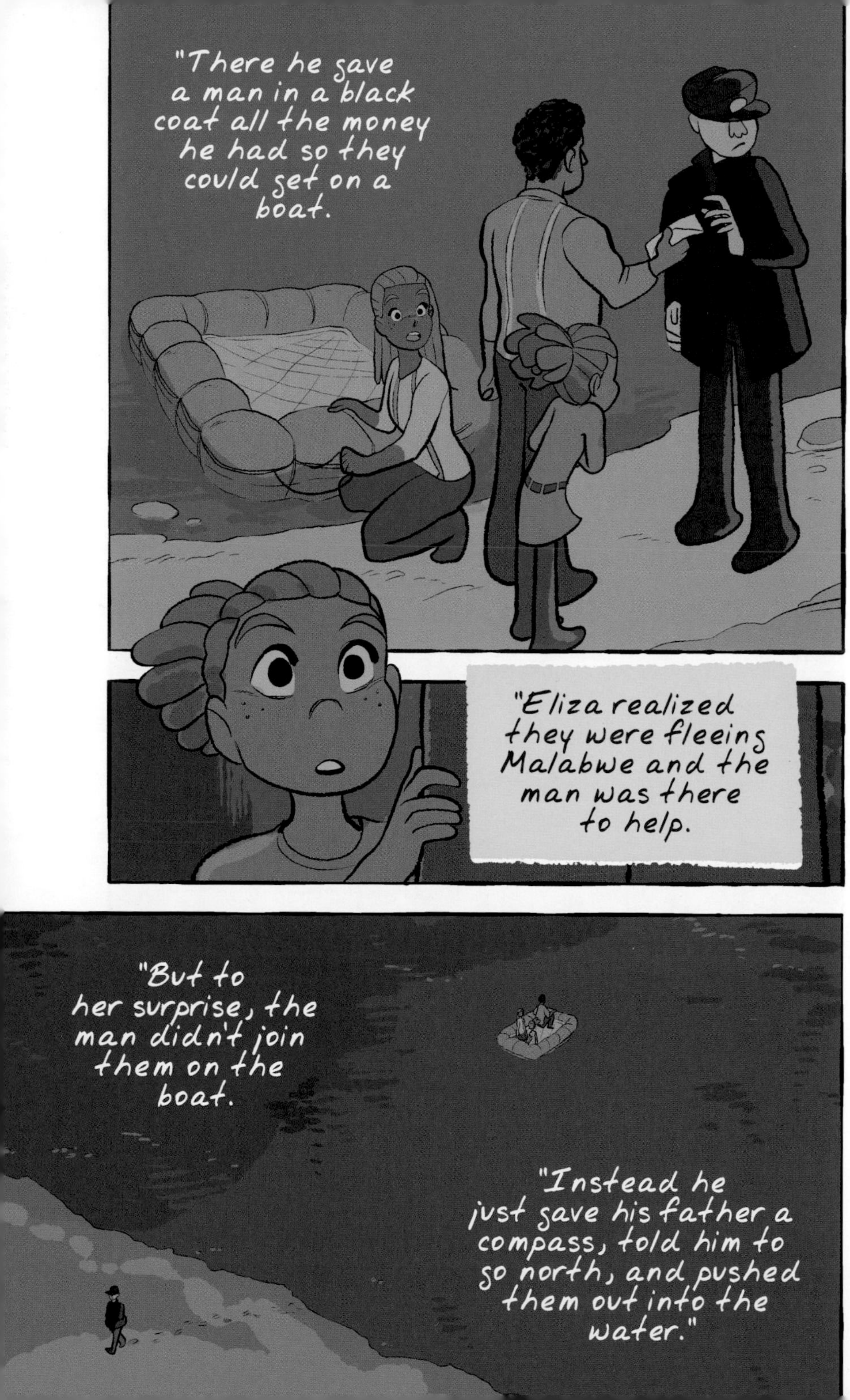

"There he gave a man in a black coat all the money he had so they could get on a boat.
"Eliza realized they were fleeing Malabwe and the man was there to help.
"But to her surprise, the man didn't join them on the boat.
"Instead he just gave his father a compass, told him to go north, and pushed them out into the water."

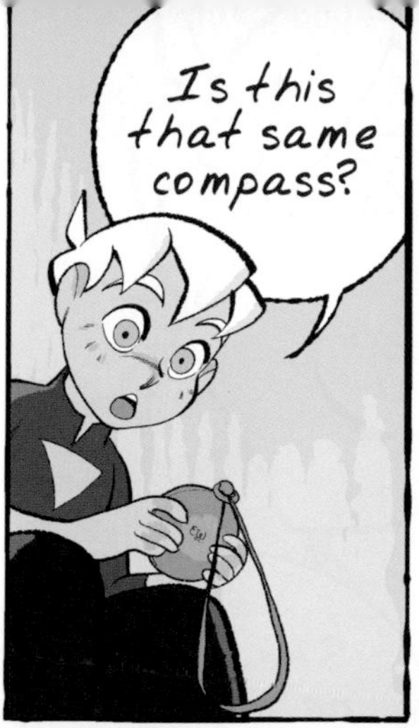
Is this that same compass?

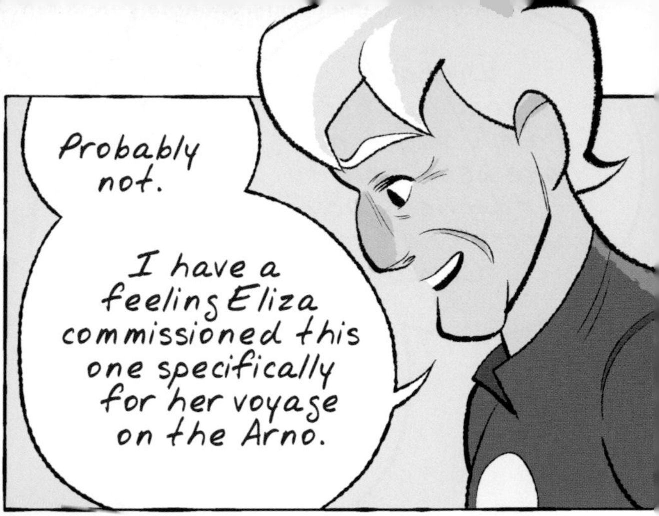
Probably not.
I have a feeling Eliza commissioned this one specifically for her voyage on the Arno.

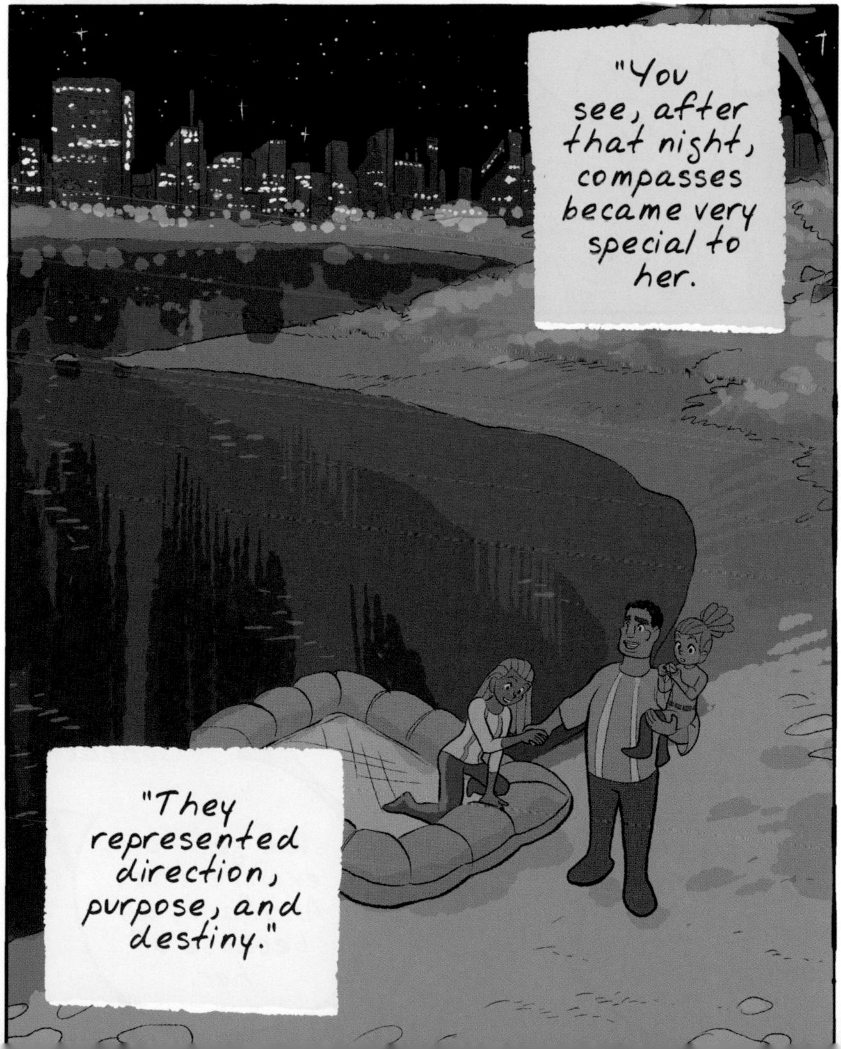
"You see, after that night, compasses became very special to her.
"They represented direction, purpose, and destiny."

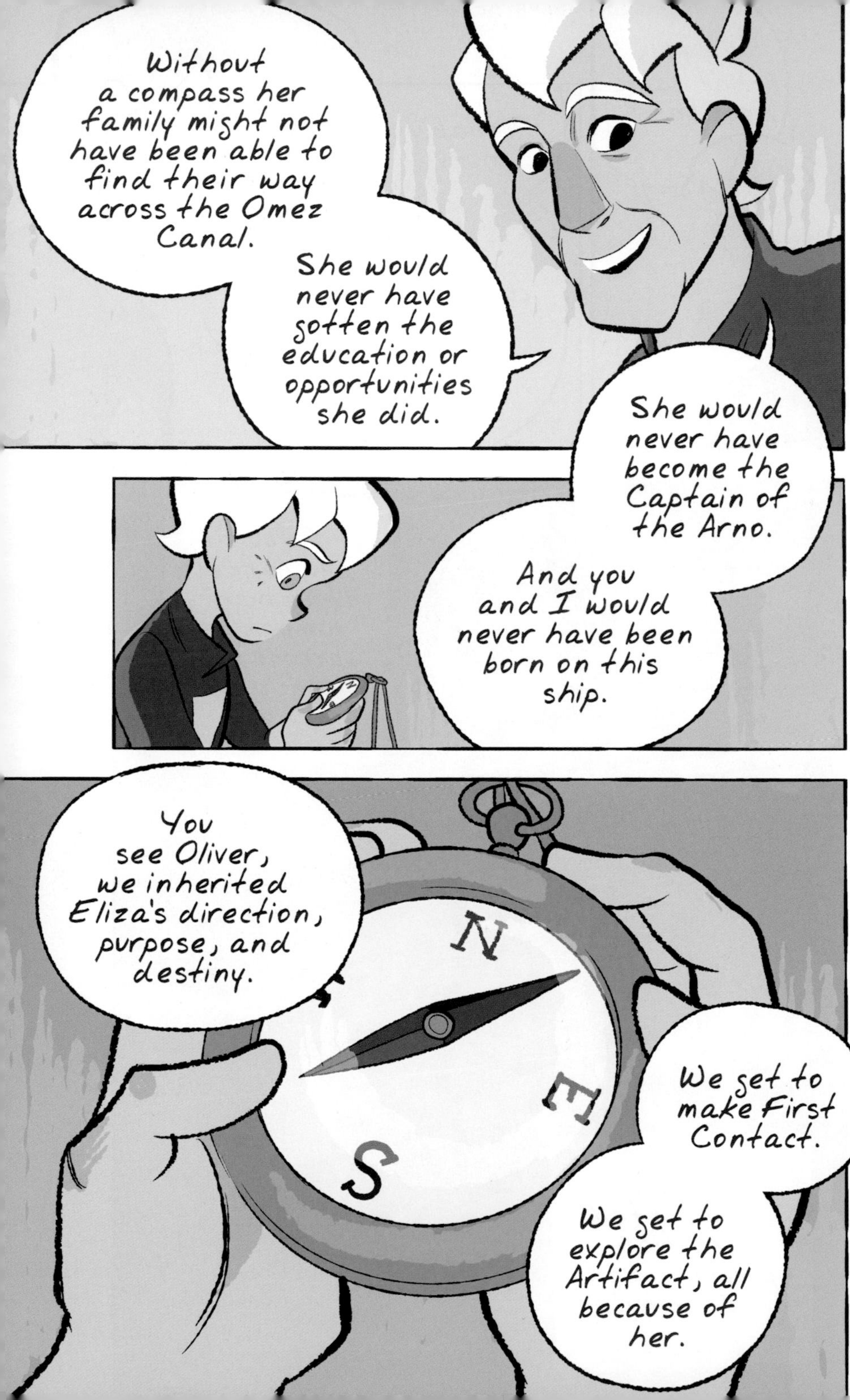
Without a compass her family might not have been able to find their way across the Omez Canal.
She would never have gotten the education or opportunities she did.
She would never have become the Captain of the Arno.
And you and I would never have been born on this ship.
You see Oliver, we inherited Eliza's direction, purpose, and destiny.
N
E
S
We set to make First Contact.
We set to explore the Artifact, all because of her.

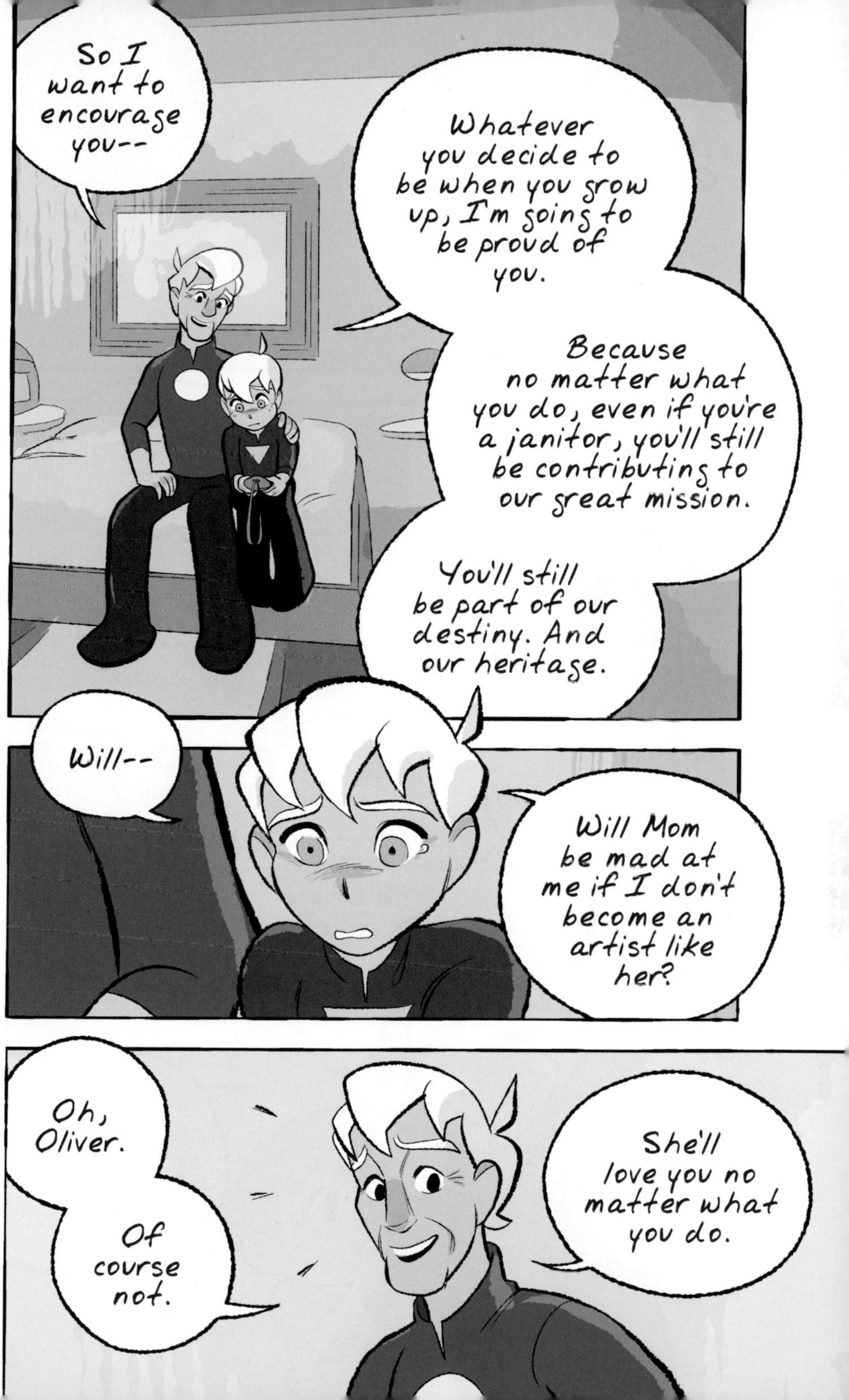
So I want to encourage you--
Whatever you decide to be when you grow up, I'm going to be proud of you.
Because no matter what you do, even if you're a janitor, you'll still be contributing to our great mission.
You'll still be part of our destiny. And our heritage.
Will--
Will Mom be mad at me if I don't become an artist like her?
Oh, Oliver.
Of course not.
She'll love you no matter what you do.

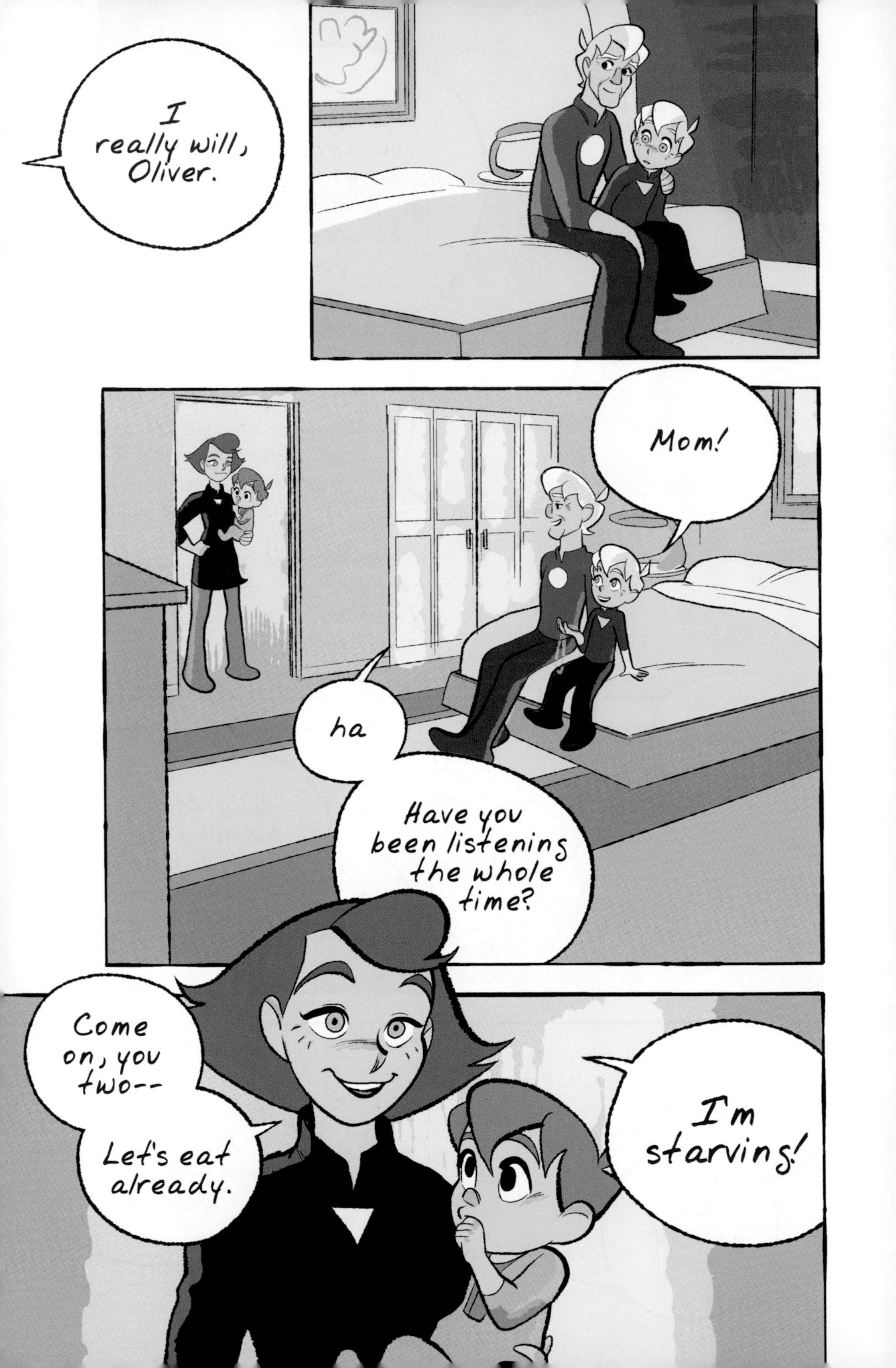

I really will, Oliver.
Mom!
ha
Have you been listening the whole time?
Come on, you two--
Let's eat already.
I'm starving!

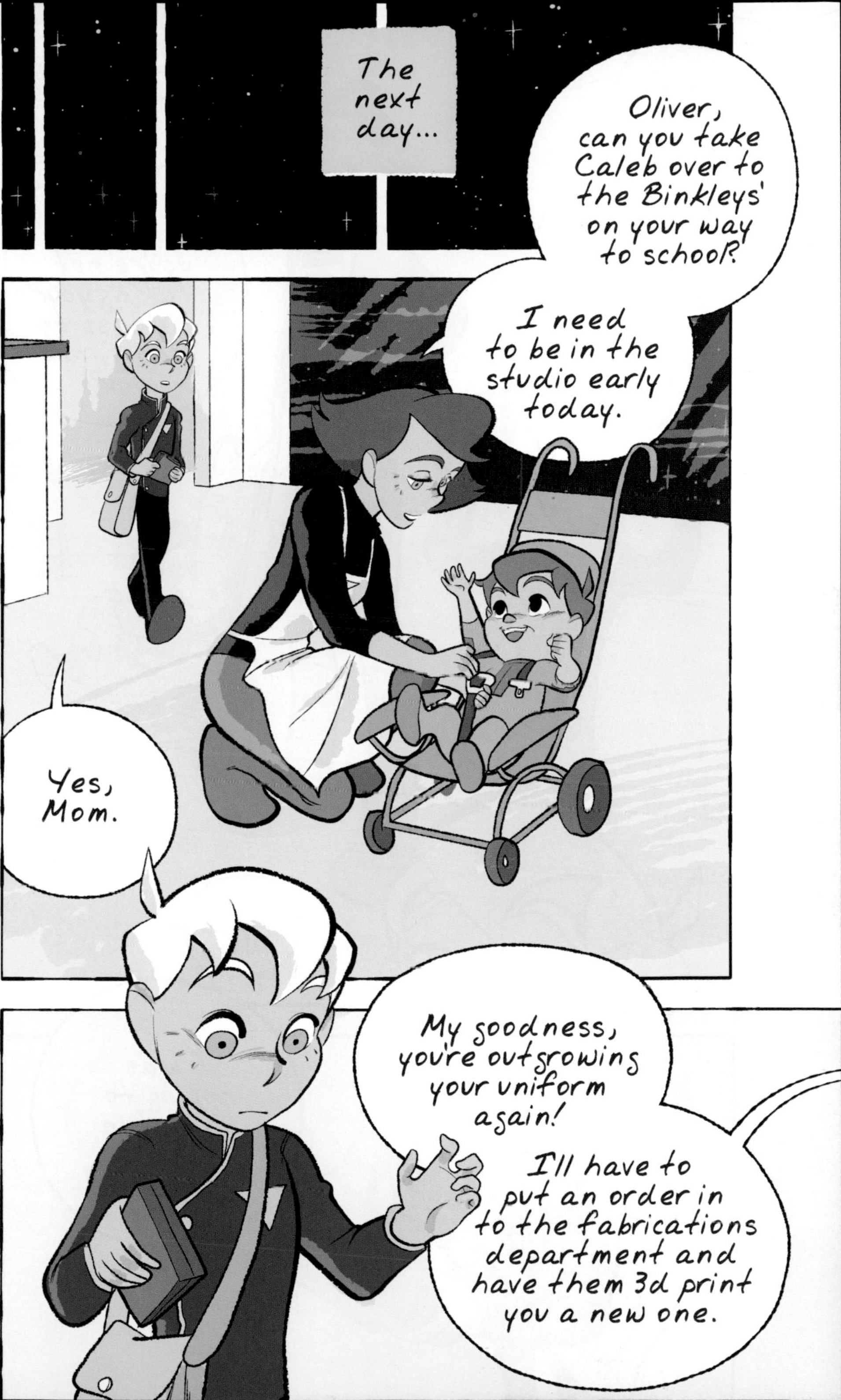
The next day...
Oliver, can you take Caleb over to the Binkleys' on your way to school?
I need to be in the studio early today.
Yes, Mom.
My goodness, you're outgrowing your uniform again!
I'll have to put an order in to the fabrications department and have them 3d print you a new one.

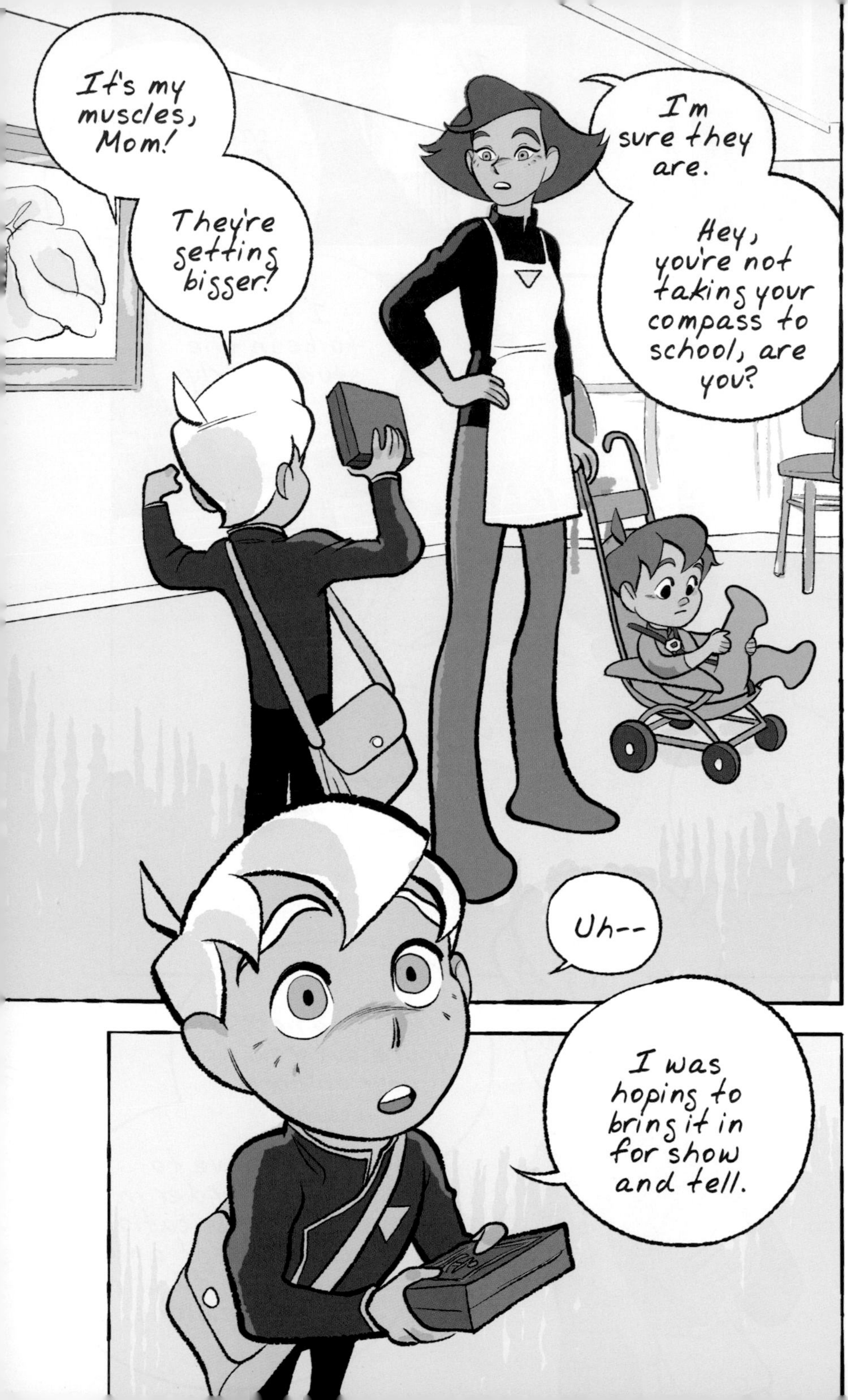

It's my muscles, Mom!
They're getting bigger!
I'm sure they are.
Hey, you're not taking your compass to school, are you?
Uh--
I was hoping to bring it in for show and tell.

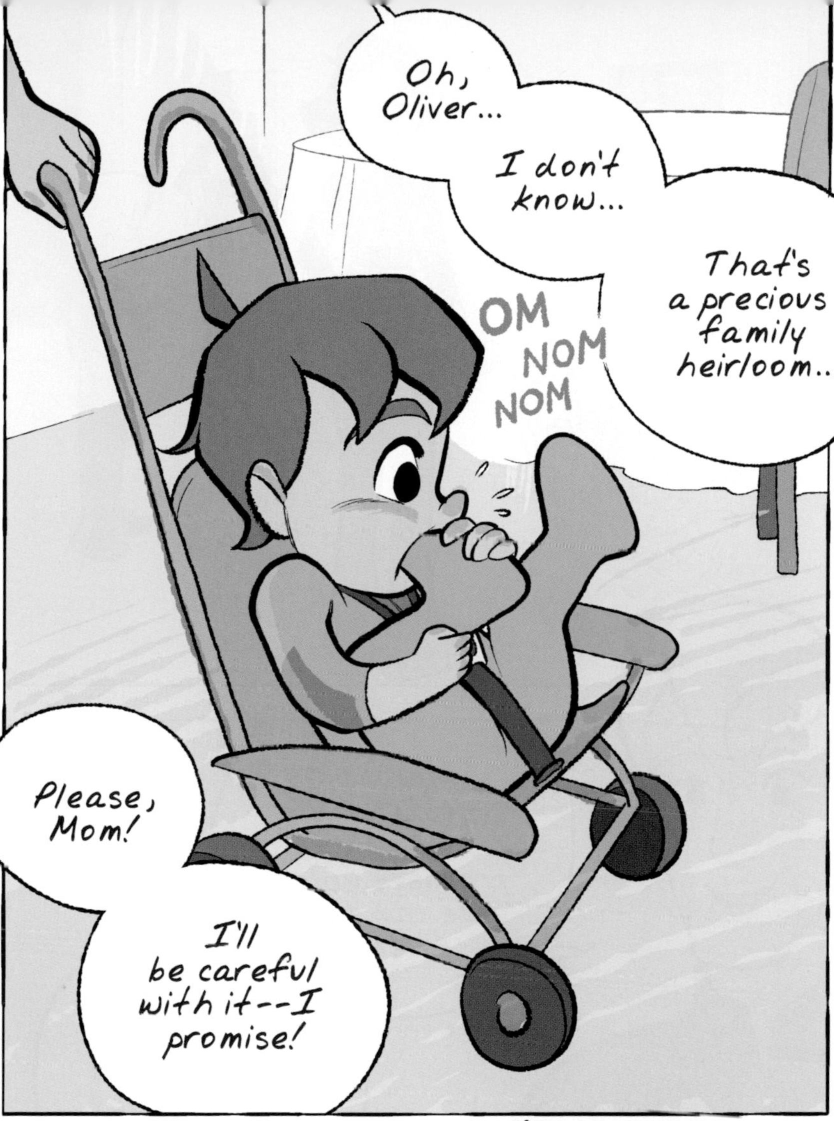
Oh, Oliver...
I don't know...
That's a precious family heirloom...
OM NOM NOM
Please, Mom!
I'll be careful with it--I promise!

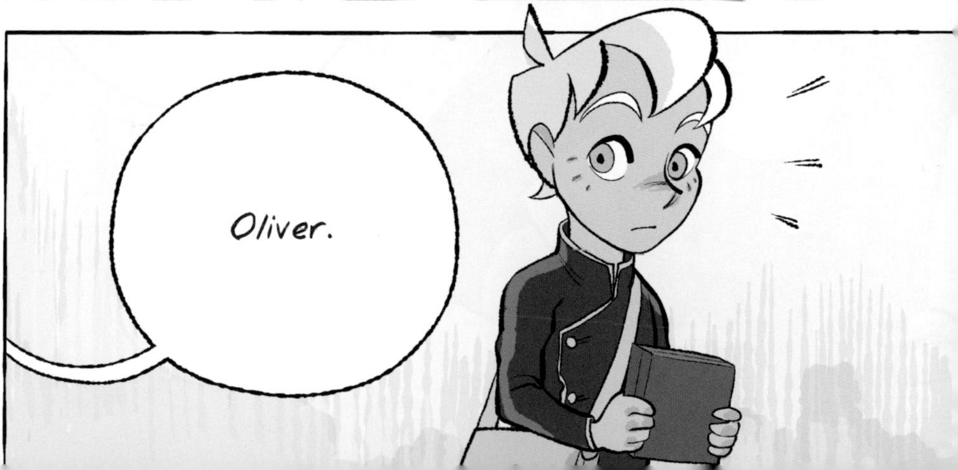
Oliver.

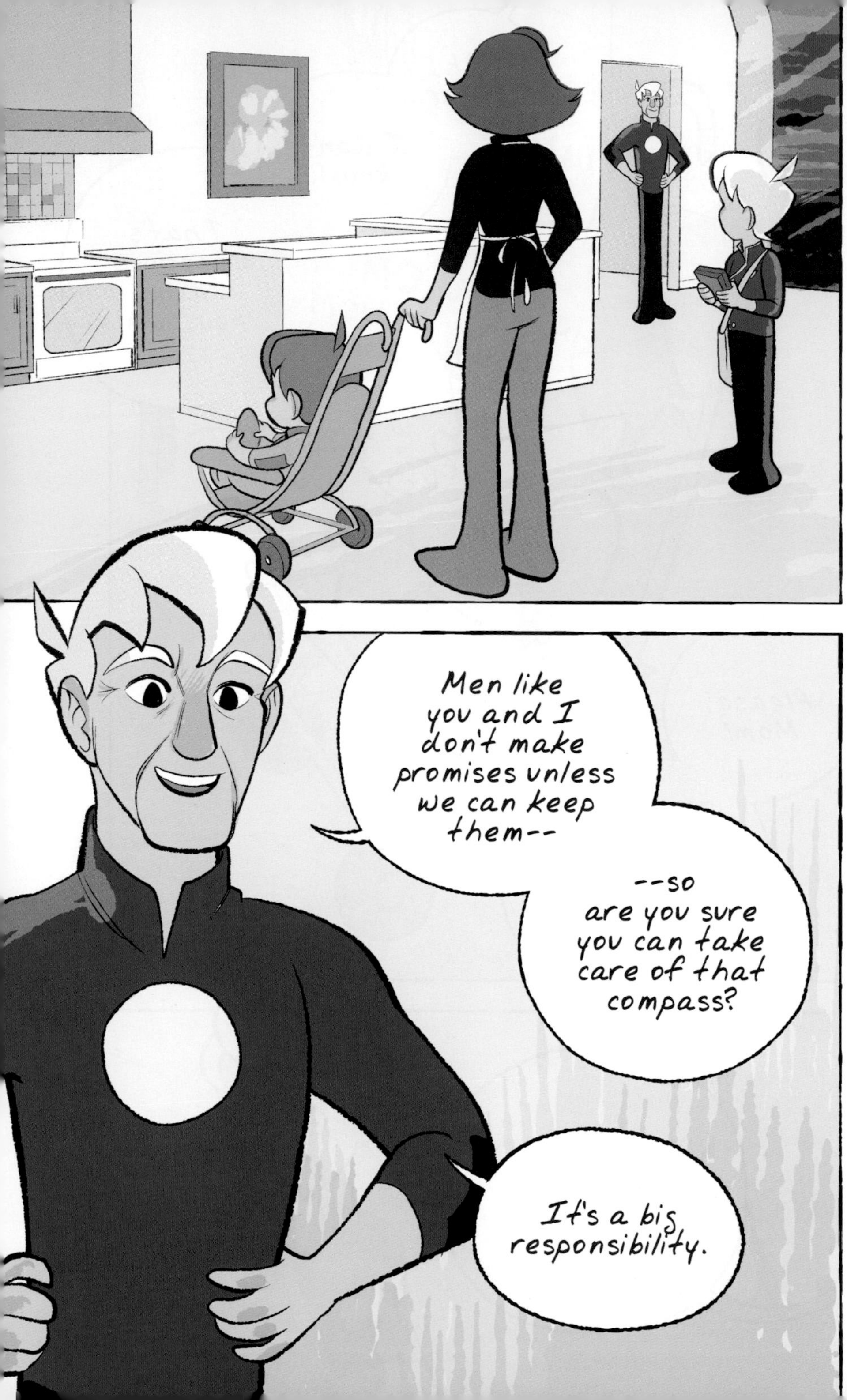
Men like you and I don't make promises unless we can keep them--
--so are you sure you can take care of that compass?
It's a big responsibility.

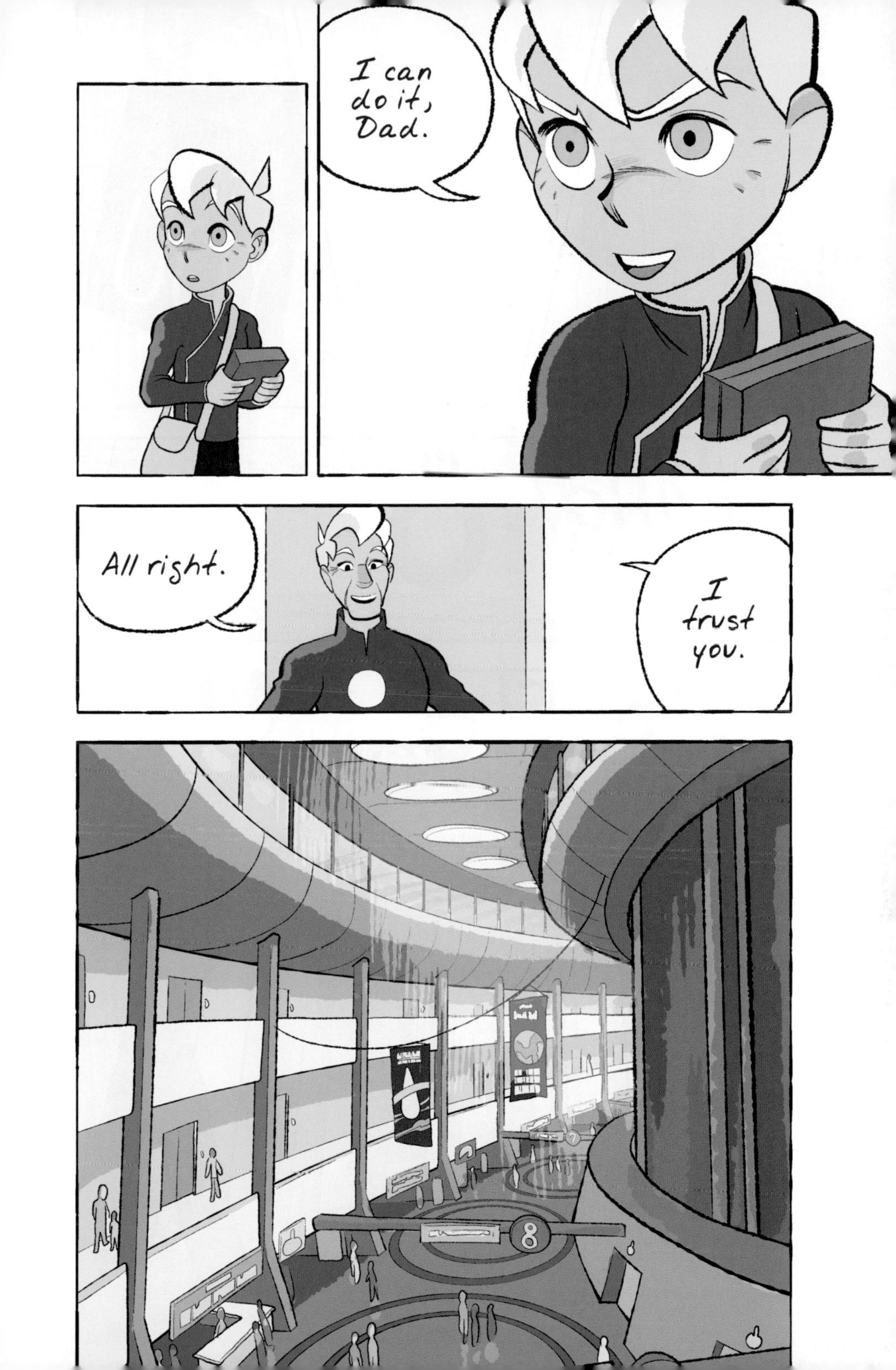

I can do it, Dad.
All right.
I trust you.

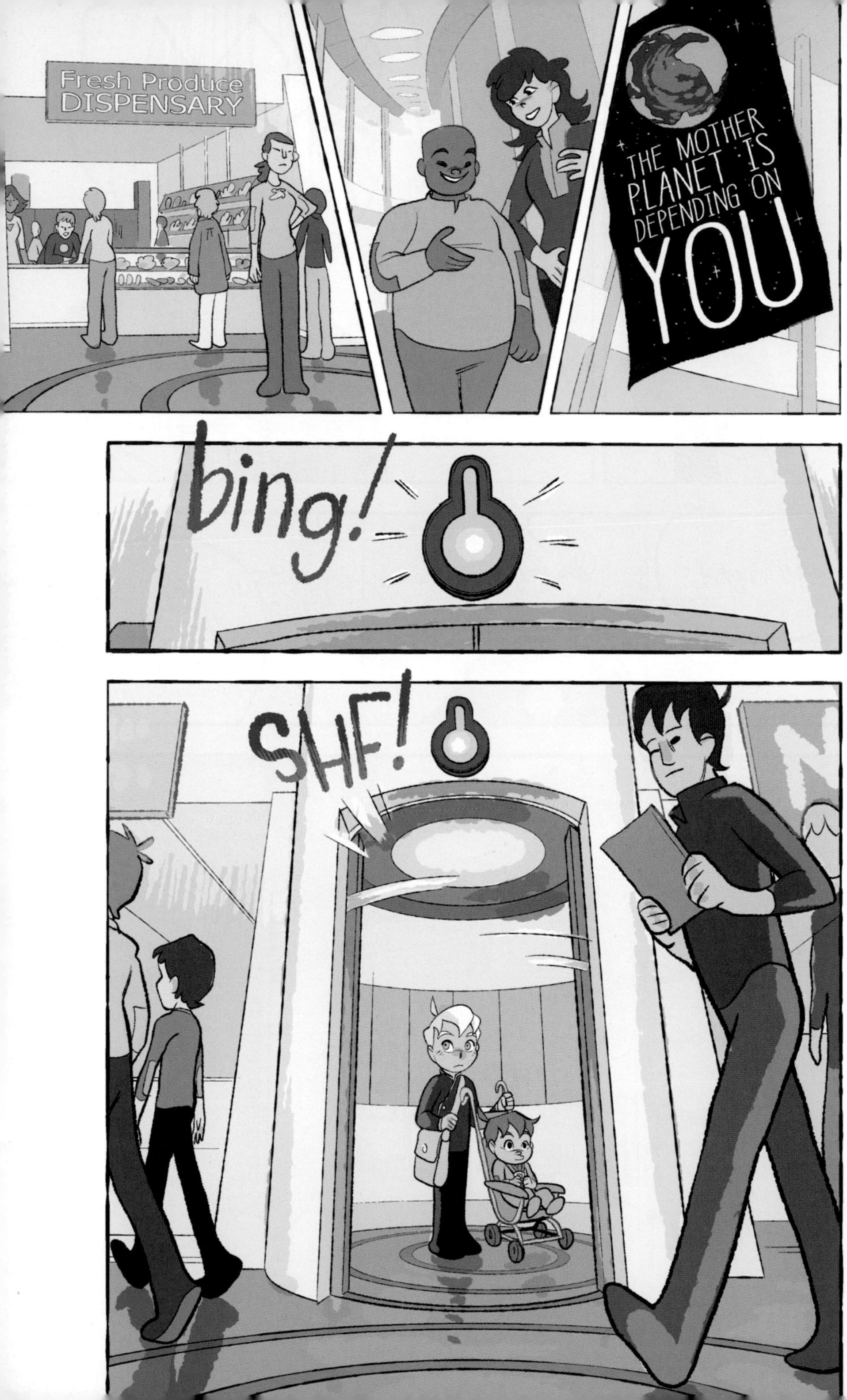
Fresh Produce
DISPENSARY
THE MOTHER PLANET IS DEPENDING ON
YOU
bing!
SHF!

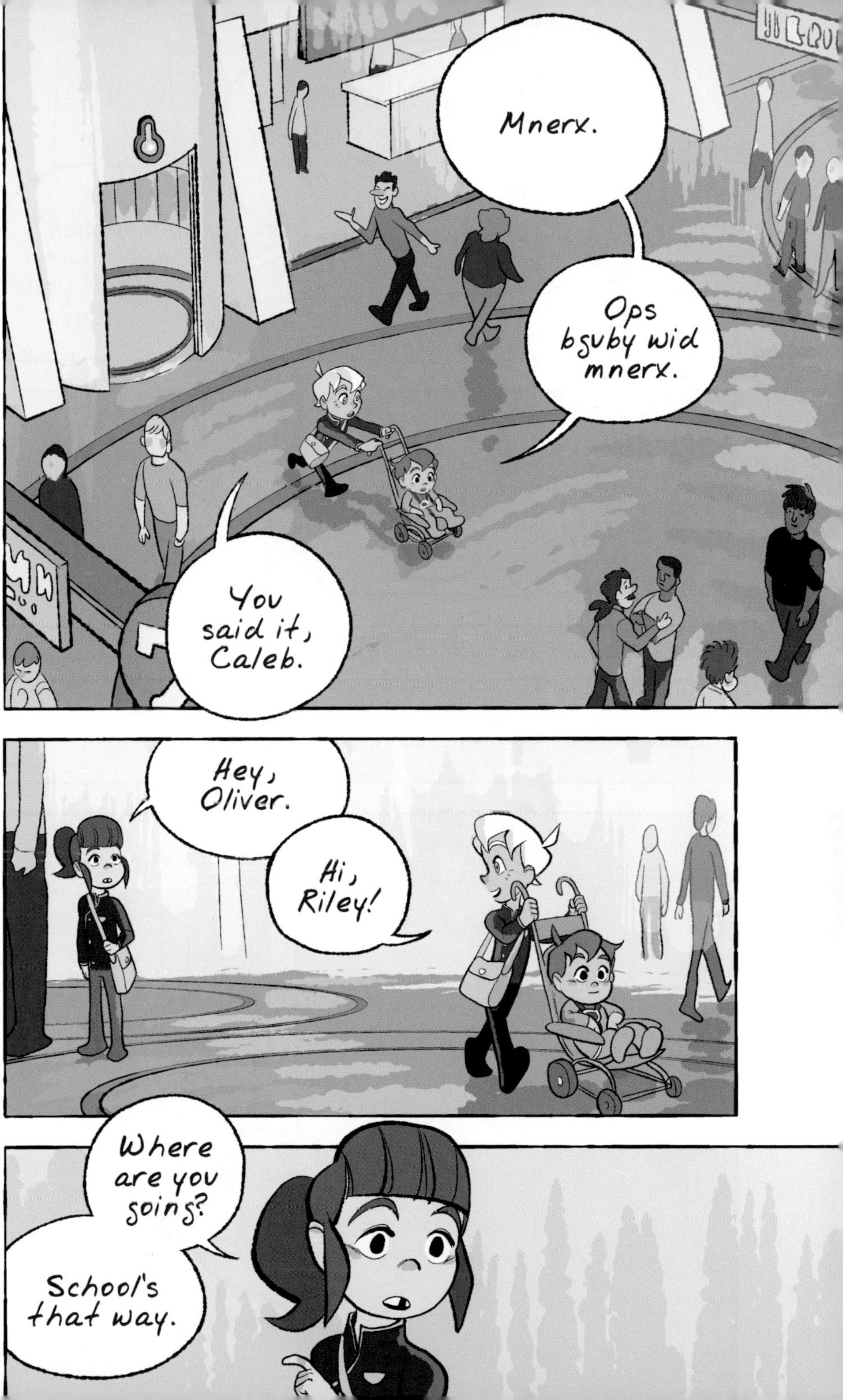
Mnerx.
Ops bguby wid mnerx.
You said it, Caleb.
Hey, Oliver.
Hi, Riley!
Where are you going?
School's that way.

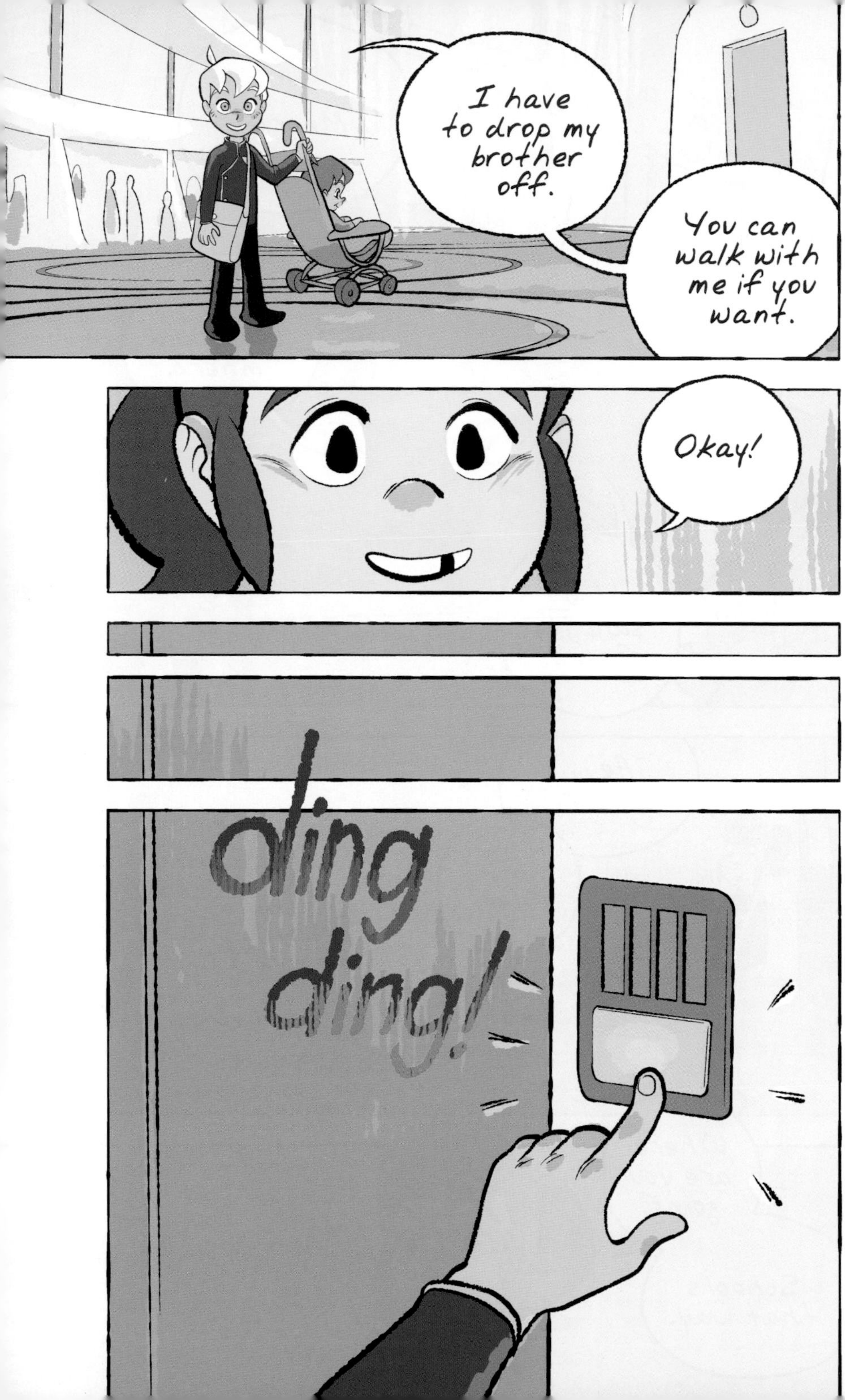
I have to drop my brother off.
You can walk with me if you want.
Okay!
ding ding!

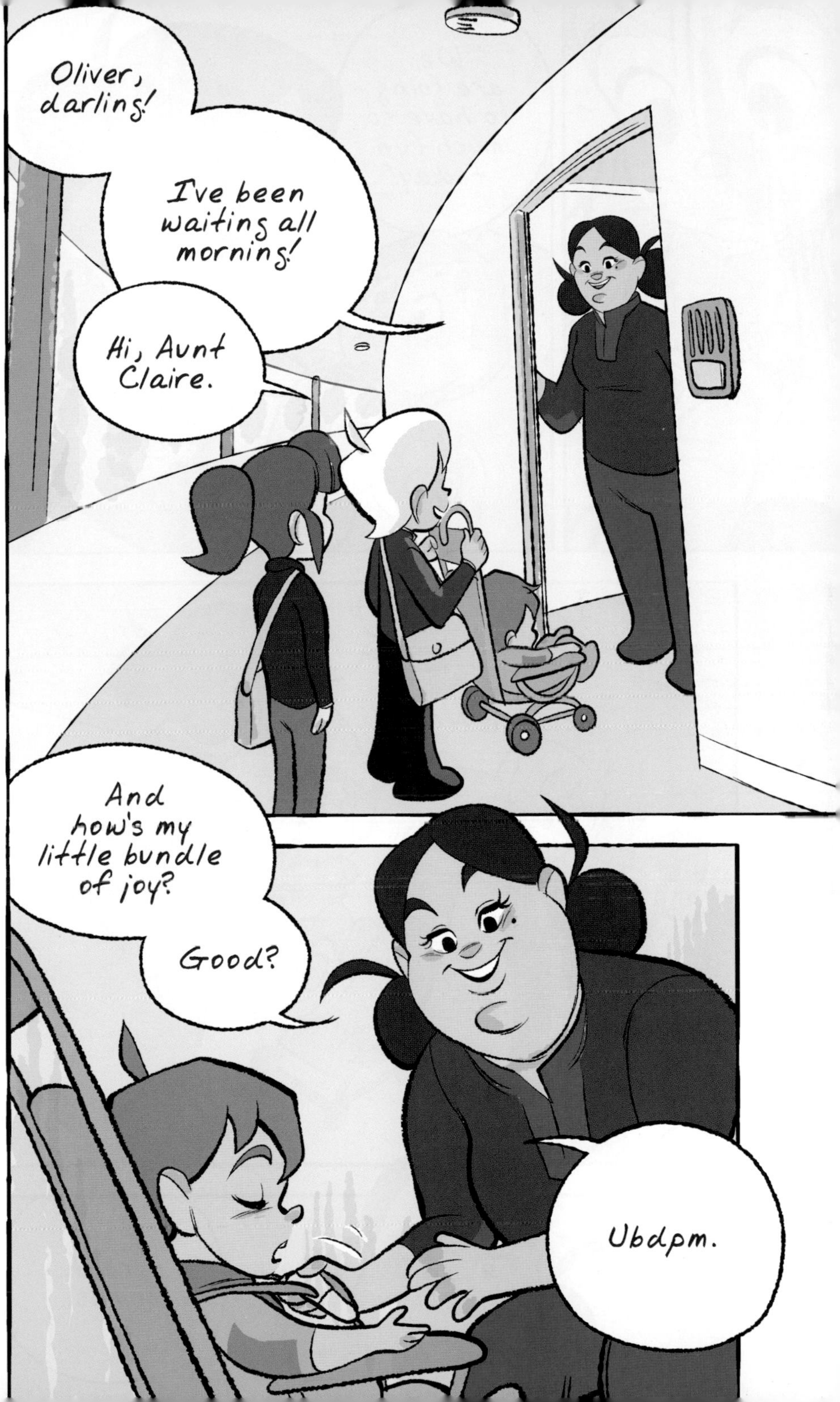
Oliver, darling!
I've been waiting all morning!
Hi, Aunt Claire.
And how's my little bundle of joy?
Good?
Ubdpm.

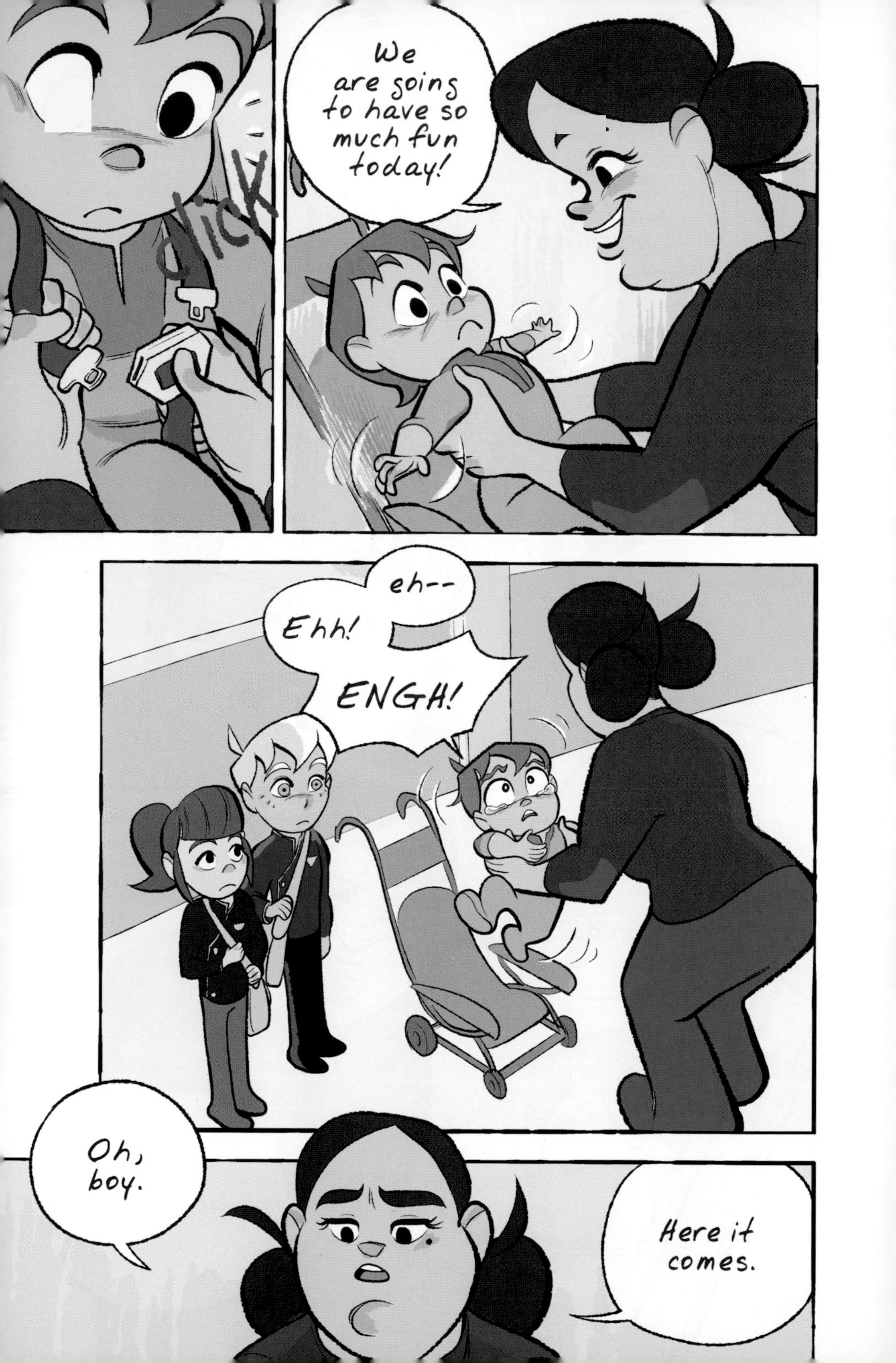
click
We are going to have so much fun today!
eh--
Ehh!
ENGH!
Oh, boy.
Here it comes.

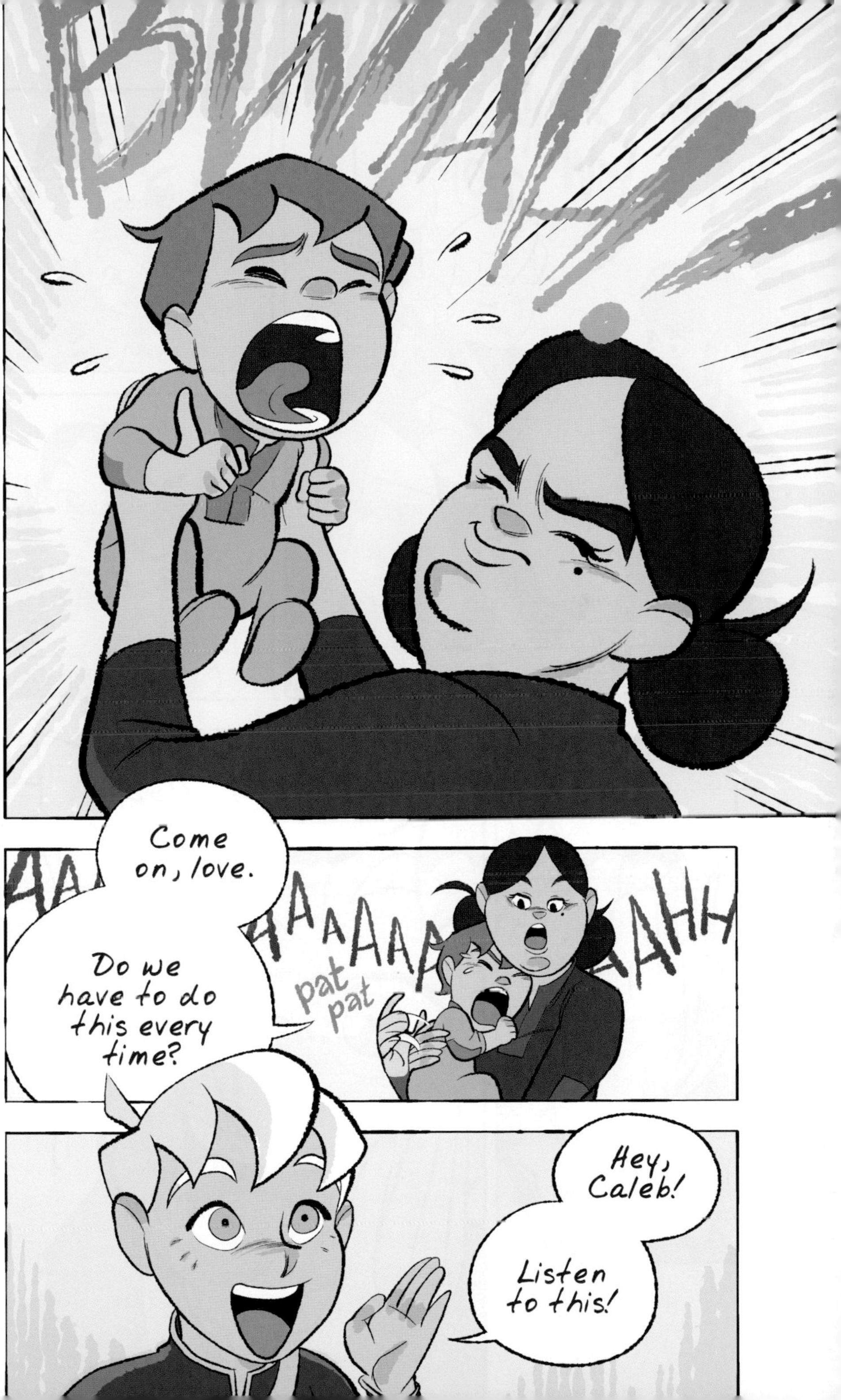

BWAAH
Come on, love.
Do we have to do this every time?
AAAAAAAAAAAAHH
pat pat
Hey, Caleb!
Listen to this!

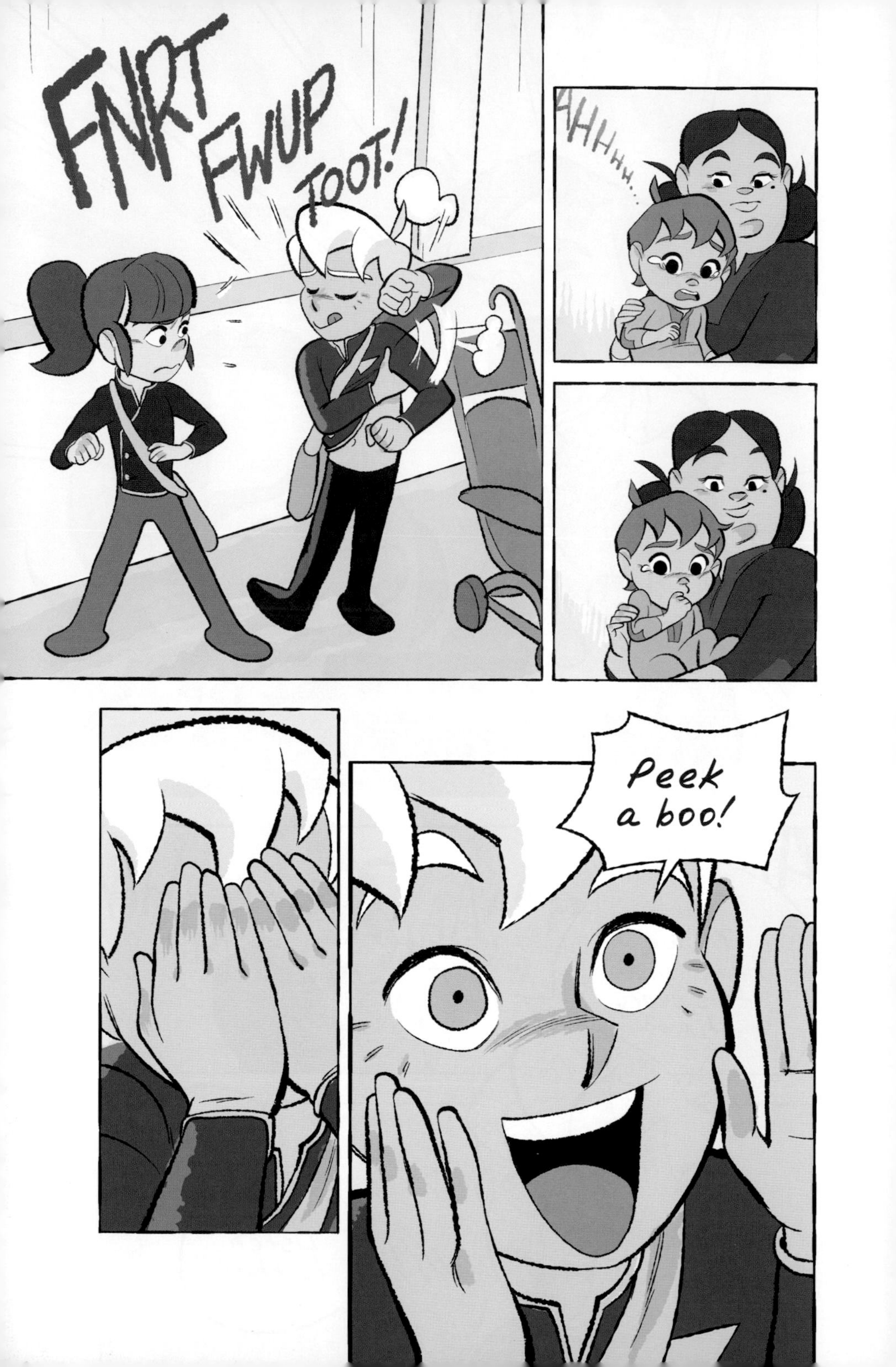
FNRT
FWUP
TOOT!
AHHhhh...
Peek a boo!

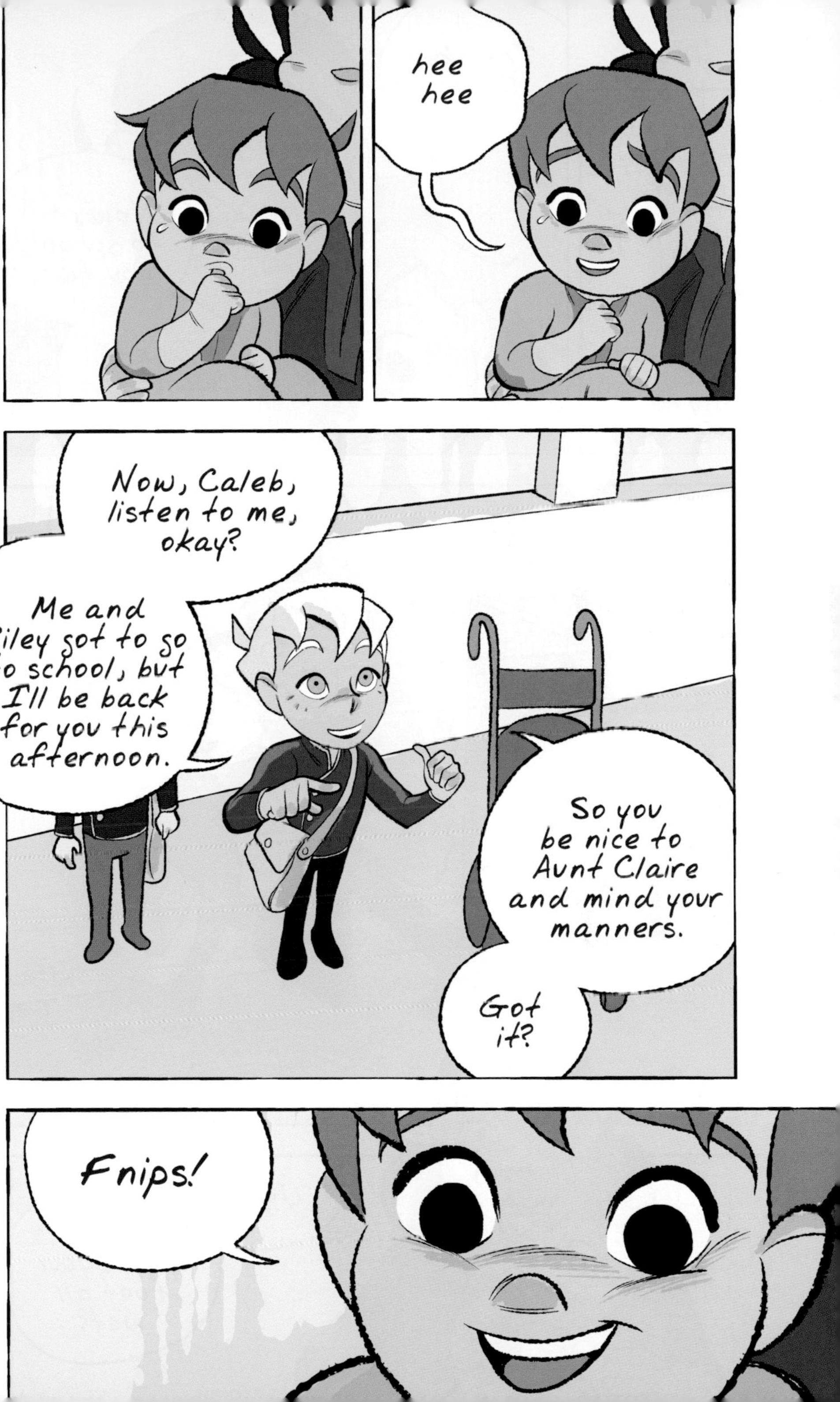
hee hee
Now, Caleb, listen to me, okay?
Me and Riley got to go to school, but I'll be back for you this afternoon.
So you be nice to Aunt Claire and mind your manners.
Got it?
Fnips!

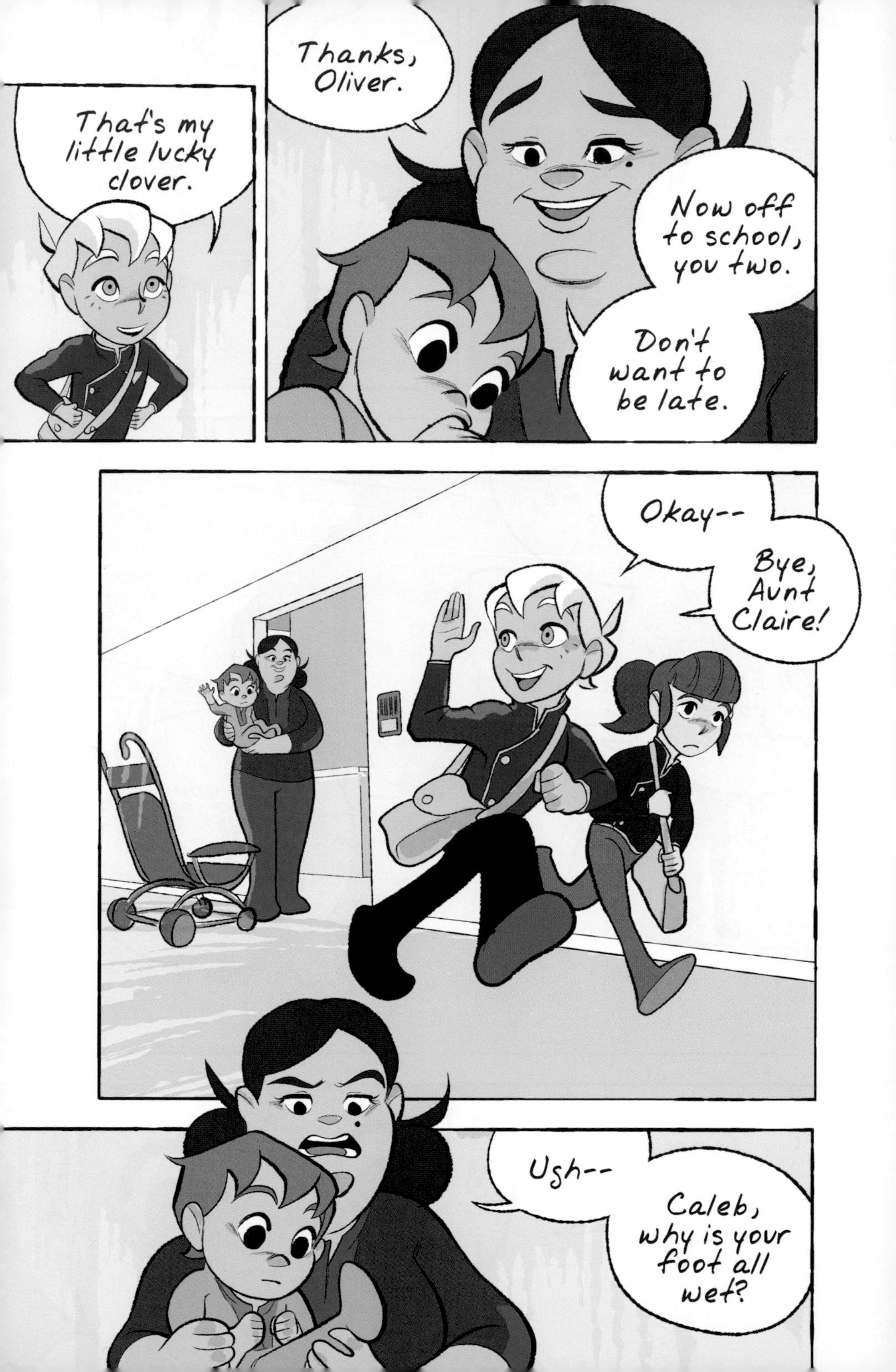
That's my little lucky clover.
Thanks, Oliver.
Now off to school, you two.
Don't want to be late.
Okay--
Bye, Aunt Claire!
Ugh--
Caleb, why is your foot all wet?

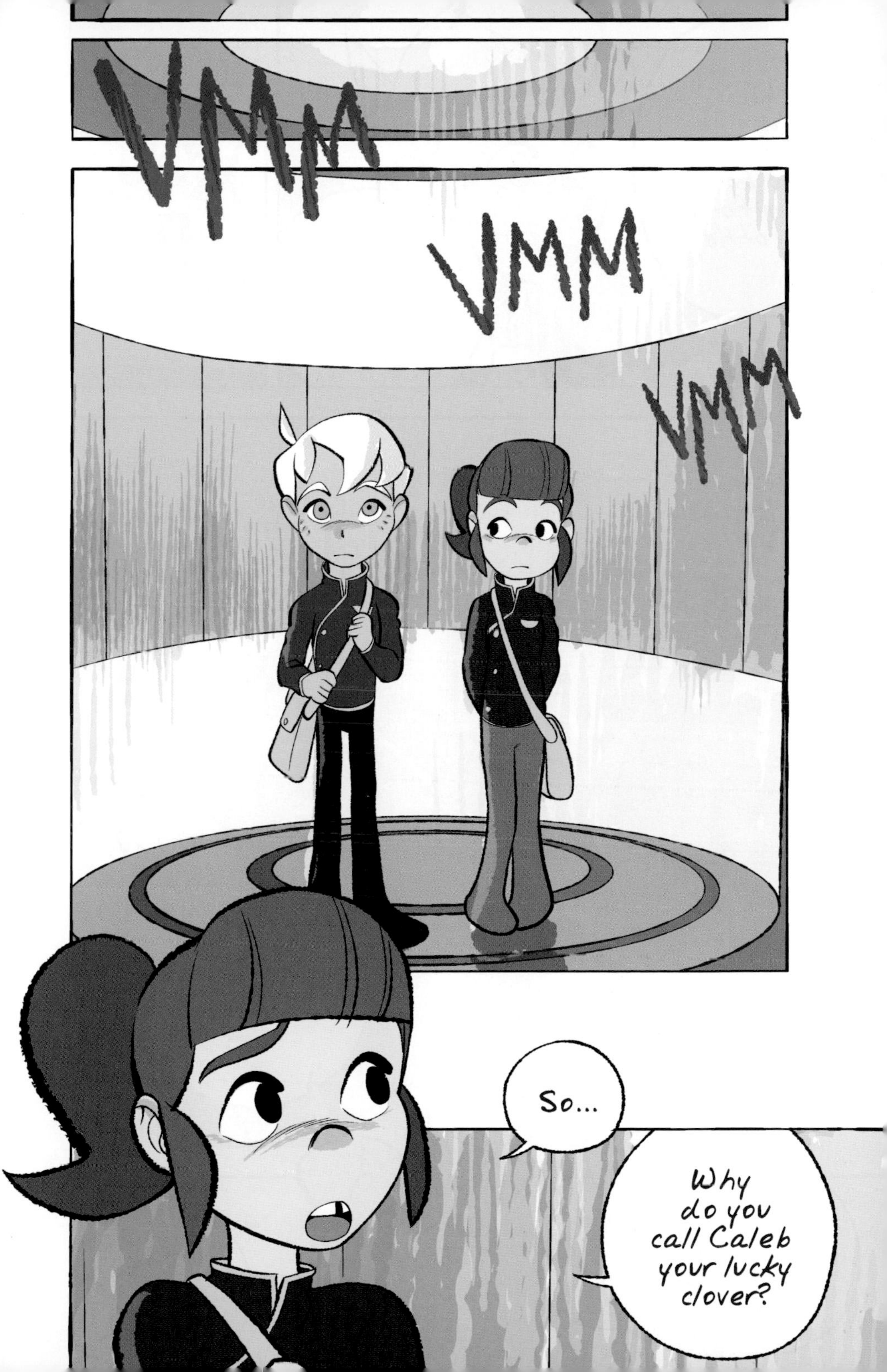
VMM
VMM
VMM
So...
Why do you call Caleb your lucky clover?

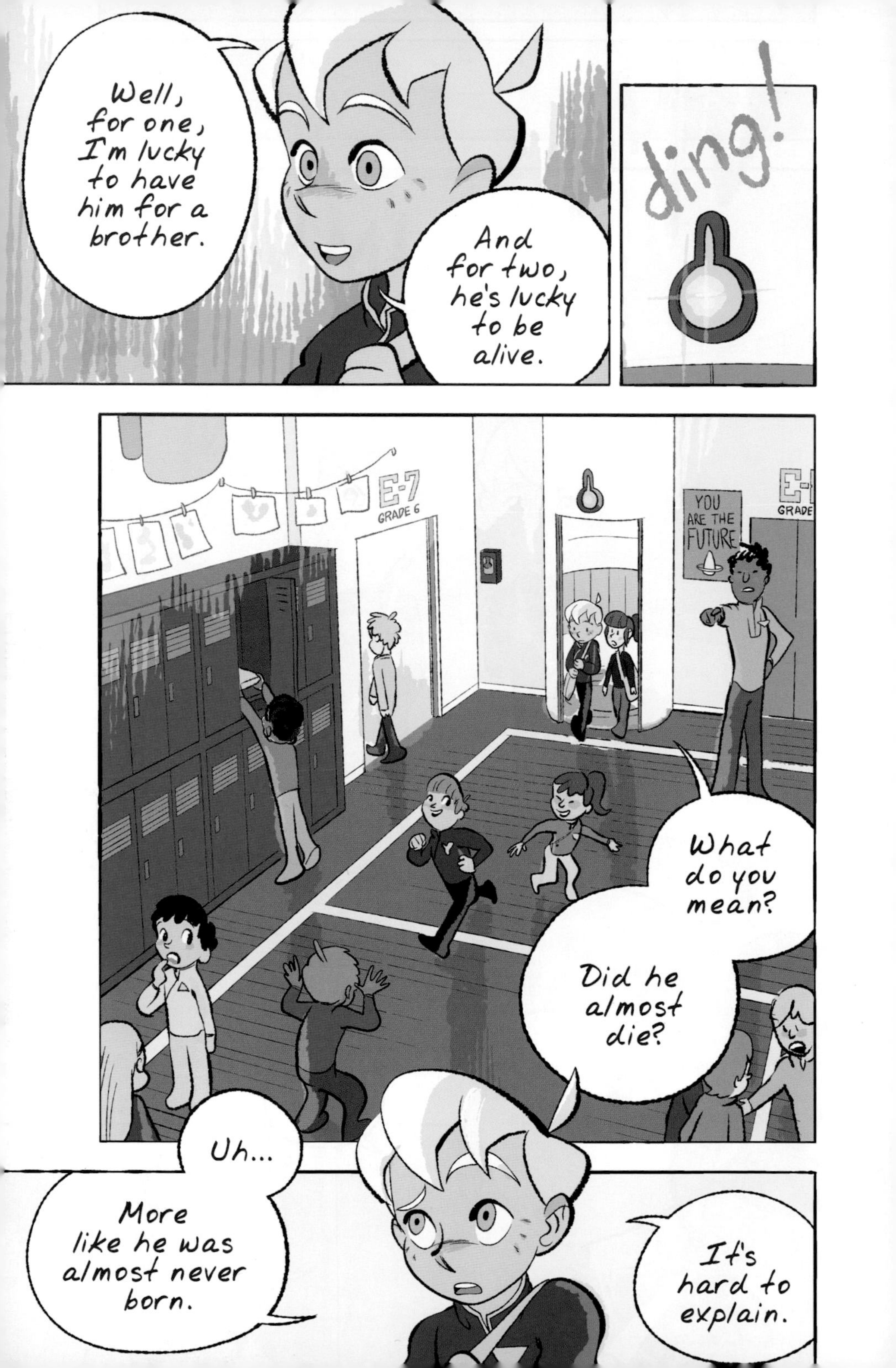
Well, for one, I'm lucky to have him for a brother.
And for two, he's lucky to be alive.
ding!
E-7
GRADE 6
YOU ARE THE FUTURE
What do you mean?
Did he almost die?
Uh...
More like he was almost never born.
It's hard to explain.

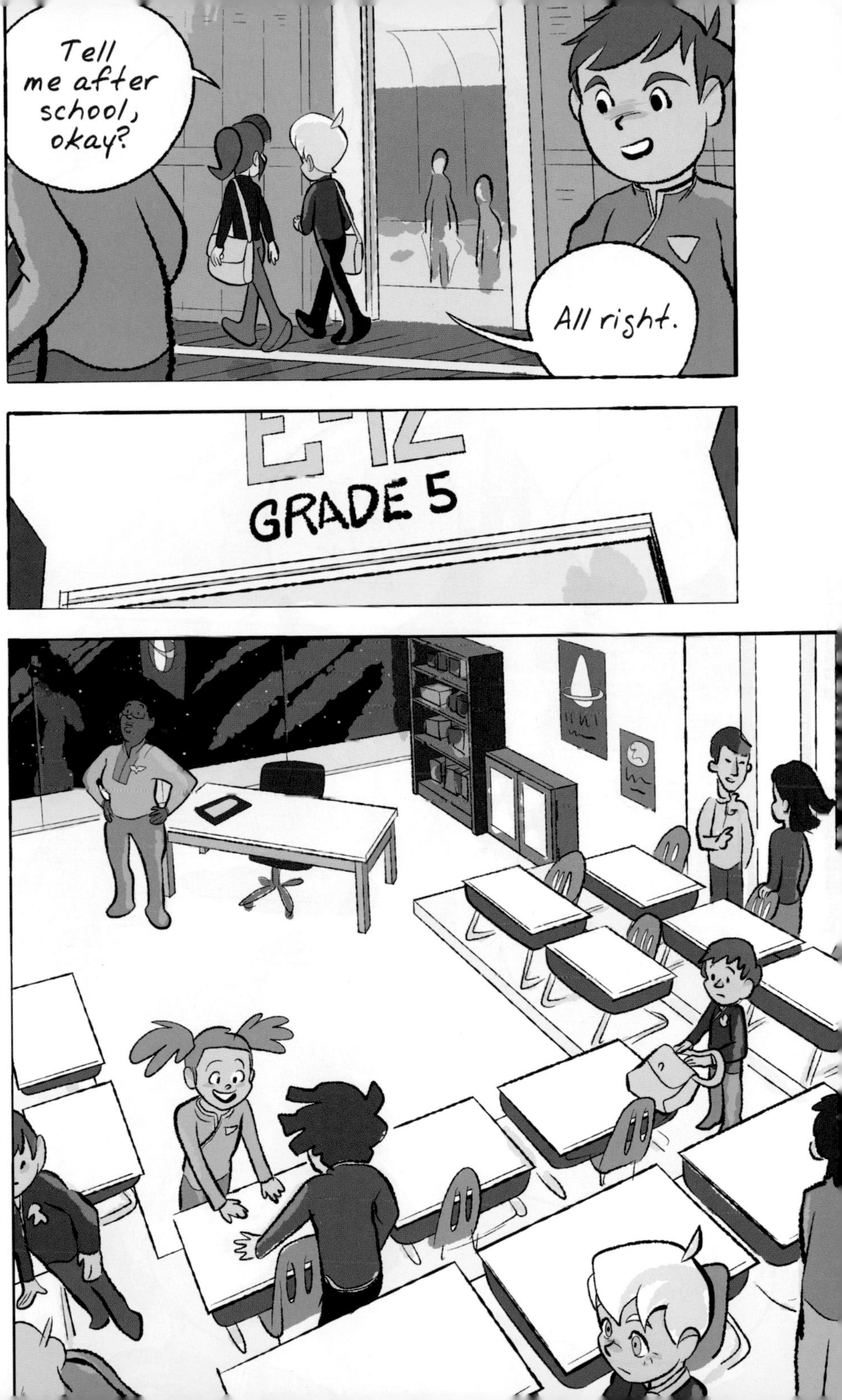
Tell me after school, okay?
All right.
E-12
GRADE 5

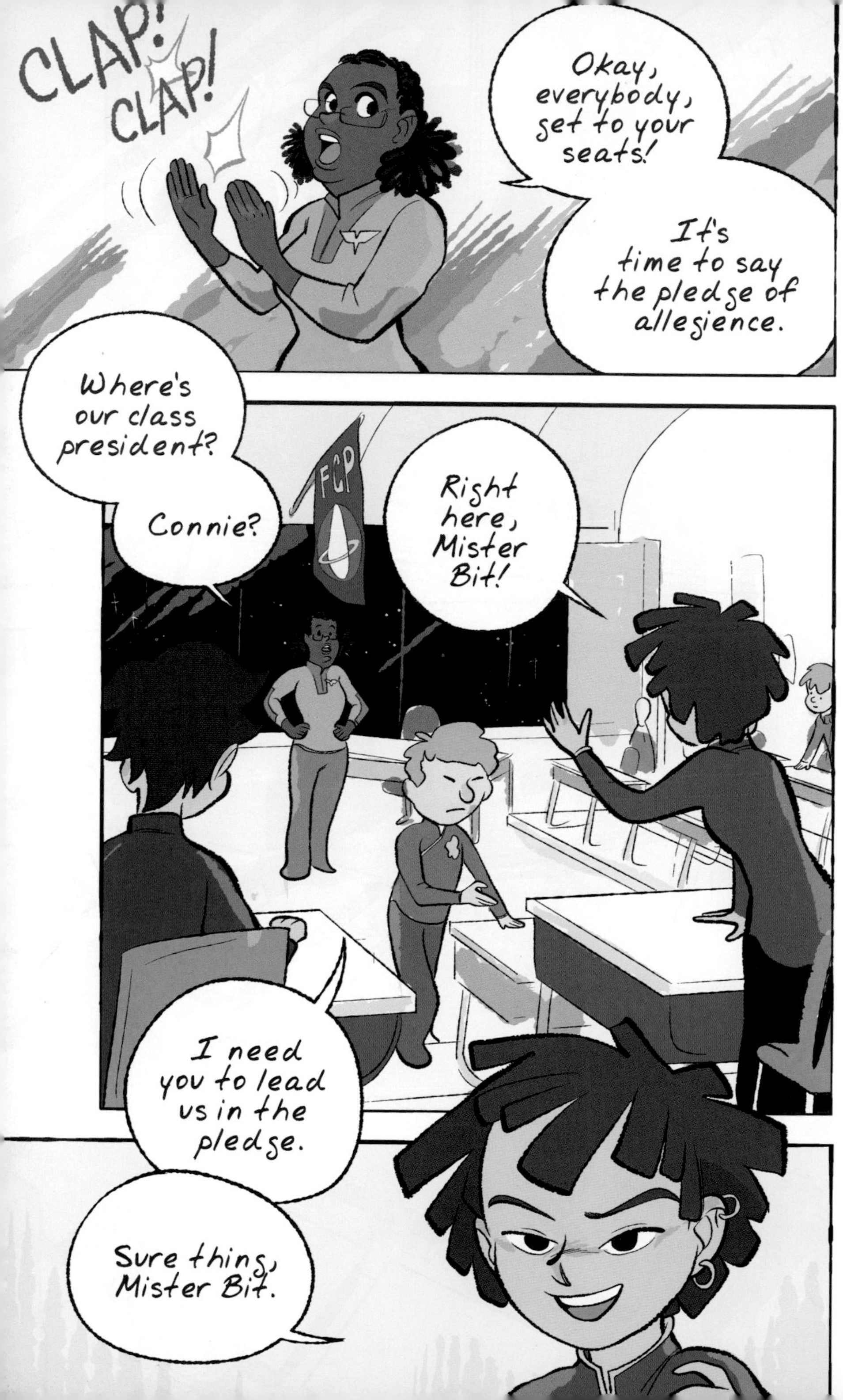
CLAP! CLAP!
Okay, everybody, get to your seats!
It's time to say the pledge of allegience.
Where's our class president?
Connie?
FCP
Right here, Mister Bit!
I need you to lead us in the pledge.
Sure thing, Mister Bit.

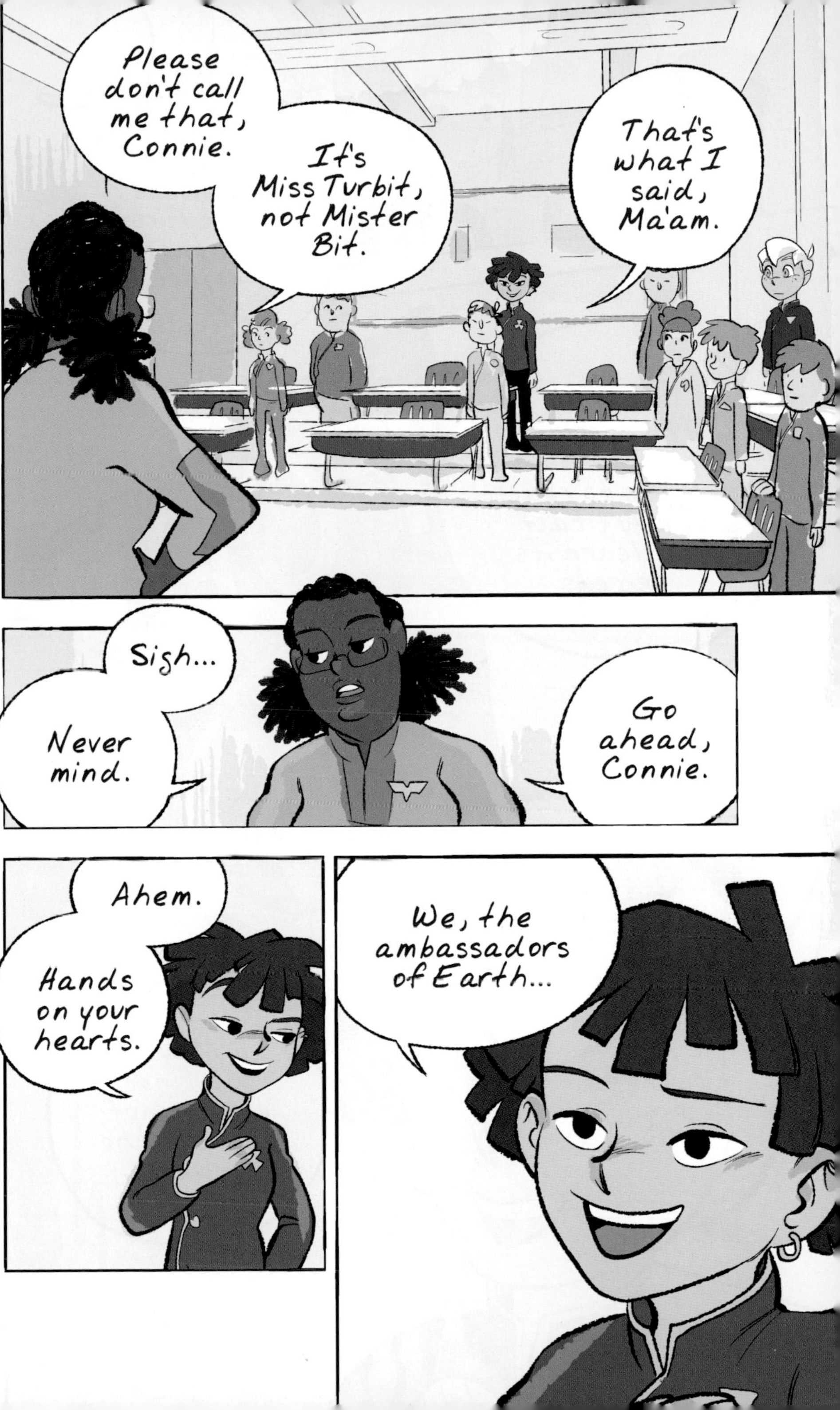
Please don't call me that, Connie.
It's Miss Turbit, not Mister Bit.
That's what I said, Ma'am.
Sigh...
Never mind.
Go ahead, Connie.
Ahem.
Hands on your hearts.
We, the ambassadors of Earth...

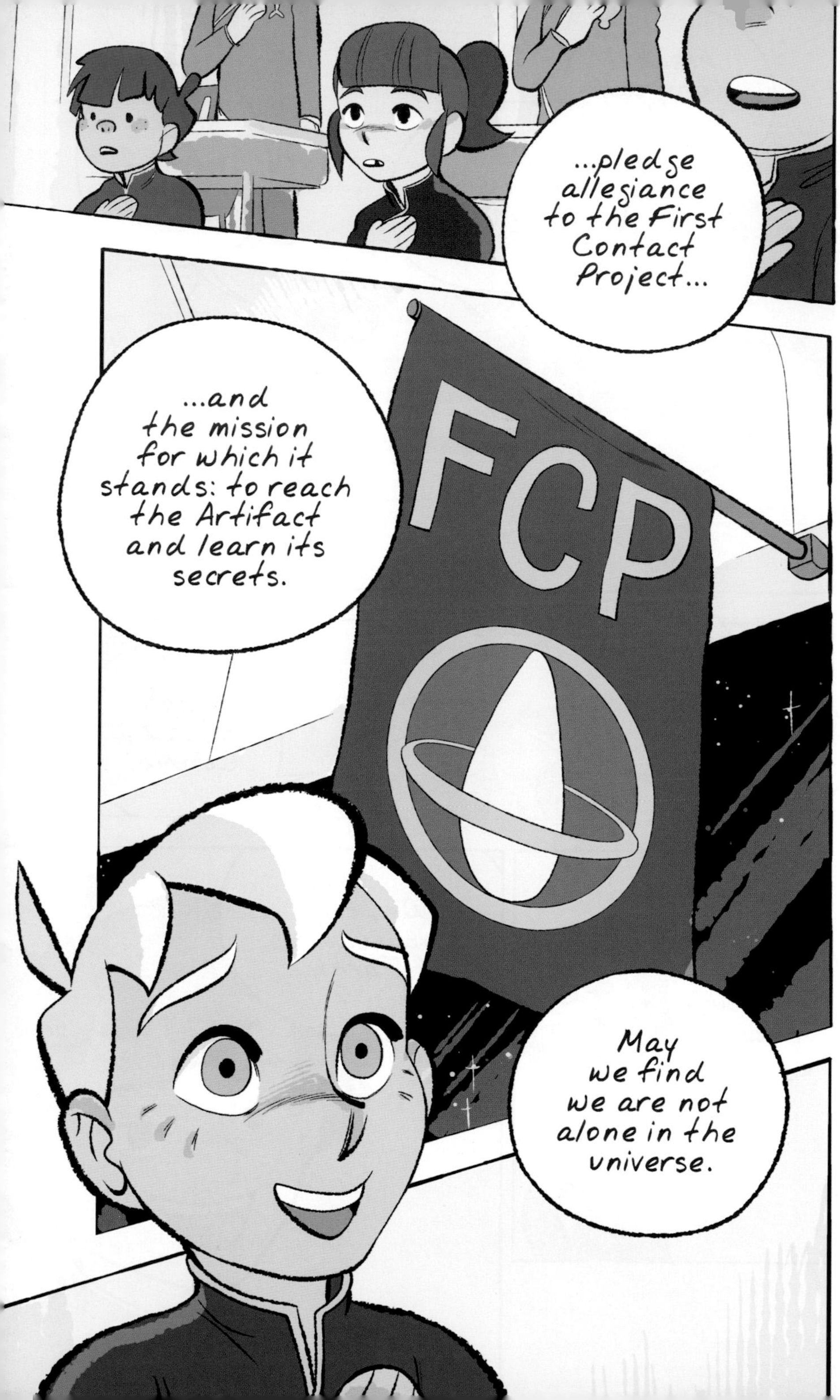
...pledge allegiance to the First Contact Project...
...and the mission for which it stands: to reach the Artifact and learn its secrets.
FCP
May we find we are not alone in the universe.

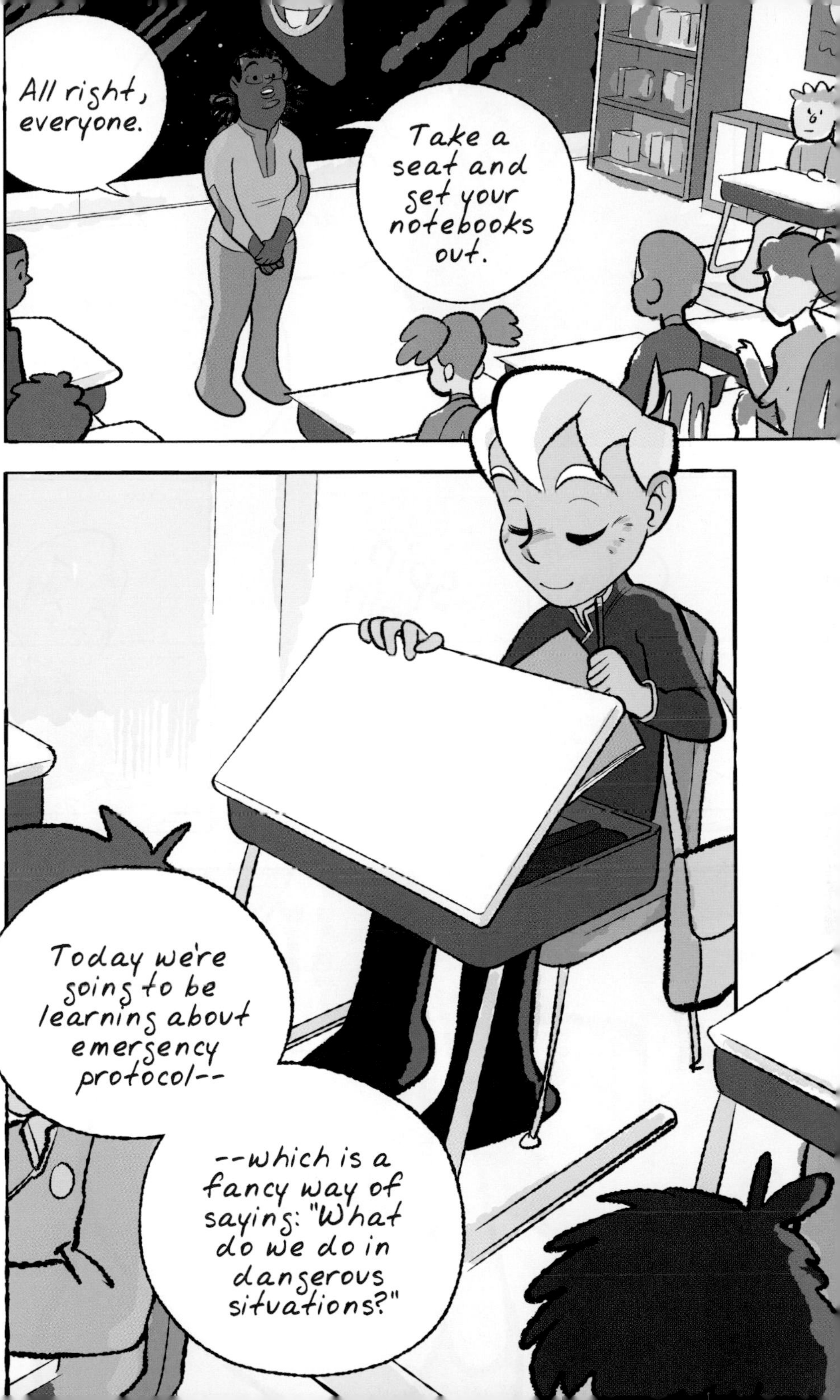
All right, everyone.
Take a seat and set your notebooks out.
Today we're going to be learning about emergency protocol--
--which is a fancy way of saying: "What do we do in dangerous situations?"

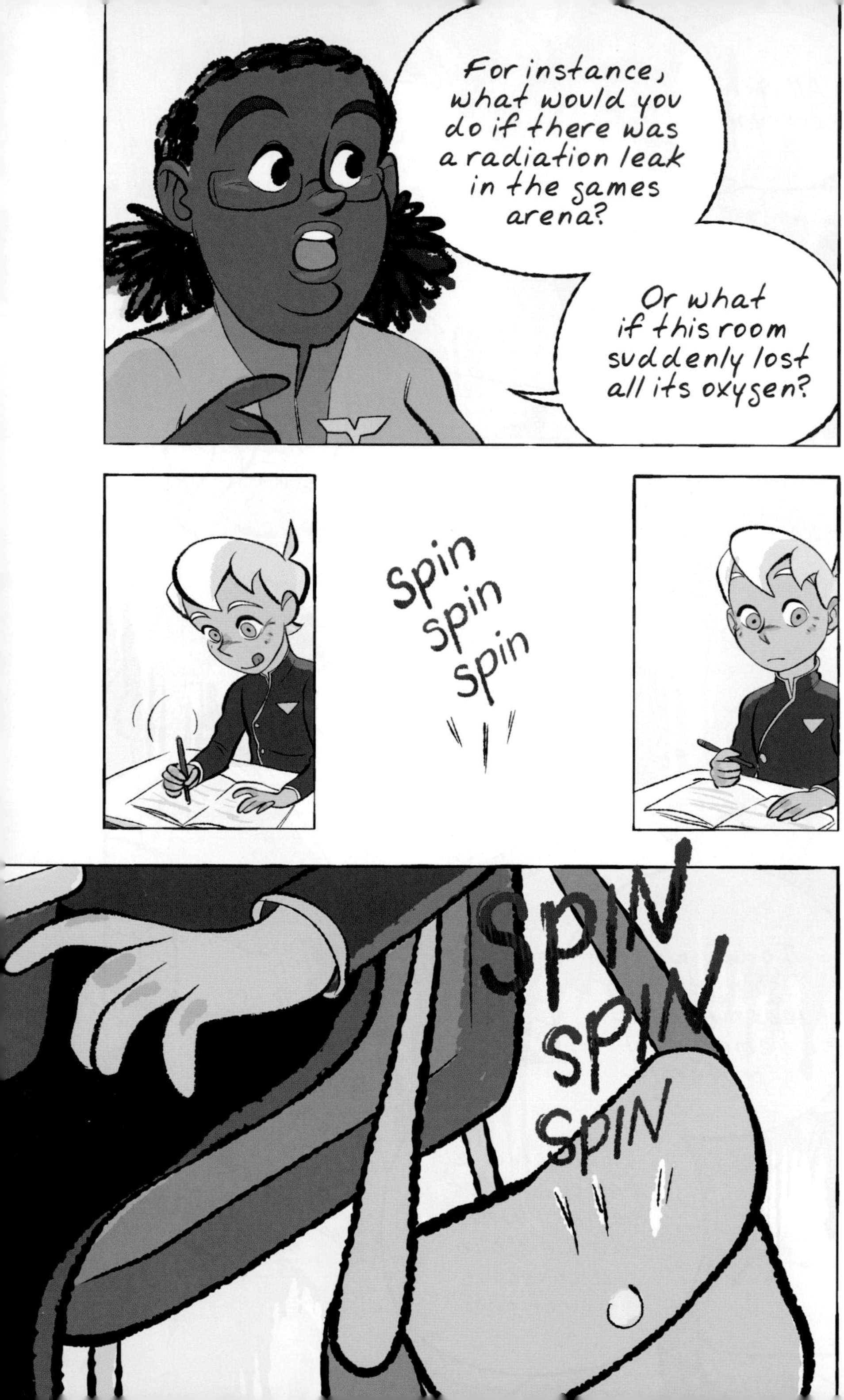
For instance, what would you do if there was a radiation leak in the games arena?
Or what if this room suddenly lost all its oxygen?
Spin spin spin
SPIN SPIN SPIN

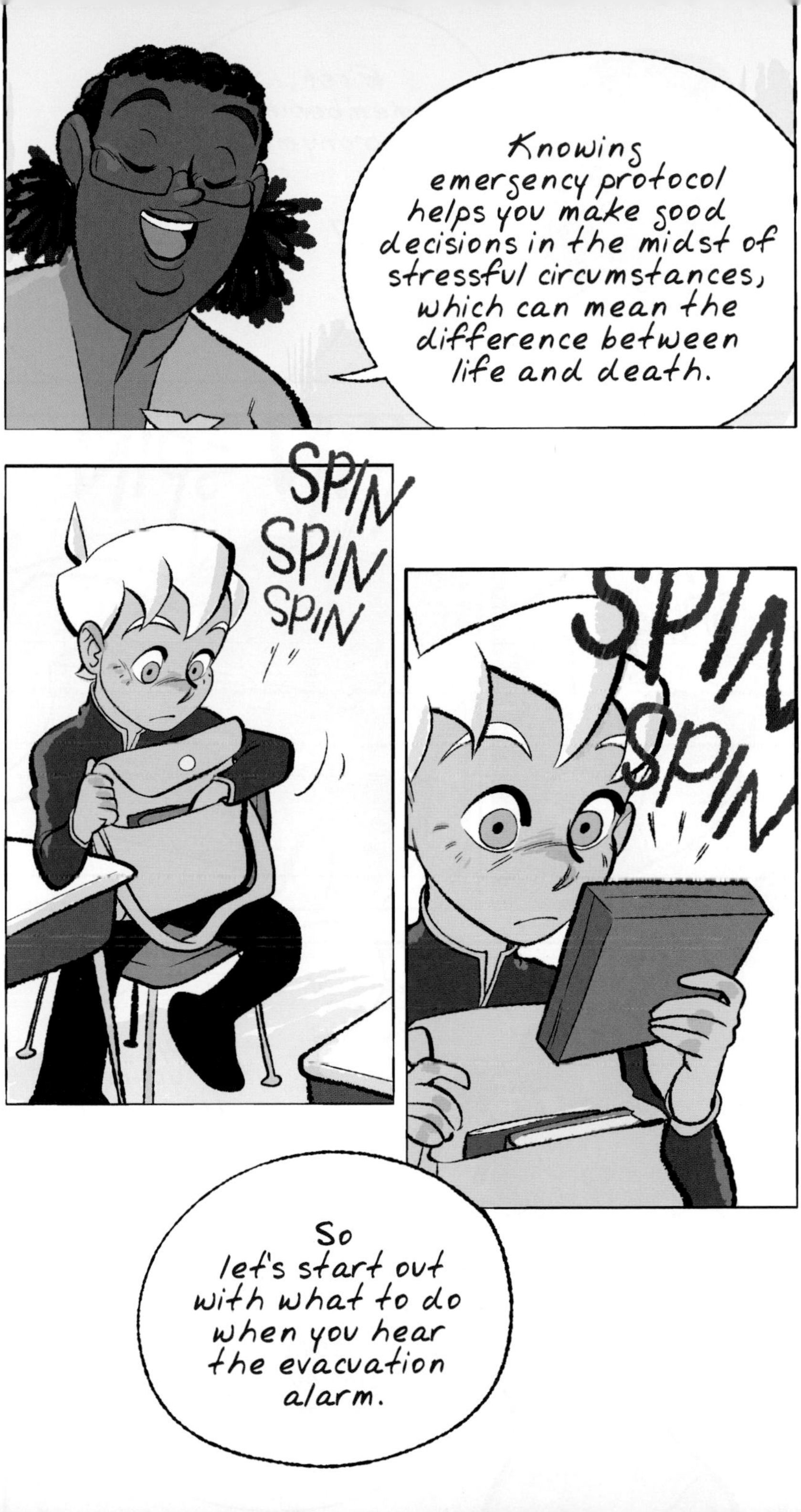
Knowing emergency protocol helps you make good decisions in the midst of stressful circumstances, which can mean the difference between life and death.
SPIN SPIN SPIN
SPIN SPIN
So let's start out with what to do when you hear the evacuation alarm.

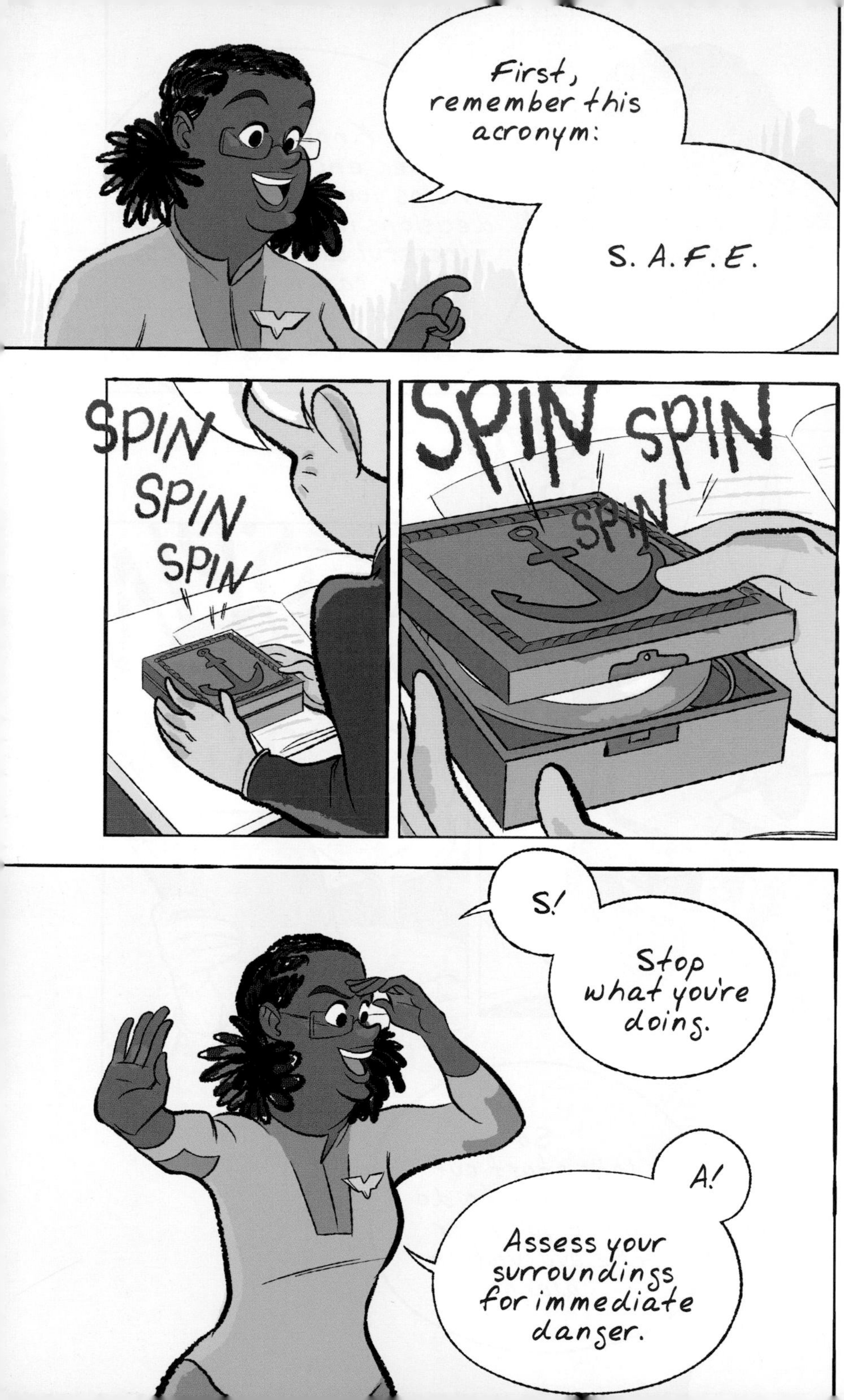
First, remember this acronym:
S. A. F. E.
SPIN
SPIN
SPIN
SPIN
SPIN
SPIN
S!
Stop what you're doing.
A!
Assess your surroundings for immediate danger.

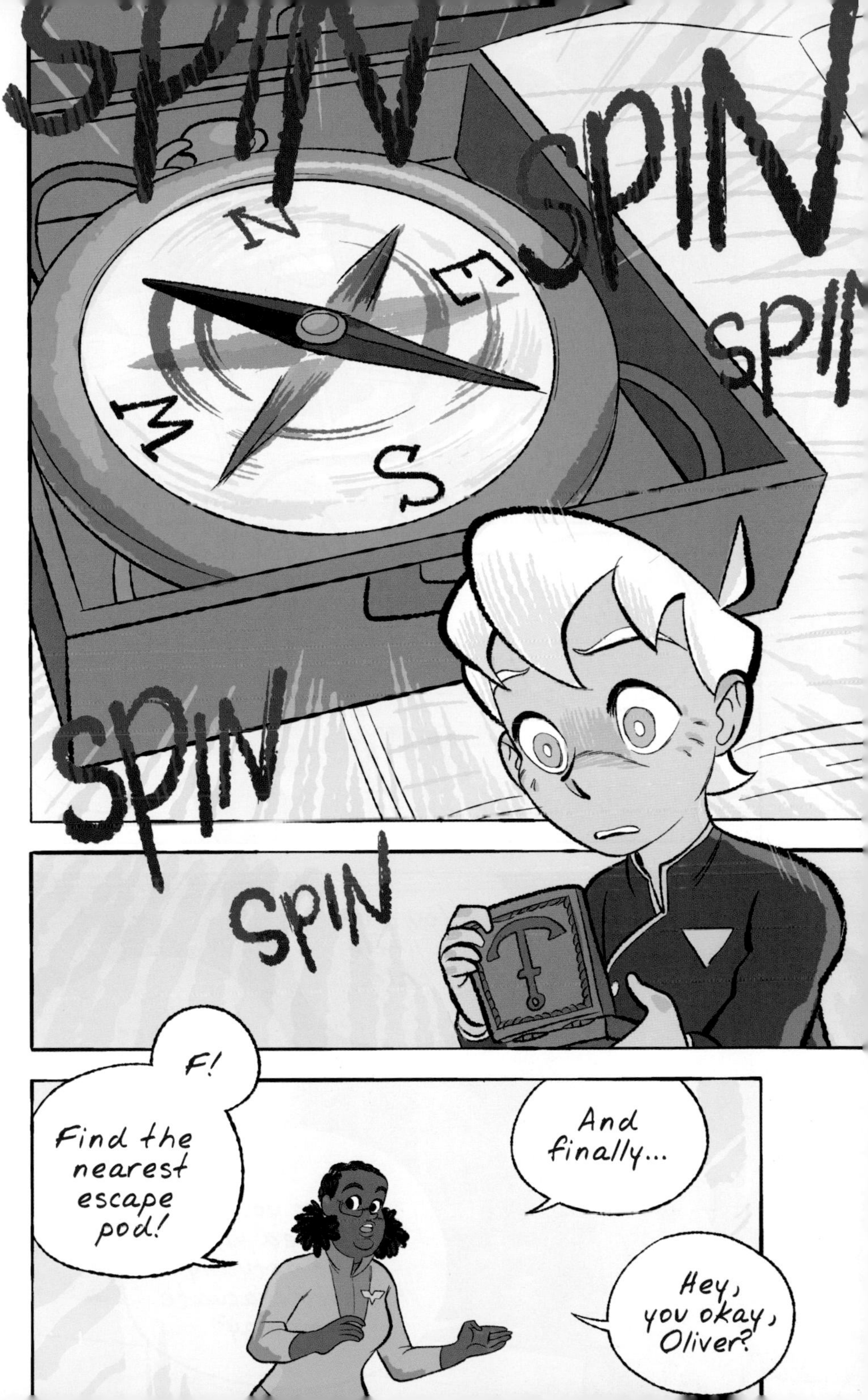
SPIN
SPIN
SPIN
N
E
S
W
SPIN
SPIN
F!
Find the nearest escape pod!
And finally...
Hey, you okay, Oliver?

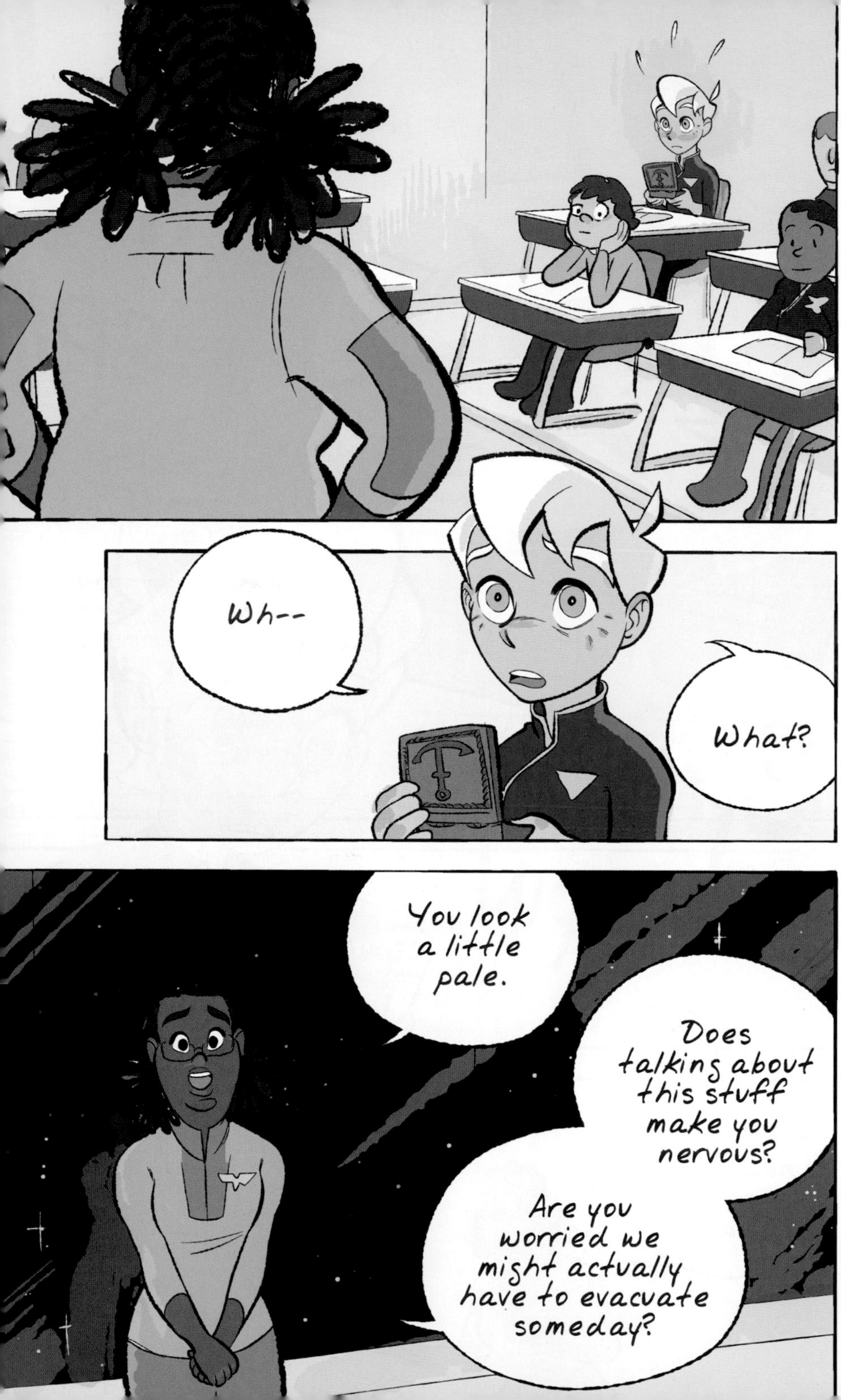

Wh--
What?
You look a little pale.
Does talking about this stuff make you nervous?
Are you worried we might actually have to evacuate someday?

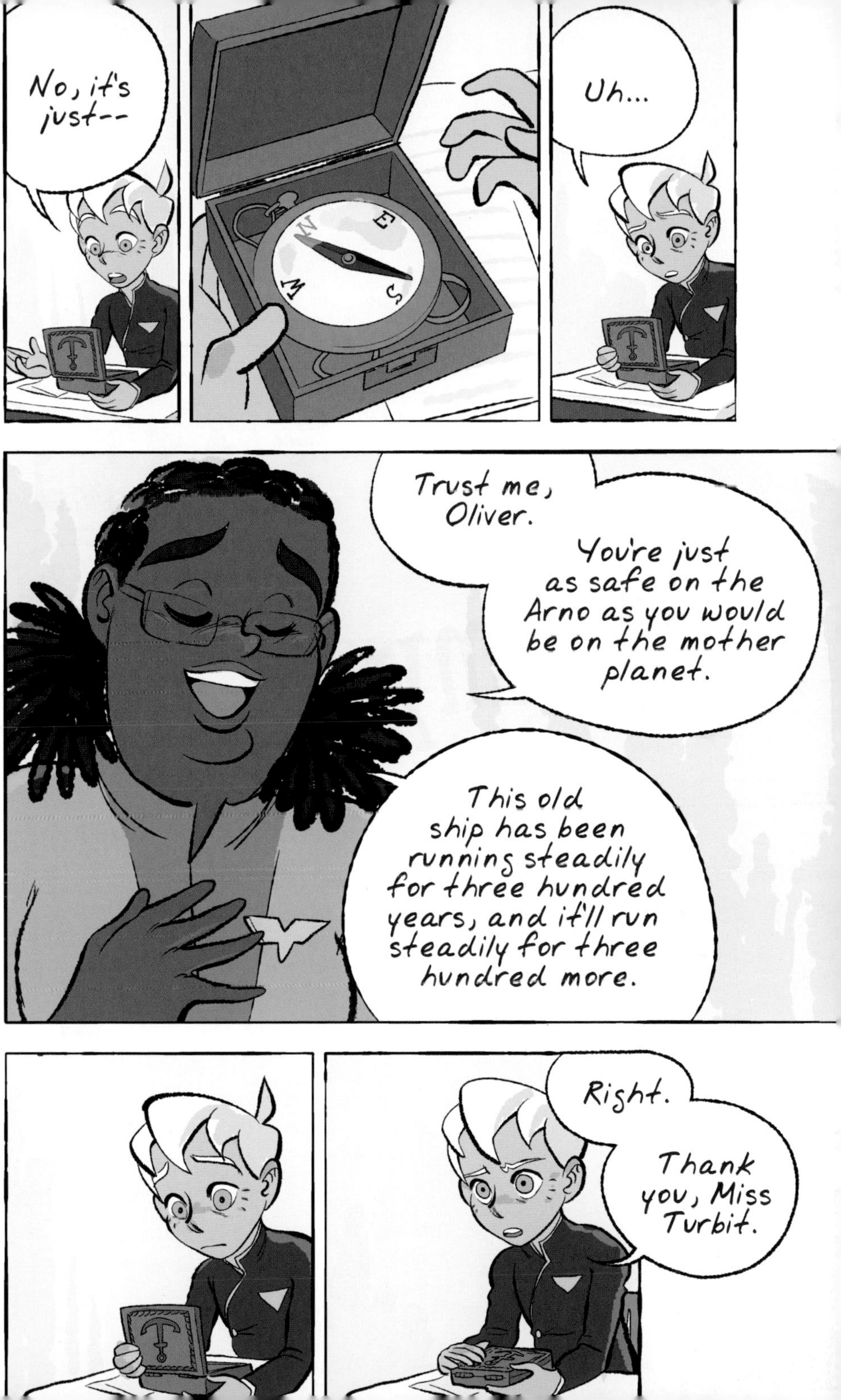
No, it's just--
Uh...
Trust me, Oliver.
You're just as safe on the Arno as you would be on the mother planet.
This old ship has been running steadily for three hundred years, and it'll run steadily for three hundred more.
Right.
Thank you, Miss Turbit.

Li'l Amy

by
Stephen McCranie

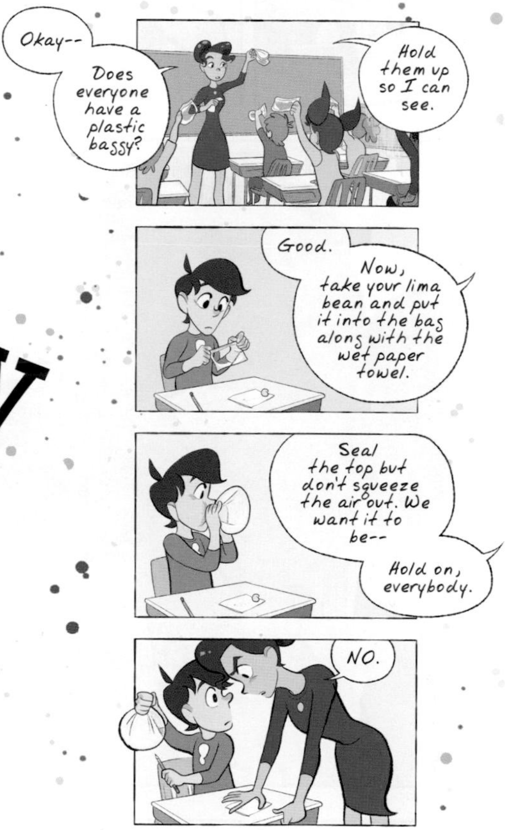
Okay--
Does everyone have a plastic baggy?
Hold them up so I can see.
Good.
Now, take your lima bean and put it into the bag along with the wet paper towel.
Seal the top but don't squeeze the air out. We want it to be--
Hold on, everybody.
NO.

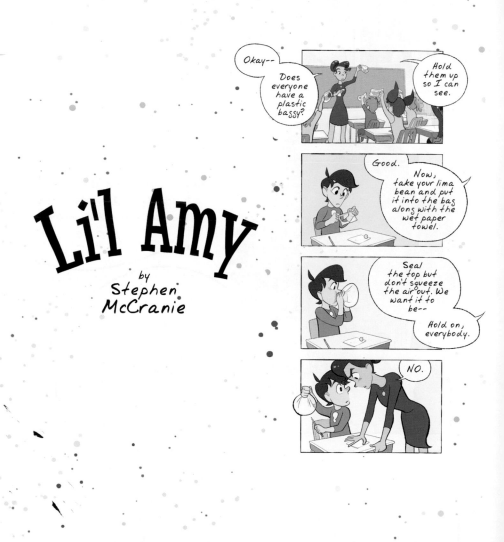

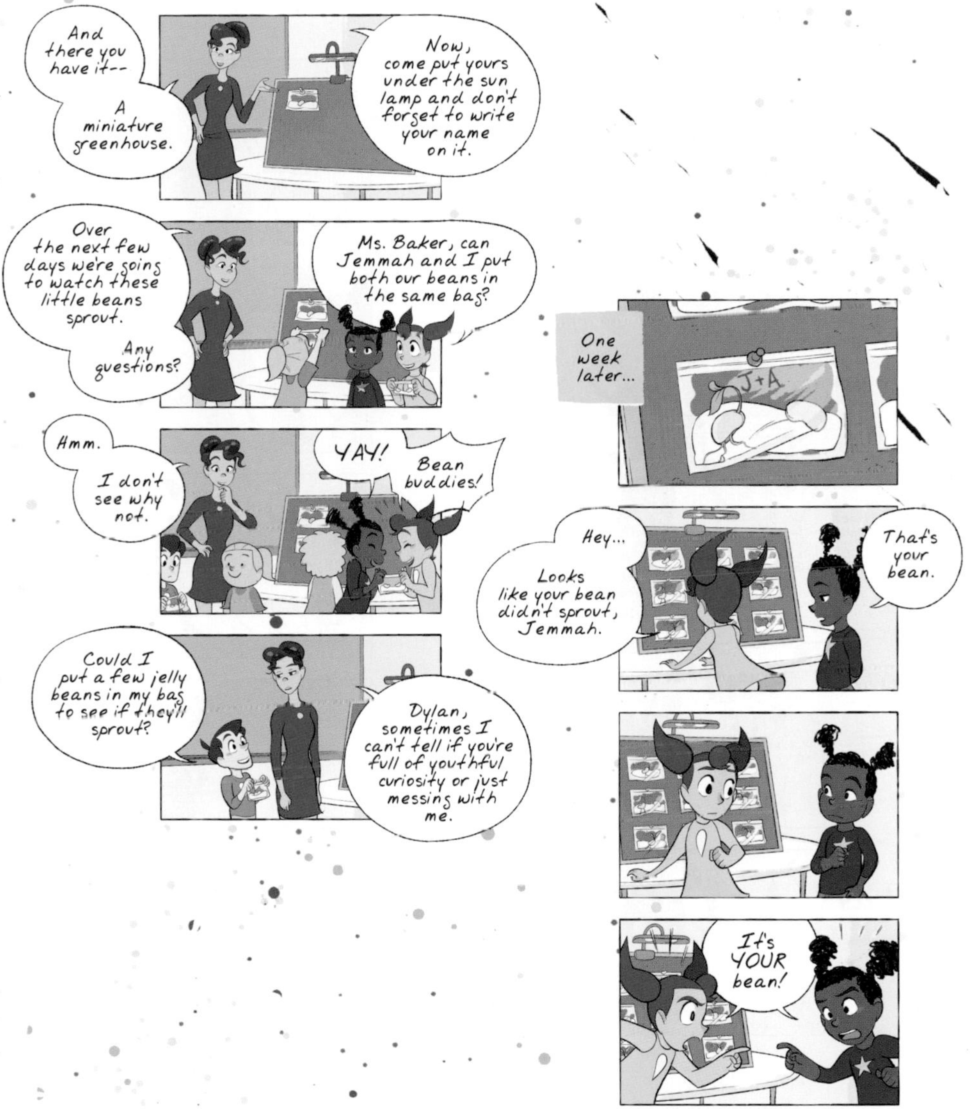
And there you have it--
A miniature greenhouse.
Now, come put yours under the sun lamp and don't forget to write your name on it.
Over the next few days we're going to watch these little beans sprout.
Any questions?
Ms. Baker, can Jemmah and I put both our beans in the same bag?
Hmm.
I don't see why not.
YAY!
Bean buddies!
Could I put a few jelly beans in my bag to see if they'll sprout?
Dylan, sometimes I can't tell if you're full of youthful curiosity or just messing with me.
One week later...
J+A
Hey...
Looks like your bean didn't sprout, Jemmah.
That's your bean.
It's YOUR bean!

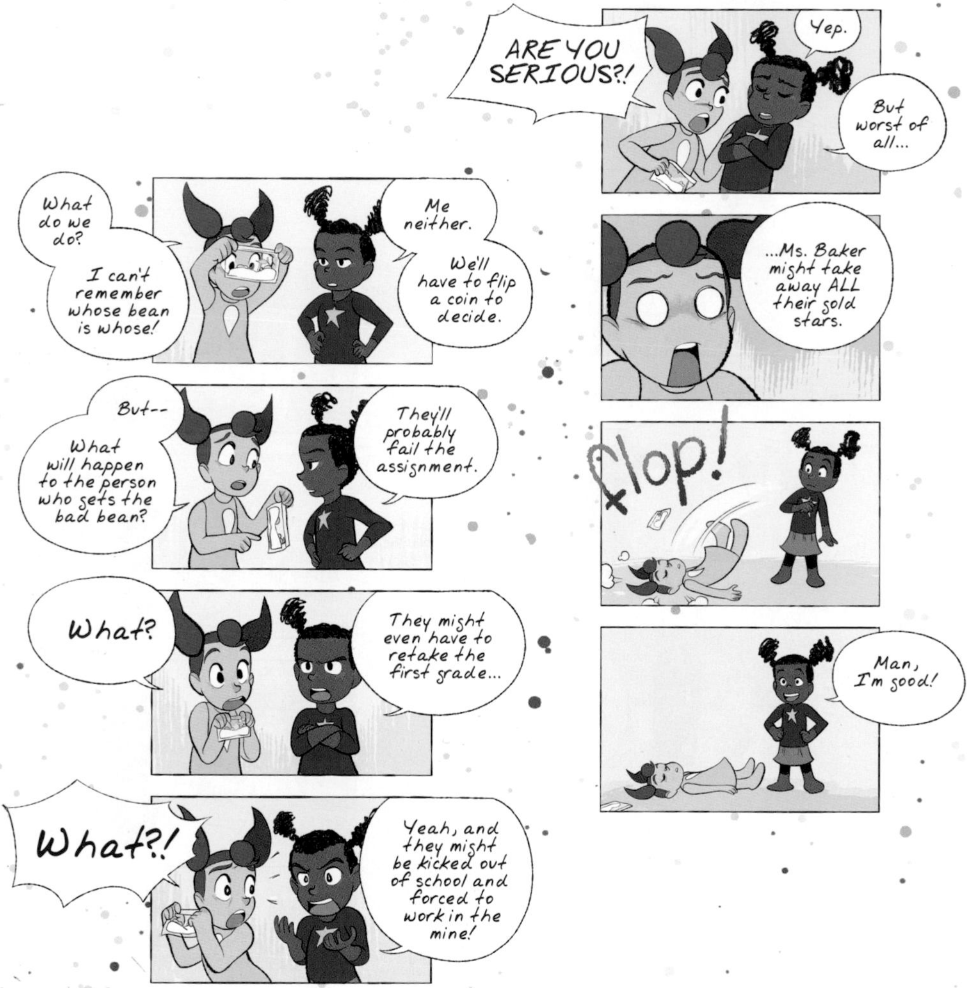
What do we do?
I can't remember whose bean is whose!
Me neither.
We'll have to flip a coin to decide.
But--
What will happen to the person who gets the bad bean?
They'll probably fail the assignment.
What?
They might even have to retake the first grade...
What?!
Yeah, and they might be kicked out of school and forced to work in the mine!
ARE YOU SERIOUS?!
Yep.
But worst of all...
...Ms. Baker might take away ALL their gold stars.
flop!
Man, I'm good!

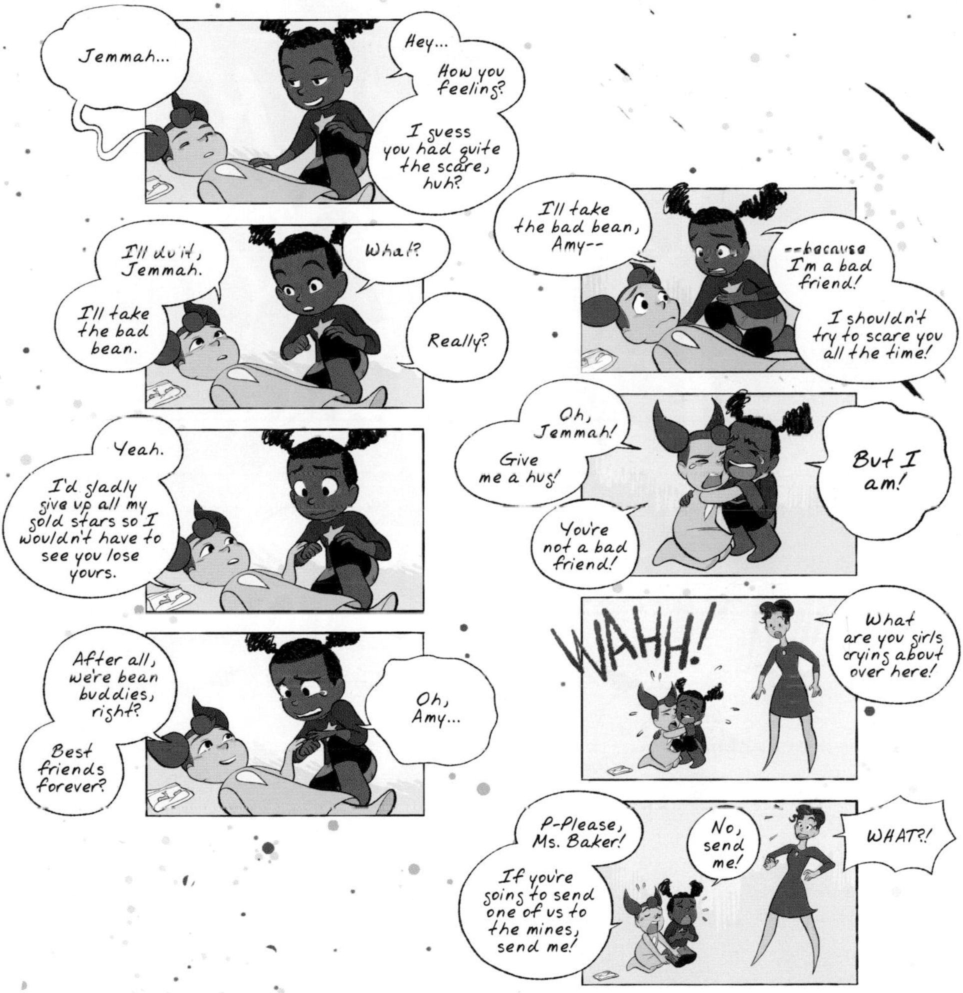
Jemmah...
Hey...
How you feeling?
I guess you had quite the scare, huh?
I'll do it, Jemmah.
I'll take the bad bean.
What?
Really?
Yeah.
I'd gladly give up all my gold stars so I wouldn't have to see you lose yours.
After all, we're bean buddies, right?
Best friends forever?
Oh, Amy...
I'll take the bad bean, Amy--
--because I'm a bad friend!
I shouldn't try to scare you all the time!
Oh, Jemmah!
Give me a hug!
You're not a bad friend!
But I am!
WAHH!
What are you girls crying about over here!
P-Please, Ms. Baker!
If you're going to send one of us to the mines, send me!
No, send me!
WHAT?!

COMING SOON . . .

Stephen McCranie's
SPACE
BOY
10

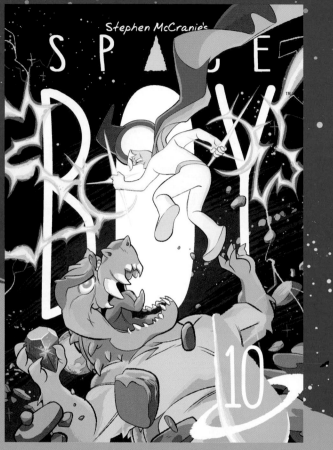

THE ORIGIN OF SPACE BOY REVEALED!

Deep in space, the Arno closes in on their destination . . . the artifact. Oliver spends his days in school, with his little brother, and battling Wargles! After his father, Wyatt, gave him a family heirloom, a compass, Oliver fears he broke it when the needle starts spinning uncontrollably. This new discovery alarms his father who begins to suspect that the ship they all live on may be in grave danger. However, Wyatt's warnings and suspicions only bring dismissal and rebuke from his superiors along with a demotion to the maintenance crew. Will Wyatt and Oliver figure out what's happening to the Arno in time to save everyone? Find out in the next volume, available June 2021!

YOU CAN ALSO READ MORE SPACE BOY COMICS ON WEBTOONS.COM!